SWORN IN BLOOD

A BLACK FATES NOVEL

Christine Roi

Book design by Alison Cnockaert
Cover by Natalia Junqueira

ISBN 979-8-218-33731-5 (paperback)
ISBN 979-8-218-33732-2 (eBook)

www.christineroi.com

CONTENTS

For the girls who just want to be loved like a Hozier song
(and fucked like one, too.)

... Sorry, Mom.

CONTENT WARNING

This story contains graphic content that might be troubling to some readers, including, but not limited to, depictions of and references to:

Intimate Partner Violence

Forced asphyxiation

Severed appendages

Murder/assassinations

Dismembered bodies

Torture

Sexual Assault

Trauma

Your mental health is important to me. Please be mindful of these and other possible triggers and seek assistance if needed.

PROLOGUE

THE VOW

The late hour cast the office in almost complete darkness. Even the moon hid its face as the stars guttered like dying candles. Only black skies peered through the blinds covering the window. The carpet felt thin beneath my denim-clad knees, the hardwood beneath pressing into them like stone. It had only been days since I'd told my sister I wanted to work for the family. This was the rite that was required of me.

Kaia, my sister and new boss of the family, stood over me with a glass of wine in one hand and a gold dagger in the other. The dagger that had been our grandfather's just as this office had once been.

"First you say the words," she said as she set the wine down on the desk behind her.

The blade glinted in the low light of Nonno's office, now her office, above the club. Muse was silent, having been closed and cleared out for hours. Kaia lifted the blade to her palm and quickly sliced the soft flesh. I winced. She didn't.

"Say them."

The air in my lungs started to burn, the only sign that I'd been holding my breath. With a shaky exhale, I looked up at my sister and began.

"I will walk the forest in the dead of night,
I will stalk the predators among the trees,
I will know no peace if our enemies roam free,
For their blood is my wine,
Their souls are my fee."

My sister squeezed her fist and a drop of blood fell into the glass of wine. As I knelt, she handed the dagger to me. The steel bit into my palm as I made my cut. Kaia held the glass below to catch my blood. Bright red swirled into the dark burgundy liquid.

"Drink," she said as she held it out to me.

The coppery tang of our blood mixed with deep, rich berries and earth on my tongue. I handed the glass back to her. She sipped from the glass and placed it on the desk.

"Rise, wolf."

TARAXACUM

It began with a voice. Talking to me from above. From miles away. Not clear, but like sound traveling through water. Only one or two words got through at a time. They were there, leaving a trail back to my mind. Distant but present as the full moon, I could feel my body.

"Come on. Open those beautiful eyes and look at me."

Large warm hands stroked my arms, my hair, my face. Every touch renewed awareness of my existence. Cold emptiness had started to pull away from me like an ebbing tide. Feeling began to work its way back into my body. As though his touch woke the nerve endings that had given up and chose to start fighting to feel him instead. Breath came more easily. Thoughts floated through my mind. I was safe. I was with him.

I was alive. I was alive. I was alive.

WHAT CAN I say? Sometimes the bad guy really does want to kill you. Benjamin Camden was the impossibly beautiful billionaire women around the world dreamed about. Gossip sites followed the tech investor all over town, wondering which supermodel he would make Mrs. Camden. He showed me a good time over the last few weeks. Of course, he did that while leading me on a fucking wild goose chase.

It wasn't until the deceptive playboy had me tied to a chair that I realized he was playing me. I realized too late that I'd walked right into the middle of a human trafficking scheme and paid the price. Then my sister went missing. West, my friend and the strip club's bouncer, had to pull my ass out of a bind and bring me back to life.

Laying in his bed in almost the middle of nowhere, I thought about how quickly my life had changed in just a few weeks. I got lucky. That was the truth of it. Without West, I would be dead. Probably dumped into the ocean or dismembered. It wasn't hard to imagine the sparkling beads of my dress glinting in the disappearing light as what remained of me sunk to the bottom of the ocean. Then the face of the body changed. Became slightly older. My sister. I pushed the thought from my head.

The large cotton t-shirt I'd been sleeping in was the only thing I had worn since waking up in West's cabin. Not that I had any other options. The room was small but nice. A small armchair faced the bed from one corner and a bureau was on the opposite side. The cushions were abused like someone had sat there for hours on end. The bed I was sitting in was pushed up against the only window in the room. Its wooden headboard was as rustic as the rest of the furniture.

Soft sheets enveloped me. They smelled like West. Cedar and clean laundry. Dove grey in color, I threaded them between my fingers in the early morning light. An IV drip was pulled from my arm three nights ago by West. A small purple bruise winked back at me as I examined where the needle had been. Because I apparently wasn't in enough pain, I prodded it, sucking air in through my clenched teeth at the light sting.

A clicking ratchet being turned told me was West outside working on his Bronco. Again. If he wasn't chopping wood, checking on me, or going into town, that was what he occupied himself with. The man was probably trying to avoid becoming bored to tears just waiting for me to get better.

It had been about ten days since he'd brought me here. Truth be known, it was hard for me to keep track. He found me inside the utility closet Benjamin had dragged me into, weakly clinging to life after being given a lethal dose of what turned out to be a sedative. At the time I was near death. The first half of that time, I was in and out of consciousness. "Barely here." That's how West put it.

Kaia, my sister, had known about the girls. About the trafficking. And now she was missing. When she sent me looking for the missing dancers from Muse, our strip club, she suspected it might have been an act of aggression from one of our rivals. Or maybe a jealous boyfriend. The moment I discovered the truth, I told my sister what to look for. Had sent her to the docks to look for shipping containers filled with abducted women.

She did everything I asked of her, despite being boss of the family herself. Kaia warned me to be careful around Benjamin. Hell, everyone told me not to trust him and now my sister was in danger because of my piss poor judgment. Possibly even...

I squeezed my eyes shut to force the worst-case scenario from my mind. Throwing the blankets off of myself, I headed for the bathroom. My gold-rimmed irises looked back at me as I splashed some cold water on my face. She was alive. She had to be alive. I grabbed West's shearling-lined denim jacket and headed out to the porch. The rustic cabin wasn't very big. In fact, minus the bathroom, it was really only two rooms. Plenty of room for a broad-chested giant of a bouncer and the pocket-sized assassin he had taken pity on.

My bare feet felt the threat of every splinter on the worn wooden porch as I crossed it. A brisk breeze sent goosebumps up my bare legs as I leaned against the railing and watched him work. West ducked under the popped hood, the muscles in his arms twisting under the short sleeves of his worn white tee shirt while he tightened something with the ratchet again. The clicking sound permeated the otherwise quiet air.

"Did I wake you?" West asked without lifting his head. Of course he heard me come out. I didn't make a move he wasn't aware of these days.

"No," I said with a sigh. "I've been awake a little while."

He stood up and put the wrench down on the open toolbox next to him, then wiped his grease-covered hands on an old red rag. Our conversations had been short since he'd told me about my sister. I didn't blame him for what happened, but it felt strange talking to him now. Something about being rescued. Or the way he was acting around me. It could be in my head. Maybe the damsel-in-distress role was just not for me.

"Are you hungry?" West asked as he pushed the sweat-damp tendrils of hair that had come loose from its knot out of his face with his forearm.

I gave him a weak smile and shrugged. Keeping food down had been a challenge ever since I'd come to. I shuddered at the thought of vomiting up another dinner. He approached the porch and walked up the short steps, placing a still slightly greased hand on the railing.

"You have to eat something, Lili." He walked past me into the cabin. "Come on. At least have some toast."

Toast. I could do toast. Maybe. I followed him inside, too tired to feel embarrassed that he was spending this much energy on taking care of me. After washing his hands in the small steel sink, he popped a piece of bread in the toaster and leaned against the counter behind him. A look of appraisal mixed with concern set in as he let his eyes rake over me. He must have decided I wasn't looking very good because he then put on the kettle for tea.

"I'm glad you're walking around. You look steadier than yesterday."

I nodded absently. This was the longest we'd talked in days. Since I'd first woken up to hear everything he'd told me, I'd not been able to stay awake for long. Before I could muster up an interesting response, the toast popped out. Ready to eat. Then possibly vomit. I eyed the bread warily as he slid it toward me on a plate. A small smirk curled on his lips.

"It's not going to bite you. You bite it. That's how it works."

"Dick."

I rolled my eyes and picked up the bread. It smelled good. Grainy, hearty sourdough. My mouth watered. Oh, I did actually *want* to eat it. West's eyebrows raised as I took a bite off of the corner. After that bite seemed to go down fine, I took a slightly larger one with more confidence. The tea kettle sounded its whistle, alerting us to the hot water. Soon, a cup of steaming hot mint tea was sitting in front of me. Alternating bites and sips, I soon had more solid food in my belly than I'd had in a week. West watched silently until I'd cleared my plate.

I took another sip of tea and watched the tea bag sink to the bottom as I set the cup down. Nausea tugged at me as I squeezed my eyes shut and let out a breath as I tried to force unpleasant thoughts from my mind again.

"Are you alright?"

I nodded. The tea had been fine. The toast, too. But imagining my sister's lifeless corpse sinking into a dark abyss was too much to stomach.

2

LAVANDULA ANGUSTIFOLIA

Worries gnawed at me with sharp teeth as I watched West wash and put my dish away. I looked around the room, looking for a distraction from the thoughts that coursed through my mind like a relentless ticker tape, taking in the details for what felt like the first time.

Wood paneled walls. A slice of tree trunk on metal legs sat in front of the beaten-up deep red sofa. In the kitchen, there were mismatched plates, mugs, and glasses, except for a pair of tumblers next to a half-full handle of bourbon. A tall stack of worn novels old enough to either be the previous owner's or purchased secondhand. I couldn't make out the titles. The only art was a single framed photo of a misty mountainscape. Mounted next to the cabinet over the sink was a telephone. With a freaking rotary dial.

"Why do you have a landline? And a phone that was made in the 1970s?" I said over a sip from my steaming cup of tea, batting my eyelashes like I was waiting for hot gossip.

He smirked, shaking his head.

"I picked up the phone at Goodwill. The landline is because the wireless signal is awful up here," he glanced over his shoulder at the object in question. "Besides, it may be from the 1970s, but it works just fine."

"The avocado green really classes up the place," I laughed. In a weird way, it was kind of true.

As I looked at the chipped finish on the decades-old device mounted to the wall, I remembered that my mobile phone had been with the security guards from the party. Maybe Benjamin had retrieved it from them while playing the doting boyfriend. I wondered how he could have explained my disappearance to them. If he explained it at all. He was their boss, after all.

West looked at me expectantly. I'd gone quiet imagining all of the things Benjamin could possibly have gleaned from possessing my phone. Sure, it was password-protected, but he owns several tech companies. He has to have a way around that, right?

"Is it listed?" The question was moronic but helped take my mind off things I had no power over. Not right now, anyway.

"To my father. Joe Hale. This is his cabin. It was, anyway," he said as he turned to face me, wiping his hands on his jeans. "He didn't have a phone when it was his place."

"And it's yours now."

He nodded and looked around the space as if to confirm his ownership of it. To a stranger, this smattering of things would seem completely random. Just a bunch of stuff from a thrift store. But it was all him. Everything in here felt like West.

"When he died, he left this to me. Lanna is still pissed about it."

I squeezed my eyebrows together and angled my head to one side, trying to shake loose the memory of someone with that name. Lanna?

"My sister."

Right. The sister who had saved my life in the back of West's Bronco. The sister who had kept my heart beating until they could get me here. The one who'd given West everything he needed to keep me on this side of life while he watched over me. I looked down at the bruise on my arm.

After another sip of tea, I stood and tugged down the hem of my shirt. His shirt.

"Do you mind if I use your shower? I can't remember the last time I bathed," I said as I gave myself a sniff. Lie. I remembered every second of showering in Benjamin's bathroom before the last Eros party, his ice-blue eyes glued to my body as he shaved. I blinked away the memory of his gaze.

"In there," he said as he pointed over his shoulder. I didn't want to tell him that there was no way I could forget where the bathroom was at this point. I was pretty sure the tile pattern would be forever imprinted on my knees. Between the fits of vomiting and the IV I'd been on, I'd spent as much time in that room as I had in his bed.

STEAM ENVELOPED ME as I stood in the old cast iron tub and its plain white curtain shielded me from the rest of the world. The water was as hot as the cabin's old water heater would allow. I watched it stream over the wolf tattoo on my sternum in scalding rivulets. It still wasn't hot enough to scald the memory of the last several weeks off of me. Before my sister went missing. Before I nearly died from a sedative overdose, I had been foolishly falling for a man who wanted only to keep me out of his business.

Every time I closed my eyes, I saw Benjamin towering over me. The rage in his cold blue stare. The way his arms felt around me. Like the squeeze of a serpent around his prey. I remembered the feel of him on my skin. His lips. His tongue. And the prick of the needle going into my thigh.

A light knock thudded on the door. I blinked myself back to reality. How long had I been standing here?

"You alright in there?"

"Yeah," I shouted. "I'll be out in a little bit."

Taking a moment to ground myself in reality, I started looking around for soap as the meager breakfast I'd eaten threatened to climb up my throat. My shaking fingers wrapped around the dark green bar in the little chrome wire tray. Hot water started to cool from my lengthy shower as I began the business of cleaning up. My body gradually connected with my mind to make me whole again. The familiar scent of cedar floated up my nostrils as I lathered away.

"I'M SORRY. I didn't mean to be in there so long. That shower has really good water pressure," I said as I squeezed the towel into the thick black waves of my still-wet hair. The cool air touching my exposed legs felt refreshing on my newly cleansed skin.

West's head popped up from behind the open refrigerator door.

"I didn't mean to bother you. It's just, you were in there a while. I thought you might've passed out."

"I'm fine," I said as I draped the towel over the back of the barstool. Bereft of any other clothes, I was in another one of West's overlarge short-sleeved shirts and a pair of boxers. It wasn't much, but at least it was clean. Still, I would've killed for a bra and my own underwear. It's the little things that make us feel human, right?

West closed the refrigerator and leaned against the counter. He crossed his arms and looked me over. Started at my toes and worked his way back up to my face. Something about the way he was looking at me made me aware of every inch. A flicker of some thought crept through his expression as he cleared his throat. Rounding the counter, he moved to face me with a more casual expression.

"Now that you're eating again, I should probably pick up some more food. Do you want to come? It might be good for you to get some fresh air." He took off his flannel and dropped it over my shoulders.

"I don't think my appetite is what it was before," I joked, stuffing my arms into the shirt's gigantic plaid sleeves.

"I'm sure it'll be back in no time. Come on."

"West, wait. I don't have shoes!"

He paused for a moment with his hand on the doorknob. Then long, heavy strides had him standing before me in a blink. I yelped as he scooped me into his arms with a playful grin. The feel of his big warm body against mine wasn't something I'd prepared myself for, so I told myself the flutter in my stomach was from residual nausea and definitely nothing else as I snaked my arms around his neck. I wasn't enjoying this. Definitely not.

"You can stay in the truck," he laughed into my hair.

Tiny threads of shame wound around my middle. I shouldn't have been enjoying this. Any of it. I shouldn't have felt happy or safe. Not when my sister certainly wasn't. Despite being wrapped up in West's hold, in his clothes, I couldn't shake the guilt that crept up around me.

COFFEA ARABICA

I t wasn't until halfway through the drive into town that I realized how far we were from it. And the word "town" was being applied very loosely. While I knew we were in the San Bernardino Range, we were well removed from all of the developed ski resorts Angelinos liked to frequent. What West defined as civilization consisted of a small post office, a diner, and a general store that also apparently included some laundry services called "Suds' n' Spuds."

"Now be a good girl for me and wait here," West had said with a wink. I sent him off with a smile. And a middle finger.

Sitting in the car while someone else does the grocery shopping made me feel like a kid again. Only this time there was no Kaia to keep me company. Just the sinking feeling I was never going to see her again. The thought had my breakfast burning in my stomach like a hot coal.

West had only been inside for about five minutes when I had started to make a game of trying to guess what he was picking from the shelves he was wandering through. It was easy to see a man his size stalking down the aisles. Watching his man bun bob through the store, I wondered if he could feel me watching him.

Once he was finished selecting what I decided was deeply boring healthy food and some smutty magazines, he approached the counter and exchanged pleasantries with the small man behind it. He was laughing with the elderly store attendant inside as he put his food into a brown paper bag. The attendant handed him his change. In his worn but somehow gleaming white tee shirt, West's tattoos stood out like storm clouds of ink on an ocean of golden brown skin. Staring. I was staring.

I was watching the tentacles of his octopus-skull tattoo undulate with his muscles as he hefted up the bag when my view was obstructed by a small female hand.

A petite blonde woman was touching West's arm. His face was still relaxed as he smiled at her. Did he know this woman? He said something to her and she tossed her head back and laughed like it was the funniest thing she'd ever heard. Whatever it was, it couldn't have been that funny. I huffed out a sigh, annoyed that she was delaying him. The cab of his Bronco was starting to feel too small. Even though the windows were down.

I clenched my hands into tight fists at my side, then loosened them with a deep breath. A surge of irritation tightened my fists again. Irritation I had no right to feel. He was bending over backward to take care of me. He was allowed to talk to other women. They'd always been drawn to him. Hell, it was this side of a month ago that I'd had another man's tongue down my throat. Who was I to claim ownership over West? He was my friend.

"Come on," I muttered to myself, shifting in my seat.

West said something else to the blonde woman and gestured in my direction, excusing himself from their conversation. The small blonde turned to look at me. He didn't see the grimace on her pretty face, but it told me enough. She was interested in West and I was not part of her plan. It was an effort to smother my smile at her discomfort.

The bell on the shop door dinged as West came out, groceries in hand. He passed the bag to me as he climbed into the driver's seat. I looked down into the bag and smiled. Bread, eggs, peppers, potatoes, onions, and coffee. A big bag of coffee. I picked it up and took a deep whiff.

"I don't know if your stomach is ready for that yet, but I can make a pot when we get back," West said with a half-cocked smile in my direction. "You still need to drink actual water. Coffee doesn't count."

Coffee fucking counts.

THE QUIET RIDE home set my mind wandering again as the wind whipped strands of unbound, wet hair into my face. Thoughts of Kaia in certain danger, Daniel staying with a stranger while his mother was missing, and what was happening with the family without their leader circled me like vultures. I'd failed Casey. Though I had found out what happened to Isabelle, I never discovered what became of Casey. I worried she was an abandoned body in the desert just like her friend had been. I'd failed her. I'd failed everyone who mattered to me. Here I was being pampered and protected like a princess when all I could think about was everything that had gone wrong. One question kept floating to the surface. I set the bag of groceries down and turned in my seat, pulling my legs up on the soft leather.

"How did you know where to find me?"

West glanced at me and blew out a breath. The ends of his hair danced their way out of the knot on his head as the wind from the open window whipped them free. His hands flexed on the steering wheel. Bracing himself for the conversation. This wasn't going to be good.

"Your sister."

"What do you mean? Kaia told you where I was?"

"She thought that someone from the Arawn Clan might try to attack you. Kaia explained that someone called Ronan Arwan had people who were causing problems, I guess. And she didn't know who she could trust to look out for you. So she asked me to follow you while you were out with, uh," he stopped himself from mentioning the man we were both thinking of now.

I pushed the hair out of my eyes and looked out at the road ahead of us, letting the wind blow Benjamin away from my thoughts and back to the man beside me. West couldn't have followed me everywhere. He was at the strip club, Muse, often before I was which meant he stayed in the Los Angeles vicinity. But he could have driven out to Las Vegas. He could have seen me off of the highway, burning the remains of Henry Johnson. A small wave of panic swept over me. What did he know?

"How long were you following me?" I asked quietly.

"Since the Bootlegger burned down. Only in LA. I couldn't... I wasn't able to track you everywhere else."

He had followed me to the Eros parties. I'd seen someone standing in the shadows as I waited for Benjamin to find me at the first masquerade. A tall man in a skull mask. Watching as I sat on Benjamin's lap and he coaxed an orgasm out of me in front of strangers. As he put his fingers into my mouth and watched me lick them clean.

My cheeks heated as a different sort of dread took over. West knew exactly how close I had let Benjamin get to me. Despite my sister's warnings. Despite his own. I didn't know if I was more embarrassed about the exposure or my carelessness. I blew out a breath and looked away, out the window as trees whipped past.

"You were there the entire time?"

His eyes slid to mine. A curt nod was my answer. Oh god. I slumped down in the chair and wished for the ground to open up and swallow me whole.

4

SYMPHYTUM OFFICINALE

On the drive back to the cabin, I kept picturing everything West could have witnessed. Every intimate moment. Benjamin always found a way to paw at me in public. Hell, he'd almost had me on the beach in Santa Monica. We'd been only steps away from everyone on the pier as he nearly mounted me beneath a lifeguard tower. Had West been there watching me come undone for Benjamin?

We ended up spending the rest of the day in silence. Though the silence had started with discomfort, it eventually became companionable. Tired of the interior of the cabin, I brought the Hemingway book I'd been reading outside and sat on the porch as West cut wood. All I'd had to busy myself with were my own thoughts and West's collection of worn-out second-hand novels. The sound of the ax falling was perfect for drowning out the thoughts I was trying to escape and the pang of cowardly regret for trying to escape them in the first place.

When it came time for dinner, I was able to get down a few potatoes, an egg, and more tea. West was still quiet. I hadn't dared to ask any questions even though they swarmed my mind with their stinging desire for answers. I couldn't.

Instead, I did the dishes. Then he insisted I go back to bed after that. I welcomed the break from consciousness.

EVERYTHING WAS ALWAYS quiet at four in the morning. The 9-5 set had gone to bed hours ago. They slept deeply and comfortably on their boxed mattresses, waiting for their phones to wake them up because nobody seemed to own an alarm clock anymore. The party crowd enjoyed their delivered late-night tacos or each other behind closed doors.

The rubber soles of my boots made little sticky noises against the wood floors of the hallway. It was quiet. The bedroom door was ajar and I could hear my target's deep sleeping breaths. As I entered, I looked around. A feeling of déjà vu seeped into my bones. I've been in this room before. I approached the bed with my needle in hand. Black hair was fanned over the pillow. Olive skin covered a bare shoulder.

The point of the needle dropped in with ease. They would be found in their bed, presumably asleep forever. A small voice comes from the hallway.

"Mama?"

Dark curls. The same olive skin. The small boy looked at me with horror in his familiar eyes. I looked back at the bed. At my sister.

THE NIGHTMARE JOLTED me back to consciousness. Every time I closed my eyes, I was looking down at my sister's body. Looking at my nephew who was alone in the world because of me. Waking up in a strange place, I sat staring into the dark. I tried to collect myself and whispered a curse as the memory of my dream clung to my mind like cobwebs.

Nudging the door open carefully, I tried not to make a sound as I walked on quiet steps past West sleeping on the sofa. A book was lying flat against his chest as though he'd fallen asleep reading it. Still in his clothes, too. My footsteps whispered past him as I went into the kitchen to look for a glass.

"They're in the next cabinet."

I jumped and turned around to see West watching me from the sofa. He marked his place in the book and put it down on the coffee table. Tilting his head to one side and then the other, I heard his neck crack.

"I'm sorry. I thought you were asleep," I apologized as I reached for a glass, standing on tip-toe to grab it from the irritatingly deep shelf.

"Are you feeling alright?" His voice was husky. He had been sleeping. Maybe he'd only just nodded off.

"Yeah, I just. I've always had a little trouble sleeping. I guess now that I'm getting better, my brain is back to its usual bullshit." I let out a breath and continued. "Anyway, I was just getting some water."

The wind made a whistle and a whooshing sound from the slightly open kitchen window. I went to the sink and filled the glass with water from the tap, then slid the small window closed. Leaning there against the counter, I took a sip and then a breath. West eyed me for a moment before sitting up to speak.

"Why?"

Wondering how much I actually wanted to tell him, I decided to go with the usual nightmares. I didn't want to get into what I'd dreamed of tonight. It had been so long since I'd told anyone about what our father used to do to us. The last person I'd shared that with had been our grandfather after our last Christmas with our parents. I'd told Benjamin I'd had nightmares about my father, but I didn't tell him exactly what was happening in them.

"It's a PTSD thing, I guess. Usually, I sort of relive some stuff with my dad. The kind of things that stick with you."

West's brows furrowed as he angled his head. He was working it out. He wanted to know more but wasn't going to press me.

He'd already seen me at my most vulnerable. It would be stupid to be embarrassed by these details that weren't my fault. His silence was enough encouragement for me to continue. I drew in a breath to steel my nerves. "When he was really angry with us or just had a bad night, he would come into our rooms really late and take it out on us. On really bad nights, he'd strangle us or keep his knee pressed into our chests until we couldn't breathe.

Like even our breathing was offensive to him. Eventually, it was too hard to fall asleep without being terrified."

My stomach clenched and I took another sip of water. Glancing over at West, I noticed his hands had balled into fists even though his expression was blank. He was waiting for me to finish.

"So, if I don't fall asleep without some background noise or something, I can have pretty vivid nightmares about that. About other things, too."

It was a minute before either of us spoke. I was sure I'd over-shared. I showed him how damaged I really was. Who would want to know something like that? West stood and walked to the little shelf over the sink. After a pause, he stepped closer to me. Golden skin and delicate tufts of hair revealed themselves as his shirt lifted. Taking down the bottle of bourbon and another glass, he grabbed my glass and poured a little for me. Then he poured some for himself.

"Come on," he said as he guided me to the sofa. I sniffed the bourbon as he moved his pillow to sit down, but left space for me to sit beside him. I'd been here over a week but hadn't actually sat on the sofa. Since West was sleeping out here, it felt like the last bit of his territory, and I wanted to respect that. The leather was still warm from his body. We sat and drank quietly for a minute.

"So, do you have this problem a lot, then?" West asked, taking another pull from his glass.

"Not every night, but most nights since my parents died. My grandfather used to put on old records for me."

"That's terrible."

"It's…it is what it is. The dreams tend to happen more when I'm stressed or worried. Which is pretty much always." I tossed back my bourbon and settled back against the sofa, letting the smoky honey flavor coat my tongue. West sat leaning forward with his arms braced on his knees, eyes on me.

"And background noise helps?"

I nodded. "Sometimes I'll put on the TV and set a sleep timer. Or watch something on my phone. Like streaming Netflix or something. Or I'll listen to music." I paused and gave him a sidelong glance. "Kaia used to help me with them when we were growing up. She'd lay in bed with me and tell me that it was over. That he was gone and we were safe."

West sighed through his nose as he got up and walked to the kitchen, taking my glass with him. He returned with a refill and set it on the table, then knelt at my feet with his hands braced on the sofa around me. His eyes were filled with anger and remorse. Even the jagged scar through his eyebrow looked upset.

"I'm sorry," he said roughly. "I'm sorry that happened to you. I'm sorry that I couldn't help your sister."

"You helped me," I said after a beat. "I'm only here because you helped."

Up this close, I could see how little he'd slept. How tired the last few weeks must have made him. The dark circles beneath his eyes and the pallid look to his usually warm face. I wrapped my arms around his neck and pulled myself closer to him. Like my body needed it. To feel the certainty of him. This man, my friend, had shown up when I needed someone most.

"Thank you," I warbled.

It never once occurred to me to blame him for anything. Not for what happened with my sister. And it felt freeing to tell him about the dreams. About my father. I pressed my forehead to his. With a shuddering sigh, he wrapped his arms around me and gently stroked my back. We sat like that for a while, just holding each other. Anchoring the other to the world.

AFTER MY REVELATION, I didn't go back to bed. Instead, we sat and talked as we never had before. Drinking and laughing until we were both too drunk to hide from other unpleasant subjects. Of course with almost no food in my system, I was drunk before West was. But tipsy West was a treat. His normally booming laugh turned into more of a giggle after a few too many.

It was nearing two in the morning when West turned to me, the look on his face reminded me of something. Like he was weighing his words. The look informed me that whatever he said next was going to make me uncomfortable.

"Were you in love with him?"

Oh god. I leaned back and looked at him, squinting my eyes to clear my slightly bourbon-addled sight. His eyebrows furrowed, awaiting my reply. A tightness pressed in on my chest. I didn't want to talk about Benjamin. That's definitely who he was asking about.

"I was a fucking idiot," I laughed, trying for a lightness I didn't feel in my gut. "But I wasn't in love, no."

Maybe near it. As near as you could be to falling in love with someone without actually being in love. Remembering the way he kissed me. The way he listened to me pour my heart out. The way I gave him almost every part of me. It had all been an act. That fact didn't make his betrayal and my foolishness sting any less.

"You two put on a convincing show."

The bourbon had me imagining the bitterness in his tone. But it could have been there. That grinding stone quality in his voice. He could have just been angry for me because he was a good friend who had witnessed the result of my foolishness. I rested my head on his shoulder and sighed.

"Well, that was kind of the point. He told me he'd intended to distract me and he did a damn good job of that. I never expected to actually let my guard down around him, but because I'm so fucking broken I let him in." I leaned forward and put my empty glass on the coffee table. "I think I might just swear off of love. I clearly can't trust myself."

Finally succumbing to my exhaustion, I moved his arm to lean against his broad chest and closed my eyes with a sigh. The cedar scent of him wrapped around me like a warm blanket. As I decided that I could fall asleep right here, West tilted my chin up. My eyes fluttered open to meet his. The large, calloused pad of his thumb stroked my cheek, wiping away a tear I hadn't noticed I'd shed.

It was almost as if there was some kind of tug. Some sort of pull. Towards him. Towards West? What was happening here? *That's it*, I thought. *I'm losing my damned mind.*

We sat there silently, his large hand cupping my jaw. His thumb continued stroking as his gaze became thoughtful, searching. He sucked in a breath, ready to say something, then seemed to think better of it. Warmth stirred low in me as I let myself lean into his touch. Suddenly I was brought back to another night I'd had too much to drink. When he was in my home, kneeling before me I felt the pull. The tug. The same one I was feeling now.

I let my gaze travel down his sculpted jaw to the golden skin peeking at me through the open buttons of his henley. Each was undone to reveal the delicate brown swirls of chest hair beneath. All except for one. The bottom button remained. Suddenly, I was losing my mind over a fucking button. Imagining what it would feel like to let it warm under my touch. The smooth, round edges. Pushing it through the hole that held soft cotton together. Threading the fabric through my fingers. Fisting it. Dragging him toward me.

That button. That fucking button was going to be the death of me. I licked my lips and looked up at him again. Our eyes connected and we watched each other. Standing on the edge. Both waiting for the other to jump.

If this were any other man, I wouldn't think twice. But this was West. Possibly my only friend in the world. He'd been taking care of me for days. He wasn't just being nice. It wasn't my sister's request that put the worry in his eyes. Or the soft touches he thought I didn't notice, like he was reassuring himself that I was there.

His eyes dipped to my mouth as he sighed.

"Maybe you should go to bed."

The energy of the room had shifted without warning. We were walking on a frozen lake and I plunged beneath the surface. West stood and offered his hand to pull me up. His other hand pressed to the small of my back and practically forced me back into the bedroom. Tired and confused, I simply agreed quietly and told him to sleep well.

I am such a goddamned chicken.

WEST'S BED SURROUNDED me with his comforting fresh laundry and cedar aroma as I stared up at the dark ceiling. Still awake. Still drunk. As I thought about our conversation, how at ease I'd felt with him. Something about the way he looked at me made me feel unsettled. What the hell was that? Was he going to kiss me? Did he want to kiss me?

Did I want to kiss him?

It felt like he'd wanted to. That much was clear. It felt like I'd wanted him to. That was the part that had me biting my nails. How could I trust myself now? After everything, all the bullshit from Benjamin I'd dealt with. It was so hard to just lean in to what I was feeling because my stupid heart had literally almost gotten me killed.

Every instinct I had told me I could trust West. This man who had saved my life. This man whose scent wrapped around me like a warm embrace, heating my blood. We'd spent almost every day for the last six years together. Still, I couldn't trust anyone with my heart. Not even me.

But I could at least trust him with my body. Anything, anything, anything was better than the feeling of my utter helplessness.

My mind drifted back to the night he drove me home. I'd blocked out the way he'd looked at me. The way his hands had felt on my legs as he carefully removed my shoes. And the spark his touch had struck in me that night that had never been extinguished. Just ignored. Like shutting a door on a room engulfed in flames.

Confused and tense, I needed to relax. I couldn't get another glass of bourbon because I'd have to slip past him on the sofa. I got out of bed and reached for the door. I'd been leaving it open a crack because it somehow felt safer knowing he was near. The light was still on, so I knew he was still awake. I pushed the door closed as quietly as I could. I didn't want to shut him out, but I couldn't let him hear me. After the way the night ended, it was easier to let him believe I needed to be alone.

Crawling back into bed, I pushed my hand into his boxers, between my thighs. My thoughts about our relationship had clearly been at war with my body because I was already wet. Thinking about West was a welcome distraction from the thoughts about my sister that had been chasing me like wild dogs. I pleasured myself, letting my mind wander to the man in the next room.

I imagined walking the short distance between us. Begging him to touch me. His big, warm hands coasting over my body under the threadbare shirt he'd given me to sleep in. His mouth finding the sensitive peaks of my nipples, tugging and licking. Straddling him and riding until we were both sweaty and screaming. I wanted it. Wanted him. A moan burst from my lips as I came. Pressing my face into his pillow, I sighed.

A second sigh came from the next room.

5

ARNICA MONTANA

Thwack! Thwack! Thwack!

The cracking sound of splitting wood woke me. Hard grunts met with continuous, resounding thumps. Only slightly hungover, I rolled myself out of bed. A foggy head had me dry-swallowing pain relievers after relieving myself. Quickly blowing through the living room to grab a wool blanket from the sofa and wrap it around myself, I let myself outside. The soles of my feet moved gently over the deck, careful not to surprise the man who was swinging an ax.

West was standing next to a pile of split logs. His long waves were gathered in a topknot and sweat poured over his bare chest down to his worn tan work pants. I watched his arms work, his shoulders flexing as he split another piece of wood with a grunt. He rested his ax across his shoulders, noticing me on the porch as he did so.

The grunting, sweating, and ragged pace of his breathing. He sifted his fingers through loose strands of hair and I wondered how those strands would feel in between mine. The thought did something to my insides. To my brain. The things I had started to picture...My stomach did a little flip at the same time my chest squeezed, a sensation that left me lightheaded.

My spine straightened, seeming to realize where my mind was wandering.

It was so easy to distract myself with these ideas that I didn't stop to think about how stupid I would be to do anything about them.

"Are you feeling alright? How did you sleep?"

I glanced at him again, his head now cocked to one side as he assessed the change in my demeanor.

"Lili?"

"Hm?"

West asked me something. Damnit. I cleared my throat and asked him to repeat the question. When I thought about him this way before, they were always passing fantasies. Images that wandered through my mind as I pleasured myself on lazy afternoons. Today they seemed to linger. There was no way he knew what I was thinking. The direction my thoughts had taken. Against the side of the house. Sliding those pants down his hips. Panting. Groaning.

"You alright?" He asked.

I swallowed, gave a small nod, and hoped he couldn't read my thoughts at all. *Please don't read my thoughts.*

"Did you sleep well?" He said with an expectant look on his face. I nodded. After pleasuring myself with the thought of riding him on that sofa. Sure. I slept great.

"Did you?" I asked.

He gave a small smirk and blew out a breath, turning to look at the pile of split logs. I sighed skyward, trying to regain control of myself. After assessing the mountain of wood he'd created, he leaned the ax against the stump he'd been using.

"I need to go to town." His tone caught me off guard. Though he was still winded from splitting logs, he managed to sound irritated. Had I done something to upset him? Sleeping on the couch all these nights may have been taking its toll.

"Okay," I said meekly. Maybe I'd overstayed my welcome. We'd known each other for years, but we'd never spent this much time together. Maybe he just wanted to be alone and I was invading his space. I picked at my nails as I mulled over what I could have done as he approached me. Kindness softened his features as he looked up at me.

"I need to pick up the mail from the post office. I won't be long. Make yourself some toast," he said, as he gently tucked a strand of hair behind my ear.

"You're very brave to trust me with a kitchen appliance in the middle of a forest," I joked and bit the side of my lip, trying to ignore what that touch did to me. The way it curled my toes.

His eyes dipped to my mouth and then back to mine as he bit back a smile. My stomach did the little flutter thing again.

"I trust you with toast."

IT'S FUNNY HOW your anxious thoughts will always wait until you're alone to gang up on you. Like they can sense prey at their most vulnerable. I hadn't been by myself since West brought me to this cabin and now my worries were screaming inside my head. Closing in on me in the forest of my mind.

My sister. Daniel. The girls. The family. From where I stood, I had no idea what I could do for them. Being powerless was eating me alive from the inside out. I needed to do something.

The avocado green phone looked at me. I could make a call. But who could I trust? Outside of West, there were only a handful of people in the world who would want to keep me from harm. There was Lupo. He'd been my grandfather's bodyguard for years. Practically a second father to me. But could I risk endangering him? Would his son be enough to shield him from the risk of helping me?

Nico had done exactly what his father did for our family. He stepped up to be a bodyguard to the family's new boss when my grandfather died. My sister had trusted him implicitly, but now that she was missing in action I wasn't sure. What role was Nico playing in the family now that the Caccias were out of the picture?

I stared at the phone. Maybe it would be worth the risk. Calling Lupo. If I could remember his goddamned phone number. The phone looked back at me. Mocking me like a little green monster.

After deep cleaning the kitchen, I didn't have much to do. There was no grout to scrub. I organized the mail on the counter. Someone called Emmit Monroe had sent West a few letters. They were open. He wouldn't know if I'd read them or not, would he?

"Mind your business, Lili," I said as I traced the edge of an envelope with my finger. West had been keeping me hidden from the outside world. Nursing me back to health. If he was working with someone else, he had ample opportunity to do away with me. It couldn't be anything to do with the family. Besides, Emmit was a man's name. Nothing to worry about. Not that I should worry about worrying about anything. No, of course not. Wouldn't that be stupid of me?

Annoyed with my own brain, I decided this anxiety wasn't going to work itself out. So I took a shower. Brushed my teeth. Flossed. Like, put floss between every tooth and rocked it around. It was when I was dressing in the bedroom and noticed all of the tactical knives on the dresser that an idea came to me.

Deciding that West probably didn't want me throwing knives in his home, I stepped outside in a flannel and a pair of his overlarge boots. Then I looked for a target. The trees shot up around the house, enclosing me in their shade and scent after only a short distance. I tread through the dirt and crunching pine needles as I searched.

A few yards away from the clearing I'd left lay a discarded tree stump that had been ripped from the soil. Being so low to the ground, I decided that wouldn't do. It wasn't large, so I walked over to it and grunted as I hoisted it onto a nearby boulder. It was more of an effort than it should have been. My muscles barked in protest. The wood winked at me, mocking me with a tiny knot in its center.

The belt I'd wrapped around my waist made for a decent enough holster. The tactical knives were weightier, presenting more of a challenge than my sleeker throwing knives. A swift, brutal flick of my arm buried the first knife in the wood. It felt like taking in air after holding your breath. The second sank in with the familiar plinking sound of the metal blade hitting a hard surface.

Plink! Plink! Plink!

After several dozen more tries, sweat was pouring down my face. If you'd told me I'd been there for hours, I wouldn't have been surprised. Each of the knives stood out from the center knot of the upended tree stump pinning one of my worries to the wood. A low whistle came from behind me. I jumped.

"Not bad," West said, leaning against a tree.

"I didn't hear you pull up. How long have you been standing there?"

"Long enough to see you make that old stump regret the day it ever crossed paths with you," he laughed. "How long have you been able to do that?"

I shrugged and adjusted the sleeves of the flannel I'd wrapped around myself, trying to think of when I'd first learned this particular skill. Wearing West's clothes had been relaxing at first and I loved sleeping in them, but his massive body made for an annoying fit on my small stature.

"About fifteen years?"

He gave me an impressed nod and approached the stump, pulling the knives free from the knot. A twig snapped under his heavy footsteps. Flipping one blade in his hand, he arched that damned scarred eyebrow at me. I fought a smile at that, biting down on the corner of my lip to resist the urge.

"So, I brought you a cheeseburger. From the diner in town. Fluffy bun. Juicy patty. Melted cheddar cheese. Just the way you like it. Fries too. I'll let you wrap your lips around that burger if you can make that same shot with your eyes closed."

"Don't you know how incredibly dangerous that is?" I said as he closed the distance between us. He was wearing a fucking henley again. I eyed the collar, noticing he'd decided to fasten two buttons today instead of just the one.

"Does that mean you're not going to do it?" He leaned in. The bastard was goading me. Oh, I could do this.

"No," I breathed, grabbing the blades from his grip. Ignoring the way my skin sparked when his hand grazed mine. "It just means you have to up the stakes. I want more."

"What do you want, Lili?"

It was so tempting to ask for something ridiculous. Something tempting. Something that heated my blood. Something I knew would be a bad idea. Instead, I said "I want a bath. With bubbles and everything." I cocked my chin up at him. He laughed, shaking his head with a grin. "Do we have a deal?"

"Bubbles and everything."

I tossed him an arrogant smile as I flipped a blade in my hand. Stepping forward, I started to line up my shot when his hand shielded my eyes. Fine. Blind. As I put the other blades back in their makeshift holster, Kaia floated into my mind. She was always far better at this than I was. My grandfather taught me the skill. Kaia had made me a master.

I squeezed my eyes shut and adjusted my grip on the first blade. With a hard whip, I made my shot. It gave a metallic ping as it connected with the stump. From behind me, I heard a small grunt come out of West. I threw the next one. Then the next. And the next. When I'd thrown the final knife, I opened my eyes.

Each blade found its home near the center of the stump. One had struck true. I turned to West and smirked before strutting with swinging hips to the stump to retrieve the blades. He finally found his words as I yanked each one from the splintering wood.

"How the fuck did you do that?"

"I told you I've been doing this for fifteen years. If you think that was impressive, you should see Kaia do it." My stomach tightened as I thought about my sister. I took in a deep breath and walked back into the cabin as I tried to let it go. Poking my head out of the door, I painted a smile back on my face. "I'll take that bath whenever you're ready, Hale."

6

MATRICARIA CHAMOMILLA

My sister. He had my sister. She sat before me, zip-tied to a chair under a bare bulb. Construction sheeting hung around us, ready to catch everything that would leak from her. Things that have come out of the many men I'd tortured before. The tears. The urine. The blood. A rough olive hand gripped her white Armani-clad shoulder. The gold signet ring he'd had made for himself glinted in the light: R.C. Raoul Caccia.

"Did you think you could just replace me?" He smiled as the words oozed from him. "Some fucking legacy. Our family name is shamed by you. My daughters. I was cursed. Cursed with you. With her."

He dragged a blade along the curve of Kaia's cheek. She made no sound. No move to fight him.

"She has so much of her mother in her," he said wistfully. "So beautiful. So strong. So stubborn."

The blade glided to her throat to meet his other hand. He turned to show me his bared teeth. Not a smile, exactly.

"Not like you. You're not like your mother. That sanctimonious woman. You got her mouth. Her nose. But the eyes. Those are my golden eyes looking at me now, aren't they?"

A protest died on my tongue. I tried to step forward as his hand tightened *around Kaia's throat. My feet stuck to the ground. I couldn't help her. Rage coursed through my blood at my powerlessness.*

"That's not the only thing you got," he sing-songed to me with a mocking laugh. "My little misery. You like to make them suffer. To watch them fade away. You like," he paused, deep in thought. "You like to watch them bleed," he snarled as he plunged his blade into my sister's heart.

THE SCREAM FELT trapped inside me. It rattled my ears as I tried again, not able to open my mouth. Blood coated my face. No, she couldn't die. I'd let him take her. I let her die. She died right in front of me and I did nothing to stop him. No. I was not like him. A whimper followed my swallowed screams.

"Lili, wake up," a rough voice filled my ears as everything around me shook. "Lili!"

Darkness greeted me as I peeled my eyes open. True, middle-of-the-wilderness darkness. Pine-scented air from the open window cooled the space as I struggled to take it into my burning lungs. Careful, tired eyes looked down at me as I took labored breaths.

"Kaia," I said with a sob. "He killed her."

"It's not real. Your sister is not dead. You were having a nightmare. You were screaming," West said evenly, like a cowboy talking to a spooked horse. "This is real, Lili."

I nodded and looked around, trying to ground myself in the space as tears spilled down my cheeks. Dresser. Bedside table. Tiny clock. Framed flag. Skull mask. *Her blood. Her blood. Her blood.* Green eyes. Scar. I swallowed the memory down.

"I'm sorry. I didn't mean to wake you," I said, my apology thin and watery.

West gave a tight smile and looked around the room. Like it had been an effort to look directly at me. It wasn't enough that I was keeping him from his bed. Now I was waking him in the middle of the night. Embarrassed at my outburst, I looked down at my hands fisted in the sheets. West sighed and stood as he walked back to the door, ready to resume his reading in the living room.

"Wait, West?"

He turned, standing halfway through the door.

"Stay? Here," I said, pulling the blankets open for him. "That couch can't be comfortable. It doesn't look very comfortable," I offered with an attempt at a laugh.

West looked away, probably at the sofa I'd just mentioned. As he turned to leave again, I let desperation seep into my next words. I was asking too much. I had to be. But I didn't care.

"Please don't leave. Please."

For a while, he just stood there. I looked down at myself. Still sweaty, though the cool breeze wafting in had dried most of it. I was covered, thanks to his gigantic tee shirt. Looking up at him, I started searching for something more dignified than begging but came up empty.

"Stay," I whispered. "Please."

For a moment, he just stood there.

"Hang on," he said with a sigh, "and scoot over."

He disappeared into the living room. For a breath, I thought he had decided not to come back. Then he was in the doorway again. I'd moved to one side of the bed. The light on the bedside table clicked on as he turned the little switch. Then I could see he'd come back with a book

Not comfortable getting beneath the covers with me, he laid atop them with his pants still on. The mattress sank with his weight as he tucked a pillow beneath his head. Anxious to get my mind off of my father, I offered West a small truth.

"My great-grandmother was a circus performer."

"Hm?" The soft, confused hum was the only sign he'd heard me as he adjusted himself on the bed.

"Throwing knives was her act. She taught my grandfather how to do it. He taught Kaia and me."

He gave me a thoughtful look, then opened the book he'd brought in with him. Looking down at the open pages before him, he cleared his throat with a soft grunt.

"Alright. Where I left off, Gatsby was waiting for Daisy to come over to Nick's house. Let's see what happens next."

Nestling into the pillow, I watched him read from F. Scott Fitzgerald. Listened to the rich sound of the words as he read out loud, describing Gatsby and Daisy's tortured romance. I pulled the blankets around myself and breathed a sigh, hopeful that West's voice would protect my slumbering mind.

A GENTLE HAND stroked my hair as the other squeezed my fingers, warming them after the lethal dose of drugs had begun to release their grip on me. Lips brushed against my knuckles as they began to speak.

"Come on, Trouble. If you don't wake up, I'll have to start sparring with someone my own size."

The hand squeezed mine again. A kiss pressed it followed by an uneven breath.

AFTER FALLING ASLEEP to the sound of turning pages, I woke to find West curled around me. Protecting me from enemies he couldn't see. I turned to look at him. The little lamp was off and the book was on the table. Eying West's mouth, I remembered the way it felt pressed against my hand. It was relaxed with sleep, like the rest of his face. Unguarded, free of something I didn't know he'd been holding onto. I pressed a grateful kiss to the corner of his lips, relieved he hadn't stirred awake at my touch.

A mournful bird sang a two-note song outside, adding its music to the sawing breaths of the man next to me. We'd fallen asleep side by side, but the two of us were now shoved onto his side of the bed. I settled back against him again, trying to keep the feel of his protection around me for a little while longer.

"Good morning," he muttered, the sound of his voice was thick with sleep. He pushed himself up on an elbow and looked down at me.

"Hi."

"Any more nightmares?"

I shook my head. Up this close, I could see the ridges and valleys in his green irises.

"Good." West rolled onto his back, moving the muscled arm that had been around my waist to rest beneath his head. "That sofa really is shit compared to this."

I sat up on my elbows and looked at him. Aside from the fact that he was rumpled by sleep, the man looked good. Still in his clothes. Still on top of the covers while I was under the covers, also wearing his clothes. What a gentleman. I smiled to myself.

"This is your bed, you know. You're more than welcome to sleep in it. I'm the crasher here."

He cracked open an eye, raising his scarred eyebrow at me. I raised one back at him.

"I don't know how much sleep I'm going to get next to someone who snores all night."

West was unprepared for the pillow I launched at his face. His muffled laughter put a smile on my face.

"Come on, I'm hungry," I said as I hopped out of bed, feeling more energy than I had in days.

BACON SIZZLED ON the stove. Since I'd started eating again, he was determined to get as much food into my stomach as possible. I wasn't sure that was the approach I would have chosen, but I wasn't going to say no to the man making me breakfast. Especially when it felt like something from out of somebody's fantasy.

"Have you heard anything from your sister about Daniel? Is he alright?"

West glanced up at me from cutting vegetables in the kitchen.

"I talked to her on my way to town yesterday. He's doing fine. Not eating very much. I told her to keep him out of school, so her neighbor watches him while she's at work."

He took the pot off of the coffee maker. Two blue-speckled enamel cups were filled with the piping hot liquid and set on the counter.

"She said he's been asking a lot of questions. He wants to know what's happening," he said with a wince.

My gut turned at the thought of a stranger watching Daniel. Of course, I couldn't control the situation. I should've just been grateful for the help. I threw myself face down on the sofa with a defeated flop. The poor kid. I should have been there for him. He must have been so frightened.

"Popcorn," I mumbled into the cushions.

"What?"

I lifted my head.

"Daniel loves popcorn. If he won't eat anything else, she can make him popcorn. He won't be able to resist."

The sizzle of eggs hitting a pan accompanied West's hum of acknowledgment. Feeling like a useless leach, I got up to finish fixing the coffee cups. I'd never drunk a black cup of coffee in my life, I wasn't about to start now. After dumping a little cream and sugar into my cup, I hopped up on the counter and watched West prepare our food. Offered him his cup with just a dash of sugar. Took a sip from my coffee. For the first time in weeks, a sense of normalcy washed over me.

I resumed my position on the sofa with the steaming cup and a plate of eggs with a hash that smelled heavenly. Salty, buttery, savory. Guilt yanked at my insides as I thought about the gorgeous man making me breakfast compared to the terrible conditions my sister could be experiencing. If she was alive at all.

West would have the gym's phone number. Watching him approach from the kitchen, I thought about asking him for it. Lupo was at the gym more than he was at home. I could reach him there. He would be able to help me. Tell me what to do.

"Breakfast comes with a surprise this morning," West said with a tentative smile. He grunted softly as he hefted a box he'd left by the door onto the coffee table in front of me and gave it a soft tap. He slid a blade through the packing tape on top and pushed it toward me. "I forgot to give it to you yesterday. Open it."

I looked up at West. He was doing so much for me. Asking more of him felt selfish. He nodded encouragingly toward the box and I smiled. Later. I would ask him later.

Pulling the cardboard flaps apart, I looked down into the box. The first item was folded gently on top. My leather jacket. My things. This was a box of my things! I pulled out my hunting knife and its holster, holding it up to show him like a child holding up a Christmas gift. He nodded.

"My sister was able to go over to your place. It was in pretty bad shape, but she packed up some clothes and things for you. I'm sorry it took a while to get here."

"Will you stop apologizing to me? You literally saved my life. You just made me breakfast," I laughed.

I kept digging through the contents and folded as I removed what might've been all the panties I owned, as well as some bras, jeans, tees, socks, and a few sweaters. Then my hands found a clunky mass at the bottom. I squealed with joy as I pulled it from the box. My boots! West chuckled.

"I thought you might want those."

I continued to dig and found the thigh holster containing my throwing knives. Thankful I didn't cut myself on any of their sharp edges, I gently set them on the table on top of my jacket. West scooped eggs and potatoes into his mouth as he cleaned his plate and headed back into the kitchen.

"I better get into town," he said through a mouthful of egg.

"Again?" I tilted my head in confusion. He was going every day. Even with us going through more food, it seemed like a lot.

"The mail doesn't come out here, so I have to go get it."

I nodded and winced, thinking of my likely overstuffed mailbox back home. Still, it seemed odd that he'd be getting mail every day. Even if he was corresponding with this Emmit person, it was excessive. Especially when these jaunts to the post office took hours.

Trust. West had not given me any reason not to trust him. I could give him that. Even as thoughts of him working up a sweat with the blonde waitress from the general store pushed their way into my mind.

"Are you waiting for a new Big & Tall catalog or something?" I joked, holding out my arms to display the massive shirt I wore. "I can start wearing my own clothes now."

West laughed and grabbed his keys off of the hook.

"I'll be back in a little while," he said as he closed the door behind him.

7

MEDICAGO SATIVA

ater and grit met my fingertips as I pushed my hunting blade down the whetstone. Cabin fever was getting to me, but sharpening my knives gave me something to do. The grinding friction combined with the singing steel was like a tuning fork for my thoughts, giving me a sense of control over the worries that nipped at me in every unguarded moment.

Who took Kaia and was she alive? Was it Benjamin? Could I go to the family for help, or were they the ones to betray us to begin with? I was leaning heavily toward Benjamin. Whoever Benjamin was working with had grabbed my sister. She had set the meeting with him in the first place. He knew I would report to her. She was a reputation risk at best. A legal liability that would destroy his empire at worst.

Nico, her bodyguard, would have died for my sister. Just as his brother had died for our family. His father, Lupo, was getting chemotherapy when my sister was taken. Nico was by his side. Whoever took her knew that her bodyguard wouldn't be with her, which meant that they could have had help from one of our guys.

It occurred to me that one of our guys was probably working with Ronan Arawn. The Irish mafia boss had help from the inside when they burned down our restaurant. He seemed to be hell-bent on taking down the

Caccia empire. What had started as a tense rivalry had recently become blind hatred.

The Caccias were the dominating presence in Los Angeles. Men who served us were paid handsomely. They were loyal. But not all of them. There had been unrest when my sister took power. Vocal objections. Ozzie. He'd still pulled at the leash every chance he could get. Getting rid of my sister sounded exactly like something he'd want to do. Maybe he'd seen his chance and taken it. The very idea made my stomach turn.

I had to call them. Tell them I was alive. Lupo would help me. With Nico still in the family, I wasn't entirely sure how to approach him. But his father would never betray me.

Steel bit at my fingertips as I finished sharpening an edge. A frustrated grunt tore out of me. This was becoming tedious.

"Son of a bitch," I muttered as I brought my cut fingertip to my mouth, tasting the coppery tang of blood as I sucked at the injury. Completely cut off from technology. From everyone. The walls of the cabin felt like they were starting to press in on me. I shot up from my feet to open a window.

A breeze swept the scent of pine through the room as I resumed my position on the floor. We never took vacations when I was growing up. Our father treated us more like pets or experiments that he did children. Nonno was never allowed to have us for more than two days when my parents were alive. Once they were dead, he was too busy running his empire to take much time off for us.

After Kaia took over as Boss, we got so busy with work that the idea of a vacation completely evaporated. But we got away for a few hours. Just a few. A morning at the beach. An evening concert. A day at a theme park with Daniel.

Now that I was in the woods, god knows how many miles away from Kaia, asking for a week together felt greedy. I would kill for just a few minutes.

Leaning backward on my hands, I uncrossed my legs to stretch them across the worn area rug. My stomach tightened as I looked down at the array of newly sharpened blades. I thought about the workshop that was likely untouched. About all of the plants that likely needed my attention. All of the ingredients that were going to spoil if they weren't dealt with soon. The world, my world, was reaching out to grasp at my mind. Trying to pull me back in. With a deep breath, I put my tools away.

It was time to get back to work.

WHEN SOMEONE LEAVES you alone in their home, they assume you're going to go through their things. At least, they should. I had opened every drawer. Dug through every cabinet. Climbed the counters to look at the top of the refrigerator. Looked around until I found something ancient. Something of use.

The fucking Yellow Pages.

I sat on the kitchen counter and leaned against the wall, waiting for the old man to pick up. Lupo Ricci hadn't changed his home phone number in decades. I'd never called him there. The answering machine played his outgoing message. I hung up and dialed again, hoping he'd just been indisposed. After the second unanswered call, I looked at the clock and realized he'd be at the gym. One Two. The gym that wasn't listed.

"Shit," I muttered to myself as I hung the handset back on the phone's hook. The sound of tires on gravel told me that West was back from town. Like an attention-starved puppy, I fought the urge to run out and meet him. My nails clicked against the yellow laminate countertop, tapping as I wondered if he would have the gym phone number.

Deciding it couldn't hurt, I hopped off of the counter and walked onto the porch, then down to the gravel driveway. West was hauling a bag of laundry out of the Bronco. The henley was completely unbuttoned today, highlighting the muscles that peeked out from underneath. I couldn't help but admire the man.

"Hey," I said as casually as I could. "Do you remember the phone number for One-Two's? Or do you have it?"

"You shouldn't be making phone calls," he said as he hefted the bag onto his shoulder. I watched the tentacles of his bicep tattoo ripple with the movement.

"Why?" I asked flatly. I never responded well to being ordered around.

West gave me a skeptical look, as though the answer to my question was obvious. He took a step closer so that when he bent down to speak to me, we were almost nose to nose.

"You're off the radar here. We don't want anyone to come looking for you."

He brushed past me, taking the porch steps two at a time to get into the cabin. I stomped down the gravel driveway, following him back inside. This was not going the way I'd planned.

"No one at that gym knows me by the sound of my voice except for the one person I'm trying to get on the phone. I really don't think it's an issue."

Dropping the bag onto the floor, West whirled on me with thunderous intensity. We stood halfway inside the house, halfway out. He propped his hands on the door frame, dwarfing me. The wood groaned under his grip.

"They know you're alive, Lili. There's no way that they don't. Your apartment was ransacked. The club is being watched. You really think they're not looking for you? Waiting for you to screw up so they can kill you?"

"Who is they?!" I shouted. "I don't even know what I'm up against here!"

"You know goddamned well who."

His eyes flared with rage, stoking a torrent of anger in response. I stepped closer to him and gritted my teeth. Fingers circled my wrist and yanked me inside, closing the door behind me. A muscle ticked in West's jaw as he read my expression.

"What am I supposed to do? I can't stay here forever. They have my sister, West! She's all I have left," I shouted, trying to disguise the crack in my voice. I would not let myself cry. "She could be dead already and all I've done is play house with you and feel sorry for myself."

West's jaw worked again. He stepped aside to let me through the door. I walked inside and sat at the kitchen counter, turning the stool to face him. Picking up the laundry bag, he stormed into the bedroom and shut the door behind him.

I looked at the keys to the Bronco. It would be so easy. Easy to just jump in the truck and leave. The thought of abandoning West here kept my ass in my seat.

After about twenty minutes of silence from the next room, I got up and sat on the sofa with the copy of Sense and Sensibility I'd started. I'd been lost in the rainy hills of Devonshire when West reemerged and stood awkwardly in the center of the room as if he were still deciding on something.

I peered over the top of the book, doing my best to ignore him and failing miserably. He dropped an envelope on the coffee table before me and walked out the front door again. A phone number was written on the back of the envelope, with the number 12 scrawled above it. Not 12. One. Two.

8

CEDRUS LIBANI

He stayed outside. I sat inside, experiencing violent shifts from righteous anger to sour regret on a near-hourly basis. The phone remained on the hook. Mocking me with its green glare. *You got what you wanted*, it seemed to say. *Ungrateful wench.*

West went back and forth between cutting wood and working on his truck, which had to be fit for professional races by the end of the day. How much work did that thing need? I was thoroughly pickled in guilt and shame for how terribly I'd behaved.

He'd only been trying to help me. He didn't have to be doing any of this. It was so hard to believe I was even worth the trouble. Why was he doing it in the first place? This was above and beyond friendship.

After the sun went down and he was still outside, I decided one of us was going to have to apologize before he got pneumonia from the steadily dropping temperatures. Having shoved myself into a pair of jeans and a purloined sweater, I grabbed a pair of coats and went onto the porch.

"I've always loved that smell," I said weakly as I slowly walked down the steps.

West looked over his shoulder at me, then went back to sipping from a flask. A cement fire pit was crackling with roaring flames as he sat on one of the large round chunks of tree trunk cut into stools. Bronze and gold-tinged bits of dark hair peeked through the hasty knot he'd tied behind his head, lit by the flames before him. I took a few steps and sat on the one beside him.

"I'm sorry," I said, offering the coat I'd brought out for him. "I know you're right. You're just trying to help me and I'm not trying to complain or impose. I guess I am imposing. It's just that I don't know what to do and doing nothing makes me feel like shit. My sister is missing and it feels like I can't do anything to help her right now. I don't even know if Benjamin took her or if it was someone in the family who wanted her out of the way."

I looked down at my hands, wringing my sweater-covered fingers together out of discomfort. Apologizing to people was never a strength I possessed. Even though it killed me, I forced myself to continue.

"I feel powerless. I hate feeling powerless."

"Yeah, I know what you mean," he mumbled, not looking at me. Staring into the fire. This mood had been coming and going for days. Like he couldn't decide how to behave with me now that I was around all the time. Every time he'd stopped himself from saying something, I'd felt it. It seemed like our all-night conversation had possibly been a one-time thing. A log tumbled and sparked. We watched them disappear. Then he asked, "How are you feeling?"

"I feel alright. Only sort of worn out now. Getting a little stir crazy though," I said with a sigh. West hummed his agreement with a soft laugh. The fire popped and crackled as we watched it. The words came out before I could stop them. "I just keep wondering how it happened."

"How what happened?"

"How I let my guard down so easily. I keep wondering how I could have been so stupid. And then I can't stop thinking about how much I hate myself because all of this is my fault." The last words came out in a croak as my throat tightened. This wouldn't end in tears. I wouldn't let it and forced myself to take a deep breath.

"You shouldn't hate yourself for what happened. Sometimes we let ourselves want things, even when we know we shouldn't," he said, staring into the fire.

"I have a hard time believing you'd ever be so impulsive," I swallowed as I wiped away a stray tear. "You'd never do anything like that, would you?"

West looked at me sideways. With a small laugh to himself, he turned and put his arm around my waist. The other hand tilted my face up to meet his gaze. In his smokey green eyes, there was a sort of earnestness mixed with something else. A finger traced over my jaw and sent a shiver through me. Our breath fogged together in the cold night air. I knew, absolutely knew, what he wanted to do. His nose grazed mine as his breath fanned across my lips. It felt like I'd stopped breathing altogether.

"Fuck it," he growled.

The grip on my jaw firmed and pulled my face to his. Soft, sensuous lips brushed mine in a kiss that felt half-sure. When my mouth moved against his in what I hoped was an encouraging gesture, he softly grunted. His hands had been on me a hundred times. A thousand. Our bodies had been pressed together before. Moved together. Sweat together. But when his mouth covered mine, it was like touching him for the first time.

Little explosions sang along every nerve. Warmth pooled low in my belly. My hand fisted the fabric of his pants, desperately fighting the urge to pull him closer. Maintain some sense of control over myself. The tips of his fingers drifted down and around my neck, until they were tangled in my hair. As his tongue licked the seam of my lips, soft cedar-scented tufts of his beard tickled my chin and I let out a giggle. West stilled and pulled away like the noise had startled sense back into him.

Clearing his throat, he murmured, "I'm sorry." Before I could find my words and tell him that I wasn't sorry at all or reach out to pull him back, he walked into the cabin. I felt the cold in his absence and pulled my arms around myself.

The Bronco roared to life in the driveway and West drove away into the night. I sat there with one hand over my mouth, staring into the flames. After extinguishing the fire, I went to the bedroom and closed the door.

THE HIGH OF what had just happened had worn off quickly as I picked at my nails and thought about the last time West had that look on his face. The one he had right before he kissed me only minutes ago. We had been in my apartment. He'd driven me home from Muse. I'd been drinking and he took my shoes off for me. Kneeling on the floor, as he lifted my feet out of my shoes, he looked up at me with that same expression. Then he told me to go to sleep and left.

When it was clear that he wasn't coming back anytime soon, I changed into one of his shirts and pairs of boxers and climbed into bed. I turned over and looked at his side, still thinking about what had just happened. Then I screamed into my pillow like a teenager.

West kissed me. He kissed me. We kissed.

Something between us had shifted. It could have been when he rescued me. Or even before that. But I felt it and I knew that he did, too. Like a form of magnetism. Or gravity.

It felt like we were two cars hurtling down a highway, bound to crash into each other. I'd felt it then, just as I was feeling it now. Want. Dread. There was no way we were headed toward anything but disaster. He deserved someone better. Someone stronger. Someone who wasn't going to bring him down with them. I told myself I needed a distraction, and I was too damned selfish to push him away. West's words drifted back to me.

Sometimes we let ourselves want things, even when we know we shouldn't.

DAWN STARTED TO peer through the window, illuminating the bedroom with soft blue light. I lay perfectly still, waiting to hear any sign that West had returned. Deep, even breaths sounded from behind me. When I first opened my eyes, I thought about Kaia. Daniel. The family. Benjamin. But setting eyes on West had pushed those thoughts away. As he had the night before, West was fully clothed and curled around me. His large body was a wall, defending me from the world.

Unsure about how long he'd been gone, how long he'd been here next to me, I uncovered myself and scooted back toward him, wanting to feel his warmth. I didn't stop until his chest was pressed against me. Half asleep, he draped an arm around me.

"Go back to sleep," he muttered.

Selfish. I was so selfish and filled with want. It was easy to lose myself in the urge to touch him. Be touched by him. The desire for him was something I could be certain about when the rest of my life felt lost at sea.

The memory of the last man I'd been intimate with threatened to douse what was building in me. Lingering at the edges of my mind as I wiggled into West, adjusting for comfort when I felt what was pressing against his zipper. My hips rolled in little circles. I kept moving, grinding my ass against his growing erection.

"Lili," he growled. "What are you doing?"

I was silent, continuing to move against him. His body betrayed the intention of his question. Against my ass, his hips made small thrusting movements to meet mine. We had only barely kissed. Instead of having a conversation about it like adults, I was grinding against him. In the small hours of the morning, he was as weak as I was. The arm that had wrapped around me pulled my body firmly against his. I squeezed my thighs together, looking for relief from the ache that had started to build.

A small pit of fear opened in me as memories of Benjamin flooded my consciousness. His rough, dominating touch. The aggression I'd mistaken for passion. Deciding not to let him have another victory over me, I turned to look at the man lying next to me.

"West," I panted.

"Use your words. What do you want, Lili?"

Tilting my chin up so our lips grazed each other, his beard brushed my cheek as I whispered, "Touch me."

He slipped his other arm beneath me. His breath warmed my face as I licked and nipped the curve of his stubbled jaw, urging him on. With one hand still pressing me against him, his other teased the edge of my boxers. *His* boxers. I arched against him as he buried his face in my neck.

"Touch you where?" He asked, not entirely a question. The other hand wandered up, up, under the shirt to find my breast. Massaging one, then the other.

"Please," I breathed. With his length pressing into me with every thrust of his hips, I wondered how he would feel inside me. The thought alone made me squirm. The hand playing with my waistband plunged beneath the elastic, seemingly done with toying with me. His chest rumbled with a moan at the wetness he found waiting for him.

"Oh, you are Trouble."

Curiosity got the better of me as I slid my hand between us and rubbed the heel of my palm against his arousal. Selfish need had my fingers curling around his shaft, aching to know exactly how he felt. How I affected him. He groaned into my neck, pressing himself into my hand. As he did, his fingers brushed against my slit, teasing every inch of me.

I opened my legs, dropping one around his to give him more access. He obeyed my silent command, centering his focus on my clit. Like a match being dragged across sandpaper, the sweet friction promised to ignite me from within. A work-roughened thumb stroked the bundle of nerves, causing my thighs to shake.

Small moans fell from me, delicate compared to the sound of his thunderous growls. The tips of his fingers tested my center, dipping in slightly and withdrawing. Moving up and down my slit as his thumb continued its brutal strokes.

"Fuck" he growled. "You don't know what you do to me, Lili."

My hips jerked as he pushed two fingers inside of me. The hand that had pressed me against him moved down, pushing against my pelvis to give the fingers he curled inside more leverage against that spot that he seemed to find with no trouble. Our eyes locked as he pressed his forehead to mine. We both knew exactly what we were doing and had no idea at the same time.

As his green eyes flickered with something, I wondered if this was a mistake. Maybe I was taking advantage. Surges of pleasure fought the raging doubts in my mind.

His hips rutted against my palm and my ass. I couldn't stop the scream that burst from my lips as release barreled into me. My legs reflexively clamped around his hand as I rode it through my orgasm.

He buried his face in my hair, hot ragged breaths warming my neck as he slowed his thrusts against me. Once his grip on my shaking body loosened, I turned to face him. My eyes drifted to the front of his pants. Where his erection had been a dark spot now appeared. Then my gaze met his. I was surprised at what I saw. He looked almost... angry with me.

Doubts gnawed at me as West got out of bed and left the room, slamming the door shut behind him. We had crossed a line. Or at least I had.

9

CINNAMOMUM VERUM

Sweet. Tapdancing. Jesus.

What just happened? We just pawed each other like horny teenagers under the bleachers, that's what. What is wrong with me? West's hands were all over me. I tried not to think about it. Tried not to think about how he felt in my hand. Or about how I wanted more. But this was fine. It was just pent-up energy letting itself out. We were steam and this cabin was a kettle. My life was already complicated enough. I didn't need to add this mess to it. We could just be friends who fooled around and leave it at that, right?

Too embarrassed to leave the room, I let myself fall asleep again. The sun had been warming the bed for hours when I finally opened my eyes again and rehearsed my speech about letting off steam. Then I heard a woman's voice coming from outside. Curiosity quickly doused any lingering embarrassment as I shoved myself into some clothes and hurried to the window, ignoring the anxious hope that I wasn't about to see that damned waitress.

Long dark hair piled in a messy bun and an oversized pink hoodie were all I could see from peeking through the curtains. West was smiling at her, leaning against what had to be her car. A yellow Volkswagen bus that had seen better days. Alright, so not the blonde waitress, but who?

I shut the front door behind me as quietly as I could but was immediately sold out by a squeaking plank on the porch. West's smile faded as he glanced up and the woman whirled to look at me. Beautiful, kind brown eyes met mine.

I took her in for a moment. West's relaxed posture. Their matching noses and eyebrows. Well, minus a scar. It wasn't hard to guess who this was.

"Hey! It's good to see you moving around," she said, quickly walking toward me. I blinked and tilted my head, slightly confused. "Lanna," she said with a hand on her chest. "I'm not surprised you don't remember me. I'm -"

"You're his sister," I confirmed with a nod toward West, trying not to sound too relieved. *Oh god*, I thought, *what were they talking about?*

"Unfortunately," she smiled. West grunted at the insult. "And you're Lili. Lilith," she said, quickly correcting herself.

"Lili is fine," I grinned. "You saved my life. You can call me whatever you want. Sorry I couldn't introduce myself when I was unconscious."

She chuckled. West crossed his arms and grunted, clearing his throat.

"My little brother was just going inside to make us some coffee," Lanna said, her eyes sparking with mischief. "I want to talk to my new friend."

I shot West a helpless look as he passed me to go inside. I didn't do well with new people. He knew that. What if I said the wrong thing? He only shook his head and laughed.

"Come sit," Lanna waved me over to the steps, straightening her black leggings before sitting down herself. I glanced down at her pink shearling boots and looked up to see her giving me an assessing once-over. It was tempting to ask for information about West, but there was only one subject I truly cared about.

"So," I said as I sat, "how's my nephew? Where is he?"

"Good, I think," she said with a tired sigh. "He's with my neighbor."

I angled my head, waiting for her to continue.

"He's been quiet, but he's eating and sleeping normally. Thanks for the popcorn tip, by the way. He's eating it by the box. At first he had a lot of questions, but I guess he didn't like my answers because he stopped asking after a while."

"What did you tell him?"

"Well," she sighed. "I told him you and his mother had to go away for work. That neither of you could call."

I tucked my tongue into my cheek and nodded, trying not to seem ungrateful. Daniel was like me. Never very good with strangers. This was my fault. I couldn't imagine what everything had been like for him. And it was all my fault. The sound of a spoon clinking in coffee cups filtered through the kitchen window as we sat there in silence for a moment.

"If you have any children's books around, he'll like those. Or movies about super heroes. But he can't watch Star Wars yet."

Not without me.

Lanna nodded thoughtfully.

"Also," I added. "Keep him inside. Away from other people. Just to be safe."

Another nod. A minute passed. Then she blew out a breath.

"I'm glad I finally got to meet the famous Lili," Lanna said with a small smile, changing the subject. I raised my eyebrows at her.

"Famous?"

"You're all my brother talks about," she said. She lowered her voice to imitate West's. "'Lili said the funniest thing' or 'Lili kicked my ass today.' That one's my favorite. You'll have to show me how to do that."

I laughed as I heard the door swing open. West eyed the two of us cautiously as he elbowed his way out with two steaming blue coffee cups. Lanna smiled up at her brother as she took the cup from him. He returned her smile, not sparing a glance my way as he handed me my cup. She watched him go back inside before she spoke again.

"I do have something to say to you," Lanna said, her voice taking on a more serious note. *Here it comes*, I thought. *Don't get my brother mixed up in your mess.* I had nearly gotten myself killed. What did she think that was about? I leaned against the railing, bracing myself for what was certainly coming next.

"When he got home from his last tour, he wasn't the West you know now. He was shut off. All darkness," she took a sip from her cup and winced at the black coffee. She tossed an accusing glance toward the house. I glanced down at my cup, holding it up so she wouldn't see that he'd made mine with cream and sugar. "He slept on my sofa for weeks. Barely bathed. Hardly spoke. I didn't know what to do."

Lanna took another long pull from her coffee, despite it being black which was clearly not her preference. This was certainly not where I thought this conversation was going. With a puff of air through her nose, she continued.

"I suggested he get some exercise. Maybe work out some tension at least. That's when he met you."

I thought about the near-silent man I'd met at One Two. All muscle and hardly any smiles. I'd been surrounded by unsmiling men my entire life. It hadn't scared me then. But I'd felt drawn to him somehow. Recognized the broken look in his eyes. I sipped from my cup, bracing myself for the scolding that would follow this lengthy preamble.

"And you gave him a job at that strip club, which I don't love, by the way."

I chuckled, looking down into my cup. Lanna's face was serious when I looked up again.

"Then he started training with you. I think working with you gave him a sense of purpose."

Lanna put down her coffee and stretched her hands, fanning her fingers out like a cat stretching after a nap. With a roll of her shoulders, she looked at me again.

"When he got home from his last tour, he was angry all the time. Sad, too. But after he started working with you, the hard days seemed to be farther apart." Lanna seemed to weigh what she wanted to say next. She took down her hair and put it up in the same nervous way I'd seen West do a thousand times. "He started therapy. Moved out. I know some things may never get fixed, but I can kind of see the old West again. I think you did that."

"I don't know how much I did. I just took advantage of his generosity, I think," I joked, trying to brush off the pain that pressed in on my chest. I glanced at the door, wondering about the man on the other side of it. Lanna shook her head at my joke and took another sip of coffee. A small wince followed. Definitely didn't like black coffee.

She was kind and warm, just like her brother on his better days. The more I looked, the more I could see the other evidence of resemblance between them. The shape of her eyes. The wave in her dark hair.

"Breakfast," West called out from the open window. "Come on."

With a small smile, she shrugged and stood from the porch, brushing off the back of her pants. Looking down at me, she offered a hand to help me stand.

"He helped me too." The confession tumbled out of me as I rose. She nodded. It felt incomplete. He'd more than helped me, but I didn't know if I had words for what he'd done.

WEST HAD LIT up around his sister. They laughed over stacks of pancakes he'd whipped up for all of us. He talked and joked with her so much that it filled the awkward space between us. It was enough to ease my worries about Lanna catching on to the weirdness she'd dropped in on.

After his sister left us with big hugs and headed back down the mountain, West went into town. Again. He'd left only minutes after his sister. I didn't have time to say a word to him alone. But it did give me time to call One Two and leave a vague message on Lupo's answering machine. I'd stashed the number in my box of things, digging it out once I had time alone. After West had been so adamant about not calling, picking up the phone had felt like a betrayal. But I'd done it anyway.

West being gone also gave me hours alone to think about what we had done this morning. And the look on his face afterward.

Angry. He'd been so angry with me. Then he acted like nothing had happened at all. What was that about?

I'd come to only one conclusion. That blonde woman in the store. He'd been leaving me to go see her. He was angry with me because he was seeing her. I made him cross some line and ruined our friendship because I couldn't keep my hands to myself. Sure, he kissed me first. He crossed the line. But I had pushed him well beyond his boundaries.

I was sitting on the kitchen counter, eating a grilled cheese sandwich I'd fixed for myself when he finally walked in. His hair was down around his shoulders but rumpled enough to tell me he'd been messing with it a lot. The flannel he'd thrown on this morning had its sleeves rolled up.

"Where've you been?" I said with a mouthful of cheese and bread. Agitated, he held up a brown bag from the market as if in answer.

"For four hours?" I asked with an incredulous look. "Yeah, right."

He rolled his eyes and dropped the bag on the counter next to me. Muttered something inaudible. The words left my mouth before I could stop them.

"Were you with that blonde woman? The waitress? Is she your girlfriend?"

West snorted. I dipped my sandwich in some ketchup and took another bite, trying my hardest to be casual. *You don't own him,* I thought. *He can see whoever he wants.*

"She's not my girlfriend."

He started unpacking the bag. Apples, orange juice, laundry detergent. Each item slammed onto the counter. Punctuating whatever thoughts he wasn't sharing with me.

"So you're not dating her then?" The question was half muffled by another bite. God, I was acting like a jerk.

"We've been on a few dates," he huffed, not meeting my gaze.

"Well, I'm sorry. I didn't know you were dating someone. I wouldn't've pushed you to do anything," I said with a swallow. Hard crisp edges of bread scraped down my throat. It was so easy. Easy to take out my frustration on him. He was a safe space and I was ruining it with my moronic jealousy. *Stop it, Lili.*

I took a sip of water and looked him over as I wiped my mouth with my wrist. Trying to retain some level of almost destroyed dignity, I stayed perched on the counter. Tried to seem casual. He stopped unpacking the grocery bag, and instead just stared into it.

"Does that bother you?" He inclined his head, ire lacing every word. His eyes locked on mine with simmering anger. Hell, even the scar above his eye looked like it was scowling at me. I deserved it.

Stop it. Stop it. Stop it.

"Nope. Do what you want. Do her. If you haven't already." I finished my sandwich to demonstrate just how little I wanted him to think I cared about the situation and set the empty plate into the sink.

"Lili. Does it bother you?" His eyes moved from my face to the sink and up again. I looked down at my glass and brought it to my mouth for a sip. I shrugged, not meeting his gaze. My insides felt tight with nerves like my body was preparing for a fight it knew I was losing.

"Why would it bother me?"

"You know why."

I didn't respond, instead taking another sip of water. Breath was trapped in me, making the small sip feel like drowning. Even without looking, I knew West's eyes were pinned to me as he moved to brace his hands on the counter, caging me in. My thighs grazed his forearms and I felt my cheeks flush under his stare. I tried to breathe. Where did all of the oxygen go?

"I'm not seeing her anymore. The waitress," he said, his bared teeth made his voice sound like it was dripping in acid.

"Oh," I whispered, looking down, away, anywhere but into those green eyes that were burning a hole right through me.

"Oh," he snorted. "That's all she has to say," he muttered the words angrily as he pushed away and stalked out of the house.

Stunned for a moment, I just sat there and stared at the floor. A blink brought me back from feeling like prey hoping for mercy. I looked around and noticed the bag still sitting on the counter. My fingers dragged the bag closer so I could look inside. There was only one item left unpacked. I pulled out the small blue bottle and examined it.

Bubble bath.

10

HAMAMELIS VIRGINIANA

The pan clattered against the steel sink as I rinsed it out. Washing dishes had nothing to do with the fact that I could watch the driveway through the kitchen window. I didn't hear the Bronco start. I could just barely see the doors opening and closing. As I rinsed my dish, I kicked myself for opening my stupid mouth.

West's boots clunked on the steps, then the deck. Then he came through the door again with what looked like a large backpack in hand. The khaki-colored camouflage and matching flag patch told me it was from his military days. After getting a better look at the long asymmetrical shape, I had a pretty good idea as to what was in it. It wasn't a backpack. It was a rifle case.

"I haven't been entirely honest with you," he said as he put the case down on the table. His voice was low. Different from the frustrated notes I'd heard last. Propping my hip on the counter, I folded my arms. Whatever the explanation was…Whatever he was about to tell me, I could deal with it. After everything he'd done for me, I owed him an open mind.

"I've been going to the range to dial in the sights. It's been a while since I used this," West said, patting the bag. "It takes a while."

I couldn't stop myself from chewing my thumbnail. He didn't need to give me an explanation. He didn't need to be doing any more than he already was. Not when I was eating his food, drinking his booze, sleeping in his bed. That didn't stop me from asking more questions.

"Were you a sniper?" I blurted confusion probably all over my face.

"No. But I had that training. Sniper training. It was part of my SEAL program."

I nodded, remembering the framed patch on his dresser I'd seen when I first opened my eyes in this place.

"You were a Navy SEAL," I said. "I saw your patch in the other room."

"Yeah. I was a sailor in the Navy before that," he said, looking at me expectantly. Like he was waiting for me to judge him. For what, I didn't know. I angled my head and looked at the bag on the table, then back at him.

"Did you eat anything while you were dialing in your sights or is snacking while sniping a no-no?"

He laughed. An actual laugh. And something in my chest loosened at the sound.

"I didn't eat, no."

"Ah," I nodded. "Well, that explains your mood. I can fix you a grilled cheese. It's the closest I can get to cooking without burning this whole cabin down."

"Sure. That sounds good."

I took the pan off of the drying rack and wiped it down with the kitchen towel. West took the gun out of his bag. I'd never seen a sniper rifle before but I had no idea it came with so many parts. Fetching the bread, cheese, and butter out of the refrigerator, I stole casual glances at him as I watched him walk to the wall and pull the framed picture away from it to reveal a safe. My eyes popped open. He punched in his code and a small chirp sounded as it opened for him. How had I not heard this?

As I made his sandwich, I tried not to think about it. Tried not to think about the fact that he wanted to be ready. Ready to fight. Ready to protect me. From who? I wondered if I should call Lupo again as I looked over my shoulder to see him put away the dismantled pieces of his rifle into black foam next to a disassembled 9mm pistol. The safe shut with a click and I quickly turned back to the stove.

"It's almost ready," I said over my shoulder.

West walked toward the kitchen, grabbed the paper bag from the counter, and then went into the bathroom, closing the door behind him. I heard the water start and plated his sandwich, wondering if it would be cold by the time he got out of the shower.

ABOUT TEN MINUTES went by. I resumed my position on the kitchen counter, this time with a small pour of bourbon instead of water. Kicking my feet into the cabinet below me, I glanced down at the sandwich on the counter. A sip of bourbon had me wondering if West was ever coming out of the bathroom when the door opened. He appeared, still in his clothes, as steam billowed out around him. I probably had that dumb, confused look on my face. A smile curled his lips when he noted my narrowed eyes.

"I think," he said as he casually strolled toward the kitchen, "I owe you something."

West looked down at the sandwich, then up at me. He extended a hand to me. Trying to keep wariness from my eyes, I took it and hopped off of the counter. I tried not to think about the feel of his hand on mine. Or the idle stroke of his thumb across my knuckles. For a man who had stormed out of the bedroom this morning, this touch was surprisingly intimate. What was this? I felt more confused than ever. Before I knew it, we were in the bathroom.

It was dark, illuminated by one candle sitting on the sink and light pouring into the small window from the full moon. Before me sat the iron bathtub, full and steaming.

"One bath," he said, warming my ear with his breath. "Bubbles and everything."

I chewed on my lip and looked back at him. I was met with the expression I'd noted before. Earnestness mixed with...I didn't know. But there was a look in his eyes that had become clear to me now. Want. Whether he said it or not, I knew it was there. Something he was fighting. It took my breath away. Shaky fingers curled around the hem of my shirt as I quickly pulled it over my head.

"I'll leave you to it," he said, averting his eyes as he turned to walk away. My hand shot out to his before I could change my mind.

"No," I breathed. His eyes were pinned to mine, not daring a glance down to my breasts as their dusky pink tips furled at the exposure. I let my hair down in an inky black waterfall around my bare shoulders. West's gaze traveled down with the movement, allowing the sweep of hair to guide his view to every inch of bare skin.

I let go of his hand and took a small step backward, moving my fingers to the button and zipper on my jeans.

"I know you've seen me naked already," I said with a wry smile. "And baths are so lonely."

His eyes were sharp. Honed in on me.

"You were half-dead when I undressed you, Trouble. I wasn't looking for fun."

Trouble. It was his new nickname for me. I had to admit, I sort of liked it. As I slid the jeans down my thighs along with the panties I'd been wearing, I thought maybe it suited me. A small step had me standing completely naked before him. West's throat worked as he took in every inch of me. Dipping to where his hands had been only hours ago. Biting my lip was the only way to keep my grin contained. Our eyes met as he shook his head at me.

"You're looking now."

He swore softly. I laughed and turned toward the tub. Steam curled around shafts of moonlight as small bubbles fizzed under my fingertips. One step had me in the water. Though I knew it was hot, it was no match for the blood pumping through my veins. I lowered myself into the tub, eyes pinned to West. He hadn't moved except to place his hands on the doorframe over him, muscles straining from his iron grip on the wood.

I dipped below the surface, letting myself sink to soak the mass of hair on my head. The water pressing in around me matched the blazing heat roaring through my blood. Another distraction. An escape from cabin fever. The invading thoughts of my sister. My mind wanted to torture me with worry. My body wanted to free me from that anguish. Wanted West's body to be the liberator of my pain.

When I rose, I glanced at the door to find it empty. It was only for a moment. West appeared with two glasses of bourbon, the one I'd been drinking and his own. He set his glass down on the sink. I reached a hand out for it and noticed the clink of ice. He jerked the glass away from me and knelt next to the tub. After placing the glass on the metal soap tray, he fished a cube out and brought it to my lips to trace their shape.

West's eyes followed the ice as it slowly melted against my skin. The sharp cold moved down my chin to slide along my jaw and down my neck. I watched his expression darken as his touch drifted across my collarbone. The ice disappeared at the hollow of my throat. Another cube was in his hand before I could breathe a word.

My eyes didn't leave his face until he moved, placing himself behind the tub. Instead, I tracked the hand that picked up where he'd left off, skating down my chest to a nipple that tightened at his touch. A soft gasp spilled from me at the contact. A dark laugh sounded behind me.

"Do you know..." he started. Fuck, his voice dropped an octave. My toes curled at the sound. "How hard it's been not to touch you?"

His confession was nearly lost to the touch of his hands. How hard it's been not to touch me? Like he'd been caging himself. How hard it's been. Like he'd been tortured. The confession was laced with agony.

Before I could process another word, the ice moved around my breast until his fingers cradled it. His arm snaked across my chest and the cube grazed the inside of my other breast. Hot breaths fanned across my neck as I let out another gasp, my hands gripping the rim of the tub.

"You," West murmured, "have the softest skin. And you sound so sweet when you come."

His hand flattened against my stomach as his teeth grazed my ear. I arched against the tub.

"Lili, you're more beautiful than you have any damned right to be."

A soft lick followed his teeth, trailing down my neck. He planted a kiss at the base. My core tightened at the touches. The teases. The way his beard felt against my skin. I could come just from this. His other hand, I'd somehow forgotten the other hand, found my breast as the first moved down my stomach. Lower.

"Especially when you're jealous."

A knuckle dragged across my center in a single teasing stroke. My back arched again as I sucked in a breath. He stood slowly, taking his hands away from me. I looked up at him as he took a pull from his bourbon. Disappointment must have shown on my face as he smirked down at me.

"Enjoy your bath," he said. And left.

11

MELISSA OFFICINALIS

West was asleep on the sofa when I got out of the bathroom, a crumb-covered plate and an empty glass on the coffee table beside him. Swearing in every Italian curse word I knew, I went into the bedroom and slammed the door behind me. I had spent the rest of that bath drinking and scrubbing, trying to undo the aching need that he'd created. He'd teased me into a stupor I wouldn't soon forget. After tossing back the bourbon he'd left for me, I had shaved everywhere I could with what had to be his sister's razor. I'd washed everywhere. Even between my toes. I'd washed my hair and braided it to control the insanity of air-dried waves. They say that idle hands are the devil's playthings. My hands needed to stay busy or I was going to ring his damned neck.

As I drifted off to sleep, flashes of things floated into my mind. Like a television switching between channels. Except everything felt real. A ripped evening gown dropped beads everywhere, clacking on metal and carpet. Blood. Sweat. Hands-on my face as a voice was begging. Pleading with me.

"Come on, Lili. Stay with me. Open your eyes!"

Another voice said *"I need to hook her up to a drip. She needs an antagonist now or we're going to lose her."*

A hand brushed hair off of my face in gentle strokes while a wet washcloth was pressed against my forehead. A whiff of cedar. Soft words from a tired, broken voice.

"You know, sometimes I can smell you on my clothes after we train together," he said. *"I put off changing for as long as I can so I can smell you a little longer. Like vanilla and something. What is that smell? Wake up. Wake up and tell me."*

Burning pain, like a pulled muscle or a sprain, tightened my chest. Focused, deep breathing lulled me to sleep as I tried to forget the sound of fear in his voice and the crushing feeling that stirred in my heart.

THE CORRIDOR WAS long. White. Absent of any color. Except for the color blue. I looked down at them again. Rolled them around in my hand.

The offices were empty. Even the ornate office of the head man in charge. I pushed the door open and strode to the desk. Right where I'd met him the first time. I leaned against the edge, just as he had done.

They were surprisingly warm to the touch. His eyes. For as blue as they were. For as cold as they had seemed. Benjamin's ice blue eyes were warm, cradled in my palm.

THE HOUSE WAS empty. Again. West had left. Again. I got out of bed and looked for him, expecting to have an awkward conversation. Or not talk at all. What were we even doing besides dancing around each other like a couple of idiots? I looked around the room for the gun bag. Noting its absence, I decided he'd gone to the range. Again.

After calling the gym again to no avail, I proceeded to eat two slices of toast with unholy amounts of butter on them and smeared in blackberry jam. Then I started picking up things around the room, deciding that I was going to start memorizing the phone numbers of everyone I knew as soon as I had the opportunity. I marked West's place in the book he'd been reading. Folded the blanket he'd been using. Smelled the shirt he'd been wearing. Cursed myself for smelling the shirt. And did it again.

It only took me two hours to clean two rooms from top to bottom. Well, two rooms and the kitchen. And the bathroom. The grout in the bathroom had been surprisingly tidy. Not satisfied with sitting in the freshly cleaned space, I stepped outside with my throwing knives and started hurling them at my makeshift target. Relief pooled in me as I realized my body finally felt whole again.

Hurling steel at a target had always helped to hone my thoughts. Daniel was safe. The billionaire I'd been mixed up with wanted me dead. My sister was missing. Either the family she was in charge of or the billionaire was responsible. If someone in the family was trying to start a power grab, they would also want me out of the way. If I was going to get out of this, I had to tackle one problem at a time.

I needed to get back to Los Angeles.

IT WASN'T LONG before I heard the rumble of the Bronco's engine.

"You hungry?" I heard West call from the driveway. "I've got lunch."

"Oh yeah? What have you got for me this time?"

I approached the Bronco, untying the hair I'd secured atop my head.

"Patty melt on rye for you. Club sandwich for me."

"Pickles?"

"Oh, I've got a big pickle for you," he smirked. The paper bag hit the hood with a plop.

"You're disgusting," I giggled.

My laughter was interrupted by the shrill, insistent ring of the phone piercing the air. We both heard the shrill ringing. Fear clamped down on my insides as I imagined the possibilities. Daniel could be hurt. Lupo could be calling with a warning. Or Nico. Had something happened to Lupo? Was that why he hadn't been answering? Why he hadn't called me back?

West's steps were swift as he strode inside to take the call. My boots crunched in the dry leaves and pine needles as I hustled after him, taking two steps for every one of his. He dropped the bag of food onto the counter as he picked up the phone. That damn thing hadn't rung once since I'd been here.

"Yeah," he barked.

It wasn't a greeting. It was a dare to speak.

"Yes, it is. She is," he said into the receiver. "No. Almost."

He paused and looked at me, still listening to the person on the other end. Who is it? I mouthed the words to him. Ignoring me, he answered the caller in rough short sentences.

"She's fine."

He was still looking at me, but his gaze hardened with irritation. I would have melted from the accusatory look in his eye if I wasn't trying so hard to listen. Trying to hear anything on the other side of this conversation. Lupo. This had to be Lupo.

"I don't know. I'm finding out."

He glanced to the mail stacked neatly on the counter. Then to me. His mouth tightened as he turned toward the wall.

"No. She'll call you later. Tomorrow."

The phone was back on its hook before I could speak. West looked down at his boots, flexing his hands.

"Who was that?"

"You know who that was."

"Why did you hang up? I needed to talk to him!"

"I didn't even know that you called him, Lili. I thought you were just going to let him know you were alright. And you gave him this number?"

His tone was sharp, matching that angry look that had returned to his face.

"He doesn't know where I am or where this is. He just knew he needed to call here for you. Lupo is a safe person. I don't know where my sister is. I need to find her. I need to figure out who wants her out of the way. If it's the family. If they want me out of the way too. He can help me."

"You don't know that."

"Yes, I do," I growled. "Lupo was my grandfather's bodyguard. I know to you he's just an old man running a boxing gym, but to me he's family. He would never hurt me and neither would his son. Nico wouldn't have let them take my sister which is why they moved while he was away. I don't have anyone else to turn to and I can't just sit here. I can't do nothing. Don't you understand that?"

I opened the door to retrieve the knives I'd left buried in the wood. Spending time with West was one of my favorite things, but questioning my judgment made me want to stab something. I turned and said, "I can't trust a lot of people, West, but I'd trust him with my life."

THOUGH MY PRIDE had demanded I leave the room, my stomach kicked me for not taking the patty melt with me on the way out. Or maybe at least the pickle. The stump was splintered to hell by the time I heard the front door close. My stomach growled in response. Glancing over a shoulder as I lined up my next shot, I spotted West carrying bags to the Bronco.

"Leaving again?" I called as I threw a dagger.

The front door shut again. Not only was he bailing on me again, but he was also not talking to me.

"Typical," I grumbled, throwing my second blade. The silent treatment was not going to work on me.

Boots crunched behind me, approaching me slowly. Without turning to look at him, I said, "If you leave now, this argument is going to be very one-sided."

Arms locked around my chest, pinning mine to my sides. My reflexes were slow. I'd been overly confident about my safety. Only by seconds, but enough for me to lose my last blade. The steel thudded into the dirt. Not West. This was definitely not West. I fought to widen my stance as the man behind me lifted me. I kicked and screamed, but remained locked in his hold.

"Not today, sweetheart," a rough, raspy voice laughed. "Hold still, you little bitch."

Another man appeared from behind a tree, stalking toward me with a gun in his gloved hands. I looked down at the hands attached to the arms squeezing the breath out of me. My ribs ached from the compression. I couldn't get another breath down to scream again. Latex gloves. This was an execution.

West left me and now I was going to die. Killed in the middle of nowhere by two goons I'd never even seen before. Who were these assholes? As the man walking toward me lifted his silenced pistol, a hole appeared in his forehead. My would-be executioner fell to the ground, revealing West walking toward us with a pistol. He hadn't left. He was here. And he was saving my ass. Again.

"Fuck!" the guy behind me sputtered out. Dropping me like a bag of laundry, I fell to the ground on my hands and knees. They barked at the sudden impact. The man was large and slow, trying to keep me between him and West's gun. My fingers wrapped around the blade I'd dropped and flung it. Steel penetrating flesh squelched as it found its mark between his shoulder blades. His groan of pain was silenced by a bullet.

West's knees hit the pine-covered ground, breathing shaky and hard as his hands went to my face. His eyes were wide but still burned with anger. West's hands turned my head, tilted my chin up. He searched me everywhere he could touch or see for any sign of injury.

"This is a terrible time to say 'I told you so', in case you were wondering," I wheezed, trying to get air back into my lungs.

"Come on," he said as he threaded his arms under my own to help me stand. "We've got to go."

I gave a weak nod and followed him to the Bronco. The cargo area was already filled with our things. He'd known this was coming and had been preparing. Because I messed up. Again. Somehow this was my fault. As we pulled away from the cabin, I wondered how we'd been found.

12

TRIGONELLA FOENUM-GRAECUM

Where are we going?"

West glanced at me as we sped down the mountain road, putting as much distance between us and the cabin as quickly as possible. Either he didn't want to say or he didn't know. I didn't blame him. I was still trying to make sense of it all. I glanced at the bags in the back, to the one West had packed full of my things. My ribs ached as I took a focused breath.

It just didn't add up. Lupo couldn't have told anyone where we were because I hadn't told him. West hadn't told him. He would have deleted the message after he heard it, which meant only he had the number. Lupo was family.

Family.

Only one person had seen us at the cabin.

"You need to call your sister."

West let out a low curse as he patted his pockets down for his phone. If Lanna was in danger, then Daniel was in danger. And if Daniel was in danger...I pushed the thought out of my mind. Flexing my hands, I blew out a breath, trying to dissipate the building fear and right my thoughts. The smartphone slipped from his grip and slid across the leather seat to the floor. I leaned down, trying to grab it as it slid by on a turn.

"She went to my place, right? Someone must have followed her. Wait, how did she get in?"

The phone slid past my fingers. I grunted in frustration and fed my arm under the seat, trying to reach it. I wouldn't forgive myself if something happened to West's sister because of me. My loose ends wouldn't hurt one more person. Securing the device with my index finger, I curled it to drag the phone close enough to grab it.

"Got it," I breathed, sitting up with another grunt. Handing the phone to him, he shook his head.

"Call her, I need to drive."

I held the phone up to his face and heard it unlock. No wallpaper photo? Even I had a photo. Only a couple of apps. Wow. Alright, not important. Scrolling through the contacts to find her didn't take long.

"You only have like ten people in here."

"It's a burner," West said with an eye roll. "My real phone's still at my apartment."

Bags packed, ready for us to leave. A burner phone. Honing his skills as a sniper. Maybe I needed to start giving West a little more credit. I dialed Lanna's mobile and left a message, begging her to call back when she had a moment.

"She'll probably be at work right now. Doesn't answer her cell when she's working. Call the hospital. It's the second number."

An automated answering system gave me options for departments in the hall. I gave West a troubled look.

"ICU," he said, glancing at my confused expression. "She works in the ICU. Ask for Dr. Lanna Hale. Say it's a family emergency."

I gave him a flat look, silently screaming at him. *Of course, I know it's an emergency.* Whoever answered the phone in the ICU told me to hold after I repeated West's instructions. Smooth synthesizers played a Duran Duran cover as I waited, watching trees whip past at an alarming speed. A click sounded as Lanna answered the phone.

"Lanna, it's Lili. Uh, Lili Caccia. You must listen to me and do exactly as I say. Act like you're having a normal conversation. Keep your answers simple. Say yes if you understand."

"Yes."

West glanced at me, worry all over his face.

"Okay, I think someone is following you. They have been since you went to my apartment. Has Daniel left your house since then?"

"No."

Good.

"Has he been outside?"

"No."

Relief loosened my tightening shoulders. If the people following Lanna hadn't seen Daniel, there was a chance he could have been moved to a safer location without their knowledge. I hoped they had no idea where he was. If we were lucky, they didn't know he existed at all. There was only one other person in the world I could trust. A plan started to shape itself in my mind, increasing in clarity with every passing second.

"Is he with your neighbor now?"

"Yes."

"Alright. When you hang up the phone, I need for you to text message your neighbor. Have them take Daniel to the address I'm about to give you and leave him there. The person at that address will know what to do."

West's knuckles went white as his grip on the steering wheel tightened. After I give Lanna the address, I add another instruction.

"Lanna? When are you done at work?"

"Seven."

I pulled the phone away from my ear to look at the time. It was just after one. Somehow everything that had happened made the hours seem longer.

"When you get off of work, go to the gym called One Two in Silverlake. We'll meet you there."

Our conversation was interrupted by a coworker checking on Lanna. She told them everything was fine and thanked them for asking. "Lanna? Did you get that?"

"Yes."

"Good," I said. "Thanks."

After hanging up the phone, I started typing an address into the GPS app. West looked at me with an inquisitive furrow that begged me to explain what I'd just told his sister to do. I wanted to. Needed him to know that he could trust me the way I trusted him.

"I'm having Daniel taken to Lupo's house. I'm going to call him and leave a message to let him know to expect a package at home. One that he needs to get in person. We're going to meet your sister at One Two's. We need to make some other stops first."

"What exactly did you have in mind?" His voice was flat. Not irritated, but not thrilled about a lack of control over the situation.

"We need money," I said with a look out the window. "And I know exactly where to get some. A little business I have that no one knows about. Not even my sister."

West took the phone from me as I held it out to him. Glancing from the phone to the road and back again, he let out an astonished laugh.

"You own something called Laundrette Fluff & Fold?"

"You know I like things clean. Besides, technically Flora Hunter owns it. We can get cash from there. I haven't been there to cash it out in a few weeks, so there should be quite a bit there. Close to a month, actually. Mostly in quarters, but still."

An impressed grunt came from the driver's side. With our next steps in place, my body started to catch up with my mind. I blew out slow, even breaths as I took in my surroundings and tried not to think about, well, everything. Everything that had happened. Everything that could happen. Anxiety bubbled in me as West and I headed down the mountain, back to Los Angeles and all of the nasty possibilities that awaited me there.

13

SAPINDUS SAPONARIA

Any financial expert would tell you not to have all of your funds come in from one revenue stream. Diversify, you know? Most wise guys would tell you the same thing. My grandfather owned several businesses before he died and those businesses became my sister's. Kaia was the expert in this area. Even when I set eyes on our accounts, I knew she had more money coming in than she was telling me about.

After working for her for about one year, I decided I needed to follow her example. Find a way to get cash that had nothing to do with the family. A backup plan. A safety net. So I bought a laundromat. At the time, I thought I was a genius. Passive income I could cash in on just by dropping by. I even cleaned it up! Using some of my family dues, I made it a nice place with upgraded equipment, polished concrete floors, and vending machines with every kind of laundry soap I could find. Not to mention snacks.

West pulled into the tiny parking lot of Laundrette and parked, turning the key to shut off the engine. I pulled my hair into a messy bun atop my head and hopped out. Tiny nervous flutters pulled at my stomach as I thought about revealing this secret to him. No one in my life knew about this. He would know more about me than even my sister did. It felt intimate. Dangerous.

West rounded the truck, shutting my door behind me.

"How are you going to open up the machines without a key?"

"Who says I don't have a key?" I smiled. Glancing at the window, I noted that the hand-lettered pink and gold sign needed to be repainted. "Open 24 Hours" was starting to look like "pen 24 hour." Heavy, booted footfalls followed me inside.

The scent of fresh laundry always makes me feel better. It's one of the few simple pleasures in my life. As a child, my mother would ask me to help her fold the laundry. Fresh cotton passing through my fingers. Linen and denim. Socks balled into pairs with rabbit ears. They all smelled of lavender and soap with a touch of bleach.

Even now, when we were being hunted by nameless thugs, the scent was comforting. Air conditioning cooled my cheeks as I made my way down a row of washers. Empty of customers, I went directly to the vending machines lining the back wall. I turned to West.

"Can you give me a boost?" I asked, pointing to the acoustic tile panels above me. Without a confirming word or gesture, he bent down and wrapped his arms below my hips. I squeaked with the swift change in height, bracing my hands on his thick shoulders as a reflex. With my ass being squeezed by West's arms and my breasts practically resting on his head, I decided to try not to think about it and get my next task done quickly. Very quickly.

West's breath warmed my stomach. Instead of focusing on the fluttering feeling that followed, I decided to focus on the fact that even the acoustic paneling was free of lint and dust. I really needed to give my janitor a raise. The panel moved easily to reveal the small metal box I'd placed on the vending machine framing. Taking the box in one hand, I replaced the panel and patted West on the shoulder.

He set me down and I went to my knees, glancing up at him as he watched me with a look that was either impressed or amused. My fingers dialed the combination lock with the speed only muscle memory could provide.

"Here we go," I mused.

Three keys. One for the change dispensers. One for the vending machines. One for the laundry machines. I held them up and jangled them. West extended a hand to help me off the floor. I took the laundry machine key off of the ring and handed it to him.

"Alright, maybe you can get started emptying the coin boxes? I'll get the cash out of all the other machines," I said as I looked around the room. As he started toward the first machine, I opened the trash can next to the wall as another idea came to me.

"Wait."

I'M NOT SURE how much a big-box store-sized detergent box full of quarters weighed, but West made it look easy to carry two of them. Well, sort of easy. A stifled grunt here and there told me they weren't light. Both change machines were at their capacity, bursting with bills. Same with the vending machines.

"Do you think the Beverly Hills Hotel would accept payment in quarters?" I joked as we climbed back into the Bronco. West chuckled. Between the bills and all of the coins, we probably had close to thirty thousand dollars. In all honesty, I would have slept in the truck but I had a feeling it wasn't big enough for a man his size. He glanced at his watch.

"We need to be at the gym soon."

"Yeah," I nodded. "I want to get there before she does."

The shortening days had chilled even the warmest California weather. As we pulled out onto the road, I rolled up the window. West leaned over and adjusted the heater, sparing me a small glance before focusing on the road again.

I went over everything we needed to do in my head. Everything that would follow. The layout of the gym. How to protect Lanna. We had devised a way to lure out whoever was following her. It was simple and possibly stupid. While he didn't completely agree with my approach, we were short on other options and West was the only one of us who knew how to use a gun.

"I'm teaching you how to shoot when this is over," he grumbled while practically swallowing his second cheeseburger when we had stopped for lunch on the way to the laundromat. I had been too enamored with my Double-Double and perfectly crisp fries to argue with him.

When we arrived at One Two's, it was practically empty. Only two of the trainers remained. They were putting equipment away after their clients were long gone. Each of them waved at us, more than used to West and I showing up in the middle of the day.

"They have to get out of here," I said quietly. West headed in their direction. I looked around the space and rolled my shoulders. We had twenty minutes to set our trap.

14

CURCUMA LONGA

When you have a photographic memory, it means that you can remember the things you see with picture-perfect detail. Photographic memory was what helped me get near-perfect grades growing up. When I got to college, I took a human anatomy course, a physiology course, and more for my minor in biology.

Thanks to the graphics in my textbooks that outlined different systems in the human body, I learned where I could slice to do the most permanent damage. I knew where the tip of my blade could plunge and twist to sever a joint. I could picture exactly what cuts to make to make a man fall to his knees for me and never rise again.

A lone streetlight illuminated the otherwise dark parking lot. To a passerby, One Two looked closed for the day. All of the lights were turned off. With West and I in our respective hiding places, it also appeared completely empty. A flare of headlights caught my attention as I peered out of the window.

"She's here," I whisper-shouted to West.

The weathered Volkswagen pulled into the parking lot. It didn't take long to notice the unmarked utility van parking across the street. Lanna looked around, confused by the darkened gym. With an uncertain grimace, she tried the door and found it unlocked.

I leaned against the pillar I'd hidden behind and unsheathed several throwing knives, adjusting my grip so they'd be hidden by my sleeves.

"Lanna," I said in a broad and friendly boom as I turned on the lights with an elbow. "So good to see you."

Here I am, I thought. *Come and get me.*

I kept smiling at Lanna as I watched three figures dart across the street.

"When I say so, get down," I muttered through my teeth. A flash of confusion crossed Lanna's face but she gave an almost imperceptible nod.

Two figures came closer, almost through the door, when I threw my first blade.

"Get down!"

The knife didn't strike the intruders, but instead pierced the lamp over their heads. Sparks rained down, distracting them for long enough to get Lanna out of harm's way. She dropped to her knees, curling behind a dangling punching bag as it took bullets meant for her.

Sand hissed to the floor from the punctured bag. The first of the goons charged toward me with his weapon drawn and took a bullet in his chest. He collapsed before me as the second fired his gun. Loud metallic pings sounded as the lockers took fire behind me. I dropped to my knees and made a deep and brutal slash to his thigh, severing his femoral artery. Death wouldn't take long.

Another shot came from behind me. Then the thick sounds of flesh hitting flesh and men hitting the ground. My gut tightened with concern. I didn't notice the hand that circled my ankle, pulling my leg out from under me with a violent tug. The man I'd thought dead from the shot to his chest dragged me toward him, sand stinging my skin with every pull.

"Fuck!" He shouted as I threw a handful of sand into his eyes. I loosed the hunting knife from my belt and cut his Achilles tendon, causing him to drop to the floor like a bag of laundry. Loud, long wailing screams poured out of him until they were silenced by the knife I drove through his soft palate.

MY HANDS SHOOK as the adrenaline left my system. Small waves of nausea coursed through me as I watched life leak out all over the floor before me. Lanna crouched on the floor, hands still over her ears and eyes squeezed shut in fear. I walked to her huddled figure and squatted in front of her, touching her arm as gently as I could manage with trembling fingers.

"Hey," I said gently. "It's okay. Everything is okay."

Lanna yelped as she opened her eyes, terror twisting her features.

"You're safe." I wrapped my hand around her arm to pull her up with me. A gunshot rang out from the locker room. Lanna screamed.

"Clear," West shouted.

Lanna looked at my hands, one shaking around her arm and the other clutching the still-bleeding hunting knife. Her expression dripped with fear. My stomach roiled at the sight.

"You killed them," she whispered, more to herself than to me. I shrugged, too tired to confess to Lanna that this was far from my first kill. I wondered if she'd ever seen a man die outside of a hospital. With a pat on her arm, I stepped toward one of the corpses on the floor. His thigh wound still wept with blood, but it slowed to a trickle as the mass of it spread across the finished concrete.

I bent over, taking the corner of his blazer in my hand to wipe across my bloodied blade. The material was fine between my fingers. He was too well dressed to be a hired gun. This guy was connected. Sheathing the knife at my back, I ran my hands over him. Another clip. A laughably small knife. A gold chain around his neck. Wallet in his jacket pocket.

The lump of folded leather was hard to miss. Why do so many men treat their wallets like a mobile file cabinet? I glanced over my shoulder at Lanna, who was still watching me intently. Though the wallet was overflowing with receipts, it was also laden with cash. I slipped my fingers into the billfold and removed the money.

"Here," I said as I held it out to Lanna. She looked at me skeptically. "It's not a bribe," I laughed. "Just a thank you. For Daniel."

The money sat in my extended hand for a moment. It was an offering. I was grateful for her help with Daniel, but I also needed her understanding. Men had been following her. Threatened her life just to get to me. The money wasn't just an offering of gratitude. It was an apology. I would never have wanted to involve her in any of this. West's involvement was bad enough. Stuffing down the swirling clouds of guilt, I shoved the wad of bills toward her again.

Lanna carefully took the money in her hand as West came out of the back rooms. Blood was splattered over his hands. His face. His shirt. He arched an eyebrow at the money but said nothing. Lanna turned to her brother who put a bloody reassuring hand on her shoulder.

"Are you hurt?" He asked with worry in his eyes.

She shook her head. I stepped away from them to let West explain what had happened and went to examine the other body. The familiarity of his face tugged at my brain like a nail on a loose thread. I'd seen this man before, but where?

My hands skimmed his body from the boots up, removing weapons as I found them. This one carried no wallet on him. There was a money clip stuffed with bills, which I tucked into my bra. And the phone in his breast pocket, which had a bullet lodged into its screen courtesy of West. I stashed the wrecked device next to the wallet and returned to Lanna's side, placing a hand on her shoulder.

"Well, the good news is that these guys aren't following you anymore. The bad news is you can't go home for a little while, but hey welcome to the club."

Leaving Lupo with three dead bodies and blood stains everywhere seemed like a real dick move. Lanna was sitting down, putting her mind back together while West pulled the Bronco around back. For a while, he was stealing glances at me. Like he needed to get a better look at me. He'd seen me deal with the mess at Muse a few weeks ago. Then I remembered how angry he was afterward. Ugh.

My muscles twitched at the memory of that night. Twisting leather to keep my hold on a man's throat. Fingers desperately seeking the knife I'd dropped in our struggle. Stephen Bryant. Benjamin's business partner. He'd given me no choice. Shown me he'd been willing to kill me when he'd tried to strangle me. I showed him I was willing to kill him by opening his throat.

Once I explained to West that we were going to need to get rid of any evidence of these guys before we left, he moved quickly. It apparently didn't occur to law-abiding citizens that blood and corpses weren't something you wanted to leave lying around.

We grabbed big black garbage liners and made them into makeshift body bags. After heaving them into the back of the truck, West picked up every little piece of evidence we may have left behind and threw it into another garbage bag. I wanted to kiss Lanna when I came back inside and found her cleaning everything with Clorox. When I gave her a grateful look, she simply shrugged.

"Whatever. I'm a doctor. Blood doesn't bother me."

Closing the back of the Bronco, West turned and crossed his arms as he sagged against the rear. He was starting to look tired again.

"What's the plan, then?"

I rubbed a hand down my face and looked at the pile of rubbish we needed to dispose of. With my usual options unavailable to me, things were about to get messy or complicated. I decided complicated was best.

"Well, there's a cleanup crew that usually handles this kind of thing for the family, but since I don't have their number this next part is going to get a little DIY."

"DIY?" Lanna asked.

"Did you ever see Breaking Bad? That hydrofluoric acid thing doesn't actually work. So, right now we only have two choices. We can burn everything or we can drown it."

15

MACROALGAE

Late at night, regular people don't ask questions. If you're doing something nefarious, people would rather not know anything at all than interfere. Strangers are dangerous. Questions, even more so. Still, getting a boat to take us into international waters was easier than I thought. A trawler with a pleasantly plump captain who seemed to be living on it was our best and only option. The ease at which he agreed to help us made me wonder how much hush money he usually made.

A midnight ride with three strangers and a bunch of trash bags? No problem. This guy was sketchy as hell. But I kill people for a living, so who was I to judge?

"Someone should probably have the authorities look into this guy," West muttered as we boarded. I laughed, then wondered if he was thinking the same thing about me. Worry bloomed at the thought. I'd have to explain myself soon.

Lanna talked with the captain as he steered the boat out toward international waters. I felt bad telling her she couldn't go home. We couldn't risk having her followed again. Or worse. West couldn't lose his sister. Especially when mine was still unaccounted for.

Black water yawned open before us as we left the lights of port behind.

Even though it wasn't technically very far, it felt like it was taking longer than it should. But who knows, my anxiety can make any task last hours in my mind.

West leaned on the bulwark and looked out at the wake trailing behind us. I took up a spot next to him, feeling guilty for wearing his coat when the wind bit at us. Of course, that wasn't the only thing filling me with guilt.

"This is all so incredibly fucked," I said quietly. "I didn't want your sister to get involved in this. Or you. You've already done so much for me. If you want to go somewhere else with your sister, I can handle things from here."

I couldn't, but he didn't need to know that.

West let out an irritated sigh and scratched at his beard. Every muscle in my body tightened up, bracing myself for the blow I was certain was coming. I winced, readying myself for his judgment. It was deserved. I knew it. I could survive it. Maybe.

"Lili, I've worked at the club for almost six years. How stupid do you think I am?"

I blinked.

"You come around at all hours, sometimes covered in bruises. Other times, you just look exhausted. You said you needed my help to learn to fight, but you already knew a lot," he said, shifting his weight to look at me. "I ignored it because I like being with you."

I didn't have anything to say to that. Everything he said hung between us with the vapor of our hot breaths.

"Are you finally going to tell me what it's all for, or are you going to keep lying to me?"

"I've never lied to you," I sniffed. Looking out at the water, I debated what to say next. How much could I explain without him thinking I was, well, trash? What was the limit? "When my sister became boss of the family, we didn't have a fixer. Dante, the fixer before me, was Lupo's son. He died shortly before my grandfather did. So, I told my sister I'd take Dante's place."

"And now you're the fixer?"

I nodded, not sure if the bobbing of the boat or the conversation itself was making me nauseated. A hard swallow and some deep breaths through my nose gave me time to brace for West's eventual judgment.

"What does a fixer do?"

I shifted my weight and turned to look at him. At least he was listening. He tilted his head to the side, waiting patiently for my answer. Here goes nothing.

"Well, a fixer solves problems for the family. Usually, those problems are people. And solving people problems usually involves," I trailed off and gestured to the bags beside us.

The boat seemed to be slowing to a stop as we stood there in silence. A moonless sky made everything around us pitch black. With the motor off, I could hear the water lapping against the sides of the boat. I couldn't bring myself to look at him as I waited for his response.

West sighed and placed a warm hand on my back. For a long while, neither of us spoke. Only the water filled the silence. I just enjoyed the warmth of his hand on me in the freezing ocean air.

"Thank you."

At first, I thought I didn't hear him. Thanking me for what?

"For what?" The question came out of my mouth in a shaky whisper.

"Being honest. Telling me the truth." West's warmth surrounded me as he brought his mouth to my ear. His voice was low, rumbling in his chest as he spoke. "You can tell me that you can handle things from here but I'm not going anywhere."

THE CAPTAIN STAYED in the pilothouse while West and I unbagged the bodies and readied them for their voyage to the depths of the ocean. Heaving plastic garbage bags into the water didn't sit right with me. Just because I regularly send people to their graves doesn't mean that I don't care about the environment.

"Goodbye, fellas."

Hands floated up over the bodies in a final farewell as we watched them disappear into the pitch-black reaches below. Lanna's visible shiver shook us from all of the quiet horror we'd sunken into. The movement was enough to remind me that watching bodies get pitched overboard wasn't a normal sight for most people. I turned to West and his sister with a weak smile.

"None of us can go home," I said. "Not until we know it's safe. At least, not tonight."

West gave his sister a knowing look. I'd told her as much before. Remembering the stash of money-stuffed laundry boxes in the Bronco, I cracked my neck and sighed.

"How about a swanky hotel on me?"

16

SERENOA REPENS

Le Grande Chateau.

It's a name everyone in this city knows. Notorious for housing the wayward rock stars and movie stars of a bygone era, the Tudor-style hotel squatted in the hills of Hollywood like an all-seeing gargoyle. Lanna gave me an uncertain look as I signed for both her room and ours. Two rooms wouldn't break the bank. At least for a night or two.

We rode the elevator upstairs in silence. Lanna was likely still parsing the insanity of the events that had just transpired. West's silence was louder than the bad music coasting into the tiny space. Mirrored elevator doors meant meeting his gaze every few seconds as I tried to imagine what he thought of everything he'd learned about me in the span of just a few hours.

The bell pinged as the elevator reached our floor. The mirrored doors slid open, giving me a moment of reprieve from the staring contest I was losing. I fished the keys out of my jacket pocket and handed one to Lanna.

"You're two doors down. I'm sorry about the short notice. Will you be alright for the night?" I asked as I realized she didn't have a bag. "I think I have something you can sleep in."

"I'll be fine." Her response was clipped. Tired.

West snorted and walked toward our room.

"Good night," she said in a mocking singsong directed at her disappearing brother.

❦

THE HOTEL ROOM was luxuriously simple. A modest bathroom. A balcony with a view of the city. One dresser, one desk, and one very big bed. Each piece of furniture looked carefully curated. Antique and yet somehow timeless. Airy white bed linens called to me from their California King mattress.

"I need a shower," West said as he dropped our bags onto the desk.

Shucking off his boots, he walked toward the bathroom and closed the door. Correction, he mostly closed the door. I watched through the generous crack as he turned the shower on, stripping layer after layer until he was in nothing at all. Every honey-gold inch of his backside on display. Feeling my face flush, I turned away.

He'd seen me. From top to tail, he'd seen me. Still, watching him felt like I'd be crossing a line. I walked to the desk, looking to busy my traitorous mind with a task instead of thinking about the bare-naked West only steps away from me. As I pulled a shirt and boxers from my bag, the debate raged on in my head.

He did leave the door open.

Was that an invitation?

Maybe it was an oversight.

But if it was an oversight, why wouldn't he have closed it before he got in the shower?

Struggling to identify his motivation occupied me as I laid out my clothes on the bed and removed my shoes. A quick glance in the mirror reminded me that I could do with a shower of my own. As I slipped my socks off, I heard the knob turn and the shower silenced.

Steam billowed out of the room as West pushed the door open, walking toward his bag dripping wet with a towel slung around his hips. I commanded my eyes to stay away from the terry cloth-covered parts. Without another word, I stepped into the bathroom and finished undressing with the door closed. Mostly.

The steady beat of hot water sent me into a trance. After scrubbing myself clean of any remaining sweat or blood, I just stood there thinking about the man in the next room. Water hitting porcelain in a fog of white noise provided the clarity I needed to sort through every moment we'd had together these last few days. And the rest. Moments where I was just Lili and he was West.

I wanted him. The way he'd touched me in his bed. Teased me in his bathtub. A small emptiness had begun to grow in me. One that I'd been doing a piss-poor job of fighting. I shut off the water with twitchy fingers and wrapped myself in a towel.

West was standing on the opposite side of the bed, looking down at his phone. He'd unpacked a few things, including several envelopes that now sat on the bedside table. Apparently dressing for bed meant putting on a fresh pair of black boxer briefs and nothing else. I glanced at the clothes I'd laid out and back at him. Tiny seeds of doubt took root with every step I made in his direction.

"Is your sister alright?" I started.

He nodded, still looking at his phone. My steps were soft and slow on the plush rug.

"That's good," I said quietly. It was. The kills I'd made in front of her had bothered me, but having them around was enough to distract from the gut-churning nausea that normally followed. Of course, killing two men who were trying to kill me wasn't exactly a moral conundrum. I continued moving toward him, like a predator quietly advancing on prey.

Once I reached his side of the bed, West turned to me. I stepped to get closer until we were sharing breaths, taking in every inch of skin until I was looking up into his dusky green eyes.

"What do you need, Lili?" His voice lowered, almost to a growl. Large hands fisted at his sides. His nostrils flared. My fingernails traced up his thighs. I was delighted at the shudder that followed.

"It feels selfish to ask more of you when you've done so much for me. But," I released the breath I'd been holding. Mustered confidence I didn't feel. Licked my lips before continuing, satisfied with the way he was watching my mouth. I continued, barely above a hushed tone. Low and sweet. "West, I need you to fuck me."

My hands moved over the cotton covering him, avoiding what now strained against it. Let my fingers trace along his waistband. West's expression tightened as he examined my face. I was too hypnotized by his darkening gaze to notice the hand moving to snare my jaw. His thumb and forefinger caught my chin and tilted it up. The callused pad of his thumb rasped along the edge of my lower lip.

"Please," I whispered, hardly able to breathe.

"Lili, I'm doing my best to be a good man."

Leaning down, his beard grazed my skin as he brought his mouth toward mine, but not enough to touch. Tempting me. I closed my eyes, taking in the feeling of it all. A rough hand skimmed my cheek and tangled into my hair.

"Don't be." My lips barely brushed his as I issued my command.

West surged forward, pressing me into the wall. He kissed me like a drowning man taking his first breath of air, using the hold on my hair to give himself a better angle. Long, hungry strokes of his tongue made my blood boil. My skin suddenly felt too small to cover me. Thoughts drained from my mind as his other hand danced along the edge of the towel, trailing fingers close to the wetness gathering between my thighs.

The feel of his mouth on mine. I was surprised at how immediately natural it was. Not awkward. Not unwanted. The brush of our noses. His breath mingled with mine.

I had always noticed other women noticing him. Because I noticed him. Admired him the way someone admires a beautiful thing. The Mona Lisa. Untouchable. Unattainable.

Pulling away, West stared down into my eyes, pressing his hips against me. His hand left my hair to brace himself on the wall beside my head as he lowered his lips to my ear.

"I've spent a lot of time thinking about touching you like this," he said as he traced his finger down the fold of my towel, kissing just beneath my ear. "Thought about the sounds you made when you came for me." His teeth nipped at my neck, my ear, and my shoulder and I shivered. "Were you thinking about me when you touched yourself?"

"You heard me?"

He huffed a dark laugh as he licked down to my shoulder. A growl followed as he sank his teeth into the base of my neck. This version of West Hale was a damn beautiful thing.

"Yes," I whimpered. "I was thinking about you."

As his lips and tongue moved over the small hurt, I wondered if he'd bitten me hard enough to leave a mark. Pressing his forehead to mine, his smoky green eyes burned into mine.

"Tell me. Tell me you want this. Want me." The words were hot against my lips.

"West, I..." My eyes fell shut as his fingers moved to again graze the soft skin of my inner thighs. Forcing myself to look at him again, I told him the truth. "Yes, I want you."

"You've got me."

17

LEPIDIUM MEYENII

Large, strong hands grabbed my legs and hoisted me up. As though telling him I wanted him had snapped some inner restraint, West wrapped my legs around his waist and walked us back toward the bed. Small moans fell from me as his tongue brushed across my upper lip to take my mouth again.

He turned and sat with me in his lap, his hard length pressing against my center with only the thin cotton of his boxer briefs to separate us. Long fingers stroked down my back as I ground myself into him, enjoying the feel, the heat, the taste of him.

I couldn't ignore it. The way he looked at me. Awed. Worshiping. The way he drank me in. Savored me. Though his touch was sure and strong, I had felt passing tremors in it. Maybe he was feeling what I did. That potent mixture of fear and excitement. Jumping from a great height. Crash landing into an uncertain future. It was almost too much.

Swallowing my sighs, his mouth moved with mine. Soft deep hums of his own filled my ears. His scent, the feel of his skin against mine, the sounds he made as we tasted each other. He flooded my senses.

As I rocked my hips against him, his hand hooked into the towel wrapped around me and tugged slightly down. Only a moment passed before West pulled away, seeming to remember himself, and breathed a disappointed sigh.

"Lili, I don't have a condom."

"Have you been tested?" I asked with a wince, hoping I knew the answer.

"Yeah, I'm all clear."

Confetti cannons of relief fired in my mind.

"Me too. Also, I have a birth control implant," I said, pointing to my bicep. He chuckled at the motion. "I think we're covered."

"Thank fuck," he said as he smiled broadly.

Lowering me to the bed, he leaned over me and tugged the towel open. I shivered at the way his eyes took in every bit of newly exposed flesh. Completely exposed to him, I kept waiting to feel embarrassed, but everything about this felt right. Only molten desire coursed through my veins. No hesitation. I wanted him. He wanted me. West lowered himself, careful to balance his weight on an elbow as he took a nipple into his mouth.

Exploratory licks and kisses singed my skin. His long dark hair slipped from the knot he'd tied, brushing me in tantalizing teases. Crawling backward, he pushed himself to sit on his heels and looked down at me, splayed like an offering before him. Tonight I was his. All his. An ache was building low in my belly as I sat up to help remove his boxers, like if I didn't have him at this moment I would combust, but he pushed me back down.

"Not yet."

I cocked my head and gave him a quizzical look.

"I'm in no rush, Trouble. If this is the only time I get to taste you, I'm going to fucking savor it."

West's eyes had gone from heated to hungry. His tongue dragged along his lower lip as he rubbed at his jaw. That hungry gaze took me in.

"This is your last chance. You can tell me to stop and I'll stop. Or..."

"Or what?"

"Tell me you want this."

Silence went taught between us. He waited for my answer. I knew that if I'd told him to stop, that I couldn't do this, he would. But that wasn't what I needed.

"I want this."

He leaned forward, his hair tracing along my stomach as large hands moved up my parted legs to lift my ass. With one hand, he propped a pillow beneath me. Satisfied with my position, he leaned forward while placing my thighs atop his shoulders. A long, flat lick dragged up the length of my center and I let out a sharp gasp.

Fucking hell.

"Fucking hell," he rasped.

Laving his tongue through me, I squirmed and moaned. Then he moved his efforts upward. He took my clit into his mouth to suck and lick with deliberate strokes of his tongue. My breath grew shallow and I raked my fingers through his hair, grabbing a fistful to grind myself into him. If the sensation wasn't enough to send me over, my mind did the rest.

This was West. The occasional wandering thought had wondered how his fighting skills translated to the bedroom. His strong hands. The feel of his body wrapped around me when he was showing me a hold. A grunt or growl at a particularly delicious meal. Hell, I'd had sex dreams about him since the day we'd met. Now West's head was between my thighs. The thought sent shivers through my body. Or maybe that was his mouth.

The nearness to release wrenched a mewling sound from me as I bit into my index finger. His left hand gripped my shaking thigh to steady me. So close. I was so fucking close. The right hand found its way to my opening as he thrust a finger inside. I swore. If I was teetering on the edge before, this was going to push me over. Soft little pants escaped my lips as my hips undulated into him. Working me with his mouth, growling against me, a second finger pushed in and curled toward the spot he knew would make me scream.

As if on cue, my orgasm crashed through me. West's eyes were locked on me, tinged with a wicked grin I couldn't see as his tongue and fingers worked in tandem to destroy me. His name fell out of my mouth in desperate little whimpers. The licks and strokes of his tongue continued to work me as my moans quieted. Satisfied with his performance, he sat back on his heels.

"Perfect."

All the days we spent training in the gym, grinding it out. Sweating, fighting. Every time I faced off with him, I looked forward to his praise. A small spark of something, this feeling I'd been stifling, kindled in me. Punch, kick, stretch, breathe. I realized that I had worked harder, and got better, not just to defend myself. It was for his approval. For the smiles he gave me when I bested him. It wasn't until he was on his knees before me, taking my shoes off after a long night that it felt like it could be something more. I couldn't admit to myself what I had felt for him then. Somehow, I hadn't thought he'd see me that way. This way.

Standing from the bed, he shed the boxer briefs, watching me like he was worried I would run off. Of course, that was ridiculous. Not only did I want more, but I didn't think I could walk even if I wanted to.

After discarding the underwear, I took in the sight of him. All of him. I had been granted a new level of access. His body was painstakingly sculpted with muscle developed from hours of training. The beautiful warm tones of his skin were interrupted by a smattering of scars and splashes of black ink. The thick muscles at his hips guided my gaze all the way down to parts I'd felt grinding against me only moments ago.

A smile tugged on his lips as he noticed me taking in the sight of him. Placing lazy kisses along my body, he prowled over me and brought his face to mine. When we kissed, I tasted myself on him. Salted caramel mixed with a taste that was distinctly West.

"You're uh, really big."

"Come on. Don't tell me you haven't thought about it," he grinned against my lips.

"Cocky bastard."

He arched his eyebrow at me and I laughed. The pad of his thumb danced across my lips before he kissed me again.

The thick length of him slid through me, over my opening, rough and teasing. He moved down to nip and suck my nipples until they were stiff peaks. Moving himself slowly, he stirred frenzied need in me. If he was trying to make me lose my mind he was definitely succeeding. "West, please. Stop torturing me."

"Come on now. I know you can take a little more," he said with a wry smile, still working himself against me.

Having had enough torment, I pushed him onto his back and straddled his lap with a wicked smile of my own.

"There's my girl," he said with a dark laugh, pushing the hair out of my eyes with a stroke of his hand.

My entrance pushed against the tip of him. I moved my hips and let him enter me slowly. West looked up at me, patient, letting me set the pace. His expression was somewhere between pleasure and agony at the drawn-out penetration. The tips of his fingers pressed into my thighs, and he let out a low groan once I was fully seated.

Every nerve sizzled and sparked from feeling him in this new way. Each touch and kiss felt magnified by the awareness that we were crossing some imaginary boundary. Friendship didn't seem like the right word for what this was. If I was being honest with myself, it hadn't been the right word for a while.

Exactly what I needed. The way his body responded to mine. Anticipated what I wanted. I was the wind and he brought the storm. He thumbed my clit while I leaned back, braced on his thighs, working myself on his long shaft. The sensation was strong enough to be overwhelming. I was far from being a virgin, but the way this made me feel brand new. This was West. West. *West.* Flush with tingles surging through my body, I tossed my head back and squeezed my eyes shut to keep my brain from falling out.

Every rational idea slipped from my mind like so many grains of sand.

The only thoughts seemed to be coming from my skin. Each square inch of me cried out for more. More of this touch. More of him.

Inside me there was just one word. Over and over again. When I felt every cell reaching for him. When I breathed his name. When I arched into his caress. The word pulsed through my veins.

Yes.

An overpowering rush was surging in me like a rising tide. Tension built in me. Racing toward me. I wanted every second to last a little longer.

"So fucking perfect." West gritted out, grabbing my hip with his other hand. "Open your eyes. Feel everything."

At his command, our eyes connected. Those dusky green eyes were on fire for me. Burning into me and filled with utter fearlessness and something else. That thing I couldn't name. Didn't want to name it because it scared me more than any memory. Warm, tempting release had coiled low in my center but faded as that flicker of fear started blazing in me. West sat up and wrapped his arms around me.

"Hey," he breathed against my lips. "It's just me." A hand slid down to grip my backside and rocked me against him, his thighs moving to cradle me. This new position rubbing all of my most sensitive places. His brow furrowed, as though he could see the fear in my eyes.

"Just feel it," he whispered in a ragged breath. "Come for me, Trouble."

As if begging me to be here with him, West's mouth found mine again. His tongue was strong and demanding against my own. Fear collapsed under the weight of what he gave to me. In his arms, I felt safe. Trembling and grasping at his broad shoulders, moaning his name in a half-broken voice I didn't recognize. While I was riding through the aftershocks of my orgasm, he found his own, growling while spilling himself inside me.

The high I felt, we felt, sang like a note vibrating through both of us as we sat panting with our heads pressed together. West smiled as he brushed my errant black strands away from my face to kiss me gently.

"Please tell me we can do that again," I panted, still trembling in his arms.

"I don't think I'll be able to stop now," he said as he pressed a soft kiss to my shoulder.

WE LET THE sweat we'd worked up dry and cool with the breeze coasting in through the open window. I'd found my way into the nook under his arm and lay my head on his broad chest. West roused from sleep as I adjusted myself against him.

"Don't leave," he muttered, eyes cracking open to look down at me.

"I'm not. Just readjusting."

He squeezed me against his side and hummed with approval. This feeling. Somewhere down in my gut, a soft warmth had been expanding in me. I'd felt his skin against mine many times but hadn't appreciated it. The texture was almost velvet beneath my fingertips. I traced his curves and edges. Soft tufts of chest hair brushed and tickled my palm. When I reached his collarbone, I started again to learn the landscape of him. Somehow, he was more tangible to me now than he'd ever been.

"What are you doing?" He breathed, sounding more awake than he'd been a moment before.

"Just looking."

"You've seen me."

"Not like this," I purred as my fingers drifted over him again.

"Be careful touching me like that." The words came out rough and low. My fingers continued their survey of his landscape and drifted further south. West clenched his jaw as I wrapped my hand around his thickening length. A long stroke coaxed out a curse. "Lili..."

I sat up and looked down at the intimidatingly large man who was now at my mercy. It was too tempting, too delicious. Turning to face him, I edged myself down and uncovered him. What had started to build was hard and proud in my hand.

"Lili."

I smiled at his shifting hips, moving with every stroke of my hand. The way he was looking at me was enough to make me want to hop on top of him again. But this wasn't about me. It was about him. I let my nose graze his thigh. Then followed it with my tongue.

"I never thanked you for taking care of me. So now I'm going to take care of you."

18

MORINGA OLEIFERA

The morning came quickly and slowly. It seemed as though no time had passed between going to bed with West and waking up next to him, but I could remember every tantalizing second. The taste of his release as I sucked him. The languid motions of his thrusts after he woke me in the morning. The feel of his callused hands on my body. The way my thighs squeezed around him as I came. I could still smell him on my skin.

The way he looked down at me, smiling. I'd always loved his smile. But this morning, in his hold, I could see something new. Not the panting breaths or the cords of hard-earned muscle that surrounded me. Something unguarded. I'd never forget that, either. I'd hold onto it. Beautiful things like that, like him, had a way of slipping away from me.

West pulled a shirt over his head as he came out of the bathroom. With a quirk of his lips, he leaned against the dresser as his gaze raked over me. The weight of his stare was becoming too much to ignore. Adjusting the strap of my bra, I looked up at him and smiled.

"What's that look for?" I laughed.

He simply sat down at the desk to put on his boots, the bemused expression still painted across his face. Looking up at me through his eyebrows, he said casually, "Just thinking about how good you are with that dirty mouth."

After tugging a loose white tee over my bra, I pulled my hair free of the neckline and tossed him a cheeky wink.

"I guess you can add that to the short list of my good qualities."

"Don't do that," West frowned.

"What?"

"The self-deprecating thing."

I shrugged. He crossed the room and cupped my chin, looking down at me with a reverence that threatened to stop my breath. I tried to look away as the pad of his thumb swept over my lips.

"Look at me," he commanded. "Your lips around my cock was the second most beautiful thing I've ever seen. But waking up with you in my arms was the first."

A pained thud in my chest was the only reaction I'd allow as I started to lose myself in those eyes. Terse knocking sounded at the door, saving me from a feeble attempt at remembering any words in the English language. Still, I silently cursed myself for not putting up the "do not disturb" sign. The knock sounded again, followed by an annoyed voice.

"It's Lanna. Open up."

He scratched at the hair on his jaw and I bit back a smile, remembering the feel of that beard on my thighs. West's hand went to the gun tucked into his jeans as he opened the door with the other.

"Good morning," West cringed as his sister came storming into the room. He looked out at the hallway behind her and shut the door.

"Am I going to work today or not? The hospital called looking for me and I had to give them some bullshit excuse about a family emergency."

"It's probably not the best idea," I said quietly.

Lanna's eyes scanned the room as we waited for West to weigh in on the subject. They landed on West's discarded underwear, still sitting on the floor by the bed. I quickly inspected the ceiling for cracks. It was a very interesting ceiling.

"I don't think you should go in," West said. "Tell them you're going to be out of town for our grandmother's funeral or something. That should buy you a few days."

She huffed a sigh and looked around again. Her eyes were flooded with exasperation as they fixed on me.

"Listen, I'm willing to look the other way because I don't want to be any more involved in whatever's happening here than I already am. I get the sense that the less I know, the better. Am I right?"

"Yeah," I said with a nod. "Look, it's just for the best that you lay low for a little while. At least until we know you're out of harm's way."

Lanna looked at her brother, who had been packing, and nodding along as I spoke. He tucked the last of his things away and gave a pat to the zipped-up bag.

"Fine," she said as she turned back toward me. "I'm hungry. Are we stuck in these rooms, or should we risk a bullet to the head for some eggs?"

I snorted.

"Breakfast burritos?" West suggested, with a grin just for me.

THE THREE OF us sat inside of a taqueria on Melrose, eating our breakfast in silence. It was the loudest silence I'd ever experienced. Minus the occasional chewing or slurping, the eye contact was loud and uncomfortable. Lanna looked at me. West looked at me. I looked at my burrito. Lanna looked at West. West looked at Lanna.

The ride over here had been just as quiet. After an undisturbed evening, West seemed confident that we were no longer being followed. Our previous stalkers were now at the bottom of the ocean. It seemed that no one had been sent to replace them. I was wondering how long the peace would last as I took the last big bite of my chorizo con huevos burrito when Lanna finally broke the silence.

"Why are you being so quiet?" Lanna asked, looking at West again. He shrugged. I washed my bear-sized bite down with a Mexican Coca-Cola and cleared my throat. I did everything in my power to avoid making any more eye contact with either of them. Being stuck between two siblings felt awkward. Especially when I'd just slept with one of them. "And you keep smiling. I almost died yesterday. That's something to smile about?"

"You did not almost die," West retorted. "Everything went according to Lili's plan. And I slept well, that's all."

"Right," Lanna said with a glance in my direction.

"I should connect with our friend to see about the little one," I said. If we didn't have anyone following us, it was the best time to see Daniel. I needed to see that kid. It would settle at least one small part of the raging anxiety in me. We would need to move Lanna to a safe location before we could do that. I didn't want to burden Daniel's guardian with another bystander. That kid was enough of a handful on his own. While thinking that over, I took another swig of my soda.

"So you two are what exactly?"

I nearly choked. West looked to me like I had the answer. Granted, it was the safest talking point. Lanna could have brought up the bodies we'd dumped in the ocean or the attack at the gym. The way I'd killed with ease. Still, it was too damn soon for this conversation. And definitely not something I was ready to answer.

"Friends. Very good friends," I stammered. Trying to cough through the sip that almost killed me, I decided to change the subject again. Seriously, I was not ready for this conversation. "Before you and I meet our friend, I want to get us set up in a safe place."

West gave a tentative nod. A *we're not done with this conversation* nod. I swallowed. Then he asked, "where?"

"My sister's house."

<h1 style="text-align:center">19</h1>

RUBUS IDAEUS

It took everything in me not to search the faces of West and his sister for something. Approval, maybe? I didn't have many friends growing up and I never got to go to slumber parties. Or have friends over at all. But I'd be lying if I said that there wasn't some small part of me that wanted to impress them.

The large white Georgian mansion was a silent monolith behind the towering cypress trees that kept it hidden from passersby. Everything that made it a home was absent from it, giving the exterior a colder face than the one I knew. The house peered down at me, as though it was wondering where I'd been. Its accusatory windows glared. *I know,* I thought. *I should have been here.*

Turning to glance at my companions, I tried to see the house through their eyes. The proud white columns. The hydrangeas. The garden. It was a luxe haven. A compound that was as opulent as it was secure.

West put a hand on my shoulder. Lanna was standing behind him, looking at me. I gave them both a tight smile.

"This was my grandfather's house. Kaia and I moved here after our parents died. It's hers now."

"Do you have a key?"

"I have a code."

We approached the front door. Kaia had replaced the locks with key-pads, a decision I was now grateful for. The keypad beeped as I typed in the code she'd given to me. A number only I would know. Not her birthday or mine, or even our mother's. But the day I'd taken my vow.

The heavy lock clanked as it disengaged. Resistance met my palm as I pushed the door open, slightly sticking to the frame from weeks of disuse. Cold air blasted us.

"Shit," I muttered as I walked to the thermostat and turned it down.

West and Lanna followed me in. Lanna softly shut the door behind us. Unsettled, my eyes coasted around searching for anything out of place. But it looked just as Kaia left it. The realization tugged at me. She thought she'd be coming back. Why wouldn't she?

"I know it looks like something from out of Architectural Digest, but I promise you, this place is basically a fortress."

West looked around but stayed in the center of the foyer like he was afraid to touch anything. I shrugged off my jacket and tossed it on the bench in the entryway.

I walked to the window and tapped on the glass.

"Bulletproof. Courtesy of my grandfather."

West blinked. I pointed to the bookshelf under the stairs.

"That's a security door. There's a panic room with a steel security panel on the other side." I looked at Lanna who was still eyeing the very carefully curated decor around her. "I'll show you how to get in and how to lock it."

She nodded.

"So this is Kaia's house," West said casually as we walked into the large marble kitchen. "It's a lot friendlier than I imagined. I always thought she lived in some ivory tower somewhere."

I looked at the crayon drawings taped to the pantry door. There was a small tug on my heart as I remembered my nephew, who was undoubtedly scared and confused. Soon. I'd see him soon.

"She's a mom," I said softly. "This house is for family only. For her. For me. But mostly for Daniel."

Lanna walked toward the island and let out an appreciative whistle.

"You grew up here?" West asked, as though he could feel my need to change the subject.

"Sort of," I sighed as the memory of a house that still felt haunted by my father floated to the surface. "My old room is Daniel's room now. Up in the converted attic. But I moved into the granny flat above the garage after college."

"Show me."

FLIPPING OPEN A picture frame in the foyer, I grabbed the small gold key hanging on a hidden hook and walked out the front door. West's steps were a steady beat behind me.

I paused with my hand on the doorknob.

"This is," I started, nerves tugging on my stomach with every breath. "I don't let people in here anymore. Kaia doesn't even come in here."

West's brows furrowed, waiting for me to continue.

"It's where I do my work. For the family. Just," I cleared my throat, trying to slow my racing heart. Showing someone this, showing West this, felt more personal than anything. Like opening this door would let someone into the tangle of thorns and briar that was the real me.

"Uh. Don't touch anything."

Here goes nothing.

Beakers and flasks were turned over and left to dry next to the sink since I'd last washed them. The large work table was empty, except for the mortar and pestle that I'd used weeks ago. Plants growing in terrariums seemed to be struggling without their usual care. I filled the mister and set to work on them. West followed me around the room, tucking his large arms into his sides. A grizzly bear in a greenhouse.

He paused beside a large glass terrarium, examined what was inside, and looked at me. I paused to look at the terrarium and the white flowers within.

"What's this one?"

"That's a white egret orchid. They can be a little bit fussy, so it stays in there."

"What do you use it for?"

"Nothing. It's sort of rare and, well, I just think it's pretty." I closed the terrarium I was tending and walked to his side, pointing at the white blooms inside. "The flowers look like little birds. See?"

I looked up at him again to see him fighting a smile.

"What?"

"Nothing, I just," West gave a thoughtful look around and paused. "You keep surprising me."

A little knot of worry settled in my gut. I sighed and wondered how long it would be before I surprised him with something he disliked. The fear clung to me like cobwebs. West placed his large hand on the small of my back then leaned in to press a kiss to the delicate flesh behind my ear as he whispered.

"I like it."

BEING IN MY sister's room was an incredibly strange thing. When I was growing up in this house, we were not allowed in the primary bedroom without our grandparent's permission. They told us it was about boundaries. About a year after we moved in, our Nonna became bedridden. Our grandfather didn't want to leave her, so he'd had an entire hospital bed moved into the room with all of the possible bells and whistles.

Since my sister became head of this house, she'd made it over entirely. There was a guest room, where I'd told Lanna she could sleep. Daniel's bedroom and playroom made up the converted attic. An office sat beside the primary bedroom. All of it got an overhaul. The primary bedroom was no exception. Wallpaper was swiftly exchanged for deep sage paint. Old-world antiques were swapped out with modern wood fixtures. A gigantic platform bed made up of frothy white linens now sat in place of the two beds that were here before. It was as though she had scrubbed our grandparents from the place completely. All that was left was their memory. At the moment, that felt like a mercy. Even though I could still pick up the smell of my grandmother's perfume.

"She's sleeping. Please be quiet."

"Don't bother her."

"She needs rest."

But every once in a while, the door would be left open just a crack. My grandmother was propped up in her hospital bed reading a book, glasses perched on the tip of her nose. If I was sneaking by and she caught my eye, she would peer over the top of her book and crook her finger to beckon me into the room. I crawled under the blankets and read with her. It was always some tattered romance novel. Her favorites were the kind where all of the men had fancy titles and the women were debutantes in high society.

One rainy afternoon in early October, the viscount was just about to ravage his beloved Sophie in the garden when my grandmother dropped the book into her lap. I screamed. After that, there were no more stories.

I hadn't realized I'd been standing like a statue at the foot of the bed until West said my name for what was apparently the second time.

"Hm?"

"I said," West began, "Is it alright if I sleep in here? With you. I can take the sofa if that's better. I didn't want to assume anything..."

I turned to look at him. He was bracing his hands on the top of the door frame, leaning into the room as though he was waiting for my permission to enter. The irony forced a small laugh from me.

"Actually, I was just thinking that I really don't want to sleep in here alone."

LANNA TOOK THE spare pair of work gloves from me and stepped into the garden. She wanted to join me after I'd shown her how to use the panic room. How to lock the steel door. In our lush green surroundings, I simply watched her explore the buds with her own eyes. Though trepidation marked every step forward, her gaze held a thorough fascination I recognized. Gorgeous and deadly. Delicate, but lethal. It was what I felt for these plants, every time they did as I willed with years of tending and care.

"This garden was given to me by my grandfather. Of course, then it was all tomatoes and vegetables. All of the things were grown to feed people. Now…" I trailed off, letting a dangling Angel's Trumpet bloom rest gently in my palm. "It's a nursery of a different sort, I guess."

Lanna eyed the flower in my palm. I gave her a small smile.

"So you planted all this just to kill people?"

"No," I laughed. "Every plant has a different purpose. Some of them are for killing, yes. Others are for sedatives or truth serums. But there are a lot of things that are for in between. Stabilizers. Emulsifiers."

She turned her attention toward the belladonna and I kept moving through the garden. Lily of the Valley grazed my knuckles as I passed. Squatting down to examine the delicate flowers, I looked up at Lanna.

"These are Lily of the Valley. Convallaria majalis. They're beautiful. They smell amazing, too. But the berries are toxic."

I lifted a large leaf to show her a spray of small red berries erupting from narrow stems.

"A small amount can cause disruptive digestive issues," I looked up at her again to see if she caught my meaning. A small nod urged me to continue. "Eating enough of them will do more than that. They can stop your heart."

My boots crunched on the gravel lining the small walking path through the garden as I stood. Lanna stuffed her hands into her pockets and looked around casually.

"This is a lovely little garden of death," she said with a laugh.

"More useful to me than tomatoes these days. Besides, I'm a shit cook," I laughed. Brushing past her carefully, I picked up the tools I'd brought in with me. The back door closed and West stepped outside, looking around at the wisteria vines that had begun to wither with his keys and jacket in hand.

"Gardening is generally seen as women's business," I said as I started toward Lanna again. She cocked her head to one side, narrowing her eyes.

"It's funny, though. Women's business is dirty," I continued, placing the second set of pruners I carried into her palm. "Sometimes it's cruel. Even bloody."

Lanna's posture straightened, nervous to be standing so close to me. It practically vibrated off of her. I sighed and put the pruner in the bag, which slid into the crook of my elbow under its weight.

"This is my family home. I do..." I looked around at the garden, then back to her. "I would do anything to protect my family. Do you understand?"

She was still for a moment. Her dark eyes met mine as she nodded. West walked toward the Bronco, pulling his hair out of the collar of his jacket.

"We've got to go," he called across the yard. I nodded and held up a finger, asking for a minute.

"Do you feel safe for a few hours alone here?"

I knew well enough what it was like to be alone in this house. Childhood had taught me how well everything was hidden. Even from inquisitive minds. With my sister's office and the granny flat locked, it would be safe enough to leave her behind. Besides, this doctor would certainly know better than to handle any of the poisonous plants before her.

"This is the prettiest fortress I've ever seen. I'll be fine," Lanna smiled. "Say hi to Daniel for me."

I grinned and gave her a confirming thumb's up, heading out of the garden toward West. The excitement I felt about seeing my nephew overwhelmed the nerves that pricked at being alone with West. After spending the night with him, I knew things had permanently changed between us. The road ahead was paved with uncertainty. Staying away from him would have been the wiser choice.

But it was also an impossible one.

20

OENOTHERA BIENNIS

Our ride to Lupo's house was tense and quiet. Neither of us knew what to say to the other. With Lanna around, all we'd done was marinate in the memory of the night before. And the morning. The roar of the Bronco must have announced our arrival because Lupo was standing on the front step of his home when we pulled into the driveway. As I stepped out of the truck, I noted the tree that was fat with oranges only weeks ago had now started to shed its leaves, readying for winter.

This house was like a second home to me, but now I felt like a visitor. Lupo's face didn't make me feel any more comfortable. Despite his ongoing cancer treatments, the old man was looking well. But frosty. Irritated.

Daniel sprinted out of the house before my feet could hit the pavement. I couldn't help the smile or the sense of relief that came over me at seeing him.

"Zia!" He shouted, wrapping his arms around my hips in a tight hug. Air rushed out of me as my shoulders sagged with relief. Knowing he was safe and seeing it with my own eyes were two entirely different things. This feeling of reassurance was irreplaceable. I brushed a hand through his dark curls. It was only a couple of weeks, but he already looked bigger.

"Hey, buddy. I missed you so much."

Daniel looked up at me and smiled weakly.

"Where have you been?"

My mouth quirked to one side. That wasn't a question I could give him an honest answer to. There was a small squeeze on my stomach as I looked down into his adorable face.

"Well," I sighed. Thankfully, before I could figure out a vague enough lie, he was distracted by West walking up behind me.

"Who is that?" Daniel asked.

"You're full of questions today," I laughed. "This is my friend. I was staying with him."

West knelt to Daniel's height and extended a hand. Daniel took it, his tiny fingers doing their best to wrap around West's in a strong handshake.

"What's your name? Mine's West."

"Daniel Caccia. It's nice to meet you," Daniel said in a polite and formal voice that melted my damn heart. Something he definitely learned from his mother.

"It's nice to meet you too."

"Let's go inside," I said as I nudged him toward the house.

Lupo was leaning against a post with his arms crossed. He stood and opened the door for us, grabbing my elbow before I could step inside.

"We need to talk. Right now. Come on," Lupo leaned into the door and told West to help himself to what was in the kitchen.

We rounded the house to the garage, stepping in through the small side door. Boxes with his wife's name written on them were stacked to the ceiling against the back wall. The old wooden workbench was covered with a stained canvas cloth, hiding whatever it was that he'd been working on.

The door slammed and locked behind me. I let out a breath. Tried not to think of another slammed door and the feeling of cold, imminent death submerging me in its depths. Another breath slowly pulled me back into the room. Lupo's weathered hand gripped my arm, finally snapping me out of my momentary stupor.

"What in the hell is going on? I haven't heard from you in weeks. No one can find your sister. I thought you were dead until I got that goddamned message. Then this stranger shows up on my doorstep with this kid and another message from you. What's happening here? Where in the hell have you been?"

"Which question do you want me to answer first?" I said, leaning against the workbench. Running my finger along the top, I pulled it up and inspected for dust.

"Don't be cute with me. I'm too fucking old for cute."

"You're not old."

"Don't change the subject. Explain. Now."

"Alright," I conceded. Then I told Lupo everything. Well, almost everything. He didn't need to know what was happening between West and I. Hell, I couldn't make heads or tails of it myself. I certainly couldn't explain that if I'd tried. Lupo sat on the rusty metal stool beside the workbench and looked up at me.

"What are you going to do?"

"I was kind of hoping you could tell me," I said with a chuckle. Lupo let out a hoarse laugh and dragged a hand down his face.

"You must be really screwed if you're asking me for help."

"Yeah, kinda," I shrug. "I'm trying to lay low. For all I know, the entire family has turned against us and I'm next on the execution block. What am I supposed to do about that?"

"Well, first you need to figure out who's in charge. Nico will know. He's still working for the family, but he's my son. He's family to us first."

I nodded. Nico was a loyal soldier, but he served Kaia for years. More than that, he'd been like a brother to the both of us. We played together as children. Spent holidays together. If he'd been with her when they'd come to take her, I doubted they'd have made it past the door.

"He's coming over on Sunday. Make sure you're here for dinner. Bring food."

I let out another laugh and sighed. Lupo stood up and walked toward the door leading into the house. We stepped inside and were met with the sounds of animated dogs with Australian accents. West sat on the sofa beside Daniel, who was completely engrossed in the program. Remus, Lupo's old bull terrier, looked up at me from his perch beside West.

"Get down," Lupo grunted. Remus let out an agitated harrumph as he lept off of the sofa and walked to his bed in the corner.

Lupo kept walking through to the kitchen. I looked back at West, his eyes following my every step. When we reached the kitchen, he started pulling down glasses from the cabinet. I grabbed a box of rosemary crackers from out of the pantry.

"So," I started, crunching on a cracker. "How's it been? With Daniel?"

"He's a good kid," Lupo said, looking into the refrigerator. The weak light from within made every worry line look deeper. Sadness seemed to wash over him as he turned to me, holding a pitcher of orange juice.

"Well, I'm sure Kaia would be happy to hear that."

Lupo set the pitcher of orange juice down on the counter and gave me a frank look. What did I do?

"Do you know his father?"

I blinked.

"I'm not playing with you, kid," he said. His anger stunned me. What did he care?

"I'm not playing with you, Lu. I really don't know. Kaia never told me who. She got pregnant while I was at school," I said in a raised whisper. This house wasn't big enough for this conversation. And why did I feel like I was betraying my sister just talking about this? I set the box of crackers down and tilted my head toward his to speak more quietly. "She never told me she was with anybody. I've tried to ask her about it. She just shuts down."

Lupo gave me a weary look and started pouring juice. After staring down into the glasses for a moment, he turned toward the door.

"Daniel, come help me with these glasses."

The little guy came bounding into the room. Lupo returned Daniel's smile as he took two glasses filled with juice and carefully walked back into the next room. Watching the door, Lupo waited until we were alone again and sighed. When he turned to me, I could swear he had tears in his eyes.

"He has Dante's smile."

Dante! I could kick myself. Kick myself and then throw myself down a flight of stairs. And then drag myself into traffic. Of course, it was fucking Dante! That man always had eyes for my sister. Always. Even when we were kids, she was his queen and he was her knight in shining armor. Until he wasn't.

I was silent the entire ride back to the house. At first, West talked about Daniel. How good of a kid he is. That Kaia was raising him right. I was glad they apparently liked each other. I'd heard all of it and none of it. My sister had a baby with a man who'd grown up by our side. I had always thought of them as family. To me they were. But Dante had always meant more to her. She just never told me.

When we stepped inside the house, I could smell popcorn in the air and heard the television on, tuned to some reality show.

"Is that you, West?" Lanna called from the living room, a nervous rattle in her voice.

"It's us," West reassured gently.

As he went to talk to his sister, I climbed the stairs. My ears were ringing. My mouth was dry. Soon I was in the bedroom. Then I turned on the shower. There was no paternity test. No DNA to confirm. But I knew Lupo was right about Daniel. Daniel is Dante's son. Dante was Daniel's father.

He'd been a good man. An honest man. Practically a brother to me. Why would she keep that from me? Every time I asked her, she shut me out. I'd been away. Not known she was even in a relationship with someone. Was it so easy to lie to me?

What else was being kept from me?

21

SILYBUM MARIANUM

The business of cleaning myself always helped to clear my mind. When I finally got out of the shower and I couldn't think about it anymore, I was alone in the bedroom. Scrubbed. Shaved. Scoured. My skin was raw, almost too tender for even the softest of my sister's bath towels. West had stayed in the living room to talk to his sister. At least some siblings were talking.

I shook my head at the unfair thought. Kaia was literally being held captive god only knew where and I was mad at her for keeping a secret that wasn't really my business to begin with. It wasn't fair. But emotions weren't right or wrong and I was still furious.

Angry pacing seemed like something people only did in movies, but I was doing it. West entered the room but took a step backward when he saw me making laps.

"You okay?"

I muttered something like "Yes", I think.

"I'm going to hop in the shower," he said as he went into the bathroom.

Continuing my pacing, I tripped over West's bag and spilled some of its contents. Fantastic. Not only was my mind a mess, but I was also making a mess. Along with some of his clothes, half a dozen envelopes tumbled out.

Muttering curses to myself, I picked them up to shove them back inside with the clothes. Unable to resist, I flipped through them. Letters. All of them from Emmit Monroe.

He'd brought the letters with him? Why would he have done that? A small cloud of anxiety thundered in me as I slipped a letter from its envelope. I had ignored my curiosity. Wanted to give him his privacy. But why was it so important that he have these letters with him? Whoever this Emmit Monroe person was, they were important to West. Privacy be damned, I couldn't deal with any more secrets so I opened up the letter and began to read.

> *Hale,*
>
> *The pigeon flies the same route every day. Eats at the same feeders. It doesn't fly over the ocean. Only to the five boroughs, a magic city, and a desert oasis not far from home.*
>
> *Emmit Monroe*

"What the fuck?" I muttered. Was I starting to lose my mind? I read the letter again.

"Hey," West's voice echoed from the bathroom. I turned to find him standing in the doorway with a towel draped around his hips. The water from his hair was still dripping over his shoulders.

"What's this?" I said, holding up the letters.

"Letters from a friend."

"From a friend. They must be important to you if you needed to bring them with you," I looked down at the letter in my hand. Emmit wasn't a woman's name, was it? I dismissed the stupid jealous thought with a long blink. "Who, I mean, what does it mean?"

"What does what mean?" West repeated my question. Buying time. He took slow steps toward me, palms up like he was approaching a dangerous animal. Anger bubbled in me at the sight.

"The letter," I snarled. "This is obviously written in some kind of code, which is incredibly cheesy by the way. Who's the pigeon?"

His jaw tightened as his eyes narrowed. West glanced at the door and crossed the bedroom, closing it softly. I guess we were about to have it out. Or maybe I was hoping for that. I really needed to fight with someone. Kaia wasn't here for me to scream at, after all. To rage at. To ask her what other secrets she was keeping from me. So I could rage at West about his. My shoulders tensed as I sat on the bed and gave West a "well, I'm waiting" expression. He closed the distance between us, stopping when his feet bracketed mine.

"It's Benjamin Camden."

"Benjamin?"

My stomach bottomed out at the sound of his name.

"Camden is the pigeon."

I held the letter up to look at it again, only to have it torn from my fingers by West. He held the letter toward me, moving his finger along the text. "It says that he's been staying close to home, and he hasn't traveled internationally. Only to New York, Miami, and Palm Springs."

I raised my eyebrows in surprise. Not a bad code. Easy to see that it was a code, but still...Benjamin.

"So, they're tracking Benjamin. How? And who is this Emmit person?"

West dropped the letter onto the bed and picked up the ones I'd put down next to me. He flipped through them until he found the envelope he wanted and held it out to me. My eyes locked on his as I tugged the letter free.

Hale,

*I've been doing some birdwatching. Spotted a common wood
pigeon in the woods with Brent. It was out on a limb with a
bird of prey, though I couldn't make out the breed.*

Emmit Monroe

My eyebrows knit together in frustration. An effective code, but my brain was too lost in anxiety and irritation to try and decipher it. West tugged a pair of grey sweatpants up under his towel.

"I'm sorry, but what the fuck does that mean?"

And who was this goddamned Emmit person?

"Woods with Brent. Brentwood. Benjamin is in Brentwood. He's meeting with someone but he couldn't see who.'"

"So you've just been getting these coded messages from this Emmit whoever for how long exactly? You still haven't told me who they are, by the way."

"I asked for their help while I was," he paused, his mouth twisted to one side as though begging himself not to say what he was about to say. He sighed. "He started following Camden when Kaia asked me to follow you."

"Were you two ever following me together?"

"No."

"Does this Emmit person know where my sister is?"

"No."

West sat down on the bed and leaned against the headboard. Placing his arm behind his head, his bicep flexed as he stretched to get comfortable. An assessing gaze swept over me.

"What's going on with you right now? You've been weird all night."

I ignored his question and stood to look out the window, facing away from him to think as I chewed on the small edges of my nails. Dodging my questions and answering them with his own was grating on me. Why wouldn't he tell me who this Emmit was? With a deep breath, I walked back toward the bed and sat on the opposite side. He tracked every second of it, raising his eyebrows at me in expectation.

"So what were you planning on doing with this information?" I asked.

"At first I just wanted an extra set of eyes on him. Then I wanted to make sure that he wasn't hurting you. Or that he couldn't again," he said, breaking eye contact to look down at his hand that flexed and relaxed again. "Now, I don't know. Benjamin might know where your sister is. Or he knows who does."

I lay down and nestled into the pillow, pulling the covers up. Looking up at him, I wondered what it would be like to be normal people. What it would be like to share a space with him. To share a bed every night. If he were mine and I was his. This casual intimacy felt fleeting. I blinked the thought away as I remembered I'd felt that way about Benjamin and been slapped in the face by his secrets. Nearly killed by them.

"Do I ever get to meet Emmit?" I asked weakly.

"His name isn't Emmit."

"What do you mean?"

"It's an anagram," West said as he pointed to his tattoo, the dark letters inked on his golden skin. As realization dawned on me, I let out a small sound of understanding. A soft click sounded as he turned off the light and climbed into bed. I rearranged the letters of the false name in my mind.

Memento Mori.

22

PAEONIA LACTIFLORA

There was so much noise. Everywhere. Beeping machines. The doctor giving orders. My sister screaming. Blood. There was so much blood. Nurses were plying her with words of encouragement. I didn't know what to do with myself. Then there was crying. Not from her, but from someone new. It was all too much. Too overwhelming.

"Come here," Kaia said.

The hospital room had emptied. It was just us. Me, my sister, and the little boy in her arms. Black hair topped his head in soft tufts. He was so small. So new.

"Here," she said, holding him up. "You take him."

Little eyes opened to look up at me. His skin was so delicate. He had that new baby smell. He was so soft. So breakable.

"I've got you," I cooed. "Zia's got you."

The monitors in the room stopped beeping. A space that was filled with chaos was now as quiet as the grave.

"Take care of him."

"What?" I said as I turned to look at my sister. But the bed was empty.

LUPO HAD TOLD me that Nico was coming to his house for dinner. It was clear he didn't want to explain to his son about Daniel or me over the phone. The rest of the family had always known how close the Riccis were to the Caccias. He might have been worried about a tap on Nico's line.

Despite wanting to know everything that he knew, I hoped Nico had the sense to keep his mouth shut around Daniel. As far as the kid knew, his mother was away on business and was in no danger. I wanted to keep it that way for as long as I could.

Aluminum containers covered in white cardboard looked up at us from his small kitchen table. when Lupo asked me to bring food to his house for Sunday dinner, takeout was the obvious choice. Each dish had its content written on top of it in black marker. The one marked "meatballs" smelled especially delicious. I'd had Pal's delivered and the smell was doing things to my insides, helping me to forget dreaming about my sister.

West pulled the garlic bread out of the oven and set the pan on top of the range. We'd arrived only a few minutes before and Lupo told us to "make yourselves comfortable and set the table" while he "took care of a few things."

After unrolling the aluminum containers enough to remove their tops, I walked over to the utensil drawer to grab flatware for the table.

"You know your way around here pretty well," West observed.

"I used to come here all the time," I said simply, setting down forks at every seat. I'd still not mentioned Lupo's suggestion about Daniel's father. With Dante's death, he'd never occurred to me as a possibility. In hindsight, it was incredibly stupid of me not to think of it. Kaia never wanted to discuss it. That should have been a red flag.

"Hey," West grabbed hold of my wrist as I came back for knives. He pulled me into his arms and stroked my back. "Are you alright?"

"I'm fine." The words were a tight lie. He looked down into my face and narrowed his eyes. He wasn't buying it. Lifting his hand to push loose strands of hair behind my ear, his forehead creased with concern.

"You don't have to lie to me, you know."

"I know," I breathed. He brought his mouth to mine, readying to kiss the lies right out of me when Lupo walked in. The old man muttered a curse under his breath and shook his head.

"Dinner's ready," I coughed, untangling myself from West's hold. He stuffed his hands into his pockets and took a step backward.

"I was wondering what was taking so long. Now I know."

The front door opened and closed quickly. Grateful for the distraction, Lupo stepped toward the door to check on the arrival. I heard Daniel shout Nico's name. The two of them barreled into the kitchen after Daniel loudly told him we were having meatballs and baked ziti for dinner.

"Zia brought garlic bread, too!"

"Lili's here?"

Like he'd seen a ghost, Nico's eyes set on me. Anxiety screwed up my insides as I wondered what he was thinking. Then he looked to West, who gave a brief nod in greeting. I wasn't sure how much time these two had spent with each other. Probably only passing polite moments at the club. Neither had seemed to deem the other a threat as their posture remained relaxed. Or maybe they'd both been practiced in schooling their body language. Lupo cleared his throat and gestured to the table.

"Talk after dinner. I'm starving," he said as he pulled a chair out and sat down. "Nico, grab the wine. And a glass of milk for the kid."

Daniel pulled out a seat beside the old man and grinned as he sniffed at the food laid out on the table. He hungrily eyed the meatballs and then glanced at the baked ziti. Then looked back at Lupo with wide, curious eyes.

"Is this like mac and cheese?"

"Kid, this is a million times better than plain old mac and cheese."

⤙

BEFORE LONG, DANIEL'S stomach was full of noodles and cheese. Lots of noodles and cheese. Honestly, I wouldn't be surprised if the kid was half cheese. After he refused to eat a meatball, Lupo offered to put on a movie. But only if he would eat the meatball. Daniel was comfortably watching an animated feature in the next room as Nico refilled his tumbler with the last of the chianti. I gave him the quick and dirty version of what happened with Benjamin.

"Honestly, I'm just glad to see you're alive. I thought he might have killed you. Your sister told me you were with him and when you didn't come back, I-"

"No," I said, with a glance at West. "Kaia had someone looking out for me."

Nico looked down at his empty plate with a sigh. Shoulders slumped, his next words were quiet.

"I failed you, Lili. I'm sorry."

"You have nothing to be sorry for. You were with your dad. How were you to know?"

Lupo walked back into the kitchen and resumed his place at the table.

"With me doing what?"

"With you at the hospital getting your chemotherapy treatment. When Kaia was... when she disappeared," Nico said. He looked at his father and then to me.

"I'm not mad. Not at you, anyway. But I need your help."

"Anything. What do you," he let out a shaky breath. Tears lined his eyes. Two fingers pinched the bridge of his nose. "Lili, I still can't believe this. I thought you were dead."

I stood and rounded the table, bending to hug him around his shoulders. Nico reached up, placing a hand on my arms. After giving him an extra squeeze, I resumed my seat at the table.

"I'm alright. Really. But I need to help my sister. That starts with you telling me everything. What's happening with the family?"

"Ozzie. He's running things now."

"Did he kill my sister?"

"No. Fuck no. He's too big of a pussy to do that. But he saw the chance to "make things right" and he took it. That's what he keeps saying. I don't think he killed her, but I think he left the door open for something."

My brows pressed together as I took my seat again. West leaned forward, a forearm braced on the table.

"What do you mean? The door open for what?" He asked.

"For her to be abducted. And I think Ozzie helped. At first, he was talking like she was coming back. Saying he was keeping her seat warm. But now he acts like she's dead."

The turn of my stomach made cheese and red sauce feel like a terrible idea. My eyes squeezed shut as I took a deep breath, hoping not to hurl my guts up all over the table. West put a hand between my shoulders and made small calming circles. I glanced at him and gave a flat smile, grateful for the steadying touch.

"So Ozzie is in control of the family," I gritted out. "Does he think I'm dead, too?"

"No," Nico said. "He's had guys looking for you. A few of them didn't come back."

I shrugged. Four. Two at the cabin. Two at the gym. I thought about their faces. No one I recognized, which meant Ozzie had been doing his own recruiting. Preparing for his takeover.

"He took the seat without winning it from the rightful owner," Lupo said with a low growl in his voice. One I hadn't heard in years. Steel and rage flickered in his eyes.

"What does that mean?" West took his hand off of my shoulder and rubbed his jaw.

"She," Lupo said, gesturing to me with his half-empty glass, "is the rightful head of the family. If Kaia was dead. Lilith is Boss. That's the chain of command."

Nico took his father's glass and filled it with the last of the wine. Lupo took a swig and looked at West, who still seemed confused.

"Chain of command? You make it sound like an army," West said with an inquisitive furrow in his brow.

"It can be. With the right leader. In the Caccia family, there's the Boss, the Underboss, the Capos, and then there are the soldiers. That's how it's always been. Lilith is boss after Kaia."

"Because she's her sister?" West asked.

"Because she's the Wolf. The Wolf is the underboss," Lupo said as he looked at me.

West's face twisted in confusion.

"The Wolf?"

Nico nodded. "The Wolf. It's what we call the fixer for the family. But it's more than that. They're also the protector of the family. Like a knight sworn to protect their king. She swore an oath. She's bound to the Boss."

"Forever," Lupo said as his son looked at him. He looked down at his hands, at the tattoos and scars, then at me. "I will know no peace if our enemies roam free. For their blood is my wine. Their souls are my fee."

I swallowed hard and looked at Lupo. He nodded with a half-cocked smile. West looked at him, then at me. Then at my chest. At the wolf tattoo I knew he remembered.

"I took that oath before you were born," Lupo groaned, stretching in his seat like he could feel the years sitting on his bones, tightening his still-impressive muscles. The three of us stared at him, waiting for what he was going to say next. Which, if I'm being honest, was a huge mistake because Lupo can sit in silence for hours. I thanked Nico silently for finding something to say.

"So what does she do? Ozzie's guys will never just let her come back. It's already bad enough that she's in Los Angeles. He's put a price on her head. He'll kill her if he finds her. Especially because she's underboss. He'll kill her before he lets her take his seat."

West's expression tightened. I put a hand on his leg.

"She has to win her place back." Lupo looked at his son and then at me.

"Win it how?"

"Gladius."

23

HYPERICUM PERFORATUM

When I was a young man," Lupo started. "I worked in construction off and on. I'd travel around and pick up work on different sites. It was usually good money. But then I went six months without a job. Crashed on my mother's couch. She could barely afford to keep the roof over our heads, let alone feed an extra mouth."

Nico shifted in his seat and looked down at his wine. This was a story he knew well, but it was entirely new to me. I shifted with anticipation and glanced at West, who had relaxed in his seat while wearing an expression I couldn't quite read.

"While I was out looking for work, I'd go to a deli every day for lunch. For that damn capicola sandwich from Pal's," Lupo went on, looking at me with a smile. The sandwich I'd brought him every single time I'd come to the gym from the moment I started training there. He called it my membership fee. Maybe because I technically owned the gym so a membership fee would have gone right back into my pocket.

"It was the only food I could afford. One day I didn't have enough money to cover the sandwich and one of the guys who was there every day covered it for me. He brought me to Nicolò Bianchi and soon I was running around with the rest of them. One night, while I was guarding the poker hall, I got into it with a real proud son of a bitch."

Lupo drained his glass to the dregs, looking at everyone to make sure we were listening. Only Nico was looking away, still at his glass. He looked up at his father when the silence seemed to last too long. It pressed in on me as I wondered where this story was going. Clearing his throat, Lupo continued.

"Back in those days, the way we settled the score was with what Bianchi liked to call Gladius. His "gladiators" would fight each other instead of disrupting the family by trying to turn loyal brothers against each other with petty squabbles. Once the fight was over, the dispute was over. If someone died, there was no punishment."

"This scar, here on my face? That was from my first Gladius. I was good with a knife. This guy was better. He had me on the ground in seconds. I thought I was dead. But then he let me surrender. Offered me a hand up. That day, your grandfather told me everything I needed to know about him."

I smirked. Both Lupo and I knew exactly how deadly my grandfather could be with a knife. It had never occurred to me that Lupo was ever on the losing end of it. Men in the family often had scars. Scars with stories I'd wanted to hear, but never asked. I wondered how often Lupo had told his sons this story. Wondered if maybe they'd wanted to know where that scar had come from. The old man patted my arm and continued speaking, this time only to me.

"You need to take back your seat by demanding a fight with Ozzie in a Gladius match. If he's man enough to meet you. You can beat him. Take over the family with honor and no one will be able to argue. If he has someone fight for him, you'll be able to stop them from getting rid of you but you'll have to find another way to take over the family."

"What other way is that?" Nico asked.

"I have to kill him," I said. Lupo nodded.

EVERY INCH OF me felt spread thin after hours of discussing what to do about the family. Nico would be my eyes and ears, letting me know when the best time to move forward with our next steps. When the time was right, he'd tell Ozzie I wanted to crawl back like a coward to them. To make a deal for my resumed position with the family. West had said he was going to check on Daniel, popping his head back into the room to tell us he was putting him in bed. Knowing Daniel was being protected by Lupo, someone who was once considered the most dangerous man in Los Angeles, eased my worries. My heart gave a squeeze, seeing Daniel's tiny limbs dangle from West's powerful arms when he brought him in to say good night.

Nico took that as his cue to leave, giving his father a pat on the shoulder and telling me he'd be in touch. We watched him exit and sat in silence for a moment. Lupo filled his water glass and gave me his "let's cut the bullshit" look. I sat up a little straighter, bracing myself.

"You and West are... what, exactly?"

I shook my head. I didn't know what to call it. How could I explain it to anyone else? Lupo gave me a flat look and continued.

"What did I say about lying to me? I've watched you two dance around each other in my gym for long enough. Now tell me what's going on."

"I'm not lying. I don't know what we are. There's too much shit going on right now. My sister is missing. The family is in chaos. Oh, and let's not forget that I almost died. You want me to define a relationship? I have no idea."

Lupo muttered a curse and took a sip of water. I stretched back in my chair to try and look for West, hoping he was still occupied with Daniel.

"I'm just trying to enjoy it," I said quietly. Lupo grunted.

"Be careful with him."

"He would never hurt me," I said, ready to defend West's intentions.

"No. He could get hurt, though. And I think you know that." Lupo finished his water, bringing the glass onto the table with a firm clink. He drilled his index finger into the tabletop as he said, "Don't play games, kid. Not with this one."

WEST AND I sat in his Bronco for long, silent minutes. Still parked in front of Lupo's house, his face was partially lit by the streetlight over us. The amount of information that'd been laid out was a lot for me to digest. I couldn't imagine what he was thinking. *Do not speak first,* I thought. *Do not fill the silence with useless chatter just because you're uncomfortable.*

"So that's what the wolf is for," West finally said.

"The wolf?" I asked, grateful I'd been able to outlast my anxiety.

"On your chest. I saw the tattoo on your chest. That's what it's for?"

"Sort of," I nodded. "My grandfather used to tell me a bedtime story whenever I couldn't sleep. It was about a village deep in the forest, filled with kind people. The wolf protected the villagers from the monsters who came out at night. I got the tattoo when he died."

With a small nod, put his key in the ignition. Then paused to look at me, the light bisecting his green eyes.

"You're not just a fixer," he said, more to himself than to me. A statement, not a question.

I nodded. My stomach tightened with worry. Maybe he thought that I'd lied by leaving out everything else. A lie by omission. But being underboss was never something I thought about. Never an option. Not really. I was always going to give my seat to Daniel when he was ready because I thought Kaia would be there. I took my job, the Wolf, because I wanted to protect my family. That was it.

As we backed out of the driveway, I watched the lights turn out inside the house. The engine cut through the silence. Silence was one of West's signature sounds. Lost in thought? Silence. Irritated with me? Silence. The two sounds were nearly identical. Almost indistinguishable to the naked ear. But the second came laced with a tension that electrified the air in a way that only I could feel.

Before the cabin, before Benjamin and my other big mistakes, I'd fill the silence. West would eventually break and start talking to me again. Not this time. After everything he'd learned at Lupo's, he needed the ride home to digest. To decide I was a liar who wasn't worth all of this trouble, probably.

I could have explained myself to West. Told him about that night I'd offered myself to my sister. Swore an everlasting vow to protect the things I loved most in this world. Instead, I looked out the window and said nothing.

24

ARMORACIA RUSTICANA

The wood target was starting to splinter after the brutality of our throws. Kaia's and mine. We replaced the boards every month. I thought about replacing them as I pulled my knives out of the center to sheath them at my side. Deciding to challenge myself a bit more, I walked backward from where I had been standing by a few more yards. It didn't have anything to do with the fact that I could see West cleaning his gun at the table through the glass doors.

A surge of fury rolled through my veins as I threw the first blade. Chilly late-night air bit at my cheeks. The target rocked slightly at the impact. I let myself think about what I would do if West left, and how I would handle my situation. When we got back, he'd gone inside. I stayed outside. He needed space from me. I shut down the things I'd felt. The fear of his departure and what that would do to me. If he left, I'd manage. I had to. A crack sounded as I threw the next knife. I'd take back the family and use the resources at my disposal to find my sister. Or die.

Something between a scream and a growl came out of me as the last knife flew from my fingers. The final blade buried itself deeply in the wood, leaving a gaping hole where the wobbling target had splintered for good. It resisted as I tried to pull it free.

"Shit," I muttered, bracing a boot against the target's pole. With a hard pull and a less-than-graceful grunt, it came free but forced me to lose my footing. I blew out a breath and composed myself, turning to take my place again. West stood by the glass door, watching me with his arms crossed across his broad chest.

His attention seemed to break through the conflict in me. Like setting foot on solid ground after being away too long at sea. Deciding maybe the board had finally had enough, I headed inside. He glanced at me as I shut the door and then resumed gazing out the window.

"So what now?" His voice was flat, like he was lost in thought but his expression was tight. One I'd never seen before. I searched for some hint of what he was feeling or thinking.

"Now we wait."

This look on his face. What the fuck was this look?

"Wait." He says the word quietly. More to himself than to me. He'd developed a habit of doing that lately.

"Ozzie has an army at his beck and call. I need to wait until his numbers are more depleted. Until they're indisposed. That way it's more likely that I'll be able to face him one on one."

Really, I needed to figure out how in the hell I was going to deal with that. How could I deal with a man who had Ronan Arawn at his back? Ronan Arawn, the big daddy of the Irish mob. Why the fuck would he back Ozzie in the first place? Ozzie's a loose cannon. Granted, he's an easily manipulated egotistical bastard. An easy patsy for Arawn's needs. Squaring up against Ozzie meant going into a battle I wasn't sure I could win. But I couldn't help my sister with a target on my back, which meant I had to try.

"West, this stuff. It's a lot. I know," I hesitated with an uneven breath. I could do this. Do something good. For him. I mean, shit I couldn't drag him into one more mess. "I didn't tell you everything and I'm sorry. But it's something I can do on my own."

He rolled his eyes. Actually rolled his damn eyes at me.

"What?" I barked.

"Don't do that."

"Do what?"

"Push me away."

"Trust me, you don't want them to know you're helping me. Don't get tangled up in my mess, West."

A cold laugh burst from him as he placed a hand on the door frame and leaned in until I could see the brown flecks in his green eyes. My cheeks flushed at his nearness and the wildness in those eyes as he brought his mouth to my ear and whispered.

"I'm already in." His other hand circled my throat, gently. My pulse flickered under the soft strokes of his index finger. Moving so his nose almost grazed mine, his eyes blazed. "You don't need to define this to anyone, Lili. Not Lupo. Not my sister. But don't lie to yourself. You know exactly what this is."

He looked down at me, waiting for something to come out of my now-paralyzed lips. The breath I was holding burned in my chest. I glanced at his mouth, which had curled slightly into a smirk at my attention. I swallowed as his lips moved closer to mine. But like a bucket of ice water, he pulled away from me and spoke over his shoulder before heading upstairs.

"That silence is all you need to say."

Jesus Christ. Who says that? And what in the actual hell was that?

I SAT IN the living room for hours. It still smelled like baby shampoo and fresh laundry in here. The house smelled like a small boy still lived here. Maybe it always would. After West left me in a state that could only be described as confused and horny, I threw myself onto the ivory-covered sofa and turned on the television.

Flipping through all of the streaming options, I found the perfect comfort movie and sunk back into the welcoming throw pillows. Cher was getting engaged at an Italian restaurant as West's words floated into my head again.

"You know exactly what this is."

The more I thought about it, the less I wanted to go upstairs and face him. I didn't have it in me to tell him that I thought I knew what he meant to me. What all of this meant to me. The two of us were standing on the edge of something. Even though I wanted him, all of him, I knew he could do better than me. Deserved better.

I was afraid. Of course I was. My heart had been broken so many times that it was sitting on cinderblocks and rusting to pieces. If he really wanted to be with someone, settle down with someone, I was the wrong girl. It wasn't just Benjamin that made me feel inadequate. Ethan, my first real love, had cheated on me and then threw my family and occupation in my face. Told me I was trash because of it. I couldn't bear it if things with West ended that way. No one had ever made me feel like I was enough. I was worried I'd just disappoint him. Or worse.

Toeing off my boots, I pulled my legs up onto the sofa and adjusted a pillow to cradle my head as I let the movie take me away. Nicolas Cage was thanking Cher for the way she looked at the Metropolitan Opera House when my thoughts had run me ragged enough to finally nod off. Breathing in the scent of Daniel's shampoo, my sister's perfume, something in my chest eased as I laid down to sleep. And sleep. And sleep.

25

VALERIANA OFFICINALIS

Sunshine poured into the living room through its large windows as I woke to the sound of something sizzling in the kitchen. A camel-colored chenille throw blanket had been carefully tucked around me. Slowly, trying to remain undetected, I peeked my head over the arm of the sofa.

West's back was to me as he walked to the refrigerator to grab something. He propped his arm on the top, looking around for a moment. The long, dark strands of his hair were wet enough to soak the shoulders of his shirt. Without turning around, his voice lifted from the kitchen.

"Good morning."

Well, so much for remaining undetected. Sinking back into the sofa, I pulled the blanket over my head and wished the gods would have mercy on me and just end me now. I rubbed the sleep out of my eyes and, with as much nonchalance as I could force, asked if there was coffee.

"Sure," he said. I could hear the damn smirk on his face. "It's one of those single brew jobs. Come and make it."

Peeling myself out of the luxuriously upholstered cocoon, I adjusted my sleep-marred clothes and headed into the kitchen. West scraped fluffy scrambled eggs onto a plate and dropped two pieces of toast next to them.

My mouth watered at the heavenly-looking spread. The coffee machine hummed as it poured into the cup I'd readied for it.

Without looking up from the eggs he cracked into a bowl, West spoke.

"You didn't come to bed." It wasn't a question. He wasn't asking why. He was reveling in it. Like he enjoyed the idea that I'd been avoiding him. This was a taunt.

"I felt like watching a movie."

You know exactly what this is. Nope. I was not going to cave.

"What movie did you watch?"

I took a seat at the island and looked up at him, batting my eyelashes in a wide-eyed *I'm not hiding anything* expression. "Moonstruck," I said over the rim of my coffee cup as I took a casual sip.

"That's a good one," he said with a nod.

"You've seen it?"

"Sure, that's the one with Julia Roberts and Richard Gere. Right?"

"What?! No, it's Cher and Nicolas Cage."

It was a classic West trap and I'd walked right into it. To get me to argue with him. Talk to him. The same way he baited me during training. Verbal sparring. His eyes connected with mine and I didn't have to be a mind reader to know what he was thinking. *Got you.* I rolled my eyes and sipped my coffee again, trying to hide my grin.

Lanna ambled down the stairs in a pair of borrowed pajamas. With a yawn, she started fixing herself a cup of coffee.

"Is it alright if I borrow your sister's clothes?" She said as she hoisted an arm up. "I don't have anything with me."

I nodded as I shoved food into my mouth. Knowing my sister, she probably would have given them to her without asking.

West took a place at my side. I'd started to enjoy being fed by him. It was a nice change from my usual takeout and junk food meals. As he took a forkful from a steaming pile of eggs, West raised an eyebrow at me. An eyebrow that said, "I'm not going to let you forget what I said." Then his mouth said, "You should get cleaned up when you're finished. We have somewhere to be."

WALKING INTO THIS apartment felt a lot like walking into a long-forgotten storage unit of a sports memorabilia hoarder. The word "apartment" may be too generous for what I was looking at. Boxes. They were everywhere. Stacked in almost every corner with words that seemed completely random written on them in a hasty scrawl.

The space was large. Big windows looked out over the other buildings in the downtown area, letting in the meager amount of sunlight left in the cold winter evening. This loft was in the middle of an older area downtown, on the top floor of the building, with a door at the end of the hall that was blocked by a large potted ficus. It had a "hiding in plain sight" kind of thing going for it. I could respect that.

West put a hand on my lower back and pushed gently to move me further into the living room. A large leather sofa that looked oddly expensive compared to the construction spool being used as a coffee table and a bunch of wooden milk crates that were nailed together to hold up his gaming console. I wondered if the large flat screen hanging from the wall was too heavy for the precarious carpentry.

A beep came from the kitchen area, then the sound of the microwave opening and closing.

"Shit!" A strangled curse and what sounded like a plate hitting the counter.

"Clay?" West peeked his head around a stack of file boxes to look into the kitchen.

"Coming, coming, coming," the voice from the kitchen said in a hurried huff. After the rustle of some other objects and the clinking of bottles in the kitchen, I heard footsteps approaching us.

A man in a baseball cap and horn-rimmed glasses came out of the kitchen with a plate of tortilla chips and melted cheese on top. Olives, pickled jalapenos, and possibly hot sauce were scattered haphazardly all over the plate. I eyed the Taylor Swift tee shirt that also had hot sauce all over it and lifted my gaze to meet his.

"Nacho?" He held out the plate toward West, who shook his head. Then the plate was offered to me. Who was I to refuse cheese? I took a chip and popped it in my mouth.

"Clayton, this is Lili Caccia. Lili, this is Clayton Wrigley."

West had explained on the way to this building who we were going to meet. The man behind all of Emmit Monroe's letters. A former SEAL team member turned mercenary; Clayton seemed as strange as West had warned he would be.

"It's a pleasure," I said, looking around again. "Interesting place you've got here."

"Interesting is the polite word for shithole, isn't it?" Clayton said, looking at West for confirmation. "Well, Lili Caccia, welcome to my shitbox."

"Shit*hole*," I corrected. "So what's in all the boxes, Clayton?"

Clayton looked around as though seeing the boxes for the first time himself. Kind of attractive in a frat boy sort of way, Clayton's short brown hair was nearly the same color as his eyes. With a shrug and a Cheshire grin, he moved toward the sofa and sat down. West let himself into the kitchen, leaving me alone with our host.

"So," Clayton said around a mouthful of nacho. "Your ex-boyfriend wants you dead."

"Something like that," I muttered, leaning back into the sofa cushions. "You know where he is?"

"Something like that," Clayton replied, taking a generous swig of beer. West returned from the kitchen, setting a beer for me down on the wooden spool and taking a drink from the one he'd gotten for himself. Watching his throat work around a gulp, I cleared my throat and returned my attention to Clayton.

"Because Camden is a public figure, tracking his whereabouts has been the easy part. He just assumes I'm a pesky paparazzo. But he plays things very close to the chest. It's hard to pin down who he's dealing with."

"Yeah, that part I knew," I said as I picked up the bottle and took a drink. Surprised at the quality of the beer, I took another sip and settled against the back of the sofa.

"How do we get that information?" West asked, checking on me with a short sidelong glance. Benjamin seemed to be a sensitive subject for both of us.

"We could hack his phone," Clayton offered.

"You know how to do that?" I asked.

"Nope. Do you?"

West took a sip of beer and gave Clayton an annoyed look. A short, silent conversation passed between the two of them before Clayton looked at me and continued.

"He's well-connected enough to be the ringleader, but I don't think that's what's happening here."

"You think he's answering to somebody else?"

"Well, if they're trafficking people all over the world, that means they're dealing with different governments. Different lawmakers. Camden has enough money to deal with that, but he doesn't have the political connections."

"So a bigger fish with political clout."

"Do you have any suggestions? A way to find out about this big fish Camden's working with that doesn't involve something impossible?" West said as he placed his empty bottle on the wooden spool.

I thumbed the damp paper label on the brown bottle, letting it curl and peel against my fingernail. The answer was obvious. They knew it. I knew it. Both men tried to avoid looking directly at me, but I could feel them waiting for me to say it.

"We ask him."

IF WE WERE going to get Benjamin alone, we needed for it to look like he'd disappeared of his own accord. No overt attacks. This was where I came in. We needed him sedated, alive. Well enough for me to get information out of him. Security meant I wouldn't be able to get close to him, so a needle wouldn't do. Whatever we gave him, we'd have to somehow get him to ingest it himself.

Three hours and two pizzas later, we had a loose approximation of a plan. Clayton would continue to shadow Benjamin as a member of the paparazzi, keeping us up to date on every movement. Thanks to some bribery Clayton was able to find out where he was going to be next, allowing me to see Benjamin for the first time since the last Eros party. Since he'd tried to kill me.

I fought a small grimace as I lifted a slice of what Clayton called "kitchen sink" pizza to my mouth. Though watching West and Clayton talk about methods of moving Benjamin without arousing suspicion was pure entertainment, I was anxious about seeing him again. But I couldn't move forward with our plan without a closer look. If Benjamin was responsible for my missing sister, then putting him in harm's way could harm Kaia.

Our plan. As I washed the pizza down with the last of my beer, I enjoyed how weirdly nice it was to be on a team. Working alone would never be the same after this.

26

ASPARAGUS RACEMOSUS

When I stepped out of Kaia's bedroom, Lanna was exiting the guest room across the hall. She looked me over and gave a low, appreciative whistle.

"You look nice," she smiled. "Green is definitely your color."

I looked down at the olive-green silk dress I'd pulled out of Kaia's closet. A small flame of guilt flickered in me when I took the tags off of it. I'd never seen her in it and it was shoved toward the back like a secret, lost among all of her designer suits. My hands smoothed down the sides as I did a little turn.

"It's nice, right? It's my sister's."

"She has excellent taste," Lanna said. With a sigh, she picked up a book from the small table beside her and gestured to the stairs. "West is already outside waiting for you."

A small flutter went through me. Why was this starting to feel like leaving for homecoming or something? Placing my hand on the railing, I turned back to Lanna.

"I'm sorry you can't come. It's safer this way," I said. It was true. If someone attacked me, I knew how to defend myself. So did West. But Lanna didn't. For all of the help she'd been in other ways, I didn't need that kind of distraction. She would be safer with the security of the house. Still, I felt guilty leaving her behind. "I know what it feels like to be trapped indoors. But I promise you'll be able to go home soon."

Lanna's nod was small. She followed me down the stairs and went into the kitchen with her book, presumably for her own dinner. A fluttering in my stomach started as I headed toward the front door. I wasn't sure whether my unsteady steps were from anxiety or the heels rarely wore. Then I stepped outside.

Every day West Hale wore beat-up work pants and a cotton shirt and he was still a good-looking man. Maybe a little dirty. Sometimes he looked like he could use a hose down with a power washer. But still, bronze skin and long dark hair coupled with a sparkling smile made him handsome. When West was cleaned up, with his hair braided back and in a deep burgundy suit that highlighted his green eyes and a black shirt that strained against his powerful body? He was devastating.

As he approached me, my stomach did another nervous little flutter. The scent of cedar that normally surrounded him was somehow stronger, making me almost lightheaded at his nearness. Up close, I could see that he'd brushed his beard. The way he drank me in with his eyes made my already unsteady legs wobble in their high heels.

"You ready?"

Temporarily unable to speak, I nodded. His hand moved to my lower back to guide me to the truck. The heat of his palm did nothing to slow my racing pulse.

The last time I had been out on a dinner date was with a man who had tried to kill me. And I was about to set eyes on him again for the first time.

THE LIGHTS OF the city looked like scattered stars as we stepped out of the elevator onto the rooftop terrace. Lights strung overhead remind me of the patio back at the house, but that's the only similarity the spaces share.

Tiny tables with white tablecloths are scattered about. Each one has a small votive candle and an arrangement of wildflowers in its center.

This is stupid, a small voice in me cried. *This is so incredibly stupid. Why risk confronting him now?* But I told myself I needed to do it. Needed to set eyes on the man who nearly killed me. Needed to take the measure of the man who was likely connected to Kaia's disappearance.

A host guided us to our table. They must have gotten my note because we're set in the back of the space with a good view of the rest of the room. Private, just like I'd asked. West pulled out a chair and I almost stumbled in my heels at the gesture. After sitting down and scooting me in, West sat across from me to take in the room. His eyes scanned from one side to the other.

"He's not here yet," he said quietly as the host walked away.

"He'll be here."

West nodded, turning his eyes to me.

"You pulled out my chair," I grinned, angling my head. West took his seat and shrugged. "I don't think anyone has ever pulled my chair out for me."

"That's what I do on dates."

"So, is this a date, then?" I took a sip of water, unable to keep the smirk off of my face.

"Yes. We are on a date. I am buying you dinner and enjoying your company."

My stomach did the little flip thing again at West's seriousness. I glanced down at the menu, suddenly feeling guilty about the expensive restaurant. West clocked my discomfort because he shook his head and leaned forward to speak to me in a low voice.

"I make plenty of money," he said with a chuckle. "Your sister pays me very well. Ridiculously well. Also, I have a lot of hazard pay that's just sitting in savings."

His hand covered mine.

"I've wanted to do this for a long time."

"But you and I eat out together all the time."

"As friends. This isn't that. I am going to buy your dinner. You're going to tell me something I don't know about you. Then, at the end of the night, I'm going to kiss you."

His fingers caught my jaw as he leaned forward, pressing his mouth to mine. What had started as a short brush had turned into a lingering kiss as he captured my lower lip, sucking it briefly between his own.

"You said you were going to do that at the end of the night," I murmured against his lips.

"I didn't say that was the only kiss you were getting tonight."

As he leaned back in his seat, he picked up his water and lifted it to his lips. What an arched brow and a smirk, his eyes seemed to say *your move.*

"Alright," I said while clearing my throat. Holy shit, this man had game. "Something you don't already know about me."

I fought the way my mouth twisted to one side as I mulled over my options. What didn't he know? Aside from the bloody awful truth he'd only recently learned, I told him everything.

"Well," I sighed. "The first time I had to…" I made a subtle throat-cutting gesture and West nodded, "I accidentally got the guy in the eye. Right in the eye with the needle. I had been crouched in his water heater closet all night. After he fell asleep, I snuck into his bedroom to do what I needed to do. He woke up and I panicked and jammed it into his eye. It was a real mess."

West's laugh exploded from him. It warmed me from the inside. Maybe it was the way it rumbled out of him. Or the way his eyes wrinkled when he smiled. All I wanted to do was make him laugh again. Unfortunately, our unguarded moment meant we didn't see who approached our table.

"Lilith?"

Benjamin Camden and his date stood there, looking down at us. He looked exactly the same as when I'd last seen him. An expensive blue suit covered a rugby player's build. Every detail, from the sterling cufflinks and sparkling watch to his polished brogue shoes, was immaculate. That dark curl of brown hair dangled over his brow in what I now knew was calculated imperfection. My breath lodged in my chest as I met the cold blue eyes of the man who'd tried to kill me. His date, a blonde gazelle who seemed nice enough, gave me a polite smile and waved at the man accompanying me. West put his glass back on the table and left his hand within reach of the flatware.

"Benjamin, so nice to see you," I crooned, attempting to sound more relaxed than I felt. With my nerves firing like an electrical storm, it was a herculean effort.

"You look well," Benjamin said with a curious smirk, no doubt remembering the way I looked the last time he saw me. Knocking on death's door with both hands. Prick.

"Thank you," I gave a pointed look at his immaculate suit. "Are you between tailors? I preferred the more fitted look on you."

Benjamin cleared his throat, unable to keep himself from smoothing the front of his jacket with his free hand. The corner of West's mouth tipped up at the movement.

"Yes, well, I thought I spotted you. I thought it would be rude to leave without saying goodbye," Benjamin said with a bit of bite. Every muscle in my body froze as my stomach turned at the memory of the door closing behind him and the way he left me to die alone in a utility closet. I swallowed hard, fighting my body for control.

West lifted his drink to his mouth, all of the joy and warmth completely gone from his eyes. Looking me over, then assessing the man standing beside our table. His free hand flexed and relaxed. I started to wonder what West would do to Benjamin if given the chance.

"Goodbye then," I said cooly, grateful my voice remained even. Benjamin nodded, escorting his silent date away from the table. I could hear her asking who I was as they departed. Poor girl. Unable to resist, I lifted my voice to call after him. "I'll be seeing you soon, Benjamin."

I turned to West, waiting until Benjamin was out of earshot. His eyes were hard and cold, watching the man leave. Carefully measuring every inch.

"So," I said, lowering my voice. "How much do you think he weighs? I'm thinking 180, but I'm not sure. If I overshoot the dosage, I'll kill him."

"190."

27

CROCUS SATIVUS

It took two aggressively mixed filthy gin martinis for me to calm down. Not normally my drink, but I needed something in the vicinity of paint thinner to get the taste of that conversation out of my mouth. Having gotten our task for the evening out of the way, I was content to forget everything else as quickly as I could.

West let me finish the first martini before attempting to return to a normal evening. The cold, angry look had disappeared from his face.

"If I haven't mentioned it yet tonight, you look gorgeous," he started. "I'm still not used to seeing you dolled up like this."

My skin heated at the look he gave me. Then the smile. The smile that felt purely lethal. Or maybe that was the martinis.

"Yeah, well, I'm not planning on making it a regular thing."

West cut into his ribeye and brought a piece of it to his mouth, pausing briefly to speak before taking the bloody bite.

"Good. I prefer you covered in sweat."

I almost choked on my mashed potatoes.

A SHORT MAN exited the elevator on the next floor, leaving the two of us alone for the last two down to the parking garage. I looked at us in the reflection of the elevator doors. West cut a striking figure in his suit, but I still preferred him in his usual well-worn attire. Still, he looked sinfully good. His gaze met mine and I bit down on the smile pulling at my lips. He smirked. Damnit.

"Where did you get the suit?" I asked, trying to break the silence.

"I went by my apartment to pick up some things," he said nonchalantly. His fingers brushed against mine, his thumb stroked down my hand then moved away. The elevator pinged as the doors opened into the vast concrete parking garage. West gave me the "after you" gesture and walked out behind me. Our footsteps echoed in the near-empty parking lot. I searched the space for any sign of Benjamin, grateful to find nothing.

"This little dress is torture," West said, giving my ass a small slap.

The green silk dress hugged my body, flaring out a little with a mid-thigh slit. Maybe I let my ass wiggle a little as we made our way back to the Bronco. Just a little. Casting a glance over my shoulder, I noticed West's eyes blaze with heat as they raked over me. I rounded the front of the truck and he followed close behind to open the door. Before I could step in, he pushed me against the side. With one hand around my waist, he reached through the slit on my thigh to palm me through my panties. His hard, thick length ground against my ass as he whispered to me.

"I don't think I'm going to be able to make the drive home if you don't stop looking at me like that."

I hummed and pushed back against him as he played with me, sinking my teeth into my lip to keep from moaning.

"Is this what you do on dates?" I laughed.

"Only dates with you. You're already soaked for me, aren't you?"

I nodded with another hum.

"Trouble likes it a little rough. This pretty little pussy needs me, doesn't it?"

"Yes," I gasped. My hands pressed against the truck. Silk whispered against my thighs as he pushed my dress up. With the fabric hanging around my waist, I was completely exposed to him. The nearly nonexistent thong I'd been wearing felt like a complete waste of lace. My clit throbbed and I squeezed my thighs together. He dragged a finger through my slit. A knee nudged my legs apart.

"So fucking wet. So needy," he rasped.

This West was different. Taking what he wanted. I looked over my shoulder at him, watching him kneel behind me as I took my skirt in my hand to keep it up. Our eyes met. What he wanted was me and he was not going to wait for it anymore. Grabbing at my hip with one hand, he leaned in to lick through my center. Then he was lapping at my core with his tongue as he rubbed my sensitive bud with his fingers.

This man was completely out of control. Possessing me with his mouth. A small cry burst from me and I bit down on my lip again, turning my head into my shoulder to muffle the sound in the echoing chamber of the parking structure. I hoped no one could see us.

He panted and growled into the most intimate part of me. My legs started to shake at the relentless sensation. I thought could keep my composure until his hand pressed into my clit with almost brutal force.

"Oh my god," I murmured into my arm. The hand that was pinned to my hip gripped hard enough to bruise.

Release was coming fast for every nerve, scraping against every raw edge. His groans and licks were unhinged and wild. My legs shook. I couldn't take any more. Could hardly stand. I clenched around him as I came, burying my face in the crook of my arm to stifle my heaving breaths. He pressed a kiss to my inner thigh. Hands moved to pull my dress back down and support me as I leaned back against him, still shaking and out of breath.

"Fuck, did I hurt you?"

"No," I laughed. "No, you didn't hurt me. Ok, maybe a little but I liked it."

He helped me into the passenger seat and adjusted himself in his pants before closing the door again. Blowing out a shaky breath, he pushed the hair that had fallen from his braid out of his face. The truck dipped under his weight as he climbed in.

"I told you I'd kiss you at the end of the night." He winked as he stuffed the key in the ignition.

I couldn't stop the giggle that burst from me. The engine roared to life and I looked at him. A look I hadn't seen before washed over his features. Somewhere between relaxation and disbelief. It confused me. It even scared me a little. As I looked in the mirror, attempting to fix the mess my hair had become, I noticed the same expression had settled on my face. Like we both knew the answer to some evasive question.

28

GINKGO BILOBA

Sunlight poured in through the open picture windows, the big white bed like a cloud in clear blue sky. Gauzy white curtains floated on the breeze, surrounding us with their soft sounds. Benjamin was writhing under me, moaning my name in ecstasy. My fingers sifted through the curls on his chest, embracing every sensation. Loving every second. His fingers dug into my hips, pulling me closer as I rolled them against him.

He was whimpering. Begging me to finish him. I did. His cries were music. The sounds I'd been aching to hear. When I was finished with him, I climbed out of bed and wrapped myself in one of his fine shirts.

Red footprints smeared beneath me, staining the stark white marble with the last of Benjamin as I walked out his front door.

THE CLACK AND resistance of a new keyboard is an oddly satisfying thing. Clayton had set me up with a new computer since mine had been taken when my apartment was raided. When you grow up in a crime family in the twenty-first century, you learn quickly how important it is to keep your computer or phone clear of any important information. As I sipped from a cup of coffee, I thought about how convenient it was that Clayton was weirdly happy to accept his payment in quarters. The laptop he got me was sleeker and newer than mine, which had followed me to and from college. A technological clean slate.

After setting up a few new email accounts, I set up a profile on a business-oriented social media platform. Then I got to work looking for the profile of a Camden Industries employee I'd gotten to know quite well. Hell, she probably would have disappeared altogether if it wasn't for me. I sent her a direct message from my false profile.

> Juliet,
>
> After reviewing your impressive career history, I'd love to discuss an opportunity with you. If you're open to it, I'd like to have lunch with you to discuss the position in detail.
>
> Best,
> Flora Hunter

It wasn't the nicest thing, fooling her into thinking she'd have a new opportunity available to her. I knew it would work. Benjamin was selfish. Focused on his happiness. The people around him were used as a means to an end. It was likely that Juliet was sick of being treated that way. A small part of me felt bad about using that to my advantage. But it was a tiny part. Like the size of a gnat. Infinitesimal and easily crushed.

Then I worked on crushing a plate of taquitos and guacamole. West was watching the third John Wick movie and folding laundry. After I finished my meal, I watched the assassin work his way through the hotel out of the corner of my eye while relentlessly refreshing my browser. We were multi-taskers in this house. He was in the midst of a brawl when Juliet's response finally came through.

> Yes. I'm available tomorrow.

RAIDING MY SISTER'S closet for a suit that would fit me was more difficult than I thought. She was tall with lean lines and I was short with wider hips...and more going on in the breast region. After finding a blazer that fit and a dress with enough stretch in it to get over my ass, I stuffed my feet into a pair of heels, grateful that Kaia and I at least shared the same size in shoes.

Getting done up in Kaia's makeup felt like getting ready for my theatrical debut. Hair pulled back in a tight ponytail. Glasses that didn't belong to me. In today's performance, I was playing the part of a big-time CEO who wanted to poach talent away from the illustrious Camden Industries. It was essential that Juliet wouldn't recognize me. At least not immediately. For all I knew, Benjamin had poisoned the well. She could know everything about me. Be warned not to trust me. Or she knew nothing at all. I just needed a moment to get her to listen. To get her on my side. And to remind her that she owed me a goddamned favor.

Bribing the host to avoid seating anyone on the terrace with us had been easy enough. Honestly, it had been so simple that it made me question what they were paying her. It was always funny to me when "honest" businesses were the ones who seem to love screwing their employees. Mafiosos would never settle for such low pay.

Trying to ignore the merciless pinch of the pointed-toe Christian Louboutin heels I'd chosen, I kept an eye on the entrance. Once Juliet arrived, I would use the menu to hide my face for as long as I possibly could. Then I heard the host leading Juliet to our table outside. Heels clacked against the ground, approaching with purpose.

"Flora Hunter?" Juliet's voice was clear and certain. A professional.

"Hello, Juliet," I said, dropping the menu.

"Li- Ms. Caccia. You're Flora Hunter?"

I shrugged. "I noticed you're still working for Benjamin Camden and I thought you might not want to meet with me. Please sit," I said gesturing to the seat across from me. Juliet looked at the chair beside her and paused.

"I'm sorry you two broke up," she said as she decided to sit.

"Yes," I looked down at the breadbasket and tried to stifle the laughter. Broke up? Was that what he told her? "It was nice while it lasted."

Not entirely a lie. But the time spent with Benjamin had been tarnished by the way it ended. When your fake boyfriend poisons you and leaves you for dead, it tends to leave a bad taste in your mouth. Literally. It was a detail Juliet apparently had no idea about.

"He told me not to take calls from you."

I couldn't help the laugh that bubbled up. Benjamin didn't know that he was already being followed by a mercenary. And I was sleeping with a sniper who could probably snap the billionaire's neck with his bare hands. Really. Taking calls from me should be the least of his concerns. Like not answering the phone would keep me, us, from his door. Did the Big Bad Wolf stop at knocking? No. I was going to get my little pig.

With a deep breath, I steadied myself. Tried to control the urge to tell her that her boss was a piece of trash. I was cool. I was calm.

"I think he and I are due for a chat," I said, the picture of grace. "But I'd rather not drop in on him like some crazy ex-girlfriend. Is he seeing someone right now?"

Juliet looked down at her plate, worried about what the answer would do to me. I almost felt guilty knowing she was trying to protect my feelings. Like I would care if someone was dating Benjamin. Like I would be jealous. She might have cared about me more than I thought. Or maybe she was just a nice person. The thought had me feeling a little guilty but with an internal shrug, I continued.

"I'm not trying to get back together with him if that's what you're worried about. He has something that belongs to me and I want it back. That's all."

She didn't need to know that I had already seen Benjamin. We'd already conversed. I was certain he wouldn't have told her. But I needed more access to him if I was going to be able to take the next step in my plan. Our plan. Juliet nodded absently and scanned our surroundings. She could have been worried about being seen with me, but if she'd been worried about being spotted at this lunch she wouldn't have come. No one wants their employer to know they're looking for work.

"What does he have?"

I took a sip of water, trying to think of how to convey the gravity of the situation without openly saying "I'm pretty sure your boss kidnapped my sister and I need to get her back while also making him pay for such a gross infraction against me and my family."

"Something important to me. Something vital. He took it. I need it back."

"Yes, but what is it? Ms. Caccia, I can't risk my job for a vague answer like that."

I took another sip of water. My patience was dwindling. Fine. Fuck it. Generosity of spirit wasn't in my wheelhouse today, anyway. I glanced around and leaned forward. She followed my lead and leaned toward me. Perhaps she thought I was going to say something I was embarrassed by. Who knows? But I doubt she was expecting what I said next.

"Do you remember what happened to you? The little incident at the Eros beach party that could have gone much worse for you?"

She blinked.

"Yes. I remember."

"Well, I found out some things. Your boss was connected to that incident. Responsible for it and many others like it."

Tears flooded her eyes. Juliet leaned backward in a sharp jerk. Like a puppy swatted with a newspaper, her face was full of hurt and surprise. Then she looked around again. It was as though she was waiting for someone to emerge from behind a bush and take her prisoner. She was afraid.

"I'm sorry, I don't understand," she quavered.

"It's complicated."

"Explain it to me," her voice sharpened.

"This isn't the best space to do that, Juliet," I said through clenched teeth. This was becoming irritating. I wasn't here to negotiate. Telling her any of this was a courtesy. Being nice to her was a courtesy. The whole act was draining what little patience I had left. In reality, I could have drugged her. Taken her phone. Dumped her somewhere no one would find her. I rolled my shoulders.

"Then explain fast."

"No."

"No?"

"No. It's better if you don't know everything. Safer. But I will tell you this. I learned some things about him and about Eros that are highly sensitive and dangerous. I need you to tell me where Benjamin is going to be. To help to protect people from getting hurt. I can't tell you more than that."

I stood from the table and picked up my bag. Juliet seemed surprised but I didn't have time for this. She needed to know where I stood and she could reach out to me if she wished. Her help would speed things along but I'd figure out a way to find Kaia with or without her help. I had to.

Before I walked away, I placed a hand on the table and leaned over her, getting close enough to keep my voice low over the ambient street noise.

"I don't know how much Benjamin told you about me or my family, but it's best not to play games with us. We don't play fair. We don't play nicely. And we always get our dues. Benjamin crossed us. Crossed me. He takes advantage of the people he feels are beneath him and his ego is big enough that this includes everyone. Even you."

Without another word, I walked away. Part of me hoped that my words had been enough to pique her interest and do some digging on her own. Egotistical men never think they're going to get caught doing anything wrong. They think they're smarter than everyone, but they're rarely smarter than the women who make their lives happen. If Benjamin was doing dirty work, then he was letting his dedicated assistant get her hands dirty on his behalf.

29

GANODERMA LINGZHI

Working in the garden felt like coming home. Touching dirt with my bare hands. Sliding gloves on to handle more dangerous plants. I felt most myself when I was surrounded by the small wooden fence and greenery I'd so carefully cultivated.

The little white bells almost fell apart in my hands. Each one was as likely to shatter as the next. Petals drifted into my palm like snowflakes. I put them in the small wooden bowl I'd brought out to the garden. The berries from the older plants thudded into the accompanying canvas bag as I pulled them from their stems. Having collected everything I needed, I stood and walked to my little laboratory above the garage.

The mild weather of a California winter hadn't yet claimed most of the blooms I cared for. Even without my attention, the timer on the watering system had prevented a large portion of them from becoming irreparably damaged. Letting them wither and die felt wasteful. Instead, they would each find their purpose. Angel's trumpet. Belladonna. Nux Vomica. And for Benjamin, Lily of the Valley.

He was a large man. I'd have to take that into account. A small amount would not be enough to take effect as quickly as I needed it to. But a large amount would be deadly. Not that I wanted him alive for much longer, but a dead Benjamin was a useless Benjamin.

When I got into my workroom, I noticed it was already occupied. Lanna was bent over a table, reading my notes. Recipes. Processes. Studying them. I wondered if she was curious or banking the information to use against me later. While I wanted to trust her, recent experience had taught me it was foolish to trust new people straight away.

"Hello," I drawled.

Lanna's head snapped up.

"I'm sorry," she said in a rush. "I just wanted to know..."

"How to garden? Or how to make poisons?" I finished for her. "You'll be here a while. The recipes I actually use have little letters at the top of the pages. They're bisected into two different notebooks. Can't use one without the other. This one, the one you're reading, is full of trial and error, unfortunately."

I unpacked my harvest from the garden onto the worktop and got to work on processing.

"I designed them that way so no one could read them but me."

Lanna angled her head, not quite listening to what I'd said. Instead, she'd been reviewing some text.

"What's the Lullaby?" She asked, holding up the notebook she'd had her eyes on. "Based on the ingredients you were experimenting with, it seems like you'd be able to kill someone pretty quickly with it."

I squinted, trying to see exactly what she was looking at. Trying to decide how to answer. The best way to lie is to tell the truth. Just keep it simple, short, and unclear.

"I think you just answered your own question."

"So that's what you use to kill people?"

I shrugged. Did West tell her what I do? A sour knot formed in my stomach. Maybe he wasn't as understanding as I'd thought. Had to get it off his chest with someone he could trust. Was it possible that I scared him? It hadn't seemed like it bothered him. But for some reason the idea had my shoulders rising to my ears.

Lanna watched me move various pieces of equipment around. When she noticed how I was processing the various parts of the Lily of the Valley, she perked up.

"Cold distillation," Lanna observed. I nodded.

"Concentrating the dose by minimizing evaporation means I can pack an even bigger punch in a smaller package," I said as I adjusted the drip for the condensation coil I was using. With such a keen observer, there was no sense in trying to hide much. And despite my better judgement and mountain of trust issues, I started to feel like maybe I could trust this woman with my secrets.

She leaned forward, tilting her head to get a better look at what was happening. Curiosity. I could work with that.

"The trick will be to get him to ingest it on his own," I said. "This should be enough to make him sick. Sick enough to go to the hospital. But not kill him."

Yet.

"How many of your exes have you sent to the hospital? Or killed?"

"None yet," I smirked "But there's a first time for everything."

I didn't want to tell her that her brother had nothing to worry about. That he wasn't my boyfriend. That I couldn't imagine hurting him the way I wanted to hurt Benjamin. I wasn't accustomed to spilling my guts to anyone, let alone someone I barely knew. Instead, I refocused on my work and got my bottles ready.

"Benjamin's kind of a well-known bachelor, right?"

"You could say that," I said as I rolled my eyes.

"So maybe you can do it on one of his dates. Sneak into the kitchen and put it in his order. He'll get sick. Have to leave. Might even have to go to the hospital for really bad food poisoning."

I looked up from my work with what must have been pleasant surprise on my face. Maybe I wasn't the only one around here who was a little bloodthirsty. Lanna sat up in her seat a little straighter, clearly happy with my look of approval. I recognized the emotion on her face. Had chased the high all through my education. A student receiving accolades from her teacher. She was just like me.

"You just need to find out where he's going," she shrugged.

As I started the drip from the condenser into a beaker, I stood up and looked Lanna over. Perhaps the doctor was more dangerous than I thought. Maybe I even liked that about her.

DAWN CAME AND West was still asleep. I had continued working above the garage into the small hours of the morning. Lanna stayed with me until I saw that she'd passed out on the worktable and sent her back into the main house. I'd let her help me bottle a few things, figuring if she got her hands dirty, she'd be less likely to rat on me. And if all else failed, I had her fingerprints on some bottles for collateral. Still, before I lost her to Morpheus, she had picked up quite a bit. As I climbed into bed, I thought the doctor would make a fine apprentice if she ever decided to leave medicine behind.

"Were you in there all night?" West muttered with one eye open.

"Yeah," I yawned, looking for the control for the blackout shades on the nightstand.

"It's the switch behind the headboard."

"Right," I said, flipping the switch. The room gradually sank into darkness. With a roll, I saw West facing me. He reached out and dragged my body closer, tucking my head beneath his own. I looked down at his arms, each of them locked around me. The smattering of scars and whirls of ink. The skull's head with octopus tentacles. A raised mark I'd never noticed before.

"West?"

He hummed, barely awake.

"What's this?" I traced my finger over the jagged skin. The press of his stomach against me as he took a deep breath hinted that this wasn't going to be a pleasant story.

"The last mission I went on went badly," West sighed and started dragging a hand up and down my side. Like feeling my skin was somehow soothing to him. He was silent for a while, almost like he wasn't going to continue. But he did anyway.

"I'm still not allowed to say much. It's all classified. It's always classified. But there was an embassy filled with Americans. Most of them got out. My team was helping a diplomat and his family escape. I had his daughter in my arms. We almost made it out. We were on the airstrip, a few miles away. But then we started taking fire. I was shot." He tapped his forearm, to a small crater-shaped scar half-covered in an octopus tentacle. "It went clean through me and punctured her lung."

I lifted his arm and looked at the other side. Another scar I hadn't noticed. My index finger traced the shape of it.

"Whoa," I marveled. I'd never seen a wound like that. Not a healed one, anyway.

"I've seen so many people die. Commanding officers. My friends. Civilians. But I've thought about that little girl every single night. I'll never forget the way her mother screamed."

His breathing had gone shallow. No longer in the relaxed state I'd found him in. Guilt washed over me as I pulled back to look at him, placing a hand on his chest. Over his heart.

"After that, I had some mental health issues. I couldn't bounce back they retired me." He gave a hollow snort. "Retired. Like a worn-out baseball glove. Not fit for service anymore."

Unsure as to what to say, I leaned forward and kissed his nose. Then the corner of his mouth. Then his lips.

"Their loss," I whispered against him. "My gain."

⌁

EVEN THOUGH I followed every single one of the directions on the freaking box, I was doing a piss-poor job at making pancakes. Lanna chuckled at my muttered profanities while making coffee for herself. West stood up from the sofa and walked toward me with my laptop in hand. I cursed as I attempted to flip a pancake and only half of it came with the spatula.

"I think you're going to want to see this."

An email from Juliet had come through with details on Benjamin's schedule, including his next dinner reservation. I guess she had chosen a side. Though my first instinct was to be skeptical of the information, my gut told me to take it seriously. Especially after I examined it more closely. It looked like he would be taking some unsuspecting woman out to the hottest new restaurant in Los Angeles. It sounded like a classic Benjamin Camden date. His last date.

"So what's our move?" West asked as he stood over my shoulder. His hand pressed to the counter beside me as he leaned in to look at my hands flying over the keyboard. I was emailing this restaurant with a last-minute request for an important food critic who was in town for only one night. Was it a terrible lie? Yes. Did they buy it? Absolutely.

West let out a dark chuckle as he read the email I'd sent out, taking the spatula from my hand to take over pancake duty.

"You're making a mess of this," he said by way of an explanation. I shook my head with a laugh. "So?"

"We do it tonight. Call Clayton," I said as I shut the laptop. Everything in my workshop was ready. I was ready. It was time.

"Tonight?"

"Tonight."

30

EURYCOMA LONGIFOLIA

Stalking a public figure was like fishing with dynamite. Incredibly easy and ultimately unfair to the fish. Of course, I didn't care if I was being fair. Between Clayton's reconnaissance and social media, finding out the basics about what Benjamin was doing was simple. Making sure we knew where he was going to be next had been in large thanks to Juliet, who'd emailed me with his schedule.

People waited for months to get a reservation at the newest French fusion restaurant in Los Angeles. With only eight tables available, the name Mon Petit was more than apt. Lying about being a food critic was the only way I was able to get in on short notice. Unfortunately for people on the waiting list, all Benjamin had to do to get a table was force his poor assistant to bully them into submission. After all, how else was he supposed to impress the influencer he'd brought with him?

The kitchen was immaculate. With the exception of polished concrete floors and white tile-covered walls, every surface was covered in shining stainless steel. It was the neat and tidy stuff of dreams. After pretending to be a patron anxious to get away from their awful date, played by Clayton, I waited for Benjamin and his date to be seated only fifteen minutes after we'd arrived. My opportunity was near, so I watched them work. Tiny portions of food were being sent out on gigantic China plates with a gold MP monogram on the rim.

Through the circular window in the large steel door, I could see a familiar set of wide shoulders that lead up to a head of dark brown hair. Every nerve ending in my body was aware of Benjamin sitting less than twenty yards away from me. His food was finished a moment before his date's. A decadent braised short rib surrounded by tiny pearl onions arranged in a crescent moon shape with carrots and parsley oil, dotting the dish like tiny colorful stars.

Almost hypnotized by my hunger, I blinked myself back into the kitchen and quickly squeezed the eye dropper containing my special little brew over the tender beef, knowing he'd clean the plate. A man with his muscle mass needed all of the protein he could get. A tiny fillet of fish on a bed of wilted greens joined Benjamin's dish. As I watched the plates get carried out, I hoped Benjamin's date would snack on something later.

"Can I use the back door?" I asked the waitress who came to take the plates of food with a pathetic sniffle, anxious to get to where West was waiting for me.

"Yeah, totally. Bad date, huh?" She said sympathetically.

"You wouldn't believe it," I chuckled. She really wouldn't.

THE AMBULANCE RACED down the streets of Los Angeles. Benjamin's date hadn't gotten into the vehicle with him. I'd say the relationship was doomed, but she would have never seen him again after tonight anyway.

The Bronco's engine roared as West pushed it to keep up with the speeding emergency vehicle ahead of us. I flipped the passenger visor down and fixed my lipstick, trying not to smile at the thought of Benjamin's gut twisting in pain. It wasn't an emergency. Hardly. But it was enough to put him in the hospital.

A sweep of my pinky finger across my cupid's bow had everything in place. Blood red perfection. Luckily for Benjamin, the hospital wasn't far from the restaurant. Unluckily for him, everything was going perfectly. The doctor admitted him immediately, pushing fluids before even ordering any tests.

Sweaty and pale, his eyes were squeezed shut. He bent over the side of the bed to wretch again. The lavender French collared shirt he was wearing was certainly ruined forever. Blotchy burgundy stains marred the white collar and trailed down the front. Those would never come out. Pity.

Clayton had told us that Benjamin had gotten up from the table in a rush. Practically sprinted to the bathroom and remained there for twenty minutes until a waiter went to check on him and found him passed out on the floor. An ambulance was called and his date, well, she left. Didn't even touch her expensive fish entrée.

As I gazed down at him, the snarling beast in me couldn't wait to sink its teeth into his tender flesh.

"I couldn't live with myself if I didn't have you at least one more time." Prick.

The doctor came back into the room, surprised to see me standing over Benjamin. I brushed the hair out of my face and gave him a weak smile.

"Is he going to be alright?" I said in a soft, sweet voice. A doting, worried girlfriend.

"Seems to be some pretty severe food poisoning. He should be alright in a few hours."

The snort just came out, I swear.

"Sorry," I muttered. "I laugh when I'm uncomfortable."

The doctor gave me a tentative smile and looked at the chart.

"You are?"

"His girlfriend," I said, holding out a hand. "Alexia. If it's just food poisoning, can I take him home?"

"If he feels up to leaving, yes. But check in at the nurse's station before you do."

I nodded and gave the man a polite smile. Obviously, I was not going to be checking with the nurses.

BENJAMIN WEIGHED A ton. All of that muscle turned into dead weight when he was unconscious. At least, that's what Clayton and West were grousing about. After the doctor left, I pushed a sedative into Benjamin's thigh and waited until I was certain it had taken hold. A few minutes later, West and Clayton came into the room sporting paramedic department uniforms. They hefted Benjamin into a wheelchair and pushed him out the back door, where Clayton's van awaited us.

Clayton had strict instructions to get to our destination as quickly as possible while West and I followed in the Bronco. He'd made a lovely scene of being stood up by his date and walked out of the restaurant while the waitstaff awaited Benjamin's ambulance.

With a tired sigh, I pulled a bag into my lap and dug out my change of clothes. The soft, distressed denim was a welcome comfort as I tugged it over my bare legs. Arching up to get the fabric under my ass, I sat back in the seat with a flop.

"You can change when we get there."

"Relax, I'm almost done," I said as I tugged my dress over my head. Soon my tee shirt covered the sheer mesh bra West pretended not to notice. I was starting to get comfortable in dressier clothing, but nothing could replace the feel of perfectly broken-in jeans and a well-loved tee shirt. I glanced at West, still in the paramedic uniform, and grinned.

"Stop looking at me like that or I'm pulling over," West said.

"When this is all over, I'm getting you a uniform for Muse."

"You're ridiculous," he protested as he rolled his eyes, biting back the smile that curled his lips. I shifted in my seat, trying to ignore the urge to squeeze my thighs together. God, he looked good.

"I can't help it. Navy is a great color on you," I said, inching a hand up his uniform-clad thigh. He heaved a deep breath as my hand stroked him through the fabric.

"You're going to make me crash the damned car if you keep doing that. Sit down or I'm going to have to punish you."

"Don't threaten me with a good time, Hale," I said, flopping back into the seat.

Pal's came into view and Clayton's van turned into the parking lot. Though it was well after closing, it was still risky coming here. It was unlikely that anyone would use the basement without me, but I disabled the security cameras and alarm system all the same. Benjamin and I would need time to get reacquainted, and I didn't want to be interrupted.

31

NYMPHAEA CAERULEA

The human body is made up of so many little complexities. Even something as simple as our skin has hidden information. Sweat glands and hair follicles peek through the epidermis and dermis layers. Below that is the hypodermis layer, where fat and blood vessels begin. Beneath that subcutaneous tissue lay the muscles.

My eyes danced over the large masses of muscles I could slice through as I contemplated Benjamin's sagging body. Wondered what types of noises he'd make when his tendons were cut. Arteries severed. His face was still slack, deep in the dregs of the sedative he'd used on me only weeks ago. My own muscles were stiff with tension. I rolled my shoulders to loosen the building ache. Idly flipping my knife, we waited for our captive to regain consciousness.

"This is taking too long," West said quietly, cracking the knuckles on his fingers as he leaned beside me against the worktable.

The last time I was in this room, I'd been here at my sister's command. I'd been here to question an Arwan man. To torture him, if need be. I could use everything I knew about Benjamin. Make him weep for mercy until the bitter end. But I had to find my sister and unfortunately, he was possibly the only person with the information I needed.

"How big of a dose did you give him?" Clayton said from his seat on the stairwell.

"He'll be up in a minute." A sharp gasping breath sounded across the room and I smirked at the mercenary. "See?"

Benjamin looked around, assessing what was a very bleak situation for him. Confusion, worry, and recognition washed over his features as he took in the room. Then my face. I arched an eyebrow at him but said nothing.

"Lilith Caccia."

"I'm flattered you remember me, Benjamin. Welcome," I gestured to the room with my knife and rested my other palm on the table. "I'm sorry the accommodations aren't up to your usual standards. No marble shower. No California king bed."

"Why am I here?"

"Don't play stupid. It's unbecoming."

He was silent for a moment. Turning his head every which way, he took in his surroundings once more. His eyes lingered on Clayton. Then West. I could feel West tense beside me. I wasn't sure if he was growling or if the sound was coming from inside of me.

"Did you bring me in here so they could murder me while you watch?"

I shook my head, smirking at Benjamin. If he thought things were going to be that easy, he was in for a rude awakening. He looked me over and sneered in distaste.

"I see you're back to slumming it like the rest of your ilk."

The knife pierced his expensive shoe with ease. The bone in his toe split with a satisfying crunch. Benjamin's scream was so sharp, I silently thanked my grandfather for soundproofing. A lupine grin spread across my face as I watched his thick red blood bubble up through the chestnut leather.

"That's a shame. Those were nice shoes. Expensive too, I bet."

I glanced to West, whose expression had gone stony. His mouth was a tight line as he shifted his weight. He'd seen me kill but never seen me torture someone. Dread tugged at my gut. I could back off. Do the right thing and just get the information I need. The right thing became a foreign concept to me as I pictured my sister possibly rotting away in an unmarked grave.

The justice I wanted took control of my every movement. Thoughts of my sister drove my steps forward. If West decided to leave me, he'd be like every other man. I could endure that. I'd done it so many times before that the scar tissue from those wounds had numbed me. That wouldn't break me. At least, that was what I told myself as I stopped, looking into Benjamin's cold blue eyes.

"You know, my 'ilk' fronted the money for your thriving operation. Speak about them with some respect or I'll cut the lips right off of your pretty face."

If I had my way with him here and now, there would be little pieces of billionaire littering the floor like peanut shells in a roadhouse. I'd savor each moment of disassembly like some people savor a glass of wine. But I needed information from him. I had to take my time. Despite every instinct in me that was howling to tear him apart.

"What the fuck do you want from me?"

I snorted. Like he didn't know. How stupid I must have seemed to him. Every second I'd spent looking at him like a moony-eyed pup made me cringe. Still, how many girls get to torture their ex-boyfriends? A smirk pushed across my lips.

"Oh, Benji. I told you not to play dumb. It is so deeply unattractive. My sister went missing the same day you tried to kill me. Don't act like that's a coincidence," I purred, glancing down at the shoe still weeping blood around my blade. The flinch at the nickname was like a little reward. I did my best to look like a disappointed parent.

"You know exactly what I want."

Benjamin's eyes narrowed as a muscle in his jaw flexed. His breath was tight and measured. He was breathing through the pain in his foot. The beast in me growled with displeasure. It scraped through me, leaving me to fight a snarl every second I was in his presence. *Hurt him more. Hurt him better. Hurt him longer.* This would be more difficult than I'd thought.

"Fine," I huffed, turning back toward the table West was still leaning against. My hands drifted over the small bag I'd brought with me. The leather was brand new. The zipper offered satisfying friction as I pulled it open to reveal the cache inside. Small bottles lined each little pocket. Needles were safely stowed inside their tiny metal boxes.

"Benji, Benji, Benji," I sighed as I assembled a syringe. West watched Benjamin then glanced at my working hands. He leaned over to speak in a whisper, barely audible against Benjamin's sawing breaths.

"He's going to bleed out."

"He'll be fine," I said quietly. "I was nowhere near the dorsalis pedis artery. He might lose a toe, though."

Setting the assembled syringe on the cloth atop the table, I dipped my hand back into the bag and let my fingertips walk over the tops of the tiny bottles I'd gathered for this occasion. The correct bottle cried out to me, desperate for my attention. This one would do nicely. I lifted it out and turned to Benjamin, the assembled syringe in one hand and the bottle in the other.

"This is vecuronium bromide. It's a paralytic. Made this batch myself. Do you know what that means, Benjamin? That means you're not going to be able to fight me while I go to work on you. I will keep you here until I'm satisfied. I will take from you. I'll take things you didn't know you'd miss. You're going to watch me do it. Then, when I'm finished, you'll beg me for death. And I'll give it to you."

I strolled toward the chair with the syringe in my hand. Grabbed the curls of his hair and tugged his face toward mine.

"If I'm feeling generous," I smiled.

My fingers twisted into his locks. His wince was reward enough to keep twisting.

"You think you understand something about society because you struggled. Your family was poor once. But now you look down on the people you stepped on in handcrafted shoes to get where you are like they're shit on the bottom of your heel."

Every second I looked at him made me angrier. I kept reminding myself that I needed to keep him breathing. My jaw clenched, forcing me to speak through my teeth.

"My family came here and built themselves up. Just like you. They created an empire. Just like you. People know our name. Just like you. But my family will go on. And you. You will be forgotten. Everything you built will be forgotten."

Fear flickered across his eyes, those ice-blue irises that had been so hypnotizing. I'd found the heat in them captivating. Now I wanted to devour his dread like a bowl of ice cream.

32

ARTEMISIA DRACUNCULUS

In men, rage presents audibly. Breaking things. Crashing objects. Shouting. Screaming. Gunfire. Every single variety was like a familiar song from my childhood. But with women, it's different. Each reaction is like a snowflake. Sometimes it's tears. Other times it's an even voice. The reaction that should make someone run in the opposite direction? Silence.

My sister was the silent type. Her rage could be heard from miles away. Me? Not so much. I'm a talker. Rage boils in me and I bubble over. Who knows, maybe it was from bottling everything up as a kid? Back at the house, I was pacing around the garden doing both sides of my conversation with Benjamin. Imaginary Benjamin was just about to break to my will when I heard a throat clear from behind me.

"You should interrogate spies for the government," West said. His arms were crossed across his muscled chest. With the sleeves of his flannel rolled up, I couldn't help but notice the way his forearms flexed. The sight gave me a moment of reprieve from my intense embarrassment.

"I think my methods would be considered human rights violations by most countries and probably also the UN. How long were you standing there?"

"Long enough to hear you tell Benjamin that if he didn't start talking soon, you'd separate him from his favorite body part."

My eyes locked on my boots and my skin flushed. Imaginary arguments were not meant to have an audience. Didn't he know that? Hadn't he ever had it out with an imaginary enemy before? The tiny garden gate creaked as it opened. West's large boots crunched on the gravel beneath his steps.

"Hey," he said quietly.

I looked up at him. Standing next to him, I felt tiny. Of course, it didn't help that he was over a foot taller than me. Ever since we left the cabin, it seemed like West was never more than a few steps away. If someone wanted to get to me, they'd have to go through him. It was so tempting to get used to that feeling. His green eyes flashed with amusement as he tucked my hair behind one ear. The smile on his face barely held back a laugh.

"You're a very scary little murderer," he mocked.

"Watch it, buddy. I may be little, but I've got teeth."

"Like a Chihuahua."

"How dare you."

The laugh burst from him as he reached out and grabbed my waist. I let the scent of him flood my senses as he hugged me close.

"Trouble," he murmured. "Even when you're talking circles around yourself, you don't scare me."

He rested his chin on top of my head as we stood there in my garden. The flowers surrounding us could have stopped the hearts of a dozen men, but West was able to arrest mine with his words, his warmth, and his smell. A cool gust of wind rustled the leaves, filling the air with wisteria and cedar. I let all of it take me away. How is it possible that being around this man instantly changed my mood?

"Do you need to get those inside or something?"

"Hm?"

Unwrapping his arms, I missed his warmth as he pulled away from me to pick up my bag from the ground. He walked toward the garage with my bag in one hand and my hand in his other.

When we got inside, I shrugged off my jacket and tied on my apron. The distillation process for one serum had finished. After loading the centrifuge, I hung some plants and dropped others into the mortar bowl. Then I got to work on bottling the rest. West put his hands on the work table and angled his head with a small smirk.

"What?"

"I love to watch you work. It's like watching a sexy evil scientist. Or like, a witch or something."

I spilled serum on the table. The bottom corner of my apron absorbed the liquid as I pressed it to the surface to tidy up. West rounded the table and braced his hands on either side of me. His lips brushed my neck as he spoke.

"Definitely a sexy scientist. Maybe a little clumsy. But still sexy as hell."

TO BE AN attractive billionaire living in Los Angeles was probably an incredible experience. It didn't take a great leap of imagination to understand why Benjamin's ego had gotten so inflated. The messages coming through his phone ranged from flirtatious to obscene.

It seemed as though the cocktail of drugs I'd given Benjamin coupled with his terror had been a potent enough mix to make him pass out. Clayton chuckled as he placed cameras in the room, mentioning that Benjamin was in for a rough experience if he thought that exchange had been terrifying.

As I set eyes on the third unsolicited pair of breasts I'd seen in the last half hour, I set the phone down and took a drink from my soda. I'd been searching his phone for any sign of my sister. Any conversation would be a step in the right direction. Any direction. He'd either been careful not to discuss it on his device or he deleted any evidence of it as soon as her disappearance happened. Still, I had to try.

If Ozzie wasn't the one to take Kaia, then Benjamin had something to do with it. Of that, I was almost certain. He hadn't mentioned her death. That had given me hope. She was still alive. I firmly believed that now. She was alive and Benjamin knew where. I'd use every weapon in my arsenal to get her back. And I was starting with Benjamin's ego.

I opened the Eros app. He was on the Eros app. Of course, he was. When I'd met him, I'd been under the impression that women were pounding on his door begging for a chance to be with him. I hadn't realized he was using his own technology. I snorted at the gratuitous selfies he'd taken. Standing in his bathroom, staring at himself. Photos of him on his jet. In his Bentley. Would you like the luxury boyfriend experience? He was willing to give it to you.

Women who would have men crawling for them were crawling for him. They were all beautiful. They deserved better than Benjamin. I wanted to tell all of them that he didn't even come close to the Navy SEAL turned strip club bouncer who was warming my bed these days. Pulling a curly fry from the takeout container, I decided to start messaging them back. I wouldn't want to leave them hanging for a response from the ever-desirable Benjamin Camden, would I?

"What are you doing?"

"Hm?"

"You're giggling like a schoolgirl. It's very distracting."

"Oh, I'm just having a little fun," I said as I stabbed at the Caesar salad with my fork. "Is micropenis one word or two?"

West chuckled and shook his head.

"How would I know?"

"Fair enough," I laughed. "Well, Benjamin has one. Or, he does now."

Sending pictures I'd done a quick internet search for a few women on Eros and had been plenty of fun. Texting women he'd clearly been with that they needed to be checked for a fictitious skin disease was also a blast but that wasn't the type of damage I was really looking to do. The real destruction would be what happened to his pride and joy. Camden Industries.

He was still at Pal's. West helped me chain him to a wall while Clayton got the surveillance equipment online. The mercenary would be in charge of keeping him alive while I did what I needed to do. Of course, I permitted Clayton to do as he pleased with our prisoner.

After a quick look at the company website and some Forbes magazine articles, I got the information I needed right away. Then I studied Benjamin's outbox. Once I learned his style, I got to writing. Emails were sent to board members. Shareholders. Employees.

And I waited.

ACER SACCHARUM

Soft leather met my palms in a cool caress. Looking out over the beautiful wood dash, I smiled and settled back into the quilted driver's seat. My hand found the volume dial and turned up the music, enjoying every thumping beat as the song began.

The car had made quick work of Benjamin. Laying in the center of the highway, he slowly and desperately crawled toward the shoulder. I got out of the car and strode toward his bleeding carcass, the open door allowing the Rolling Stones to filter out.

He was nothing. Dust. Dirt. Roadkill.

Benjamin looked up at me like the wounded rat I always knew he was.

Mick Jagger started singing as I wondered if the devil would have sympathy for me.

NOT HEARING FROM Nico was making me crazy. It had been about two weeks since we'd seen him at his father's house and I'd still heard nothing. I looked at my laptop and checked the cameras to see Benjamin curled up on the floor. Shutting the computer and tucking it back on the nightstand, I let out a frustrated sigh.

Had something happened? Did Ozzie figure it out? Nico was a steadfast and honorable man. Much like his brother, he had a reputation for brutal loyalty. Only a fool would question his word. I hoped that Ozzie thought his loyalty was to the organization. But I knew his loyalty was to the Caccias and I was selfishly trying to capitalize on that.

"I can feel you thinking over there."

West tugged on my shoulder, rolling me until I was flat on my back, staring up at him. Santa Ana gusts were blustering outside, causing shadows to dance into the moonlit room. He propped himself up on an elbow, hair dangling around his face as he looked down at me.

"What are you thinking about?"

"Nico."

It wasn't the whole truth. Visions of my dream still clung to my mind, but once I was awake it was hard to think of anything but Nico. In the dim light, I saw his jaw harden.

"I haven't heard from him. He should have sent word by now."

West scratched his jaw and broke eye contact with me to turn on the bedside lamp.

"You're really that worried about him?"

I propped myself up on my elbows.

"Of course, I'm worried about him. I basically sent him into a hornet's nest to do my bidding. He's important to me and I haven't heard anything at all."

A hand scrubbed down his face. After a sigh he released through his nose, he looked at me.

"How important?"

"West," I sighed. "He and I grew up together. I don't think of him that way. Besides, now he's literally family to me."

Angling his head, West narrowed his eyes inquisitively.

"What does that mean?"

I pinched the bridge of my nose and squeezed my eyes shut.

"After talking with Lupo, I'm pretty sure that Nico's brother Dante is Daniel's father. Was. He died."

"You didn't know who Daniel's father was before?"

"Kaia always kept it to herself. Honestly, I was so wrapped up in my shit after Daniel was born that I didn't think about it. But it made sense. He died before Daniel was born, so she maybe didn't want to talk about it."

"How did he die?"

"He was killed in a gunfight, protecting my grandfather."

"Was he his bodyguard?"

"No."

"He was the Wolf. Before me, it was him. He died for the family and before that he," I paused and looked at West. It was hard to see in the dark, but I could make out the expression. Slightly narrowed eyes, brows furrowed. He was waiting for me to say it. "He killed people for us."

West didn't say anything. Only let out a rough sound from his throat and rolled over again, turning the light off once again. We lay there, side by side. Quiet in the dark.

"I don't know how many he killed. Or why he killed them. I can tell you why I did it or how many. I don't remember all of their names, but I can tell you," I sniffed.

His voice was soft as he said, "It's alright, Lili."

"I'm not just killing the bad guys, West," I blubbered. The confession was tumbling out of me now. Something about the last few weeks made me want to show him all of my flaws. Like a dare. Run away now. "The people I've killed for my family are sometimes bad, but most of the time they're just regular people trying to pay off debt. Or they made enemies of my family by upholding the law. Police. City officials. That kind of thing."

Wind pushed through the trees, filling the air that had been left empty by West's silence. Because I couldn't help myself, I filled it with more blather.

"I know I should have told you all this. Before you got involved in everything."

"How many people have you killed?" He asked quietly.

I shrugged. It wasn't something I kept track of. Not really. Maybe because I couldn't live with knowing that number. My mind drifted back to the cemetery where my parents were buried.

"71," West said. "I've killed 71 people serving this country. Taking orders. Killing people who were trying to kill me, yes, but that wasn't always the case."

He propped himself up, reached over, and pushed a strand of hair out of my face. West's hand stopped to cup my cheek. His nearness was like a balm, soothing the ravaged surfaces of my mind. I was starting to feel like a different person around him. A person who wouldn't have to hide everything about themselves. At least, not from everyone.

"I know what it means to do your duty. I know the choice isn't always yours to make. That you punish yourself when you feel like you're doing something wrong. That taking orders doesn't feel like an excuse."

The hand that was on my cheek trailed down to my throat. Down my chest. Over the wolf tattoo.

It was a strange thing, being close to him like this. Strange in its comfort. The way he could make me feel like I was settling into my skin. I rolled over, pushing him down to make room for myself beneath his arm. A soft growl thundered in his chest as I pressed my cheek to it. The arm I'd pushed aside found my waist.

Even with everything happening in my world, with everything crumbling down around me, being here with him made me feel lighter.

IN THE MORNING, West was still asleep when I woke. I sat up and looked down at his peaceful face. His powerful body. Sunlight cast its glow on him, leaving strands of his dark hair golden in its light. Like even the sun couldn't resist the urge to touch him. I traced the curves and swells of his lips with my fingers.

What was it about this man? I'd been beaten. Been threatened. Been near death. The amount of times I was in danger was too many to count.

Each time, I was afraid. Even if I didn't show it. I'd learned to endure that feeling. Now my heart stuttered looking down at him. This new feeling, this West feeling, was somehow more tangible than fear.

Smoky green eyes opened and West looked at me with a sleepy smile. Those eyes roved over me with an appreciative glint. It was all the invitation I needed to climb on top of him, tossing Ethan's old shirt to the ground.

"Look at you," he said, his voice rough with sleep as his hands coasted up my thighs to squeeze my ass.

"Good morning," I said with a kiss to the center of his chest.

It wasn't long before his fingers were in my mouth, enduring the sting of my teeth as he filled me from below. With his sister just across the hall, I was doing my best not to make noise. It was his fault I wasn't succeeding.

MY BARE FEET made soft padding sounds down the stairs. Before heading back to Pal's I needed to get some food in me. West had bounded out of bed and headed to the kitchen before me. I took my time and followed him a few minutes later in one of his incredibly oversized flannels.

The kitchen air was filled with butter and cinnamon. He looked up from the bowl he was whisking with a fork and grinned at me.

I wanted to let him inside. Let him see all of the ugly. All of the uncomfortable. But isn't that what I'd been doing? These last few days. Weeks? Hurling my guts up in front of him. Asking him to sleep beside me for comfort. Letting him see who I truly am. And he's chosen to stay anyway. I didn't see what I saw in Ethan's eyes when he found out what I was. Ethan, for all the hate and vitriol he spewed at me, was afraid.

Sidling up beside him, I looked over his little assembly of bread and some milky cinnamon business he had in a dish beside a skillet. He wrapped an arm around me, pulling me against him as he pressed a kiss to the top of my head. Lanna cleared her throat.

"I'm assuming you like French toast," West said, ignoring his sister. I grinned up at him.

"You mean to tell me I could have been eating French toast this entire time? You've been holding out on me."

Lanna got up from the island to fix herself another cup of coffee, leaving West the opportunity to lean in and whisper in my ear.

"Wake me up like that every morning and I'll make you whatever you want."

It was a strange kind of comfortable. Being here with him. Standing in this kitchen in bare feet. Wearing his clothes while he made breakfast for me. No one had ever done that for me. Not Ethan. Benjamin didn't count. And West...he just did these things for me. Made sure I had enough to eat. Gave me water to drink. Got annoyed with me when I didn't drink it. Which I hated to admit that I sort of enjoyed.

Maybe I never wanted to leave here. And that felt like the most selfish thing in the world.

I looked around for Lanna, wondering if she'd heard him, when I saw Daniel's drawings still taped to the pantry door. Guilt coated me like oil as my smile faded. A broad, warm hand flattened against my stomach. Nico. Daniel. My sister. What the fuck business did I have spending my morning in cinnamon-coated bliss when people needed me?

"I need..." I started.

Nothing. There was no reason for me to be enjoying myself like this when my sister was enduring who knows what. The oily feeling soaked me to the bone.

"I need to make a call."

34

CARUM CARVI

Benjamin Camden was tired of doing his business in a bucket. After pulling the hood from his head, I noted that the hard line of his jaw was now covered in a short beard. His cold blue eyes looked tired. Instead of leaving him bound to a chair, he'd been chained to a hook mounted to the wall. I wondered if he'd have the balls to cut his leg off if I left a saw down here for him.

"May I please use a real toilet?"

Now his posh London accent dropped out more frequently when he spoke. Manufactured Benjamin Camden was giving way to the real one from the wrong part of town. The word "toilet" sounds like the silver spoon fell out of his mouth. He knew he didn't have to pretend with me. Not anymore. But this broken-down facade? It was fabricated. Crafted to appeal to a part of me that still had feelings for him. Unfortunately for him, that part of me was dead. The only "feeling" I wanted was the feel of his pulse fading away in my grasp.

"The bucket works perfectly fine, Ben. Besides, I brought you more reading material," I said, holding up the tabloids and newspaper I brought for him. Setting the brown bag of sandwiches I'd also brought down for him on the work table, I hoisted myself up beside it and examined him.

After a while, it was easy to see that Benjamin Camden was a completely fabricated human being. Even if he was barely human. His usual hairstyle was perfectly coiffed, with one dark curl out of place. Intentional imperfection. All of those muscles that bulged from his bespoke suits were earned with hours of training on expensive gym equipment.

We'd shucked off the shirt that had been covered in his vomit when we brought him in. Even I couldn't stand the smell anymore. Now he stood before me in a white undershirt and the same slacks. No shoes. A bandaged foot. He didn't lose the toe, but that didn't mean I wouldn't take one or several later.

"So, Benji. Do you have anything you want to tell me?"

"No," he spat, sneering at me from his seat on the cold floor. He'd once told me about his humble upbringing, but it was easy to imagine this man as a spoiled little boy. I wondered if his parents suffered with his horrible attitude as much as I was suffering now.

"That's too bad, eggs Benny," I said cooly, shuffling the reading materials so that the newspaper sat on top. The brown paper bag crinkled in my fingers as I fisted it and placed it within his reach. I tossed the magazines and newspaper on the floor. They landed with a satisfying *plop*!

"Feel free to use the wipes I left in the bag. You're starting to smell."

Benjamin's brow furrowed as he scanned the front page of the Wall Street Journal. I knew exactly what he saw. It's the reason I picked it up in the first place.

Camden Industries at Risk of Collapse. Business burns through cash as investments yield disappointing returns.

"What?!" Benjamin's question was more of a growl than a word.

"Have a good night, Benjamin," I said sweetly.

The wrathful scream he hurled at me was cut off by the closing steel door.

PAL'S EMPLOYEES WERE happy to see me. They sent me out the door with an enormous sandwich with my favorite fixings and a box of cookies.

The little sprinkled lemon knots slid around in their box as I made the turn into the driveway, finally back at the house. The Bronco announced my entrance with a rumble as West came out of the garage.

"Where's your sister?" I asked as I hopped out. Usually, she was busying herself with tending the rest of our garden, a pastime I was grateful she'd picked up.

"I took her home. Nico sent a text saying she would be safe. She needed to get back to her life."

"He did? So no one is going to be looking for her anymore?"

West nodded.

"Is she going to be alright on her own?"

"She has what she needs to defend herself. It's better if she's there, any-way."

I nodded. Now that the family wasn't hunting her down, she didn't need to be trapped here any longer. While it was a good thing that the family wasn't looking for Lanna, I wondered if this was the way that Ozzie was running things. Kaia would never have ignored a loose end like that.

"Are you hungry?" I asked.

"Starved."

"I've got a gigantic sandwich and a box of cookies in here."

I looked around the backyard. It was beautiful at this hour. There was a small tug at my gut as I remembered the last time I was out here with my sister. Pushing the thought away, I took in my surroundings. The sun had set, but still let its light color the sky in a fading periwinkle. The trattoria lights had kicked on, illuminating the greenery that hung over the patio. I gestured toward the table.

"Grab us something to drink and we can eat here. I'll bring the food over."

CREAMY BURRATA MELTED in my mouth in perfect tandem with the salty prosciutto, sharp tomato, and bright pesto. Wood-fired bread crunched in my mouth as I took another bite. West poured more wine into my glass and then topped off his own.

"Slow down," he laughed. "You barely chewed that last bite."

"This is my favorite. It's hard to behave myself," I said through a final mouthful of bread and cheese. I swallowed and took a sip of wine, thanking him for refilling my glass. He dipped his chin and filled his own. I sat back and looked around at the space.

With a sigh, I tilted my head back and looked up at the lights sweeping in and out of the patio cover carefully nestled in amongst bare wisteria vines and lemon tree branches.

"This patio always reminds me of my grandmother. She used to make us have Sunday dinners out here every week."

I pointed to the strands hanging overhead.

"She made my grandfather put up these lights."

West took a sip of wine and kept the glass in his hand with gently narrowed eyes. He took a breath as if he was readying to speak and then sat back, setting the glass on the table.

"What?" I asked.

He gave a casual frown and a shrug.

"These last few weeks. I don't know. I guess I just feel like I'm getting to know a different side of you."

"Finding out your sparring partner kills people for a living will do that," I laughed.

"That's not what I mean," he said, rolling his eyes. Sitting forward, he put his glass down and took my hand from where it rested on the table. "You always walked around with this wall up. I feel like you've been showing me what's behind it."

I tilted my head to the side, unable to think of anything to say. The things that went through my head muddled together in an incoherent, insecure stream about over-sharing and wondering whether I should just keep quiet. But all I said was "Oh."

"You're soft," he said as he leaned forward. He squeezed my hand as his other threaded into the hair cascading over my shoulder. His finger twisted around a lock of it, watching the black silken wave curve around a knuckle. Our eyes met and my stomach dropped like I was falling from a great height. He brought his lips to mine, so close that when he breathed my name, I felt the tip of his tongue.

If West had been walking around with a wall up before, it was down now. When I met him several years ago, he seemed broken. But over time, I watched light come to his eyes. I pretended not to notice. The way his hands would linger on me for just a moment. A second beyond innocence. Beyond a platonic relationship. I pretended not to notice the way he would eye me.

It had been a long time coming. I knew that now. Let myself see it. Remember all of it. The way he'd seemed distant after I asked him about other women. Maybe he did date other women. But none of them had been right. None of them had been, well, me.

"West?" I said, still not able to shake the plummeting feeling. Why could I fight men twice my size without a moment of hesitation but I couldn't do this? I couldn't tell him how I felt. The feeling I'd been too afraid to name because it meant everything could change between us. Eight letters that would break me if they weren't returned. It was like a blossom, waiting to open. Waiting to flourish in sunlight. Or wither and die.

"Hm?"

I tried. Really. But the words didn't come. So I kissed him.

35

PRUNUS AVIUM

West let out an annoyed huff as he watched me leave to do another lap around the house. Check all the windows. Check all the doors. Make sure the alarm system is armed. Look in the refrigerator for no reason. Wipe down the counters. Fluff some throw pillows. Head upstairs to check those windows. Go to the attic and check Daniel's room. When I entered the bedroom again, I shook my hands, trying to loosen the tension building there.

"Something on your mind?" West asked.

"Other than the fact that I can't get any information out of Benjamin and my sister is still missing?"

When I called Lupo after dinner, he said that Nico was alive. Fine. Not in any sort of danger. Then he told me to be patient. Like that was an option.

West bit his lip and raised his brows. With a groan, he stretched and turned on the lamp on the bedside table.

"Alright. Let's train," he said as he got out of bed.

"What? It's late. We should get to sleep."

West let out a laugh as he walked to the armchair he'd set his bag on and pulled out a tee shirt to cover himself.

"I don't think I'm going to get much sleep with you haunting the house like this. And the house isn't going to get any cleaner than it already is."

I opened my mouth to protest as he approached me, setting his large hands on my shoulders.

"Come on, Trouble. You need it."

BEING BACK IN One Two with West felt like putting on a worn-in pair of sweatpants. It relaxed me. There was something so comfortable about settling into our old routine. Beating out everything I'd been keeping bottled up made me feel sane again. West weathered it all, coaching me like he always had. Challenging me. Throwing back everything. I struck until it hurt. Until every breath burned like fire. Until my heart rattled against my ribs like a caged animal.

When we were done boxing, I leaned on the ropes and looked at the mats on the ground. You'd never have known they were covered in blood only a few days ago. Dr. Hale had done a good job cleaning the area. West walked over to the rack on the wall taking off his punching mitts with his teeth. He said something I couldn't quite make out.

"What?"

"I said I want to try something with you."

Long strides took him to his locker. The metal door clacked against the other locker as he started digging around for something. I sat down on a bench beside the boxing ring and took a swig of water. When I set the cup down, West was standing before me with what looked like a gun. But it was green. Bright green.

"What is that?"

"I want to teach you how to disarm someone. This is a rubber training pistol. I'm going to show you how to take it away safely. And quickly."

"So you just had that in your locker?"

"I got it a couple of months ago, I just forgot about it. Anyway, let's do this."

If I had a dollar for every time West said "And now you're dead" to me over the two hours that followed, I'd have enough money to pay for the pizza I'd had delivered to the gym. During that time, West pulled the fake gun on me and showed me everything I needed to do to avoid getting shot.

He showed me how to move when a gun was pointed at me. How to attack the wrist of the assailant and turn the gun toward them. Each time I failed, he shook his head and we tried again.

West and I lay sweating on the floor of the gym, waiting for the pizza to arrive. Being here with him, panting for breath and sweating from training, was the most comfortable I'd been in weeks. Between going to Kaia's house and coming here, things had started to feel normal again. But they wouldn't feel completely normal until I had my sister back.

The pizza delivery guy pulled into the parking lot at the same time Lupo did. He came inside with the pizza guy and Daniel in tow. I paid the man and sent him on his way. Lupo took a slice from the box and handed it to Daniel.

"What are you two doing here so late?" Lupo asked.

"We had some things to work on. Besides, I could ask you the same thing," West replied with a pointed look at Daniel.

"Kid couldn't sleep."

"So it's a Caccia thing," West laughed. My last name sounded good on his tongue. Lupo eyed the green gun that had been discarded on the ground next to a still supine West and looked at me.

"You finally learning to shoot?" Lupo asked.

I shook my head and jerked my head toward Daniel. We really shouldn't have been talking about this stuff in front of him. "Just defense," I deflected.

Ignoring me, Lupo went on.

"If you're taking a gun away from someone, they're not going to just give up and walk away. You need to take them out."

West sat up from his position on the floor and took a slice of pizza from the box. He patted the ground next to him and handed Daniel a napkin as the little guy sat down.

"So it's true, she never learned to shoot?" He asked, taking a bite out of the sagging slice. Drawing it away from him, the cheese dangled from his mouth. Daniel laughed. I nearly melted.

"I don't need it," I said to Lupo. I'd always managed just fine without guns. I didn't need to know now.

"You definitely need it now," West said, taking another bite. I squeezed my eyes shut and took a breath.

"Is Zia in trouble?" Daniel asked quietly.

I gave West a hard look. We couldn't discuss what was happening. Not in front of Daniel. I wouldn't allow it. As far as he knew, his mother was still away on business. That was all the information a child should have. Lupo took off his jacket to reveal a holster strapped to his shoulders. My eyebrows shot up my forehead faster than I could think to school my expression in front of my nephew.

"Teach her to use this," Lupo said, pulling a gun from the holster. With his grandson in his care, it would make sense that he'd felt the need for added protection but the fact that he was strapped still surprised me. Still, it felt good to know that if someone wanted Daniel they would have to get through the original Wolf first.

"I've got one. You should hang onto that," West said with a small nod toward Daniel. Lupo muttered in agreement and tucked the gun away again. He pulled up a folding chair and sat down next to the younger folks still seated on the floor. I offered him a slice of pizza. He took it and shook his head.

"Pizza at midnight," Lupo picked up a slice from the box. "You eat like you're still in college."

"Don't start. We were hungry," I groused. "Why are you two here?"

"The kid couldn't sleep and neither could I. Didn't want to leave Daniel at home, and I thought I'd come here to do some bookkeeping while I was thinking about it. Didn't expect to find you two here."

"I was having trouble sleeping, so West thought we should come," I explained. "Have you talked to Nico? Is he alright?"

I couldn't hold it in anymore. Though the anxiety had been quelled by our sweat session, the worry was still there. He was supposed to be subtle. To let on that I was trying to crawl my way back to the family. Maybe he hadn't been that convincing.

"Just saw him yesterday. Went with me to the doctor. Everything is fine," he said in that stern way of his that didn't invite any follow-up questions.

I wanted to ask what was taking so long. To ask if Nico had decided not to help me after all. Maybe he'd decided the cost of sticking his neck out for me, for Kaia, was too high.

"Is she still a quick learner?" Lupo asked. He glanced at my cheek like he could remember all of the strikes he'd landed there while training me. West leaned back on his palms and looked up at me.

"Definitely. I'm still surprised she never learned to use a firearm. Isn't that kind of a normal thing in your, uh, business?"

"Yeah, well," Lupo sighed, the long night finally taking its toll on him. "Her grandfather and I had a difference of opinion on that."

36

SYZYGIUM AROMATICUM

I need you to understand something. Our family is not just blood. It's business. I've done things that would get me hard time. Everyone in this organization has. If you take this on, you will never have a normal life. Ever. Killing is not something you can walk away from. Once you get your hands dirty, they will stay dirty. Do you understand?"

I'd made my offer to my sister who was the newly minted boss of the Caccia family, she took me into her bedroom. Her newborn son, Daniel, was sleeping across the hall, and the conversation we were having threatened to wake him. Kaia gestured to her bed, where I sat. She sat down beside me and took my hands in hers. Gripped them hard enough to make my joints ache.

I nodded.

"Say it."

"I understand, Kaia."

She blew out a breath.

I looked down at my hands, then at my sister again.

"Kaia, I can't let you do this alone. It's always been you and me against everyone else. You're the Boss now. With a newborn. You need someone watching your back now more than ever. Please let it be me."

A look of resolve trickled into her tired eyes. They met mine with renewed vigor.

"Nonno will never forgive me for saying yes to this. If I was smart, I would send you back to school. He wanted to keep you out of the business."

I nodded again. I knew this. Even when I was training with him, with Lupo, it was only ever to defend myself. It was why he'd paid for me to go to college. And then a master's program. He was so proud when I'd been accepted into a doctoral program, even though I'd dropped out as soon as he'd passed away. As far as he knew, Lili, the innocent flower of the Caccia garden, would never soil her hands with a life of crime.

"IT'S NOT FANCY, but it'll get the job done."

Clayton flipped on the lights and the room slowly came into view as each florescent bulb flickered on. He was right. It wasn't fancy, but West's nod of approval told me we had everything we needed. I eyed the long corridor, lined with brick walls and a polished concrete floor. All of the windows were covered with what looked like plywood. Three unblemished targets were hanging at the furthest distance, attached to a pulley system to bring them forward for replacement.

"So you just took over the top floor of your building to make a gun range?" I asked.

"No, I took over the top floor so the people above me couldn't hear what I was doing. I made it a gun range because I hate to waste space."

"You own both floors?"

He folded his lips together and looked around the room as if to confirm for himself.

"Yup. Alright," Clayton said with a shrug. "I'll leave you to it."

The door slammed shut behind him, echoing in the stony chamber.

"Being a mercenary must pay well," I muttered.

West chuckled as he set his bag on the upholstered counter that stretched across the width of the room. While he pulled out several weapons and their accompanying ammunition, I stepped to his side and watched.

"You weren't kidding about not needing any more guns."

Looking down at the array of artillery, I saw a smirk tug the corner of his mouth. Satisfied with his arrangement, he walked to the box beside the door to dig out two pairs of goggles and earmuffs. He handed me a pair that I slung around my neck.

"Alright," West said as he held up a pistol. "This is a Glock 19. It's a 9mm pistol with ambidextrous controls, so it won't matter if you're left or right-handed. This is what we carried as a unit. It's easy to use and won't let you down."

He set it down and beckoned me closer. A soft pat of his hand on the counter directed me to stand where he wanted. Large hands circled my hips. A little flutter tugged at my gut when he gave them a little squeeze.

"The first stance is feet apart, ass out a little, hands forward so your body makes a little triangle," he said as he adjusted my body. "It's good for accuracy. Not great in a combat situation, though."

"The stance you should learn since you're right-handed," he started, angling his head to assess my posture. "Take your right foot back and angle it out a bit."

I moved my foot backward. West shook his head.

"No, that's too far." He braced his hands on my hips again, kicking my right foot out, then nudging my left so it pointed straight. After another look at my arms, he backed away. "That's called a weaver stance."

West picked up the Glock 19 from the counter and held it up, pointing to the small lever on top of the trigger.

"OK, here are the basics. This is the safety. Even if the gun isn't loaded, it should be on. Always treat a gun like it's loaded. This is how you load this gun."

He took the magazine out of the grip and slid the top back. Picking up the magazine, he started stuffing bullets into the top one by one.

"Hey, it's like one of those cartoon candy dispensers," I said.

He rolled his eyes but couldn't hide the smile in them. When he finished with the magazine, he held the gun up and slid it back into the grip. Pulling the slide back until it sprang forward, he clicked the safety back on.

"Now it's loaded."

He scooped my hair into his hands, pulling the inky black waves into a ponytail with his fist until he wrapped one of his elastics around it.

"Alright, give it a try."

The pistol kicked in my grip as I made my first shot. And tagged the outer rim of the target. My inner competitor growled. Loosing a steadying breath, I took my second and third shots.

West moved the target toward us and unclipped it from the rig. With raised eyebrows, he looked up from the paper and smiled.

"Atta girl," he said with a grin as he held it out for me to observe. Though all of my shots were scattered, they'd all hit the target. "Not bad for your first try."

"Well, you know I'm a fast learner," I said with a smile. "Let's do another one."

CLAYTON BURST INTO the room with a big brown bag about an hour later. He glanced at the targets lying on the ground, then to West.

"Is that your handiwork or hers?"

"Hers," West said with what sounded like pride.

His target was lying on the floor beside mine. I never thought guns were sexy, but knowing what West was capable of gave me a thrill I couldn't describe. Several clean shots, all made within seconds of each other, showed me that the 71 kills he'd told me about were probably done with the same precision. Quick, clean deaths.

"Not bad, Lil," Clayton said, tipping his cap to me. "Food."

He plunked the bag down on the counter and pulled out a container of fries. This guy was quickly becoming one of my favorite people. West reached into the bag, opened one of the wrapped items to see what was inside, and handed it to me. A double cheeseburger with everything on it. My mouth watered as the smell reached my nose.

"So," Clayton said through a mouthful of beef. "Camden seems like he's ready to do some talking."

I took a bite of the burger and waited for him to continue. He took another bite and chewed slowly. When he eventually swallowed his mouthful and took a sip of soda, he continued.

"He keeps talking to the camera in there, saying he's ready to cut a deal."

"How did you manage that?" I asked.

"Well," Clayton said around a french fry. "I may have let the basement get a little cold. Set the air conditioner to fifty degrees for the last few days."

West's face went hard as he set down his food. After glancing at me, he looked down at his burger.

"Are you going to make a deal with him?" His question was filled with quiet rage.

"No," I said. His hands flexed like he was readying for a fight. "Nothing is going to change anything for him. There's no scenario where I take pity on him or let him go. By the time this is over, Benjamin Camden will be six feet under."

37

BELLIS PERENNIS

Getting Benjamin tied to the chair again was an effort. West was more than willing to help me out. I think he was anxious to inflict as much pain as possible because the bindings were tight enough for Benjamin to complain. A detail I found hilarious. After West was done making Benjamin miserable with zip ties, I started.

"You know, Benji, the shop upstairs used to be a pharmacy. Back in the twenties, it was a thriving pharmacy. People would come and get their drugs. But you know what else they would get? Booze. Because down here, they were making bathtub gin. They were also smuggling in whiskey from Canada and tequila from, well, Mexico."

"Could you relieve Benjamin of his shirt?" I asked West, who cut the fabric and yanked it hard enough that Benjamin winced. I cocked my head to the side, a predator assessing its prey. Looking over his exposed torso, I let out a little laugh. "You're getting a little soft, Benjamin."

I picked up the serrated hunting knife from the steel table and sauntered toward Benjamin, dragging another chair behind me. It screeched loudly on the concrete floor.

"Now, I'm getting a little fuzzy on my anatomy. It's been a while since

I've been in a classroom. I thought I might reacquaint myself with the muscle tissue of the adult male abdomen."

Benjamin's eyes watched the knife as I gesticulated, waving it about to punctuate my thoughts.

"I was thinking we could swap stories first. Like a couple of girlfriends, you know? I'll go first. I met this guy, let's call him Henry. He was disgusting. Thought of himself as a lady's man. A playboy. He went on a date with a friend of mine. Then he killed her. Strangled her to death while he fucked her."

Isabelle's smiling face flashed through my mind as I recalled learning of her brutal end. I'd been too kind to Henry. The rage I felt then had been nothing compared to what I was feeling now. It bucked and pulled at the leash. West was still standing behind Benjamin, watching me as I spoke. No expression. No hint of disapproval, either. He'd likely seen some version of interrogation in his own experience.

"My friend, Isabelle," I continued. " She was left out in the desert by the men who cleaned up messes for Henry. Then another friend of mine went to bed with Henry. He wound up falling asleep before he could get to the good stuff with her. Then he woke up with me."

I stood up and closed the distance between us. Benjamin's eyes were bright with worry. Especially when I slid the knife against his throat, barely close enough to draw blood but plenty close enough to make my point.

"I told you what I do for a living. How I serve my family. You'll be happy to know he went quickly. Do you want to know where Henry is now? He's at the bottom of a burned-out hole in the middle of the desert."

I leaned in and whispered into his ear.

"And that's because I was feeling generous." I stood and looked down at his terrified face. "So, Benjamin. Tell me a story. How did you know where to find my sister?"

He glanced down at the knife. I pouted but removed the blade from his throat.

"They knew where to get your sister because I had your phone. The Eros party security desk let me take it. Your sister was alone at the club, with no protection because her bodyguard was with his ill father."

I looked at West. His jaw worked as he flexed his fingers.

"Why did they take her?" West asked.

"We - They were going to execute her," Benjamin turned toward West with a surprised look, like he hadn't expected him to speak, then back to me. "No one would miss your sister. The head of a major crime family's death would be celebrated. It wasn't difficult to figure out what you knew once I realized you'd been reading Henry's emails. About the product, we'd been moving. The girls. Then you poured your rotten little heart out to me and confirmed everything I'd suspected."

"Careful," West snarled.

Benjamin's jab had struck its target. *Rotten little heart*…It felt like I'd tripped and nearly lost my footing. I looked down at my shoes, unable to look at Benjamin. Unable to meet West's gaze. I had been a complete idiot.

"After I returned from the security desk to the closet and discovered you'd escaped, I decided we needed your sister for leverage. To make sure our secret was safe. To trade her life for yours. She was in our custody only a few minutes later."

My hands were shaking.

"So where is she?" I asked, trying to steady myself.

"I don't know."

Liar. Liar. Liar. It flared in my mind. Blinking in big illuminated letters. Lighting up my nerves.

"That story doesn't have a very satisfying ending, Benji."

The beast in me was foaming at the mouth as I rolled my shoulders and looked down at Benjamin. The tip of my knife was so close to his leg. *I could just jam it in,* I thought. *Sever his kneecap. Flay his thigh. Make him watch.*

I shook the thought from my head and walked toward the steps. With a nod, West understood my intention and cut Benjamin loose from the chair, shoving him down to the floor as he yanked the seat from under him. I looked down at Benjamin from the top of the steps.

"You know, Benjamin, I remember everything about being with you. You were always in such a rush. I'm going to show you what it means to take your time."

West tugged the black hood back over Benjamin's head and stood, walking toward the steps. The pathetic figure whimpered on the floor in renewed darkness. Mercy was far from my mind as I bid him farewell.

"Why don't you count the minutes until your next meal? There will be a lot of them."

⤚

"YOU KNOW IT all might be bullshit," West said as he drove us home.

I shrugged. It didn't sound like bullshit. It was confirmation of exactly what I'd feared. Anxious to change the subject, I turned to him.

"That didn't bother you?" I asked. "Seeing someone being held prisoner like that?"

"I've seen a lot worse than that."

I wondered about the man West was before setting foot in a desert thousands of miles away. Before watching his friends die. Before taking life from strangers in foreign countries.

The memory of his haunted eyes had me reaching over to put my hand on his thigh.

We turned a corner, or rather I had. He'd touched me before. Been on top of me before. But now my skin clawed and growled, aching for the feel of him. My blood prowled through my veins, jonesing for the oxytocin only he could provide.

Like the Bronco he never stopped working on, I didn't want to be another thing he'd have to fix. I looked out the window and looked at the various businesses on the street. As a sushi bar floated past, I had an idea.

"I'm going back to visit Benjamin tomorrow."

38

ESCHSCHOLZIA CALIFORNICA

When I first met Benjamin, I was taken in by everything. The whole perfect public image he created as well as the lie he created just for me. But now I saw him for what he was: a carefully constructed story to tell the public. A life so distracting that no one looks behind the curtain. And a smile that cuts like a knife, leaving you to bleed out as you drown in those frigid eyes.

"After a long night of soul searching, I thought you might feel up for a chat," I said as I casually trotted down the small wooden stairway.

Benjamin sat against the wall, knees up, feet bare. His hooded head was hanging between them. The bandage on his impaled foot needed changing. There was a distinct odor in the room now. Acrid. It could have been from an infected wound or just an unwashed man.

It was easy to imagine him digging himself out if I gave him a spoon. Of course, he'd have to get through a lot of concrete. I stood over him, enjoying the feeling of superiority that being bathed, fed, and uninjured gave me.

I tugged off the hood. He had only been in this basement a short while, but he looked like a goddamned castaway. His dark brown hair was wild and his beard had grown in. Unlike West's thick beard, Benjamin's was patchy and discolored. The ice-blue eyes that had so thoroughly done me in were now tired. Maybe even a little sad. It was difficult not to smile at the sight of his imperfect appearance.

"If I like what you have to say, you can have this," I said as I held the bag I'd brought in with me up for him to see.

"What is it?" He eyed the bag with the wariness of a broken animal. Oh, this was fun.

"Sashimi, salad, brown rice, and an ice-cold bottle of sparkling water. All from a very nice restaurant nearby. I thought you might be getting tired of sandwiches."

Benjamin's eyes widened slightly as they darted to the bag and back to my face. A chuckle burst from me at his mistrust. How rich. I looked around, noting all of the things I'd need to restock for his continued stay.

"None of it is poisoned. Unless you count the usual amount of mercury. I promise," I said with a smile.

"You want to know where your sister is," he said, his voice raw from all the screaming I'd heard through the monitor. This room was made for this purpose. No one could have heard him but Clayton, who'd been monitoring him for me. I gave him a flat look, attempting to mask the jolt of pain the words skewered me with.

"There's an encampment," Benjamin said. "It's outside of Joshua Tree. Hidden well."

"What kind of an encampment is it?" My hackles rose. I already knew.

"It's for keeping and moving product."

"Product being women?" I asked flatly. If I wasn't already planning to kill him, I would've killed him for that alone.

He nodded.

"She's there?"

"Most likely. They said they were taking her out of the city. That's where the containers are loaded. Then they're moved to shipping."

My stomach flipped at the thought. At the very idea that Kaia was crouched in a blacked-out container, making its way across the ocean on a ship amongst dozens of other containers.

"And you think she'd still be there?"

My jaw clenched. My fingers itched.

"They're not moved to the shipyard until just before. It's too big of a risk to keep them in the city for long periods."

Breathe, I told myself.

"How do I find this encampment?" The question slipped between my clenched teeth.

"You can't."

"I thought you were feeling helpful, Benji," I growled. My fingers curled around the hunting knife's grip at my back. In truth, I'd been itching to touch it since I stepped into the room.

"The only way to get to the encampment is for someone to take you there. I can't even get there without an escort."

This was some kind of test. He was testing me.

"So set up an escort."

Benjamin shook his head.

"It's not possible. I deal with the buyers and some of the accounting."

"I thought Stephen Bryant was the one doing the accounting," I deadpanned as I let go of the knife to place my hand on my hip.

"He was until you..." his voice trailed off as he considered the wisdom of his next words, his eyes narrowing slightly before looking away.

Until I killed Stephen Bryant. Until he bled out on the bathroom floor with a gash in his throat like a slaughtered goat. Benjamin had told me when he'd tried to kill me that he'd discovered what happened to his business partner. I still remembered the little choked gurgling sound Stephen made as he tried to shove the blood back in. My lips tipped up at the thought.

The basement was silent as Benjamin looked at me in horror. Maybe he hadn't realized who he was dealing with before, but he did now. When we met he thought I was toothless, but now he was seeing my fangs.

"I make sure they have what they need to do their jobs," Benjamin continued, shifting back to the subject. "There's no reason for me to go all the way out there. If they think I've given anything away, they'll cut me out completely."

Oh and what a shame that would be. I put the takeout on the ground and crossed the room to sit in the steel chair I'd had him tied to. He was finally arriving at his point. My patience was thinner than rice paper. Leaning back in the chair, I loosed my knife from its sheath and ran the edge of the blade across my thumb. Benjamin pulled his feet away, closer to the wall.

"What do you suggest, then?"

"HAVE YOU COMPLETELY lost your mind?" West growled as he slammed his hands down on the kitchen counter.

I'd come back to the house to find West and Clayton in the kitchen. Clayton had made himself at home in the living room, his mismatched socks propped up on the coffee table as he watched cartoons. West had been in the middle of preparing our dinner. So many green vegetables. Large pieces of well-marbled beef. My grandmother would be happy to see her kitchen being used properly again. She'd probably rolled over in her grave every time we made a frozen lasagna.

"If that's where Kaia is, then that's where I'm going," I said, taking a seat at the kitchen island.

"I know you want to get your sister back but fuck, Lili. What if it's bullshit? Why would he be telling you the truth?"

All good points. I shouldn't trust Benjamin. I don't trust Benjamin. But I had to at least look into what he'd told me and I didn't know any other way.

"I know. I know. But it's a lead. I've got nothing else to go on. All I need is for them to take me. We can find a way to get me out again."

"You have no idea what's waiting for you there. They could figure out what you're trying to do and kill you."

West resumed cutting vegetables, making enemies of mushrooms and shallots. Anger laced every downward stroke. The broccoli needed to watch its back.

"If my sister is out there, I have to try."

"This feels like a stupid move. What if he's just trying to get rid of you? Again."

Not ready to back down, I shifted in my seat. I knew I was going to meet with some resistance. When Benjamin explained everything to me, I was skeptical. But it wasn't like I had a lot of options.

"We can put a tracker on me. Somewhere they won't find it. Give me a few hours to look around and then come get me."

"Come get you?" West looked up from the cutting board. A look of indignation on his face. Like he couldn't believe I'd be so stupid, but he wasn't about to say it. He wasn't wrong.

"Yeah. You were SEALs, right? You did extractions. Extract me."

"I think it's a good idea," Clayton said from the living room. He stood from the sofa and walked over to the kitchen, searching for something on his phone.

"You do?" West said dryly.

"This festival she's talking about," Clayton started, "is in two days. It's easy for people to go missing at music festivals so it's not a stretch that they'd be there. This isn't far from Joshua Tree. Where did you say he told you to be?"

"In the VIP section. I'll have to find my way in. You guys can come to the festival. Keep eyes on me."

"Dress like a tart and they'll take you," Clayton laughed. "They always do."

"A tart?" I laughed.

Clayton showed me the event listing. An electric music festival. A music festival sponsored by Eros in big neon letters. West clutched a kitchen knife as he spoke, his knuckles turning white. A tremor went through his hands.

"How are you going to get them to take you?"

"I'm a woman, West. All I have to do is all of the things I'm not supposed to do in a public setting."

39

SALVIA OFFICINALIS

FIFTEEN YEARS AGO

I grew up surrounded by death. People in my grandfather's business died all the time. Funerals were a regular affair. Were it not for them, our family would have only set foot in a church for weddings and holidays.

Everyone kept telling me how sorry they were for our loss. They wanted to know what they could do. Hug me. I wasn't sure how much longer I could hide what I was feeling. Lost without my mother. That was something they would expect, but I couldn't get the words out. And I wasn't sure they would be able to hear what I had to say about my father. The relief I felt when I realized what had happened. Or the fact that I was grateful that he was gone.

Kaia was in the dining room, talking with my grandfather's associates. She wore a black suit and black heels. Her pin-straight hair was swept back in a tight ponytail. It was odd. The way she held herself, the way the men in the room treated her with respect. It was like she'd aged twenty years in a week.

As far as those men were concerned, I was just a mourning child. Some gave me uncomfortable, short nods. It was as much as I could hope for from them. Not that I wanted anything at all. Their wives kept patting me on the shoulder. Offering me a tissue without bothering to notice that I hadn't shed a tear.

"How you holding up, Lilith? I'm so sorry for your loss. You must really miss them both."

One of the attendees had leaned down to talk to me. Nico was seated on the sofa beside me but didn't look up from his video game. Her perfume was overwhelming. Her smiling face was far too close to mine and it had too much makeup on it for a funeral. I gave her a flat look.

"Do I know you?"

"Oh, well," she stammered, running her fingers through her platinum-blonde hair. "I was a friend of your father's."

"Sweetheart," Nonna said as she placed a hand on my back. "You don't owe anyone a display of your sadness. Or anything else. Why don't you go find your grandfather for me?"

My grandmother may have been talking to me, but she was looking at the blonde woman. Her face was tight with indignation. Did she know this woman?

"Go," she prompted me with a gentle push.

Deciding I'd had enough of the false niceties, I decided to do as my grandmother had asked. With a short glance backward I saw my grandmother leading the blonde woman to the kitchen. My sister was a few steps behind them.

Few people were outside. The rain had pushed the mourners indoors. Wisteria and lemon branches created a porous shield from the rain. I wrapped my sweater around myself, hoping to protect my dress from further saturation.

As I rubbed my arms, I looked around. There weren't a lot of places my grandfather would be hiding. No one lurked in the garden. All of the cars in the driveway seemed to be unoccupied. Then I saw the open doors.

My grandfather was in the garage. Working on his car. The bright blue Camero glistened under the dangling work light that hung overhead. The jacket of his suit was draped over the driver's seat. He was bent over under the hood, shirt rolled up to his elbows.

"Bambina," he said. "Can you hand me that wrench?"

His grease-covered finger pointed to the toolbox. I wasn't surprised he'd heard me approach. He always knew.

"Nonna sent me to look for you."

Nonno stood and braced a hand on the car, giving me a frank look.

"I expect that was more for your benefit than for hers. Are you alright?"

I let out a sigh and sat down in the driver's seat.

"I'm getting kind of tired of people asking me that," I muttered. He wiped his hands off and approached the side of the car.

"Mia principessa. What can I do?"

"I don't know why people expect me to be sad. I mean, I am sad. For Mama. But not for him. Father always said that death was a gift." My next words were watery. "I'm glad he's dead."

He sighed and knelt. Took my small hand in his and squeezed it.

"Death is part of our business. It's...your father," Nonno sighed again. "He never understood that it was a burden. Not for the people who pass. But for the people who are left behind."

I looked down at our joined hands. He'd lost his only son. And I was in here saying I was glad he's dead. Tears flooded my eyes as I burst into a sob.

"I'm sorry, Nonno."

Wrapping me in a hug, he stroked my hair as he spoke. After a minute, he pulled away and looked me in the eye.

"Why are you sorry?"

I sniffled.

"You lost someone too. Aren't you sad?"

His nod was slow and tired. Heaviness dragged down his shoulders. His eyes. The golden hazel hue that had been my father's and became mine. Nonno continued gently brushing the top of my head as I sniffled again, trying to stifle my crying so I could listen to him.

"I am sad. My son is gone. Your mother is gone. But, bambina. I'm sad for you. My heart breaks for you and your sister."

"Kaia seems fine. How is that possible?" I warbled.

A soft chuckle came out of him. It was a bright, odd sound. Rubbing at his eyes with the pads of his fingers, he let out another soft laugh.

"Your sister is tougher than most of the men I employ. She walks around with armor over her heart. But that doesn't mean it's not there. She's in pain, too."

We were both quiet. The rain pattering on the open garage door was loud enough to fill the silence, saving us both from things we weren't able to say out loud.

40

PSILOCYBE CUBENSIS

Tough girls in movies always kick. There's always some move where the man's head ends up between their legs and she uses her powerful thighs to suffocate him. It's sort of absurd. I'm not saying I never kick, but it's hardly my go-to move.

Kicking was all I was thinking about as my hands skimmed the too-short hemline of my mesh skirt. Having taken Clayton's direction to dress like a "tart," I looked at pictures of girls at music festivals and did my best to copy the look.

Dressed in a matching mesh pink crop top and mini skirt covered in iridescent sequin hearts, I looked just like every other girl at the Neon Hearts Festival. I patted myself on the back for a job well done. But one kick in this outfit and everyone would see what I had going on underneath, which was not much at all. And you could pretty much see everything anyway.

"You look like a Powerpuff Girl who fell on hard times," Clayton had said while stuffing his face with fruity cereal.

A festival of love. That's what this was supposed to be. We'd gotten up at the crack of dawn to beat traffic and still wound up stuck in it. As I looked around, I decided it hardly seemed worth it.

The space itself was a black void, lit only by the bodies wearing glowing accessories and the large strip of LED lights overhead that pulsed with different images and colors. As I lifted my gaze upward, the image changed to pulsing streams of light that were supposed to mimic sunlight filtering through water.

I turned to look at West. A small smile tugged at my lips. The black face paint I'd smeared around his eyes only highlighted their already hypnotizing green color as they peeked over the skull gaiter that covered the rest of his face. It was no accident that it also hid the radio he was using to communicate with Clayton.

People moved to the pounding music that set my bones vibrating. The flash of lights above us lit different faces in the crowd as West and I advanced through it. We would part ways soon, in the middle of the undulating throng. All of it was starting to feel overwhelming. My hands started shaking.

I can do this.

"I don't know how I'm going to get into the VIP section," I said as my eyes fell on the discreetly marked area of the festival. A sparse number of people walked inside, past a security guard with a list.

"Clayton says he's picking up their radio. They're talking about the lounge."

I squeezed his hand, letting him know that I'd heard. Still watching the entrance, I noticed the guard let in one woman out of a group of three. Her friends seemed to curse what they thought was her good luck.

West slowed his steps, coming to a stop in the middle of the dense crowd. A pull on my wrist turned my attention back to him. He tugged the gaiter down, just below his chin, and pulled me in for a kiss. The worry in his eyes said more than I was ready to hear.

"They're describing targets by their outfits. Blue butterflies. Yellow stars," he said, his eyes drifting down my body and back to meet my gaze. "Pink hearts."

"I'll be fine," I said, not entirely believing it myself.

He eyed me warily, hesitant to let me go. Callused fingers slipped from mine. The volume of the music went up and drowned out his next words, but I saw "you" form on his perfect mouth. I smiled at him over my shoulder, readying myself for what was coming next. As I turned away from him, a skull-masked figure in a dark hallway flashed through my memory.

Every time I think I'm doing the stupidest thing I've ever done, eventually I find a way to outdo myself. Who would willingly put themselves in this situation? There was no way for me to know what was on the other side. I let the thought of the tracker anchor me. The tiny silver bracelet that we'd decided looked inconspicuous on my ankle fed them my every movement.

Thunder clapped in the sound system as strobing lights filled the room. The sound was followed by water falling from above. An indoor storm. Screams of joy lifted from the crowd as the thunder worked into a song and the sounds of water drops.

Beads of sweat mixed with water as I danced with strangers. The rolling liquid felt like the fingertips of a lover, drifting over every inch of my exposed flesh. I let myself remember West's hands on me. His lips. His tongue. My heart beat in time with the thundering bass as I closed my eyes, losing myself in every sensation.

The charm on the bracelet bounced against my leg as I picked my way through the mass of bodies toward the VIP entrance, eyeing potential prey. Girls who were unaware of their surroundings. They were just trying to have a good time, unaware of the dangers lurking at the edge of their world. I knew they shouldn't have to live in this reality. Their joy shouldn't come with this price. But it did. It always did.

BLOCKED AWAY FROM the rest of the music festival by false hedge walls, the VIP section had a glaringly large sign over it in glowing neon letters. Eros Love Lounge. Passersby ignored it, mostly. But there was a small line of people hoping to get in. Some had passes. Others tried to gain favor with the bouncers. I took my place in line among them.

"Name?" The large bald bouncer looked like something from out of a movie in his black ensemble.

"Oh, I'm not on the list," I said as I pushed my still-wet chest up and batted my eyelashes at him. Come on, buddy. Take the bait. I bit my lip. "I was hoping to get in. A guy told me to meet him inside."

The bouncer gave me a pitying look. Then he radioed inside asking for a headcount. The response seemed to satisfy him as he stepped aside, unhooking the pink velvet rope from its blockade.

"Thank you!" I squealed.

Inside the exclusive VIP tent seemed like an entirely different event. The same music was pumping through the speakers, but that was where the similarities ended. My eyes skimmed the area, taking in details that were classically Eros. Dancing women were in ornate gold bird cages instead of on pedestals. They were even wearing feathers. Each woman was an exotic bird, trapped for the entertainment of others.

Scattered around the tent were several rugs, all topped with poufs and pillows. And draped all over the pillows, all over the poufs, laying upon the carpet were the members of Eros. Touching, tasting, and laughing in the darkened space.

My mind drifted to another Eros party. Being touched. Being tasted. I cringed.

A waiter passed with a tray of champagne flutes, filled to the brim with fizzing pink liquid. He paused by my side and lifted the tray in offer. I took a glass and nodded my thanks.

I skirted the edge of the hedge wall, a wallflower to a security guard with a monitor in his ear who'd been keeping an eye on me. I was observing, yes, but also anxious to confirm that my guardian was nearby. A narrow view through the leafy partition offered me a glimpse. The gaiter had been pulled over his mouth again. Blue light poured down on him, draining the color from his golden skin. From the smoky green eyes I wanted to see one more time.

Bodies passed before him. Throngs moved to the center of everything as the next performer took the stage. I tried to keep my eyes on him. But as the crowd moved by, I lost my focus. Lost him. Where he stood there was just empty space.

It was easy to remove the tiny vial of GHB from the cup of my bra. Even easier to dump into the champagne before me. Even though I'd measured it twice, only a large enough dose to lose consciousness for a short time, the idea that I was making myself vulnerable for even a second sent a chill through me.

The liquid sizzled and popped as I lifted it to my lips, thinking of the man in the skull mask that I'd come with. Hoping that our plan would work, that I'd find my sister and return to West, I drank as quickly as I could.

The floor felt like it was tilting beneath me. I blinked, looking for somewhere to sit. The man wearing a monitor in his ear was coming closer. He was closer, wasn't he? In the pulsing shadows, he wasn't easy to identify.

I flopped down onto a collection of inviting pillows. Oh, how I wanted to take a nap. Every instinct in me fought to stay awake. I was surrounded by strangers. No one here knew me. No one would help me. Stupid. This was so incredibly stupid.

The man worked his way between the circles of moving bodies. Closer to me still. Another man dressed in black was walking several feet behind a girl stumbling toward the bar, far enough away not to know her but too close to be a coincidence. I felt the urge to get up. To help her. To go find West. To call this off. But my legs wouldn't cooperate. My body stopped listening to me.

"Having a little too much fun, sweetheart?" The man with the monitor in his ear was talking to me. He knelt beside me. I squeezed my eyes shut to clear my vision. The edges of his body thrummed with the thumping bass. Were there two of him?

This was a bad idea.

"Come on, sugar. I'll take care of you."

Then I went down, down, down.

41

FOENICULUM VULGARE

The fire crackled in its cement pit. Hands pulled a soft blanket up around me and rubbed my shoulders, trying to give me some of their warmth. A gust of wind tore through the trees, filling the air with their unique music.

It felt peaceful here. Cold. There were no city sounds to compete with the wild mountain air. A huff of air came from behind me as he wrapped his big bear arms around me. He hummed as I leaned back into his hold.

"Are you warm enough?"

I said yes.

His hand lifted to turn my face toward his.

"Are you comfortable?"

I said yes.

He kissed me.

"Are you mine?"

THE SLIDING DOOR of a van. Metal tracks grinding against each other. A squeaking hinge. Other bodies pushed up against mine. Sniffles from someone nearby. The hours that followed came in flashes. In seconds.

My boots slid on the muddy path to the modular trailer they led us to. A foot plunged into an icy cold puddle. We were still in the desert. Somewhere it had rained recently. The inky black waves of my hair hid my expression as I cast my face down, trying my best to take in my surroundings. Worry that these traffickers had been told to find me by Benjamin's unknown partners flooded my insides. Maybe I had fallen into some sort of trap.

Our feet clambered and clanged up metal steps into a set of trailers. Upon entry, we were forced to the ground, no better than cattle to the people herding us around. I wasn't sure if my shiver was from the wet, biting cold or the way one of our captors kept looking at my exposed skin.

Each of the women in the room with me seemed to have been taken from the festival. As soon as I'd become conscious, I looked at all of them. Some foolish hope that my sister would be among them. With the trailer empty upon our arrival, I knew I wouldn't find her here. A sinking pit opened in my gut.

The first man was tall and lean. Light brown hair. A shadow of hair on his jaw. Possibly blue eyes. Maybe grey. It was difficult to tell in this light, which was almost no light at all. His associate was his physical opposite. Short. Fat. Bald. Tattooed all over but cheap, shitty-looking tattoos. The first man-made eye contact with me, then looked to his associate and grinned. They spoke with each other in a lilting language I couldn't identify. Each was armed with a pistol.

The trailer we'd walked into was connected to the second trailer through a collapsing door. Something fabric and accordion-like. Green. The only bit of color in the rooms aside from the women. From me. The mesh pink outfit seemed like an idiotic choice as I wished for something to defend my ass against the cold linoleum floor.

When we'd concocted this plan, I was supposed to look like all of the other girls. Scared. Hopeless, even. It didn't take long for my ruse to become reality.

Three other women had been shuffled into the trailer with me. Two of them had been marked over the radio the way West told me. Blue Butterflies turned out to be a twenty-something platinum-blonde girl in a blue butterfly-shaped top and matching vinyl pants. The one they called Yellow Stars was wearing a bikini top shaped like a starfish. She had chestnut brown hair tied up into tiny space buns. The third girl was the one I'd noticed staggering toward the bathroom in the VIP section. Another blonde, but shorter and younger looking. For a moment, I was jealous of her jeans because she was less exposed than the rest of us.

I made frightened looks around the room to see a whole lot of nothing. A bare floor. A closed partition. No water and a bucket for doing your business. One bucket. I wondered if this was some sort of retribution for Benjamin's current situation, but then I reminded myself that he fucking deserved it.

After another look at me, well my breasts really, the man left with his companion and locked the door behind him. The woman beside me burst into tears. The rest of us were silent.

NO ONE CHECKED on us for hours. All four of us were huddled together on the floor just to keep warm. It was still dark out. No welcome ray of sunshine to comfort anyone. Some girls cried all night. I didn't blame them. Even knowing that West and Clayton were on their way here to free me, I was still frightened. Nervously, I fiddled with the sensor in my boot and hoped the puddle didn't do too much damage.

Sleep didn't find me. It didn't find any of us. Instead, I kept my eyes down and thought about West. Hoped he'd have the opportunity to tell me what a horrible idea this was. Hoped I'd share that bed with him again. My mind filled with golden sunlight as I thought about white sheets and his soft cedar scent. It was the only thing keeping me from desperate, disappointed tears. I imagined that warm, safe place.

What a godawful idea this was. Kaia wasn't here. But I was. Why in the hell did I listen to Benjamin?

As bleary pink light started to leak in through the windows, the partition opened. A new man walked out, zipping himself up. We made eye contact. He laughed to himself, looked into the bucket, and left.

With the partition open, there was a fresh batch of things to see. Though seeing it felt like a threat. From wall to wall, it was more terrifying than the first. The one they'd shoved us into had a bucket for relieving ourselves and nothing else. But in the next room, there were several bare twin mattresses separated by folding hospital dividers.

I tried to count the occupants of that room. Hungrily searched the details for any sign of my sister. One was trying to muffle her crying in the back corner. I could hear her relatively well despite her efforts. Another was scratching at a button on the mattress she was probably sitting on, the pulling sound making a thumping tap against her nail. Then there was the last girl, the only girl I could see.

She stared at the ceiling with her body half on the mattress and half off. Lopsided and broken like a discarded doll. Stringy blonde hair clung to her forehead. Her mouth opened and closed intermittently, a fish out of water taking its last breaths. Drugged. Whatever they had given her, this woman was high enough to be hovering near death.

The man came back into the trailer, quickly followed by another new one. They started speaking in that same bizarre language to each other, sharply gesturing to the drugged girl in the next room. I tried to narrow it down as they had some kind of argument. From past brushes with the Russian mafia, I knew it wasn't that. Not anything Latin-based either. The other man grabbed the woman from under her shoulders, the other taking her ankles as they carried her out. The girl plucking the mattress button stopped. Crawling on the mattress, she poked her head out from behind the separator to watch them leave.

It wasn't the red hair or her freckled skin that caught my eye, striking me like a slap in the face. It was the familiar glint in her deep brown eyes. The same look she had when she'd tell me about her terrible boyfriend or her family problems. I couldn't wrap my brain around it.

Holy fucking shit. No. I looked at her again. I blinked, trying to clear my vision because I'd been convinced it was deceiving me. It couldn't be her. It was impossible. After all of this time, it couldn't be.

"Casey?"

42

ANGELICA SINENSIS

Women are often described as emotional creatures. Hysterical. Too ruled by their humor. In the old days, it was said that their judgment wasn't to be trusted. I've never found that to be the case. Especially not here. I knew every single woman in the room was terrified beyond belief, but it never presented itself in an outburst. Only in their eyes.

Instead, we watched. One cowered in the corner, crying. But of the six of us, five kept quiet. We watched the men come and go. Sometimes we exchanged looks when the men would check on us. Assessing the situation. But Casey had been watching longer than any of the guards.

"I asked Isabelle to go with me to this Eros party but she'd already met some guy who was whisking her off to Vegas that night. I guess being alone makes you an easy target."

Her voice was soft, but the words were low. Cold with anger. I couldn't tell if it was at the situation or herself.

"This isn't your fault," I said. Her brown eyes softened. "But it's been months. How are you still here?"

"This is where I woke up. The girls who were here when I woke up never came back after they put them on a truck. It seemed like being taken away was worse than being here, so I did what I needed to do to stay. So I didn't have to go wherever they go."

"They take girls away on a truck? But they bring them here first? Why?"

"I don't know. It's like they're checking us for temperament. Like dogs," she said.

Casey was wearing a little pleated skirt and blue sweater, dirty and filled with ragged holes. Her feet were bare and filthy, tucked underneath her to fight the cold. When the outfit was fresh and clean, she must of have looked cute. Sweet, even. It was what the men in the club loved about her. I started to get up, to try and get closer to her.

"Don't. There's a camera in this room. Not in the next one. You can't come in here."

Confused, I took my seat again. Pulled my sorry excuse for a skirt down over my ass. My arms were barely enough to protect myself from the cold in the crop top I was now deeply regretting. I crossed them in front of me as I looked at the cameras.

"Is there sound?"

Casey dipped a finger into her sweater, yanking the neck up to cover her shoulder. She looked sick. Dark circles hung under her eyes. Her usually full cheeks had hollowed slightly. The delicate shape of her face had sharpened. Everything about Casey had been soft before. Now she looked like a feral cat, turned out into the wilderness, having gone a bit too long without human kindness.

"I don't know. I don't think so. They only come back when they can see there's a problem. That's how they knew about Taylor."

"Taylor?"

"The one they took out last night. She was screaming and shouting, so they gave her something to keep her calm. I guess they overdosed her."

Something in me doubted that she'd been taken for medical treatment. Not when she was a commodity that was so easily replaced by the women I'd arrived with. My gut churned as I imagined what they'd done with her. Thought about the unmarked grave I'd dug in the desert for someone else.

It was easy to dispose of someone in these wastes. No remains would be found. Like many victims before her, her family would be left wondering. The thought of my sister in one of those graves was too much to bear.

"How many women have been through here since you've been here?"

"I don't know," Casey warbled.

I looked at her face. The cold sadness in it. Sad. But not broken. Every second, she was fighting not to break.

"Can I ask you something?"

Casey nodded. A half-empty gesture.

"Did you ever see Kaia? Here? Has she been here?"

She shook her head. I pushed.

"Maybe she came through and you didn't notice. Maybe they drugged her like Taylor?"

"I would have noticed her," Casey said, her voice hardened in irritation.

One of the girls cleared her throat as footsteps sounded up the metal steps. The tall man from our first night in. Casey looked up at him and... smiled.

The tall man pushed a hand through his greasy brown hair and picked up the bucket. I cringed. We'd all used it. I immediately understood why Benjamin asked me for a toilet. The man opened the door and left for a moment, taking the bucket with him. We all waited. I glanced at Casey, whose face immediately resumed its empty expression.

A squeak of the door opening had my head snapping to attention again. The tall man walked past all of us, no bucket to be seen, and closed the partition. In the quiet space, it was impossible to ignore the sounds coming from the other side.

As I forced my sight to the dirt-covered floor, I wondered where West was. What was taking so long? Worry flooded me as I tried not to think about my friend in the next room or what would happen to my sister if I never resurfaced from this pit. My finger fished inside my boot and furiously rubbed the small pendant that was supposed to be my savior.

After the man finished his business, he left us. No one came to feed us or give us water all night. No bucket was returned for use. The partition was open, the man had left it ajar after he departed. It felt like an hour passed before I was able to summon words.

"Casey?" I whispered. "Are you alright?"

A ridiculous question, I knew, but I couldn't figure out exactly what to say to her.

"I'm alive," she said. Her voice was flat and hollow.

THE NEXT DAY the men brought the small gathering of women enough food to not starve. Five granola bars for six women. Enough water not to die of thirst. One large gallon go share. A couple of soiled blankets to share. Even a fresh bucket. But that was it. And none of us complained.

Casey had stayed silent after our brief exchange. I couldn't ask her about what happened. Couldn't imagine how it felt. But I'd started to understand how she survived for so long.

It was because of her silence that I was surprised to hear her voice while I was using the bucket.

"Lili" she called from her flat little mattress.

I pulled up my underwear and stood up. From that angle, I could see her more clearly. Sunlight barely penetrated the filthy windows, but it was enough to light Casey's hand as she beckoned me over.

"I'm not allowed over there, right?"

"Just come here," she bit out.

With a glance toward the camera, I slipped toward her. Now that I was standing close to her, I could see the blood stains on the mattress. The sweater that was more torn than it had been before. Fresh bruises that peppered her wrists.

"They're moving all of you tomorrow," she said in a whisper so low, I almost couldn't hear it.

Shit.

"How do you know that?"

She looked toward the room full of women. Then at the camera.

"They always give you food right before. Then they move all of you out early in the morning. Right before sunrise."

A dark shipping container to the other side of the world was not my idea of a satisfying conclusion to this story. I decided I couldn't wait on West and Clayton any more. I was going to have to rescue myself. And Casey.

"Hey."

Her wild red curls bounced as she returned her gaze to me. Soothing the part of me that had become a caged beast, I closed my eyes and took a deep breath. And another. Then I looked Casey in the eye.

"I need to know everything you know about this place. I need to know how many men there are and what kind of weapons they're carrying. I need to know exactly what they do when they take girls away. And you're going to tell me right now."

43

PTYCHOPETALUM

Knowing what I knew, it was impossible to sleep. The others had curled up together under a blanket. I took up the corner closest to the partition so that I could talk with Casey. The tracking bracelet didn't seem to be working, so I took it off. If it was working West would have found me by now, I was sure of it. I fiddled with it while I told her everything I'd done to find her. And everything I'd done to Benjamin.

"You really tried to find me?" Casey asked.

"Yeah," I said softly. "I'm sorry I didn't do a very good job."

Casey shrugged.

"I'm surprised my father didn't find me first," she responded. "He's always looking out for me."

I shook my head like a dog shaking off water. Huh? Her father? As far as I knew, Casey was raised by a single mother. Everything I dug up on her when I was trying to hunt her down seemed to indicate a childhood spent with just one woman, Bethany Collins.

"What, is he like a spy or something? Like Liam Neeson in Taken?"

Casey huffed a mirthless laugh and leaned back against the wall. She looked up at the ceiling, seeming to struggle with some sort of internal debate. It was clear she'd made her choice when she breathed a deep sigh and fixed her gaze on me.

"He's a mob boss."

"What?" I must have looked surprised because Casey rolled her eyes at me.

"I know you're mafia, Lili. But Muse is the best club in LA. I wanted to dance there so bad. Only, my dad is mafia, too. My mom left him when I was little and I've only ever used her last name. It's on all of my paperwork. Even my IDs. But, my name isn't Casey Collins."

"Okay," I said, trying not to let the fact that my brains were falling out of my head read on my face. "So what is your name?"

"Arawn. My last name is Arawn."

THE SOUND OF a big diesel engine was our warning. Its approaching roar was enough for me to get up and move. Stretching to get the blood flowing into my cold limbs. I needed to get ready for what I had to do.

I crept up to the window and peeked above the frame. Two men. On a normal day, I could take down two men. At this time of night, that was all they would spare to guard the trailers. I did not doubt that more were close by, guarding the perimeter.

They'd have to come in on their own. I would only be successful if only one armed man entered. A second gunman would be deadly.

Casey explained to the girls as quietly as possible that they would have to be silent. And that when they got the chance, they should run. Find a road. Flag someone down.

The door swung open. A tall man and a short fat man were here to collect us. *Shit*. And they both had guns. *Shit!* The short man said something to the tall one and turned around to leave. I thanked heaven for small mercies as he started to walk away. For the first time, the tall man said something in English.

"Everybody up."

I stood. The other girls remained sitting. Just as I'd told them to. Then I punched him in the nose. He recoiled and reached for his gun, one hand over his bleeding nose. With a lousy grip like that, it was easy. The muscle memory was there. It was like West took the gun for me. But the gun was in my hand. And it was me who pulled the trigger.

We heard the fat man run. We heard him come up the stairs. We watched him come through the door. He only had enough time to look at his dead friend on the floor for a moment before he was a bleeding corpse beside him. I shut the door and glanced out the window. The truck was nearing the site but going slowly on uneven terrain. Its headlights were probably only half a mile away. Maybe less.

"Come on," I whispered, dropping to my knees.

Yanking the clothes off of a dead body is harder than it looks. The truck's engine roared as it neared the trailers. Only fifty yards out. Casey and I quickly put on the coats of each man. The faded brown hoodie swallowed her form. A green army jacket would have to do for me. We left the rest of their clothes for the others. Except for a leather belt, which I cinched around my waist as a makeshift holster.

"Out the back," Casey said to the others, who followed with uncertain footsteps. "Quickly. Quietly. *Now*."

They shuffled behind me like school children following a teacher out of the classroom. The door was locked. Grateful for my boots, I kicked the handle as hard as I could. A whimper came from the girls.

"It's going to be fine," Casey reassured her.

I kicked again. And again.

A small groan from another girl.

"Be quiet!" Casey shout-whispered.

A loud clang and rattle sounded as all of the women simultaneously gasped. The door swung open.

I slid the gun from the belt and undid the safety, holding it down by my side. Metal stairs thundered under our feet. Casey's hand went to my shoulder and squeezed.

"Where the fuck are we?" She whispered.

"Somewhere in the desert near Joshua Tree," I said quietly.

Large rocks surrounded the trailers, which were covered with sand-colored netting. We truly were surrounded by nothing. The truck's brakes huffed with a loud puff of air and a squeak.

"Come on," I whispered, running for the rocks. Away. We had to get away from here. Now.

I looked behind me, hoping Casey could keep up. Motioning for her to pull up her hood, I grabbed her hand and tugged her along. That mound of fire-red hair would give us away if any of the guards so much as glimpsed it.

The rest of the women ran toward other rocks. I'd told them to follow me, but they'd panicked and scattered. I silently wished them luck, hoping they'd find their way out of the desert. Casey stuck with me. Just like I'd asked her to. If I was lucky enough to find her now, I sure as hell wasn't going to lose her again.

HOW IN THE hell was I supposed to get us out of here? I climbed a rock to get a better view of our surroundings. It wasn't so much a climb as it was hastily scrambling upward. As I moved, I was simultaneously thankful for the coat that was covering me and disgusted by the combination of smells coming off of it. Like cologne and body odor.

Casey kept watch, looking toward the shouting that had rung out. And screaming. A woman screamed as men shouted at her. My stomach lurched at the sound. Told myself I couldn't have helped her any more than I could help myself, which wouldn't be anything at all if I couldn't figure out a way to leave.

As it turned out, we weren't too far from the road. It was a big road, actually. The encampment was hidden by rocks, but not far off from what looked like a highway. My bare legs scraped against the rocks as I slid down. A hiss puffed out through my teeth as I hit the ground.

"If we just go this way, we should be able to flag someone down. Maybe.

The highway isn't far. Unless the only people taking this road are people who work at this...fucking awful place."

We walked in the shadows of cactus and rocks. In the shadows of clouds as we took careful steps toward the highway. As my boots sunk into pockets of sand, I thought about running on the beach. Tried not to think about the others. Where they were. If they'd been taken back to the trailer. If they hadn't.

Casey was probably thinking about the girls. Or about everything else that had happened to her. Things she wasn't ready to tell anyone. The sun started to rise. It gradually climbed into the sky, heating our bare limbs. Our near-silent walk was cut to an end. The sound of tires roaring down the asphalt met us behind a cluster of rocks.

"There are two men over there," she said in a shaky whisper.

"Where?"

She pointed.

A pale green Bronco parked by the side of the dirt road. The hood went up. Two guys with a little car trouble. One man in a baseball cap and horn-rimmed glasses. Another with hair piled on his head and tattoos down his arms.

"It's West," I breathed, barely. My eyes lined with tears. They found me. He found me. Us.

Casey looked at me with her frightened doe eyes.

"West from the club. He's with me. It's safe," I said as I reached out to take her hand. She looked down at my extended palm. "I promise."

Clammy fingers intertwined with mine. I let her stay behind me as we emerged from behind the rocks. Clayton saw us first. Whistled. Said something that made West's head whip toward us. His lips parted in a breath I couldn't hear, but I could feel it. A sound, maybe a laugh, came from me.

Tugging Casey behind me, I tried my best to take slow steps. To give her time. But everything in me wanted to run toward him.

Shouting erupted behind us. Men screaming. West's eyes shot to the rocks behind us. He threw open the door of the truck.

"Run!"

My hand yanked Casey as our pace picked up. Sand shot up around us as bullets peppered the ground. West hauled his rifle up to his shoulder and aimed. Unlike our former captors, his shots were minimal and precise.

We came to the Bronco, rounding to the driver's side to where Clayton was firing a pistol. With his free hand, he pushed the seat down and helped Casey inside. I followed. He hauled himself into the Bronco and started it up. West took a final shot and followed.

Clayton spun the wheel as we peeled away, dirt spraying behind us with the peeling tires. The truck fishtailed out of the sand.

"What the fuck took you so long?" I shouted from the backseat.

"We lost the connection to your bracelet. It took hours to get it back."

"Hale drove us around for hours while I tried to get the signal back. I don't think we stopped except for gas. The signal came back online a little under two hours ago."

The cab was silent. Like we were all holding our breath. All waiting for another shot to be fired. Only the sound of tires rolling down the highway was heard for several minutes.

"It's good to see you, Casey," West broke the silence, speaking over his shoulder. He looked at me, reaching a hand behind the seat to squeeze my thigh.

Casey had been missing for months. I couldn't imagine what other horrors she'd endured. Or about her father. A man who'd long wanted my family dead. But I was also filled with thoughts of the women we'd left behind. The way their screams sounded. Though I knew we had no way of helping them, that we'd have been caught if we'd tried, guilt lingered deep in my gut.

44

ACTAEA RACEMOSE

The sun was burning high in the sky. It had been West's idea not to go straight home, in case we were followed. I had disappeared into my thoughts and didn't notice when we pulled into the hotel in Palm Springs. He went into the lobby to check us into our rooms while the rest of us lingered outside.

The temptation to follow him was strong. I wanted nothing but to disappear beneath the sheets with him. Just to be held by him. Get lost in his scent. His skin. But the idea of leaving Casey alone with a strange man made me feel like a real dick. So instead...

"You're going to bunk with me," I said to Casey. "I think I can scare up something else for you to wear. You can shower first. I feel fucking disgusting."

Rambling. I was rambling. What is someone supposed to say in this situation? Clayton tapped my shoulder and handed me a sweatshirt and pajama pants.

"She can wear this. It's clean."

Casey quietly thanked me as she took the clothes from my hands. I did my best to give her a reassuring smile. I've never been good at it. Comforting people.

West came out with hotel room keys and handed one to me. I was grateful

I wouldn't have to explain not sharing a room with him. That he knew exactly why we wouldn't. He'd arranged for our rooms to be next to each other. Knowing that he would be on the other side of the wall was more of a comfort than I was ready to admit.

"Wait," Clayton said as Casey and I walked toward our room just a few steps away. "I have something for Casey."

Clayton looked down at his boots and cracked his knuckles at his side. Shifting to one side so that Casey could take whatever he'd offer, I made sure to stay near. My shoulders tensed, waiting for him to say or do the wrong thing. Instead, he fished something out of his pocket and handed it to Casey. Then left without saying a word.

Casey shoved her hand into the pockets of the brown hoodie. As we entered the hotel room, Casey stopped and closed the door. She leaned against it, shutting out the rest of the world as her shoulders slumped.

WALKING OVER TO the dresser, I tugged the shirt West had given me over my wet hair. The jacket and sparkly pink little outfit got stuffed into the trash. I couldn't even look at them anymore. Casey looked like a child in Clayton's pajamas. Fragile and small.

This was not a hotel with room service. I should have known it from the way it was laid out. The way the towel scratched against my skin. But it was clean and warm. After being stuck in that deserted pit, this felt like a luxury.

"I didn't know you two were together. You can go sleep with him if you want. I'm fine. Fine alone, I mean."

"What?" I toweled off my hair. The shower wasn't near hot enough to scrub the last few days off of my skin. I washed myself like four times.

"You and West. You're together, aren't you?"

I sighed. I couldn't explain what West and I were to myself any more than I could explain it to Casey right now. So instead I just said "I'm staying here. I don't want to leave you alone and I think it's just better if I'm here right now."

Casey jolted when there was a knock at the door, waking us a few hours later. West stood on the other side with several bags of food and big green glass bottles of sparkling water at his feet. I picked it up and moved it inside.

"I thought you would be hungry. And thirsty," he said as he looked down at his shoes. Clearing his throat, he peered up through his eyelashes and leaned against the doorway. Quiet enough so only I heard him, he asked "Did anyone touch you?"

I shook my head. "I don't think so."

"Good." The word was a gruff bark. Like he'd been waiting for my answer. I wondered what he would have done if the answer was yes. Then I looked over my shoulder, briefly, at Casey.

I got lucky, as far as I could remember. I couldn't account for what happened when I was passed out. Everything was fucked. I was still processing it. But more than anything, I was angry. Angry I hadn't found Kaia. Angry that one or all of those girls were possibly hurt because of me. But most of all, I was angry at Benjamin. He lied to me.

West threaded his fingers through my wet hair and pressed a kiss to the top of my head.

"Let's never do that again," I joked. He gave me a half-cocked smile that didn't quite meet his eyes. They looked as tired as they had at the cabin. Tired and soft. I brushed a hand across his jaw, enjoying the feel of his beard against my palm.

"Go eat," he muttered.

"Good night, Hale."

"Good night."

Casey was sitting on her bed watching me instead of the television. She gave her head a little shake and pursed her lips.

"What?"

"Nothing," she chuckled as I set the bags on a small table by the window. Mini donuts, chips, nuts, and several different kinds of candy. As I kept digging, I pulled out a pair of toothbrushes and a tube of toothpaste. He must have gone to a gas station or something. I stepped back and gestured to the table.

"See anything you like?"

Casey pointed to a package of chocolate donuts.

"Gimme it."

I laughed as I picked them up and handed them to her with a bottle of water. Following her lead, I grabbed a package of powdered donuts and sat down on my bed to nibble on them as we watched reruns of Friends.

After a while, we started to talk. It began with splitting a package of red licorice and laughing about how "Joey doesn't share food." Then it became about what she'd been through. The hour had gotten late and we were both curled up in our beds talking into the dark with hushed voices when she said something I didn't expect.

"I had to let them…I had to act like I enjoyed it. Make them want to keep me. Like a toy. A thing."

I didn't know what to say. I just looked at her. Her hands were tucked beneath her chin, but she was rubbing something with her thumb.

A rabbit's foot.

Casey ended up falling asleep. She slept through the hours of television I watched. Infomercials. Reruns of old sitcoms. Some black and white Western films I wasn't at all familiar with. All of it was just light and sound. None of it helped. Casey's story kept me up. She was just a woman in the wrong place at the wrong time.

Everything she explained. All of the pain she endured. It was hard not to picture what they would do to Kaia. As I tried to fall asleep, I couldn't help but wonder what they would do to someone they wanted to hurt.

⟋

CANDLES SURROUNDED THE table. Rose petals everywhere. A string quartet played soft overtures and romantic melodies. Draped in my translucent beaded gown, the one that showed the wolf tattoo, I smiled and sipped fine champagne.

But the liquid was not gold. It turned a dark clouded color. The taste of sharp fruits was replaced with deep copper. Setting the glass back down, I wiped my mouth to find my hand stained red. I looked across the table.

Benjamin leaned forward to offer his napkin. I saw a figure standing behind him. Hood drawn over their head. A flash of steel in the candlelight. Benjamin's head tumbled from his shoulders and onto the dinner plate.

The figure pulled their hood back. And I looked myself in the eye.

45

ZINGIBER OFFICINALE

The desert sun screamed through the untinted windows of West's Bronco. Clayton toyed with the radio, earning irritated barks from West now and then. "Just pick a song and stick with it." None of it bothered Casey. She leaned her head against the window frame and closed her eyes. After our talk, she'd slept all night, waking only when it was time to leave.

If I hadn't been so consumed with my thoughts, I would have been thinking about how much sleep she must be catching up on. I'd be thinking about how terrified she must have been. How hard it would have been to feel safe enough to sleep at all.

But I wasn't thinking about that. I wasn't even thinking about my sister anymore. No. I was thinking about Benjamin Camden. Benjamin fucking Camden and the wild goose chase he'd lead me on. What was the point of that? Did he think he could get rid of me for long enough to find a way out of that basement? Or was he trying to get me killed? He'd used my love for my sister against me. The hope that I'd be able to find her was enough to lure me into a situation that was terrifying and dangerous.

I had been terrified. Even when I knew who was coming for me, I was. Voluntarily drugging myself and letting myself get taken had been the dumbest thing I'd ever done in my entire adult life.

West led Casey into the house and asked Clayton to keep an eye on things outside. As soon as my feet hit the gravel, I headed to the granny flat to collect my things. My hands gathered supplies, moving with steady precision despite my rage-addled mind.

It had all been just another one of Benjamin's plans. A distraction. I'd fallen right into his trap. Again. Only this time I came out of it ready to fight. West was still inside with Casey when I hopped into the driver's seat of the Bronco, throwing my bag into the passenger's seat and peeling away. Clayton shouted something I didn't hear after me.

Benjamin Camden. That complete asshole had only scratched the surface when getting to know me. He'd made the mistake of trying to get rid of me twice. It was clear he didn't understand me when I explained my job to him. Now he was going to see exactly what I could do.

MY HEART DROWNED out the sound of my falling feet as I strode through the crowded deli. I replayed the fantasy I'd dreamed up during the drive home in my mind. The working employees who greeted me were met with silence instead of my usual friendly response. The door in the back office clicked open after I typed in the lock code and stormed down the stairs.

"Lilith," Benjamin said. The hood was on the floor. His surprise was enough to confirm my suspicion. He'd been trying to get rid of me. Again.

"I know," I said. "I'm like a bad penny. I just keep turning up."

My stride ate up the distance between us, giving him no time to prepare for me.

"That's not...what are you doing?"

An elbow connected with his nose with a crack. Benjamin's wails were muffled by his large hands flying to his newly broken septum. They weren't there to protect his stomach from my knee or his groin from my boot. He fell to his knees, breathing labored breaths through his clenched teeth. It was easy to get the needle in. Easy and so fucking satisfying to penetrate him.

I loosed the hunting knife from the sheath at my back as I waited for the sedative to flood his system. This one was potent. It would be only a minute or two. I imagined it taking root, growing into nooks and crannies like creeping vines of ivy. The restraint killed me. My shaking fingers could barely keep their grip on the leather-wrapped hilt. I wanted to destroy him. Take him apart. It would be easy. Like a hunter field dressing a deer. As I pictured removing his innards, he started to slump. It wouldn't be long, but it felt like it was taking ages. The wrath in me gnashed its teeth, waiting to be unleashed.

"You were trying to get rid of me. Again!" I screamed.

Muffled groaning was my only answer.

"My sister was never there, was she?" I hollered the question down at him. I knew the answer. I flexed my fingers as they shook around the grip of the blade. Snarling in my veins, rage urged me to end him.

He needs to pay, to pay, to pay.

His pain made him weak. Weakness that made me sick. All of those muscles were a joke. How useless they were against me. The sedative made him even weaker as he crawled away to lean against the wall. A wounded animal. An easy target. A tremor rolled under my skin, setting the little hairs on my arms standing on end. I grabbed his hand and pulled it toward me. Angling my knife against the tip of his finger, my words were a growl.

"Where is my sister, Benjamin?"

"I don't-"

His voice broke into a scream as I severed his middle finger at the first knuckle. I clenched my teeth. Rookies start with a whole finger. It's like swallowing a fine wine in gulps. Why rush when there are so many little nuances of pain to enjoy? So many parts to play with. With a yank, the next segment of his finger was ready for the blade.

"Stop lying! Do you think you can outsmart me, Benjamin? I'm still here, aren't I? Tell me where they're keeping my sister!"

A dark stain spread across his slacks. The ice-blue eyes had gone hazy with confusion and horror. I drank his fear down like water from a stream. He never truly understood who he was dealing with.

"If she's still alive," he said between gags and panting breaths. "You'll need me alive to get to her."

Clever piece of shit. I shoved Benjamin back to the floor and stood. He cradled his bleeding hand against his ruined undershirt. Small pained whimpers left his lips as he moved away from me to cower against the wall before he passed out.

Outside of my body, I saw it. Like I was looking down at us. It occurred to me then that there, in Pal's basement, Benjamin and I appeared to each other as we truly were. He was a self-serving coward. And I was a monster.

THE DRIVE BACK to the house was short. Casey and Clayton were in the yard as I pulled the Bronco into the gravel driveway. She was seated sideways in one of the iron chairs, covered in sunlight as she read the book that lay across her lap. Someone had given her some of Kaia's lounge clothes to wear.

Clayton was leaning against the patio cover pillar, keeping watch with his hand resting atop his gun. I didn't miss the glances he stole at the redhead sunning herself. Still beyond words, I slammed the car door closed and walked toward the house. Casey looked up from her book.

"Hey," she said softly. Her dark red brows furrowed as she took in my face. The blood on my hands. I hadn't bothered to wash it off, my nerves too full of my own anger to process anything else. "Lili?"

I fell to my knees and heaved.

Monster. Monster. Monster.

Casey screamed as everything I had in my stomach came hurtling out. Distantly, I registered Clayton shouting for West. My palms felt the sharp points of gravel digging in as I hurled my guts up. Tears streamed down my face. Then a big warm hand was at my back. I retched again.

"She got out of the car and just started vomiting," Casey explained. I whimpered as I swallowed down the urge to heave again. Breath sawed out of me as I squeezed my eyes shut and tried to steady myself. Gravel on my palms. Sunshine. West's hand rubbing my back. Casey asked, "Lili, are you alright?"

I must have nodded because she accepted my answer and looked at Clayton.

"I'll get the hose," he mumbled as West pulled me off the ground, scooping me into his arms. Casey disappeared into the house, leaving West and me alone in the driveway. Still unable to form words, I just looked into his eyes. They were soft, full of worry as his hand made long strokes down my back.

My breaths were shallow as he pulled me toward him. His hold enveloped me completely. Trembling, I tried to take in more air. Tried to take myself back from the hateful, violent beast that had pried control from my twisted fingers.

I left Benjamin whimpering and bleeding in Pals without a second thought. His declaration that he'd be essential to getting my sister back was the only thing keeping him alive. But standing there, looking at him. All I could think about was how satisfying it would be to take him apart. To feel his tendons sever. To pop his joints with careful dissection.

"He deserved it," I whimpered. Again. And again. Not to West. But he answered me, anyway.

"I know," he said to me quietly. "I saw."

"Here," Casey said, handing West a cup. He thanked her quietly and held it up for me.

"It's ginger ale."

I looked at Casey who jerked her chin toward the cup encouragingly. My hands were still shaking too hard to hold anything. West held the cup to my lips, gently rocking me in his lap. Clayton hosed away my sick. After a few sips from the cup, West carried me upstairs to shower off.

46

MENTHA × PIPERITA

It felt strange to be here, at first. In the house without my sister to fill it. The house had felt like it was holding its breath. Daniel's baby shampoo scent faded from the air. Laundry didn't cover every available surface in the living room. It was empty.

Then, gradually, it started to feel alive again. As I watched the people around me make themselves comfortable in the various little nooks or dig into yet another meal West cooked for all of us in the kitchen, it started to feel like a home. Kaia would have loved it.

Clayton was hunched over his laptop at the kitchen counter the way I used to be when I was jamming out papers while visiting home during college. West was cooking something in a big pot that made my mouth water. He was just putting on some rice when I strolled over from the stairwell and stood behind Clayton, looking over his shoulder at the screen before him.

"What are you looking at?"

He glanced at me, then resumed his work. On the screen were half a dozen little displays, all with similar footage rolling at the same time. Footage of a desert outpost.

"I've been monitoring the encampment with a drone camera I set up."

"When did you do that?" I asked, surprised.

"While you guys were asleep at the hotel," Clayton lowered his voice as he noted Casey sitting in the living room, still reading from the book she'd had earlier. A small smile curled the corner of the mercenary's mouth.

"The trailers are in an encampment hidden from satellite view with anti-aerial camouflage near Eagle Mountain. Half their crew is there in twenty-four-hour shifts. When they rotate out, they head to an estate a few miles away near Joshua Tree. It's this big freaky-looking building."

"How do you know that?"

"I followed them with the drone," he said, matter-of-factly.

West cleared his throat. Clayton looked up at him and nodded.

"Anyway," he muttered. "No sign of your sister. Just like you thought."

His declaration felt wrong somehow. It scratched against my mind like an ill-fitting wool sweater. Not right. My gut clenched with a sick sort of knowing. If he saw no sign of her, that was one thing. But that didn't mean she wasn't there.

I'd plopped down on the sofa to keep Casey company while I waited for dinner. Then dinner came to me. Clayton and Casey shared the other sofa. Though he kept a comfortable distance from her, I noticed her body language was gradually becoming more relaxed around the oddball mercenary. She let the deep recesses of the sofa swallow her. Her hands were in the pockets of her sweatpants.

West's hand rested on my thigh as we sat in the living room, scooping dark orange curry into our mouths while watching an old animated film. None of us felt up to watching anything with more teeth and Casey said that she appreciated the predictability of a film she'd seen countless times before.

"I don't think I can handle any more surprises. Not for a while," she said quietly.

While everyone else placed their empty bowls on the coffee table, I let mine sit in my lap. The curry was delicious. A beautiful terracotta color and rich. The rice was fluffy and nice. Really. West was putting the beautiful marble kitchen to better use than my sister ever had. There was no way she owned all of those spices. He had to have brought them from somewhere. The cookware, though it was incredibly high-end, was old and had belonged to my grandmother. Having barely made a dent in the stewed meat and rice, I felt guilty about not finishing. A small part of me wished it was takeout. Wished it was my sister sitting next to me, watching a movie with Daniel. West stood to take the bowls into the kitchen, then took the bowl from me.

"I'm sorry," I said weakly.

He said nothing, instead heading to the kitchen to tidy up. Refocusing on the film, I tried to relax. Tried and failed. I tried not to focus on the man who seemed to always be taking care of me. How long would it be before he was sick of this routine? Lilith Caccia, the project. The fixer-upper. Guilt continued to swallow me as I watched him return with a piece of toast and a cup of tea. They were placed carefully on the table before me.

THE SOUND OF the centrifuge drowned out my raging thoughts. Sleep couldn't find me tonight. I stared at the ceiling, following shadows with my eyes and creating patterns in them. West had begged me to stay in bed. Said that there wasn't anything more I could do today. Told me that I needed rest. I'd complied, laying in his embrace until I was sure sleep had taken him. Then I slipped out. To my work.

Prune. Pluck. Propagate. Grind. Steep.

Muscle memory made everything possible. Though I glanced at my open notebooks on the worn wooden worktop, I could have done the work blindfolded. The resistance of dried berries and herbs in the mortar bowl scratched at my internally fraying edges.

"I think I can help you."

I startled and looked up from the worktable, not expecting to find Casey standing in the doorway. With what looked to be Clayton's hoodie pulled over her small frame. Deciding not to read too much into that, I put the pestle down in the bowl and propped my hands on the marred wooden surface.

"So you can't sleep either," I joked.

She shrugged and looked around the room. Her still-tired brown eyes were all the confirmation I needed. I imagined it would be a while before she slept soundly. I wouldn't blame her if she never slept again.

"You need someone to back you up with your family. The family, I mean. I can help you."

I arched an eyebrow, silently urging her to continue.

"My dad."

An involuntary laugh burst from my lips. Not at her offer. The last thing I wanted to do was laugh at Casey, but I couldn't help it. It was kind of her to want to help me, but the idea of Ronan Arawn helping me was like a Capulet helping a Montague or a spider helping a fly.

"I'm sorry," I apologized with an uncomfortable chuckle. "I'm not sure you understand how much he hates my family."

"Clayton told me he's helping the guy who took over your family. Ozzie? My dad would never do that unless it was beneficial to him in some way. If he's helping Ozzie it's because my dad can use him later."

I blinked. I hadn't been aware of any conversation between Casey and Clayton, nor had I known that they'd been talking about my problems. I wondered if she and the mercenary were more comfortable together than I had realized. Maybe that was where she got the oversized blue hoodie she was wearing now.

I could understand it. Before everything had happened, Casey was easy to talk to. She'd told me about her life and I'd told her about some of mine. We'd traded small secrets and inside jokes. An image of her ex-boyfriend I'd scared the literal piss out of while looking for her flashed through my mind. Clayton would be a welcome change from that puddle of a man.

Casey sat on the stool and folded her sleeve-covered hands on the table. She seemed to have arrived at her point but I still wasn't following. I pinched the bridge of my nose and squeezed my eyes shut, willing patience to return to me before speaking.

"What exactly are you saying?"

"Make him a better offer."

The declaration was no-nonsense. More certain than I'd heard her before. After dumping the crushed berries into a pot, I scraped out the bowl and set it back down on the table. I looked down at the bowl and took a breath. This might be a very, bad idea. But that wasn't exactly a deal breaker for me lately.

"You realize that he'll probably blow my brains out before I can open my mouth."

"I can get you a meeting with him," she said defensively.

Neither of us said anything for a minute. Though I was entirely awake, I wasn't sure my brain was working properly because it actually sounded like it might be a good idea. Working with Ronan Arawn would be a foolish gamble on a good day. A death sentence on a bad one.

But for Kaia, I had to try.

"Fine. Call him."

"I don't need to call him. I know exactly where he is. It's where he always is."

THE LATE HOUR filled the air with thick silence as Casey and I walked through the yard to head back into the house. She eyed the garden and pulled the hood of the sweatshirt she'd been wearing up over her red curls.

"Can I ask you something?" She said, her voice cutting through my foggy mind.

"Sure."

"Are you and West together? You didn't answer when I asked you before. You guys act like you care. About each other."

I blinked. I didn't know why but I wasn't expecting that. Wrapping my arms around myself, I took a breath. Then another.

"I don't know," I sighed. "He's amazing. It feels amazing. But things in my life are too complicated. I don't think I would be good for him right now." Ever.

"Oh," she lowered her voice. "I'm sorry. But you guys seem so much like a couple. The way he looks after you is-"

"We're not a couple."

Casey blinked.

"Lili."

Casey and I turned toward the house to see West standing at the back door. In the darkness, I could only make out his sweatpants and messy bun, but there he was. There was no way he didn't hear what Casey had said. Or what I had. Fantastic.

My conversation with Casey hadn't been meant for his ears. Not because it would hurt his feelings. But because even I knew what I said hadn't been the truth. He knew it, too.

"Good night," Casey said as she crept past West, into the house. He nodded at her and braced his arms on the frame, blocking my path.

"Sorry," I said. "I couldn't sleep."

"We're not a couple?"

I squeezed my eyes shut and tilted my head back in anguish. Goddamnit.

"Can we not do this right now? I don't have the brain space for this conversation."

The dark shadows of the wisteria blocked his face from mine, only allowing light to fall on his eyes. Green. Tired. Hurt. I saw his bare stomach flex with a tight inhale and slow exhale. He stepped aside, lifting an arm for me to pass.

"Right. Fine."

47

URTICA DIOICA

Standing in the doorway of the Chancer, my hands started to shake. *This may be the dumbest thing I have ever done*, I thought with a small chuckle to myself. Second only to letting Benjamin Camden trick me into falling for him, there was this. No, wait. Letting myself get captured and then having to bust out was incredibly stupid.

Walking to the long mahogany bar, my knees started to wobble. This place was nice. If I wasn't scared for my life, I would have been impressed by the thoughtful decor and impressive array of fine whiskeys. Was that a grouse or a pheasant? Before I could speak a word to the bartender, my stomach churned.

The smoking skull tattoo on his hand caught my eye as he polished a glass. An Arawn man. Just like every other man here. Scrawny compared to the other men sitting around the tufted brown leather booth that was heavily occupied toward the back of the bar. Blonde hair and a mustache. He narrowed his eyes behind his round frame glasses at me. This was definitely a bad idea.

"Two pints of Guinness," Casey commanded. "And tell Ronan that Casey wants to see him."

"You really think you can come in here and start giving orders?" He said with a glance at me. Shit.

"When Ronan finds out who's looking for him, it'll be you who's in real trouble. I suggest you get us our drinks fast and deliver my message."

The bartender muttered a curse as he pulled two pints of beer from the tap, gently placing the first one in front of Casey. The other was placed a little less gently in front of me, the head of the dark beer sloshing over the side to make a little mess on the wooden bar top. I gave the bartender a flat look. It's not like I had the Caccia tattoo on my forearm. My hair was down around my shoulders, so no one could see the one on my neck. When the bartender left to deliver her message, I turned to Casey.

"I think they might know who I am," I whispered.

"For all they know, you're just some random Italian friend of mine. But they're cautious."

"Casey, don't tell West or Clayton about this."

"I won't. It was my idea, remember? Can you just relax?"

I shrugged and eyed the beer. I'd seen him pull it. There was no way he could have done anything to it, right?

"He didn't poison it if that's what you're wondering," Casey said as she picked up her own to take a generous gulp. "Come on, you're going to need it."

With a low laugh, I picked up the glass and took a pull. Then another. And another. Gently placing the glass back on its little cardboard coaster, I looked around the room. The pub was the kind of place I could see myself drinking in if I weren't a Caccia. Wood paneling covered most of the walls to match the bar. Pale cream-colored paint covered the rest, making the black iron shelving behind the bar look that much more severe. Old mirrored liquor signs added a touch of nostalgia to the place. They reflected the low light emanating from the frosted globes that dangled over every table.

Casey's gaze migrated to the gathering of men at the booth, then the door situated behind it. The door swung open and the bartender stepped out, making his way back to us.

"He'll see you in back. Bring your friend."

It occurred to me as we made our way toward the back room that I had never actually set eyes on Ronan Arawn. Only his cronies. My eyes drifted over the men around the back booth. Each of them looked at me like I was a mouse and they were feral alley cats.

"Wait," one of the more dangerous-looking alley cats said to the bartender as he readied to push open the door for us. His grey eyes assessed me, then Casey. "Did you bother to check them for weapons, Charlie?"

The man rose from the booth, shoving the wiry man next to him out in the process. He pushed up the sleeves of his black sweater and crossed his arms, looking down at us with cruel skepticism in his eyes. His hand bore the smoking skull tattoo, but the work was lost in a sea of colorful ink that seemed to cover both of his well-muscled arms.

"You're here to see Ronan?" He asked in a thick Irish accent, looking over Casey and then me again. Casey cleared her throat, grabbing his attention.

"I am," she said with a clearer voice than I'd ever heard. "I heard he's been looking for me so stop being difficult, Killian."

The man's dark eyebrows shot up his forehead as her words seemed to shake a memory loose.

"Casey? I haven't seen you in years." His voice softened, gentler than a moment before. She nodded. "You're alright. Jesus. Come here."

I could have fainted from the sudden shift in his attitude. They embraced for a minute as he let a laugh out into her shoulder, then picked her up. As he set her back down, his eyes shot to me.

"Who is this?" Long tattooed fingers scratched at his thick brown beard with aggressive curiosity. The word "fate" was written in bold black letters across his knuckles.

"This is my friend."

"Does your friend have any weapons on her?" He glanced at the man who'd gotten up and cocked his head toward me. "He's going to give her a pat down."

Before I could object, his lean friend was running his hands up my legs and over my ass. When they reached the knife clipped at my back, I winced. He pulled it free from the holster and tossed it on the table.

"Bit oversized for a pocketknife," Killian said with a wink. "Keep that safe for her, will you, Joe?"

"I'll need that back. It was a gift." I said, trying my best not to sound threatening.

The lean man grunted and continued to pat me down, finding nothing else. Another grunt confirmed he'd finished, and Killian stepped forward, herding us toward the door.

"Best not to keep him waiting long."

Suddenly grateful for my long sleeves, a shiver covered my skin in goosebumps as the hinges squeaked. Casey and I entered, with Killian behind us. The large room was as nicely decorated as the rest of the bar. Except this room had one long table in the center of it, with a brick fireplace roaring at one side.

Sitting before the fireplace, at the head of the table, was a man who matched Killian in almost every way. The only difference was that instead of brown hair, this man had black hair peppered with silver strands. A well-tailored grey three-piece suit covered what appeared to be a lean and muscled form. The man looked up from his conversation and stood.

"Casey, my darling girl," he said with a smile and another rolling Irish accent. He approached us, searching Casey for any sign of injury. "I was so worried about you. Where have you been?"

"Hi, Dad," she said weakly. Her shoulders tensed at his increasing nearness. He smiled, which was a far cry from the cold expression I'd seen when we came in, and ran a hand over her red curls. His dark brown eyes matched Casey's. So did his mouth. When his attention turned to me, his mouth twisted into a sneer. My blood turned cold as the kindness in his eyes was immediately extinguished, turning violent when he asked the question I'd been dreading.

"What exactly are you doing bringing the Caccia bitch into my bar?"

48

ALLIUM SATIVUM

Strong hands shoved me down as Ronan resumed his seat at the head of the table. With my face pressed against it, my eyes were level with a thick cigar resting in a chipped glass ashtray with a gin logo on it. He picked it up and snipped the tip-off, lighting it with a few soft puffs. Casey had been directed to sit beside him. I was bent over the table with Killian's loaded gun to my head and his elbow in my back. Fantastic.

"Where have you been, my darling girl? I was worried something awful about you. Had everyone looking for you."

Casey looked at me, the unspoken apology bright in her eyes. With half of my face smashed into the hardwood surface, it was difficult to convey anything but discomfort back to her. She looked at her father and let out a shaky breath.

"I was kidnapped."

I heard Killian's gun cock, readying to fire a bullet into my head. Shit. My breath came out in short desperate puffs, fogging the shining surface of the table. I squeezed my eyes shut, hoping the bullet Killian fired would end me quickly.

"Not by her! Not by them. She saved me," Casey hastily spat out.

Ronan looked at Killian and cocked his head in silent command. The gun barrel left my temple at the same time as the arm pressing into my back released me. I stood, rubbing my jaw to get some feeling back into my face. Ronan nodded toward the chair next to Casey. I took it, trying to stifle the annoyance I felt at being manhandled.

"Explain," he said, taking a drag from the cigar that filled the room with its expensive scent. Killian took a seat on the other side of the table, his eyes pinned on me. He placed his gun on the table within easy reach of his tattooed fingers, the barrel still angled in my direction. I glanced at them, reading the word "love." Did his knuckles say "Love fate?" Before I could open my mouth, Casey continued.

"Well...I joined a dating service," Casey sighed, as though hoping for a partner was the dumbest thing she'd ever done. Pity tugged at me. What happened would never be her fault. If my jaw wasn't sore from the table's impact, I would have told her that.

"They have parties, mixers, where you can meet other members. I went to one and ended up being drugged by the man I was talking to. The one who asked me to come in the first place. As it turned out, he was involved in...I was..."

Casey was quiet for a moment, squeezing her hands to stop the small tremors that had affected her voice. We all watched her close her eyes and take a breath, waiting for her to go on. I wanted to give her my hand to hold. To tell her it was alright. That she was alright. But remained still, unsure if my comforting touches would be tolerated by her or by anyone else in the room.

"She was trafficked," I offered. Casey gave me a grateful look. The room was silent. Ronan set his cigar down in the ashtray, looking down at the table to summon a response that wasn't born out of pure rage.

"You were gone for two months," Ronan said quietly. "Are you alright?"

"Yeah," she rasped. "I am now. A lot happened. But," Casey sighed and looked at me. "She found me. They took her, too. But she got us out."

Ronan's dark eyes moved to me. They narrowed in quiet assessment. A small part of me wondered if he was going to eat me alive. He picked up his whiskey and knocked it back, washing whatever emotion he was feeling out of his mouth. He leaned back in his seat and said, "Thank you."

Ronan Arawn thanked me. The man who wanted my entire family erased from the city thanked me. It was hard not to remember all of the trouble he'd caused. Burning down the Bootlegger, our family's restaurant. Stealing from us. Teaming up with Ozzie to overthrow my sister. I gave a tight nod, unsure as to how to respond. His gratitude wasn't a guarantee that I'd leave this room alive. Nor did it promise that he'd give me what I came to ask for. Still, I had to try.

"I let them take me. Found out about this trafficking ring by accident. When Casey and another girl disappeared from our club, my sister Kaia asked me to find them."

"Why isn't she here now, then? Taking credit for this rescue. Using it to negotiate. Not very wise of her to miss such an opportunity."

"They took my sister. The same people that took her, I think," I said, nodding toward Casey. "I found Casey because I got lucky, but I was looking for my sister."

"So you wouldn't have bothered to find my daughter. It was just a happy accident then."

Ronan's hand flexed and bunched into a fist.

"That's not what I meant. I was looking for her. But the other girl was dead. I wasn't sure I was ever going to find her."

"Lucky for you then."

Fuck, this was going poorly. The likelihood of me leaving this room with my skull intact was dwindling by the second.

"The point is she found me. She found me and she rescued me when she could have left me there," Casey interjected with a pointed look at Killian. Was this her brother?

I could see Ronan weighing his options, dropping thoughts on each side of the scales he used to measure the burden of our rivalry. He cleared his throat, ready to roast me with whatever he said next.

"You killed Brian Donnelly."

"I've killed a lot of people, Mr. Arawn. You'll have to refresh my memory."

He gave a mirthless laugh and tapped his cigar on the ashtray. Leaning forward, he propped himself up on the arm he rested atop the table. I kept my back straight but loosened my shoulders. Unbothered. He was a growling dog. I needed to show no fear.

"Brian fucking Donnelly. One of my men. Had a family. A wife and children. He was taken by your people and never seen again. Until little bits of him washed up on the beach a week later."

A gun firing. The bright red splatter of blood and brain on white tiled walls. Suddenly I remembered Brian. Remembered exactly who killed him. It took more effort than it should have to keep from smiling at the memory of the man's death. This was it. Exactly the opportunity I needed.

"I remember Brian now," I said calmly. "Do you want me to tell you exactly who killed him? Because it wasn't me."

"Why should I believe one word out of your fucking mouth?" He snarled the question through his teeth.

"You can and you should, Mr. Arawn. I am my sister's right hand. I know how your business operates. You know as well as I do that who you do business with matters more than anything."

Ronan gave an annoyed wave of his hand in my direction, urging me to go on as he refilled his glass. I took a breath and made sure to look him in the eye before I revealed what I knew. I hoped he'd see the truth in my eyes.

"My sister asked me to interrogate Brian Donnelly after he burned down our restaurant. To learn how he acquired certain information. I had two men with me. One of them killed him before I could extract the information I needed."

Ronan looked to Killian, who nodded at what I'd said. He'd known this part. That Donnelly had burned down our restaurant. Hell, the order had probably come from someone in this room. Possibly Killian, based on the nod.

"It was Ozzie. Ozzie Grasso was the man who put a bullet in Brian Donnelly's head."

A flex of his fingers was the only reaction Ronan seemed to allow himself. Ozzie had fired the bullet into Donnelly's head to shut him up. I hoped that would be enough rope for Ozzie to hang himself with. He hadn't told his new partner that, that was for certain now. I looked Ronan over as I hoped the seed of doubt in his partner was strong enough to take root. Ronan gave a small nod to someone behind me. I heard the door swing open as that someone departed from our company. Maybe he was tiring of me already. Getting things in place to remove me.

"So, what do you want from me?" His voice was smooth. Casual. Like a king waiting for the peasant kneeling in his throne room to beg him for a loaf of bread.

"Simple. Withdraw your support from Ozzie Grasso. He's already betrayed you by killing one of your men. I'm assuming he told you I did that. Now he's taken a seat that doesn't belong to him. I want it back, but I can't take it with your men backing him up."

"Why should I help an enemy regain their position when I've got someone there who owes me?"

The door opened again as footsteps advanced from behind me. Another bottle of whiskey was placed on the table. Several bulbous glasses landed beside it with a clink. Nicer stuff than what Ronan was drinking like water. His order for more whiskey was proof enough that I'd at least gotten him to listen. My shoulders sagged with the weight of relief of seeing a bottle instead of more guns. Or a body bag.

"Because you can't trust him. He swore an oath of loyalty to us and then turned on my family. He'll turn on you as soon as you stop being useful to him. With me in the seat, you'll have a partner who is more powerful than he could ever be."

Killian picked up the bottle and started pouring into the glasses. First, he gave a glass to Ronan. Then Casey. Then himself. An empty one remained beside the bottle.

"He can't trust you." Killian's words were a low growl, contrasted by the rolling accent that made them sound sweeter than they were.

"Maybe not," I breathed, turning my attention to him. "It would be foolish for you to change your mind about me, and I don't take you for fools. But I can make a deal."

Ronan gave another irritated laugh and looked at Killian. I didn't miss the "can you believe this bitch" expression on his face.

"If I'm allowed to replace him, I will owe you," I said as I looked back at Ronan. "I'm a Caccia. A Caccia by blood. There are a lot of things that an outsider like Ozzie wouldn't know. Things I can use to help you. My name means something in this city, just like yours does. Withdraw your support for him. Support me."

To say you could hear a pin drop in the room would be an understatement. Every set of eyes was glued to Ronan, waiting for his answer. Seconds passed. Maybe minutes. He scratched his stubble-covered jaw, looking briefly at Killian, then at Casey. She put a hand on mine. Ronan reached for the whiskey, uncapping the bottle. He refilled his glass. Then picked up the remaining empty glass, filling it to the widest point of the bulb. A quick flick of his wrist had the glass sliding forward. To me.

"Lilith Caccia," he sighed. "You're going to owe me one hell of a fucking favor."

49

HYDRASTIS CANADENSIS

Being allowed to leave the Chancer alive was the only outcome I'd hoped for. Being aligned with the Arawn Clan was an outcome I couldn't have predicted in a million years. The satisfied smirk on Casey's face, as we hitched ourselves into the Bronco, told me it was exactly what she had expected.

Ronan agreed to withdraw his support from Ozzie in both the symbolic and literal sense of the word. When Ozzie was killed, and he would be very soon, his men would have nowhere to run. Nico would be safe with me and any other men who chose to remain loyal to the family. But Ozzie's crew would have to support me or die. And going to Ronan would be another sort of death sentence.

"I hate fucking cowards," he'd said between puffs of his cigar. "If any of his guys come to me, my men will be under strict orders to dispose of them. Starting with their cowardly tongues."

After our lengthy discussion about what the next steps would be, Ronan changed the subject back to family business with his daughter. Upon the change in conversation, Killian took out his phone and stood from the table. When his father nodded, releasing him from the meeting, Killian disappeared from the room.

Arawn business had waited long enough.

"So," Casey said as we pulled away from the bar. "I don't know if I can go back to Muse."

I shot her a confused look as I put the Bronco into gear. Not the conversation I'd been expecting but I thought maybe it was best to let her finish.

"I just don't think that life is for me anymore."

It would probably be a while before she was ready to be touched by someone she trusted, let alone a stranger. None of us had touched her since leaving the camp. Leaving life at Muse behind made sense. I wouldn't argue the point in a million years.

Instead, I asked...

"So, what do you think you'll do now?"

"First I'm going to eat dinner," she said. I huffed a small laugh, remembering that we'd promised to bring dinner home after running some errands. "Then I think I'm going to work for my father."

GLOWING GOLDEN WINDOWS looked over the yard like warm yellow eyes as the clouds went from pink to periwinkle, the early evening already darkening the skies. Paper bags rustled as Casey jumped out of the truck with the Vietnamese we'd picked up.

"I'm starving," she said as she shut the door behind her.

"Yeah," I sighed. "Remember, don't say a word to West or Clayton about where we were. Alright?"

Casey nodded.

"Why don't we just tell them?"

I could have said that it was because I didn't want West there. Because I didn't want a fight to start. Because I couldn't stand the idea of putting anyone in danger but myself. Not him.

"Because," I started.

"Where the fuck have you two been?" Clayton asked as he came barreling out of the house. "It's been like four hours."

Casey shrugged and hoisted the bags into the air.

"We went to my apartment. I needed clothes. Anyway, we brought food."

A lie by omission is still a lie. We had gone to her apartment. We packed a bag full of things for her to wear. Her father had paid the rent while she was missing, a detail he'd shared over a second glass of whiskey. I closed the rear of the Bronco, rolling the small suitcase with me as I walked toward the house.

Clayton took the bags of food from Casey, lifting one to sniff the contents. Without another word, he walked toward the house with Casey on his heels. I followed them indoors and looked around for the six-and-a-half-foot man I'd been avoiding all day.

"Where's West?"

"He went to the range," Clayton said as he set the containers of food on the counter. Then he gave me a strange look. Something mixed with exasperation and pity. Pity?

WEST HADN'T COME back by the time I went to bed. It was strange how quickly I'd gotten used to having him beside me. His warmth. His scent. Even the snoring. I rolled over once. Then again. Then I flipped the pillow over for a cooler touch. The door opened. I caught a glimpse of a tattooed arm. A phone landed on the bed next to me. Then the door closed again.

He'd come back. Ignoring the relief I felt at seeing him, even if it was just his hand, I wondered how long he'd been home. Where he was sleeping. If he was sleeping at all. If he hated me. I picked up the phone to look at it. The message on West's phone was clear and it was for me.

Get ready.

Nico. We had laid out our plan in detail weeks ago at dinner. He'd sent word to Ozzie. Pretended to get a letter from me. One that I'd written in the comfort of his father's home. Every word written in it was for Ozzie's benefit. In it, I said that I was "so scared" and "without the family, I have nothing." I'd gone on and on about not knowing what to do with myself and asking if he thought of a way for me to come back. I'd "do anything."

I had to tamp down the anger. The rising dread. It wouldn't be long before I was faced with the challenge we'd agreed on in advance. Gladius. A literal fight for my life. My position. My fingers fisted in the sheets as I let the phone fall to the side. I didn't know what tasted worse, the idea that Nico was in danger or that the family thought I was capable of behaving like such a coward.

Nico would suggest a Gladius match. Tell the family about his father's match. Suggest that I wouldn't be able to win against Ozzie and the man could keep his seat for good. All while half of his crew was in Las Vegas to see a fight. The real fight was going to be happening without them.

I looked down at the phone that chirped with another alert from Nico.

Gladius is on. Two days. More details soon.

It worried me. Nico was sticking his neck out for me. Of course, he was framing it like he'd be bringing me in for justice. Nico was playing on the one thing that Ozzie had none of: loyalty. As far as Ozzie was concerned, Nico was loyal to the family. And he was. My family.

50

DENDRANTHEMA GRANDIFLORA

Anxiety set my feet to walking. The house was quiet with sleep as I slipped down the stairs. Down to the living room, where I didn't find West. Instead, there was the mercenary, splayed on the sofa like a dog. I'd not heard anyone go up the stairs to Daniel's room, so I decided to check outside. With a deep breath, I stepped out onto the terrace.

Still nothing and no one. Where could he have gone? The cold night air bit at my exposed skin. Around the house, the neighborhood had gone quiet. Everything was coated in a fine layer of dew. I'd almost given up to go back inside when I saw it. A puff of steam from beside the Bronco.

He hadn't seen me. Or heard me. Facing away from the house, West was leaning against the Bronco. Still dressed. His head jerked toward me as my shoes crunched on the gravel driveway.

"You know the house has a pretty elaborate security system," I said quietly. "No need to stand guard."

West gave an annoyed huff. Maybe I was finally starting to get on the man's nerves. Maybe he was getting ready to leave. The last few weeks had likely maxed out his patience.

"Go back to bed."

Always telling me what to do. I rolled my neck, trying to lose the wave of irritation I felt at his command. This act was starting to get on my nerves. I continued to push, stepping closer so I could look him in the eye. Even in the dark.

"Why are you out here?"

"I'm not tired. Go back to bed."

"No. I'm not a mind reader, damnit. Can you just talk to me?" I let out an exasperated sigh. "God, what do you want?"

West's arm shot out to grab my wrist. With a hard tug and a turn, my back was against the truck. He leaned in. The man I knew. The one who I'd trained with every day. The one who was seemingly unbothered by the rest of the world. I'd known that there was more beneath the surface. I was not prepared for this.

"I know exactly what I want, Lili." The edge of his thumb skated along my lip. It traced its path backward. I pulled my lip in between my teeth, looking up into dark eyes. West glanced at the house.

"Get in."

He opened the door. Pushed the passenger seat forward. My feet were frozen in place.

"Get in the fucking truck, Lili."

I climbed inside, choosing the seat opposite the open door. The reprieve of distance was short-lived. West hauled himself inside. One hand braced on the frame behind me. The other encircled my thigh, giving a hard yank until my back was flat against the seat.

"Don't test me," his command was a rattling growl.

His knee pushed up between my legs. I jerked and wriggled beneath him.

"I'm not here to play games. Tell other people whatever you want about us. But I'm getting sick of having this goddamn conversation. You're the one who came looking for me. You're the one who needs something here. You seek me out when you want to feel better."

His teeth were bared as he snarled his next words. The feel of his breath on my neck coupled with the friction of his knee was doing things to me. Making my head fuzzy. I writhed in his hold.

"I've made it pretty fucking clear what I want. But in case you need it spelled out one more time, here it is. I want you. Now tell me."

The press of his body over mine. His knee between my thighs. Hot breaths against my skin as he spoke. I felt like a dog, rolling over and showing West my belly. The thought of his teeth around my neck was enough to make me squirm.

"I don't want you," I stammered, finding it difficult to get everything out. West stiffened above me. I wasn't sure he was breathing. I tried again.

"I mean, I do. Want you. I just don't want you to get hurt. I swear I'm not playing games with you. But you'll just get hurt. I can't let that happen to you."

I wasn't sure I was even making sense. But somewhere between the nonsense, it felt like I was telling the truth. West's jaw worked as he sighed through his nose, squeezing his eyes closed before he looked at me again.

"Why do you think I'll get hurt?"

I sat up, pushing him off of me. His weight. The small cab of the truck. Everything felt like it was pressing in. I couldn't breathe like this.

"Look at my life, West! My sister is missing. Aside from Daniel, everyone else I love is dead. If you...I just can't."

West looked at me before he got out of the Bronco without saying another word. He just stood there in the dark, looking at me. I almost didn't hear him as I started back toward the house. Chose to ignore the voice that found me in the dark.

"You think you're protecting me."

HEAVY BOOTS THUDDED at the foot of the bed. I stirred, noting that I'd curled up on West's pillow. He sat at the foot of the bed, peeling off his clothes until only his boxer briefs remained. I sat up and scooted back to my side of the bed.

"Where did you and Casey go today?"

I sighed and rubbed my eyes. Tugging the blanket up around myself, I looked him over. Though I was unsure if it was the late hour or the look on West's face, I couldn't bring myself to carry on with another lie.

"What do you know about the Arawn Clan?"

"Your sister seemed pretty concerned that they'd kill you. Like I told you before."

He stood and walked to his side of the bed, picking up the pillow to position it for himself. The temptation to scoot toward him and feel his warmth was almost too much. My hand fisted in the sheet. Satisfied with the pillow, he sat down and started running his hands through his hair.

"Anything else?" I asked, unsure about what I was hoping for. That he knew more? Or that this was all he knew?

"Just what I've seen in the news. Irish mob. Los Angeles based but strong ties to Belfast," he said with a small shrug as he tied his hair into a messy knot with an elastic. I continued.

"Well, Casey is Ronan Arawn's daughter. He's their boss. So she took me to see him. He and I made a deal."

West leaned back against the headboard and pulled his legs up onto the bed. I chewed my lip waiting for what he'd say next. After scrubbing his hands down his face, he propped his arm on his knee and turned to me.

"Why?"

I looked down at my lap, letting the blanket fall as my hands wrung together. My voice was quiet when I answered him.

"I needed Ronan in my corner. He was supporting Ozzie but now he's going to support me," I sighed. "That text message from Nico? It was about Gladius. In two days, I'm going back to Muse. I going to have to fight. And I need to win."

A hand covered mine. Squeezed it.

"I know. We've got some training to do, Trouble."

51

PUNICA GRANATUM

TWELVE YEARS AGO

Blood welled at the small wound on my forearm. I lifted it to examine the injury more closely. Not deep enough to leave a scar, but it stung like a paper cut. I sucked in air through my clenched teeth as pain lanced through my wound and looked at my attacker. Nonno shook his head and walked toward me, rolling up the sleeves of his pressed white shirt. We'd been out here for hours, working on my knife skills.

"No, no. You hold the blade away from yourself. Strike like an asp. Move like water." His callused fingers fixed my hold on the handle. Then he moved my arm for me in a smooth serpentine motion. Again. Again. Again as he helped my muscles to retain the memory of the movement. Satisfied, he nodded. "Show me."

His move away from me was a thing of beauty, practiced after decades. I'd seen him out here fighting for hours and hours with Lupo, always ready for any challenger. Even in his sixties, he was strong. Lean. He could move with the speed and agility of a man half his age. My strike, even with this practice, resulted in nothing more than a tear to the shoulder of his shirt. He looked down at the marred fabric and gave me a proud grin.

"Much better, mia principessa."

"Matteo!" Lupo approached us from the driveway. "You're needed at the office."

Nonno nodded and walked toward the car that idled in the driveway for him. His shoes crunched on the limestone driveway as he turned to shout at Lupo.

"Grab my jacket. My granddaughter has destroyed a lovely shirt," he said with a wink in my direction. Pushing a hand through his salt and pepper hair, he smiled. "Bambina, practice with the target until dinner."

The air was starting to get crisp as the sun disappeared from the yard. Lights glimmered overhead. The throwing knives he'd given to me only weeks ago sat on the table, waiting for me to begin target practice. The black steel blades ate up any light that attempted to touch them. I let my touch drift across their honed edges before picking them up, sliding each one into the holster I wrapped around my thigh.

"You have to mean it."

I looked over my shoulder to see Kaia standing in the doorway. She'd been here for hours, working on the family books and doing other accounting for Nonno. Just barely out of college, she was working to make the family more financially solvent than we had ever been. Based on the increasing amounts of money Nonno made, she was doing an excellent job. We weren't just making money from family businesses, shady loans, underground poker games, or unlicensed boxing matches. Now we had money coming in from online gaming. If the Caccias were small potatoes before, now we're big potatoes. Russets, even.

Kaia walked toward me, taking off her blazer to reveal the sleeveless red silk blouse beneath. The color looked as rich as blood in the waning evening sun. As I looked at her, I wondered what our mother would have looked like at this age. She held out a hand to me and I set my blades in her awaiting open palm. With her other hand, she grabbed a blade by the tip and held it up with one eye on me.

"These are for defense. To keep your attacker away from you. They are meant to save your life."

She threw the first blade, swift as a striking cobra. Bullseye.

"Someone who is trying to kill you will not hesitate. A bad throw will end you."

Bullseye.

"This knife might be all that stands between you and death."

Bullseye.

Kaia turned to me and smiled a little at what must have been a dumbstruck expression on my face, my mouth hanging open. My sister never failed to surprise me. She folded her arms across her chest and nodded her head toward the target.

"How are you so fucking good at everything?" I asked with a groan, heading to retrieve the knives.

"Practice," she said in that matter-of-fact tone that made me want to punch her.

"Practice," I repeated under my breath. "I practice."

Kaia approached me, putting both of her hands on my shoulders so she could look me in the eye.

"You've been doing this for only a few weeks, Lili. I've had years to perfect it. Give it time."

I WALKED TO the target and pulled the knives from the splintering wood. With a heavy sigh, I bent to pick up the ones that had clattered to the concrete patio. Muttered curses were my only company. Sheathing the blades in the holster, I returned to my position and began throwing again. *Mean it*, I thought.

It was after midnight by the time Nonno returned from the office, long after everyone else had gone to sleep. Except for me. One light remained on inside. Kaia never went to bed until her work was done. But only the glowing trattoria lights illuminated the patio and my target. The iron gates squeaked, alerting me to his return.

The tires hissed and crackled on the gravel driveway as the driver pulled his big black Land Rover in slowly. Lights bounced off of the waxed surface of the sedan as it crept away, leaving its passenger to walk toward me. He rubbed at his eyes with his thumb and forefinger. As he got closer, I could hear him tsk.

"Mia principessa," Nonno said with mild admonishment in his voice. "You should be in bed. You have school in the morning."

I gave a tired shrug. Even half-awake, school was easy for me. A breeze, actually. This was something I needed to conquer.

"Just once more, Nonno. Please?"

Nonno let out a tired sigh and took off his jacket, draping it over a chair at the large iron table beside us. He frowned at the ice-cold dinner of roast chicken and roasted vegetables that had been brought out to me and ignored. The tear I'd sliced into his shirt gaped with the movement. Only now the hole showed my work. I'd drawn blood.

"Alright," he said, gesturing to the target. "Begin."

52

ALTHAEA

West walked into One Two before I did, holding the door open for me and then following up behind. Even though we had been here before to protect Lanna, now it felt like we were coming home. One of the trainers was working with a boxer, filling the gym with the slapping sound of leather on leather as he hit the punching mitts.

"Home sweet home," West laughed as he approached his locker. I opened mine beside him. He shucked off his shirt and began strapping on his wrist wraps. A lump took form in my throat as my eyes tracked his flexing muscles.

I want you.

I remembered the way he caged me in with those arms. The heat in his green eyes as he told me exactly what he wanted. The broad muscles of his back flexed as he stretched, walking toward the sparring mats. My cheeks flushed at my cowardice.

"So this fight is just you and another guy?"

I blinked myself back to rational thought. Flexing my fingers in my wraps, I followed West onto the mat.

"It's a knife fight, but there aren't any rules. Submit or die. Just me and him."

"You and Ozzie?"

"I hope. But there's a chance it won't be. If he fights me, I can take over the family while Kaia's gone. If not, then I'll need to figure something else out."

"Alright," West said as he stretched. "Let's work on some defensive maneuvers."

"Don't worry," I said. "I called in an expert."

"ARE YOU SURE you want to do this?" I asked. "I don't want to hurt you."

At just after ten, the gym was dimly lit. Daniel slept soundly on the old sofa in the office. I glanced toward the shut door, worried about all the noise we were about to make.

"When was the last time you trained with a knife?"

"I've done my fair share of work with a knife lately, Lu."

"Yeah, against regular guys. Do you think Ozzie is a regular guy? Do you think he's going to let you fight someone with no skill? No."

"You sure you're up for that?" I climbed into the ring and rolled my shoulders. "The guy I'm fighting is probably going to be a few centuries younger than you. With less cancer, too, probably."

Lupo groaned as he stretched his back and lifted his middle finger into the air. West came out of the locker room and leaned against a column, arms folded over his sleeveless shirt.

"I'm going to make you pay for the cancer joke," Lupo said with a finger pointed in my direction. Then he picked up two black objects from a bag he'd brought in with him.

"Alright," he sighed. "We're going to train with these."

He tossed me a rubber knife. I laughed. Pulling the ropes apart, he stepped into the ring. With a look over his shoulder, he nodded to West.

"It's a training dagger. Rubber."

He flicked the end of his dagger. I snorted.

"You get one knife. No other weapons. No rules."

Lupo flipped the dagger in his grip, correcting the direction of the false blade. His stance loosened as he crouched slightly. The position sparked a memory of the younger man who'd trained me as a teenager, forcing me to learn to defend myself with unrestrained blows.

"They won't take it easy on you. So I'm not going to either."

He beckoned me forward. I twisted the rubber knife in my fingers and angled the tip forward. Lunging forward, I drove my knife up to catch him in the neck. My exposed gut wasn't ready for his knee. West flinched.

"Sloppy," Lupo grunted. I fell to my knees, gasping for air. Fingers wrenched my hair. "Now you're dead."

I struck his inner thigh with the edge of my false blade. Took his knee out with a well-placed elbow. He fell as I rose. A palm heel strike to his chin had him on his back. In two moves, I could open his torso. One more and he'd be gutted like a fish.

"Don't forget, old man," I said between panting breaths. "My grandfather taught me everything he knew. But I've got a few tricks of my own."

I smirked and flipped the rubber knife in my grip. Lupo smiled up at me from the mat. A small part of me felt bad for laying him out, but if he thought he could take it I wasn't going to argue. I offered my hand and pulled him up from his supine position on the floor. Once he was standing, he tucked his rubber knife into the back of his pants.

"I like the helpless routine. Gives your opponent a false sense of security. But it's a gamble."

Lupo walked to the ropes and took the bottle of water West held out for him. A ghost of a smirk tugged at the corner of his mouth as the old man took a swig. My hand absently rubbed my stomach, still aching from the blow Lupo had landed.

"Most men have a false sense of security. They think they can beat me because I'm a woman. I learned to use that to my advantage," I said with a shrug. "Can I go back to bed now?"

"You can go back to bed when I'm sure you can win."

I sighed at the ceiling. Lupo took the rubber knife in his grip and got into his fighting stance again.

"You haven't seen all my tricks, kid. Let's go again."

THE SKY WAS turning pink with the rising sun as we pulled into the gravel driveway of the house, Casey and Clayton still sleeping soundly inside.

"Breakfast or bed?" West asked as I hopped out of the truck.

"Shower then bed. Then breakfast."

I pulled my sports bra over my head, hissing at the bruises I could already feel forming in various vulnerable locations. West followed me up the stairs toward the lush white primary bedroom, careful not to wake the other sleeping residents. Each step felt like it dragged in the plush carpet like the fibers were reaching up to pull my feet back down again.

The large marble shower hissed as I turned it on, holding my hand under the stream to test the heat. As I stripped the sweaty workout clothes from my body, I didn't notice that I wasn't alone until I walked into West.

"I thought," he said quietly, "I could hop in, too. Anyway, it's big enough for both of us in there."

I looked to the shower, now billowing with steam illuminated by shafts of early morning light, and then back at him.

"Besides, as you've pointed out, I have seen you naked."

"Fine," I said with a tired smile, tying my hair up into a knot atop my head. "But no funny business."

He held up his hands, feigning innocence.

"No funny business."

The glass door rattled as I pulled it open, stepping to the side so West could get in. Despite my own nakedness, every cell in my body was fixated on him. Though it was built for two, the large shower felt smaller with him inside it. My diminutive stature left enough room for his massive frame to fit in the chamber comfortably, but not a lot else.

He rubbed his face under the second nozzle, letting the water splash over his unbound hair and beard. It streamed down the thick golden muscles of his shoulders to the delicate tilt of his lower back. Then lower.

I averted my gaze as he turned, facing me with a half-cocked grin.

"No funny business," he said.

I rolled my eyes and grabbed the soap, trying to keep the water off of my hair. The white bar frothed as I rubbed it against my skin. West shampooed his hair, watching me as his fingers threaded through the dark strands.

"You're an objectively good-looking man," I said defensively.

"You were objectifying me, then?"

He stepped beneath the spray with a grin, washing the shampoo from his hair. Cocky bastard.

"You should be used to staring by now. I'm sure you're aware of your effect on women."

He was quiet for a beat, the room filled with the sounds of water slapping against the tile as we rinsed ourselves. I could feel his eyes as they traced the suds down my stomach. Every muscle tightened at his attention. Whether or not I'd rinsed off all the soap, I tried to ignore the feeling his gaze stirred as I stepped past him to grab a towel.

West watched me dry off. Watched me shut the door. Readying for bed, I looked at Ethan's old shirt crumpled and waiting for me to put it on. The boxers with it. It felt silly now, to hang on to something for so long from someone who never truly loved me. I could feel that now. Ethan, hell, even Benjamin made me feel things. But they never looked at me the way West did.

My still-damp feet stuck slightly to the wooden floor as I padded over to the trashcan beside Kaia's dresser. Then dropped the clothes inside. The bedding was soft against my freshly washed skin, exhaustion pulling me under quickly. The mattress dipped under West's weight as he laid down sometime after.

He wrapped an arm around my waist and pulled my body toward his. His breath warmed my shoulder as I dropped my head onto his pillow with a sigh. His thumb made gentle strokes against the wolf tattoo nestled between my breasts. The remaining raw edge of my nerves was soothed with the feel of his skin on mine. A thought bubbled up as I started to drift off again.

"West?" I turned my head so our noses almost touched. "Why did you start calling me Trouble?"

He breathed a long sigh and pulled me closer to him.

"You've been trouble from the moment I met you," he said, placing a soft kiss on my neck. "Do you remember that night I drove you home? After you'd gone out with Benjamin? All I could think about after I left your apartment was not kissing you when I had the chance. And when I almost lost you, I was terrified. The way you felt in my arms, I knew you were slipping away."

His hold tightened around me, a gentle reminder that I was safe in his arms, as he loosed a shaking breath.

"I wanted to burn the place down. Waiting for you to wake up was hell. But I'd do it all again. For this. For you. I knew I was in trouble because I can't run from the way I feel about you anymore."

53

VITIS VINIFERA

The late afternoon sun burned in the sky, making a black desert of the asphalt parking lot. It would be hours before Muse opened. None of the dancers were here. No friendly faces waited inside to greet me. I looked around and saw only the cars of Caccia men filling the spaces. West watched me, leaning against the Bronco. On a normal day, he would have been arriving soon to guard the door from intruders. Now I was the intruder. And that door was beckoning me forward.

"I have to go in alone," I said, more to myself than to him. "Get back in the car before someone sees you."

"Like hell. You're not going in there alone."

"If I bring you with me, it looks like I've got backup. As far as they know, I'm desperate and alone. Ozzie won't be able to resist. It's just a way in. That's all." I swallowed, placing a hand on his chest and summoning all of the confidence I could muster with a cocky grin. "I won't lose."

THE HEAVY DOOR slammed behind me as I made my way into the dark space. Everything was the same. The same wainscoting my sister had installed on the walls and the same tile she had carefully selected. Leather-lined booths and a scattering of bistro tables and chairs around the main stage. It was good to know that even though Kaia wasn't in charge, she hadn't been erased from the space. Ozzie was holding court at the corner booth with other men gathered around him, forcing laughter at what had to be a terrible joke. Even though he was in his mid-thirties, his receding hairline and pot belly added years to his appearance.

"Look what the pussy dragged in," Ozzie shouted.

"I'm here to kneel or bleed," I said, trying to keep the rage from my voice and failing miserably.

"For Gladius, I know," Ozzie said with a bored laugh. "I get to watch you die or you get on your knees to serve me. It's almost too good to pass up."

I had to earn my place back in my own damn family. My name was Caccia. Our family owned this city. The idea that some fucking greasy usurper betrayed my sister and replaced her in her rightful seat as Boss made acid coat my tongue. I would willingly give it back to her, but I had to pry it from this asshole's grip first. I tried to keep the anger simmering in my gut from my eyes.

"Are we going to get started or not?" I growled.

"You don't give me orders, pussycat," Ozzie grunted. He turned to the man standing beside the booth and snapped his fingers. "Marco."

My stomach sank at his command. Though I knew the fucking coward wouldn't fight me himself, I was still a little disappointed. Instead of taking back the seat directly, I'd be winning my place in the family back. On to Plan B.

Marco was roughly the same size as West. West, who was a more gifted fighter than any of these guys put together, was someone I'd been trained to beat. Because of that, Marco was not an unknown opponent. But I guess Ozzie didn't know as much about me as he thought. In my experience, big also means slow. I hid the smirk that threatened to bubble up. I could do this.

"On the stage," Ozzie instructed. "So I can watch."

Ozzie's man was a stranger to me, which wasn't a surprise since my comings and goings kept me too busy to meet the soldiers working for our

Capos. But if I didn't know him, he also didn't know me. It was hard not to feel sorry for the poor bastard.

The two of us made our way up the stairs to the stage in the center of the space. Carlo followed us up. I hadn't seen him in weeks. Looking him over, I saw the distress in his eyes. He didn't want to be here. But he was doing what he had to do. I tossed him a grim smile. Marco's face was indifferent, as though this was a task that offered as much interest as waiting in line at the bank or checking out groceries.

Carlo started patting me down, looking for any weapons I might have hidden. We'd only be allowed a single knife. Two men in. One man out. Then the issue would be settled. My opponent could have been the nicest guy in the world, but right now, he was nothing to me but an obstacle. If it meant taking back what was mine, I would happily make him bleed.

Each of us was handed a knife. I tested the blade, making sure I wasn't given a dulled edge. Satisfied, I held it in my fist like a bouquet. Blade up, like a novice. My opponent tested his blade and held it properly. Alright, so this wasn't going to be as easy as I thought.

"Begin."

When my grandfather was training us, he used to say "People think of a weapon as a blunt object. A medium for destruction. Most weapons are such things. But with a blade, you must be an artist. Know where you are going to make your mark. Create your masterpiece."

As the large man lunged toward me, I flipped the blade in my palm and dropped out of his grasp. His extended hand felt the nip of my knife as it passed.

Move like water.

Again, I moved. *Chase me*, I thought. *Come get me*. His hand plunged into my hair for a handhold. A knife glanced across my cheek. I hissed at the contact. Whimpered at the way he knotted my hair into his fist for a firm grasp on me. Pulling me up to face him, we could have been lovers. Instead of a kiss, I swept the knife up his torso. He yelped like a wounded pig and released me.

Strike like an asp.

Using his free hand to press to his bleeding wound, he advanced on me again. I let him get close. Let him think he could overpower me as he grabbed my wrist, and lifted it with a strike I never intended to make. Then I put my knee in his sternum, feeling a crack at the connection. As he went down, I moved behind him and crushed my boot to the crook of his exposed knee.

Then my fingers were in his hair. My knife was at his throat. Blood spilled down his already sodden shirt as a gurgling breath sputtered from his mouth in an otherwise silent scream.

"Shit," Carlo muttered softly.

I pushed Marco's quickly cooling body forward and stepped over him as you step over dog shit on the sidewalk. After wiping the blade off on his upturned ass, I tossed it to Carlo. Ozzie started a slow clap and I internally rolled my eyes. People still do the slow clap thing?

"Very good," Ozzie said. "You'll be very useful to me. Tomorrow night you'll swear yourself to me. Upstairs in my office. You will pledge your undying loyalty to me. On your knees. In front of every man in this family. Now get out."

"Yes sir," I said cooly. My gut roiled at the command. The rest of his men turned their backs on me. All of them but Carlo.

WITH EVEN STEPS, I walked out the front door of Muse to find West leaning against the Bronco. His eyes widened at the sight of me. I looked down to find splatters of blood on my clothes. I lifted my shirt to wipe the blood off of my face as I got in the truck. It bobbed with West's weight as he hauled himself into the driver's seat.

"So you won," West grunted. "Now what?"

"I have to come back tomorrow night and swear my allegiance in front of the whole family," I said with a sigh, looking down at my boots. The roar of the engine filled the cab as we turned onto the road.

I glanced back at Muse. On the outside, it was completely unchanged. The business my grandfather had started. The one my sister had made the crown jewel in the Caccia empire.

Tomorrow night, I was taking that empire back. Tonight, I had work to do.

54

THYMUS VULGARIS

Music was pumping through Muse as the girls got ready for opening. The mood was decidedly different from the day before. As I walked past the stage, I noted that Marco's blood had been cleaned rather efficiently. I heard lilting female voices singing along to the radio and couldn't help the smile that crept across my face. I hadn't realized how much a strip club in the middle of Los Angeles could feel like home, but that's what it was. My home. Habit forced me to walk toward the back room they occupied and poke my head inside.

"Lili!" Sophie screamed as she leaped from her seat at the vanity. Her tiny frame squeezed me in a hug as I laughed. "I thought you were dead!"

"Almost," I laughed, glancing back at West. He shook his head with a chuckle. "Are you guys alright?"

"We're fine. Totally fine," Sophie smiled. "Things have been a little weird around here, but Carlo has been doing a good job taking care of things. He even stocked up our snacks."

I glanced at Maya, Sophie's girlfriend, who was watching me from the next seat at the large vanity. With a terse nod, she turned back to painting on makeup.

"Well, I have to head upstairs," I said with an uneven breath.

"See you later," Sophie said with a smile as she resumed her seat at the vanity. Maya placed a hand on her shoulder, silently checking in with Sophie as I closed the door. With a steadying breath, I forced myself to climb the stairs to my sister's office.

THE HIDDEN DOOR popped open under my palm. West remained behind me as we walked into the tiny antechamber that led to the space, still designed to my sister's specifications. I'd tried to get West to stay outside. To understand that I had things under control. He'd refused and followed. I knew my uneasy stomach wasn't because of what I was about to do. It was because I wasn't ready for him to witness this. He braced a palm on my lower back as I opened the second door to find Ozzie sitting in my sister's chair, feet propped up on the desk before him. Presumptuous fuck.

"Well, look who it is!" Ozzie jeered. "The bitch has come to kneel. And she brought her dog!"

I took a look around the room. All the players were there. My sister's men. He'd gathered every active member of the family. My eyes skated over everyone, marking every familiar face. They landed on Carlo and Gino, who had both visibly cringed at Ozzie's words. Nico was leaning against a bookcase, seemingly unmoved by my presence.

"Come on, Ozzie. Play nice," I purred.

"Sure," he laughed.

West tensed behind me but remained close. My stomach gave a small lurch as I eyed the 1911 pistol sitting on the desk in front of the meatball in my sister's chair. The well-crafted weapon had all the elegance I'd expect from my sister.

"You're here to pledge your undying loyalty. You work for me now."

"Sure," I nodded as I unclipped the knife at my back, letting the blade remain in its sheath until I needed it. "I work for you."

The door opened behind us. I didn't look to see who was coming in. Murmuring started amongst the men. They kept saying the same thing. "Arawn."

"Killian, come in," Ozzie said. "I hope you don't mind my guests. They wanted to see this."

Ozzie gestured toward the door. I obeyed. My eyes met Killian's. He and two men I recognized from the Chancer stood with hands on their weapons. Killian nodded at me with a half-cocked grin.

"My father sends his regards."

"You'll have to walk me through the ritual, dog."

"Wolf," I corrected.

"Whatever. Tell me what comes next."

"The wine," I said. "She keeps it in the desk."

"So obedient already," Ozzie laughed.

The drawer slid open. Inside was the wine and a metal cup. I heard the cup clink against the bottle as he lifted it out. Placing it on the desk, he removed the wax seal from the cork and opened it. Before he poured, I spoke.

"Add your blood to the wine. I'll add mine. I kneel and say the words. Then you drink. I drink. When we're done, you tell me to rise."

"Seems like a lot of bullshit to me but fuck it."

Liquid blubbered out of the bottle, into the metal cup. Ozzie approached me, a small knife in one hand and the glass in the other. He nicked his thumb and squeezed. Barely a drop. Coward. Then he handed me the blade. I cut into my palm. Rich red nectar dripped from my hand.

"Kneel."

I knelt.

"Say the words."

"I will walk the forest in the dead of night,

I will stalk the predators among the trees,

I will know no peace if our enemies roam free,

For their blood is my wine."

I stopped. Waited. Just a moment. Long enough for Ozzie to think I was finished. He took a drink from the glass.

"Their souls are my fee."

Ozzie handed me the cup so that I could take my drink and complete my vow. The hesitation I displayed as I took it was not out of some great internal conflict. It was a moment to control my breathing. So that I wouldn't inhale.

Lifting the cup toward my mouth, I heard Ozzie begin to cough. Like loyal pets, everyone kept their eyes on him. Without letting the cup touch my lips, without taking a breath, I performed my last bit of theater. Ozzie cleared his throat, trying to dislodge whatever was choking him up.

"Rise," he coughed.

I stood.

Ozzie walked back to the desk. I placed the cup next to the bottle and took my place in front of him. The room was tense. Silent. West had taken his place against the wall. I wondered if he'd ever pictured what our meetings were like. If he'd ever pictured this.

I glanced at the clock. A few minutes had gone by. It wouldn't be long now. A smile fought to free itself from me. Ozzie attempted to clear his throat again.

"I'm going to keep you busy, dog."

"Wolf," I smiled.

"Don't correct me."

"A dog is a pet, Oz. A wolf can't be tamed."

"What the fuck are you talking about?"

His face. Red crept into his cheeks. Capillaries had started to burst. Almost purple. He was losing oxygen. Choking to death. I glanced at the bottle of wine. Ozzie followed my gaze. Poor slow Ozzie. Finally caught on.

"I don't suppose you're familiar with Strychnos nux-vomica, Oz."

Silence. He needed to conserve his air supply anyway.

"Well, it's native to tropical regions. Easy to grow in California, though. Its fruit is poisonous. A really common, very effective poison. Do you know what it's called?"

Guns cocked all around me as I took my first step forward. Toward Ozzie.

"Put down your weapons," Killian demanded. He and his men each held two pistols, ready to take out the Capos who had come to see me kneel.

I took a seat on the desk and looked around the room. Nico remained leaning against the wall, trying to keep an even expression. Carlo and Gino were equally relaxed. The rest of the Caccia soldiers were waiting with bated breath. West hadn't moved from where he stood. With a casual sigh, I picked up Ozzie's gun and pressed the barrel to his temple.

"Come on, Oz. Tell me what it's called," I growled through gritted teeth. I dragged a finger along his bloated purple cheeks.

He sputtered. "Pl...pu.." came out in dribbling blubbers. I blew out an impatient breath.

"Strychnine."

I pulled the trigger.

A wet slap of brain matter hitting the wall smacked through the office. Pink mist drifted through the fading evening sunlight that peeked through the blinds. I stuffed the gun into the front of my pants and rolled the corpse-laden chair away from the desk.

Muse. It had been in my family for years. I'd been coming here for years. Practically a second home to me. I knew when it would be empty. It was in the small hours of this morning that I'd come here alone. I'd known where Kaia kept a bottle of wine. It was just before dawn when I replaced her glass with a cup. Penetrated the wax seal, then the cork with a needle. Injected the poison and melted away any evidence of tampering. Easy as pie.

Leaning forward, I braced my hands on the hard wooden surface and surveyed the room.

"I swore a vow that can't be broken. To Kaia. My sister is missing. Until she returns, I am in charge. That has always been the chain of command. If you have a problem with that, you can take it up with me. Or my friends here."

Each face was sour with worry. If these men played poker, they were surely losing money regularly. Except for Carlo and Gino. Gino looked thrilled at the bloodshed. Carlo looked relieved.

"Your tattoos represent a binding agreement," I continued. "It is an oath you make in blood. Loyal to us until your last breath," I said and pointed a finger at Ozzie's fresh corpse. "That's what this sack of shit chose. Betray us, betray *me*, and you choose death."

I OPENED THE small window behind the desk, desperate to get some air. Men had quickly filed out after they each made declarations of their faith. I took it all with the smallest grain of salt. Only a few could be trusted now. There would have to be a change. But I couldn't deal with that now. The wind rustled strands of hair into my face, pulling me out of the trance I had fallen into.

"What are you thinking about?" West asked quietly.

The way Ozzie's pulse felt sputtering out in my grip. How his eyes went glassy as he died. Men carrying his body out to dispose of it for me. Cleaning up the mess I made. The fact that none of it bothered me. It only felt right. My stomach made no protest.

"Nothing."

"Ms. Caccia."

I turned toward the dark Irish voice. Killian stood on the other side of the desk. His men flanked the door.

"Ronan had another message for you."

I sat in the now empty office chair and looked up at him.

"You know where to find the men who hurt my sister. He wants them dead. You help him and your debt to us is paid."

"Tell him I have personal business to attend to first. But that I'll be in touch."

Killian nodded. With a tattooed hand, he whirled his finger in the air and walked out the door. The two others followed. Only West and I remained. My head turned toward the painting on the wall.

"Lock that door."

55

JASMINUM OFFICINALE

I've never cared much for sweet things. There are only a few exceptions. Like lemon knot cookies, sugar in my coffee, or snack cakes. And vanilla milkshakes. My sister was a different story. She adored all things chocolate. On her birthday she loved yellow cake with chocolate buttercream from Magnolia. Sometimes I got frisky and brought her the cupcakes. It was only a few months ago that Daniel and I put a sparkling candle-covered cake in front of her on a warm September evening. I wished I had taken a picture of the smile on her face.

I pictured Kaia's smiling face as I typed our mother's birthday into the safe keypad behind the painting. It was an easy code to remember. A date neither Kaia nor I would forget. A day that she and I would have spent beside her grave. Before my sister was taken, she had told me to open the safe if anything ever happened to her.

The numbers beeped with a final long beep as the display flashed the word OPEN in big green letters. Metal sliding and clinking followed as the door popped free. Inside the safe were several things. A file box, keys with an address attached by a tag, a gun, and an engagement ring. An engagement ring?

It was an elegant emerald-cut diamond on a simple gold band. My mother had never worn anything so large and my grandmother never wore a ring. I lifted it from its box to examine it more closely. Inside of the band was a small engraving in elegant script.

Amor vincit omia.

Shaking my head, I put the piece of jewelry back in the safe.

After taking out the other items, I locked the safe again and covered it with the painting. Kaia's desk was still covered in Ozzie's blood, so I set everything down on the bar.

"What is all that?" West asked.

"I'm not sure," I muttered as I emptied the contents of the file box onto the leather-covered surface. Papers. Lots of papers. Kaia Caccia's Last Will and Testament. Deeds of ownership for the club, the deli, several other businesses, and the house. And a warehouse that matched the address on the set of keys.

THE WAREHOUSE WAS full of old furniture. Things from our grandparents' home. Large framed portraits were covered with sheets. As I walked around the space, I felt transported back to those Sunday dinners. She had kept it all. I thought she'd sold it. I wanted to be angry. To rage at my sister for keeping another secret from me. But all I felt was relief. West wandered over to a box of records and started flipping through them. He held up a copy of Solomon Burke and smiled.

"Big fan?" I asked.

"'Cry to Me' is one of my all-time favorite songs."

"I didn't know you were such a romantic." I laughed, shaking my head.

My eyes caught on a large canvas-covered object in the back.

"No," I whispered in disbelief.

West followed my gaze to the back of the room as I walked toward the object. We stood on either side of it for a moment. My hands coasted over the thick canvas cover. Electric cascades of anticipation licked through my veins. Our eyes connected and West gave me a knowing look. Squatting down to grab the bottom of the canvas, I yanked like I was opening a birthday gift. And there it was.

Gleaming as it had just been washed and waxed was my grandfather's 1967 Camaro convertible. Fresh white stripes cut through the ocean-blue paint. A creamy leather interior that still looked brand new. A giggle of disbelief bubbled out of me as my eyes began to sting with tears. I covered my mouth to keep from bursting into hysterical laughter.

"I can't believe it's here. It's been here this whole time," I half-whispered, placing my hand on the hood.

West's tentative smile had turned into a broad grin.

"You were right. It does look like California on wheels."

Then I remembered. That day by the beach, telling West about the hard work my Nonno had put into this car. I'd told him because I wanted to make him smile again. It was only now that I'd understood why.

"It deserves to be driven. It needs gas and probably a new battery, but it deserves to see daylight again," West said as he tilted his head to the side. "Are the keys in it?"

With a tug on the handle, he popped the door open and gestured for me to get in. My senses dragged me under in a wave of memories. Nonno's aftershave still lingered. Old Spice. The creamy leather still felt like butter beneath my fingers. He made me sit in the backseat when I was little. But I got to ride in the front with him once I was older.

My hands scrambled over the dashboard and down to the glove box, looking for the keys. They had to be here somewhere. Maybe tucked away in the visor? I flipped it down, finding not only the keys but a piece of paper. A photograph. There he was, smiling in the driver's seat, and seated beside him with a big grin on her face was a little girl with shining waves of black hair and gold eyes.

Everything came crashing down on me as I stared at the photo of Nonno and me. This little girl who'd known so little happiness, smiling without a care in the world next to the man who had been more like a father to her than her own. And I missed him. Sitting in this cabin, I remembered what his hugs smelled like. I missed him so damn much. He could tell me what to do now. He'd know exactly how to fix everything.

A tear splashed onto the photo. I blotted it away with my shirt and put the paper down on the dashboard. My hands wrapped around the steering wheel and I leaned forward to brace myself. Sharp, burning pain wrenched in my chest as a sob scraped out of me. Tears rolled down my cheeks as I took heaving, shuddering breaths.

Large warm hands turned me from the driver's seat and pulled me into an embrace. I buried my face in his neck, still weeping. Nonno had been gone for over six years now, but it felt like an open wound. I hadn't been able to say goodbye. To tell him how lost I would be without him. Ten minutes. I'd missed his death by ten damned minutes and I hadn't been able to say what I needed to.

We sat there, West kneeling beside the car as I cried. Soon my breath resumed its normal pace, in and out with only small gasps to interrupt it. I looked up into his face, which had softened as he held me.

"I'm sorry," I said in a shaky whisper, the loudest I could manage with the tightness in my throat as tears threatened to steal my voice again. He shook his head and wiped my cheeks. "I just... it smells like him."

"Don't apologize," he said, pulling me back to his chest. Gentle strokes against my back soothed me as I tried to find my breath again. The yawning ache that had opened in me calmed with every touch. When I was finally breathing normally, I pulled away and smiled weakly at him.

"I think the keys might be in the glove box."

I leaned over and popped open the small door. Owner's manual. Gloves. Knife. Keys. With a shallow breath, I slid the key into the ignition and gave them a turn. A metallic click-click-click answered me.

"Needs a battery," West confirmed. "That's normal for a car that's been sitting around. Pop the hood. I'll be right back."

"I DIDN'T REALIZE you were so fucking broken." In our last days, days we were fighting all the time, days where I couldn't get a hold of him because he was fucking other women, Ethan said that to me. I'd been crying about, I don't remember now, and it pissed him off. *"It's always something with you. You're never just happy."*

When people have said nice things to me, they go in one ear and come out the other. It never stuck. But words like Ethan's? They stuck. So when West nursed me back to life. When he saw me at my worst and stuck around. That surprised me. When I cried the body wracking sobs into his shoulder and he didn't cringe away in disgust, that surprised me.

The engine would be purring like a satisfied cat before West was through with it. As it turned out, the battery wasn't the only thing it needed, but the car had been sitting in the warehouse for years. While he worked on fixing up the car with tools from the Bronco, occasionally leaving to find this and that, I looked around the warehouse.

Clothes. Jewelry. Dishes. Things you accumulate in life. Things you never realize will have their own life long after yours is finished. My fingers traced the rim of a fine China tea cup when I heard the engine fire up again. West looked up at me from the driver's seat and gave me a half-cocked grin.

"It's far from being in perfect condition, but it'll get you where you need to go," he said with a heaving sigh. He killed the motor and got out of the car. "If you want, I can work on it. Get it fixed up again. It wouldn't take much, but finding parts will be a little bit of a bitch."

"Thank you," I said, unable to resist the urge to hug him. His arms wrapped around me and squeezed. "I think I'll enjoy driving this more than my Mercedes."

West chuckled.

"That car was nice," he murmured into my hair as he ran his fingers through it in soothing strokes. "But this one feels a lot more like you."

56

CRATAEGUS

SIX YEARS AGO

I begged. I pleaded.

Now I was here. Lupo looked me over from top to bottom, giving me a frank assessment as he circled me. In the middle of the day, the gym was empty. It was just me and him in the boxing ring.

"You've lost a lot of muscle while you've been away."

He poked my arm. My leaner bicep. My softer hips.

"I can still handle myself," I said, getting into a defensive stance. "Besides, that's why I'm here, isn't it? To get better."

"That shiner is enough to tell me you've gotten sloppy."

"The guy is still dead. I did my job," I chuckled, trying to avoid sounding as rattled as I felt. In truth, I was still thinking about it. About him.

"You could still go back to school. Still be a doctor."

"I was getting a doctorate. Not like a medical doctor. Besides, it was only the first term. I wasn't that invested."

Lupo grunted. After a playful tug on my ponytail, he took his position.

"Alright, first I need for you to show me what you got."

We circled each other, fists up. He struck. I blocked. He struck again. I blocked. I attempted a strike and was immediately blocked. Then struck. Then struck again. I did my best to deflect his blows, but I was still taking a beating.

"Quit running from me and attack!"

The front door swung open, causing Lupo to turn his head. I rang his bell for taking his eyes off of me.

"Shit, kid!"

A quiet laugh came from the doorway. I looked toward it, only able to make out a tall figure against all the sunlight pouring in. As the figure moved closer, I was better able to see the man. Tall, broad shoulders, long arms. A beard that half covered sensuous lips. A scar on his face that went through one eyebrow.

"Sorry," he said in a rich, deep voice. With a glance around, he continued. "Are you closed? The door was unlocked."

"It looks that way, doesn't it?" Lupo laughed. "No, I'm open. Welcome."

Lupo held up a hand toward me, asking for a moment while he climbed out of the boxing ring. I followed him to the edge and leaned on the ropes, eager to get a closer look at this guy.

"You a boxer?"

"Yeah. Well, I do box," the man stammered. Looked down at his feet. Then back at Lupo. "But I'm also trained in Muay Thai and Brazilian Jiu-Jitsu."

Lupo nodded, looking the guy over with an appreciative expression. After all, this guy could probably beat the stuffing out of him. He crossed his arms and smiled at the stranger, who glanced at me.

"Well, you'd be the first in here with Muay Thai under your belt but we do have some BJJ people who can work with you."

The guy nodded. I looked him over again. Dark wild hair. Either he was growing it out or just hadn't seen a pair of scissors in a while. A muscular body he'd stuffed into a pair of loose athletic shorts and a Navy tee shirt. He'd kicked off his sandals at the door. Whoever he was, he'd come in here ready to train.

"We do a one-week free trial if you want to give us a shot. Unfortunately, it's just me and her right now. Unless you want to train with someone twice your age or half your size."

"Hey," I protested. I wasn't sure why. It was true. The man was gigantic. Still, I couldn't take my eyes off of him or the octopus tentacles inked on his arm. The man looked at me with a half-cocked grin that made something in me sit up and take notice.

"Hi," he said, finally talking to me.

"Hi," I said weakly. Despite all of my other skills, I was never good at meeting strangers. Mafia kids don't get a lot of socialization. Botany and chemistry nerds got even less.

"Nice shiner."

"You should see the other guy," I joked. Lupo looked at me like I'd grown a second head. This guy didn't need to know the other guy was dead and buried. People say that all the time, right?

The guy laughed and walked toward the ring. I backed up as he climbed through the ropes to stand on the canvas in front of me.

"I'd like to give it a shot if that's alright," he said.

"Sure!" Lupo shouted his response from where he stood, looking up at the stranger and me. "Let me grab the paperwork."

Before I could say another word Lupo was disappearing into his office, leaving me alone with the stranger.

"Have you been coming here a long time?" The stranger asked.

"Sort of. I came before I went away to school. Now that I'm back, well. I'm back," I said with a shrug. With a glance at his shirt, I looked back up at him. "So were you in the Navy?"

He looked down at his shirt and then back at me, giving a small nod. The office door slammed shut as Lupo strode toward us with a clipboard.

"Here we go," Lupo said, drawing out the last word. "Just need you to fill these out and then you can use whatever you like. Got to cover my ass, you know?"

I smirked, shaking my head at the old man. The stranger was still looking at me but took the clipboard from Lupo as he held it up for him. Noting his gaze, I bit my lip and looked at my feet. This guy was kind of intense.

"Alright, kid. You're going to get it for that cheap shot."

Lupo climbed back into the ring as the stranger moved to climb out. He didn't go far, only resting the clipboard on the edge of the ring to fill in his information on all of the liability waivers Lupo made everyone sign. The old man put up his fists and approached me.

Jab. Block. Jab. Right hook. At first, the strikes were jerky. Like shifting an old transmission, my moves needed work. After a while, the motions became familiar to me again. Lupo was covered in sweat, but I was still raring to go. Wiping his face, he leaned against the ropes. The stranger tapped the clipboard with two fingers.

"Thank hell," Lupo said. He bent down to pick up the clipboard, giving the papers a quick flip to make sure he'd signed them all. "Well, everything looks good here. This is Lili. Lili, this is-"

"Hale. West Hale."

57

OCIMUM BASILICUM

Y ou want so badly to be loved," he mocked. It made me an easy target. Still, he'd only known me a few weeks. I panted after him around like a love-starved puppy, looking for attention. He wasn't interested in getting to know me. I was just a thorn in his side. A woman to distract. How could I be truly rejected by someone if they didn't know me at all?

Benjamin's words had floated into my mind. They stayed with me for the rest of the evening. As Clayton, Casey, West, and I silently ate dinner at my sister's kitchen counter. They echoed through my head as I finished my wine. As I showered off the day.

I'd been a fool for Benjamin. Seeing him tied up and tortured didn't ease the stinging regret I felt at having fallen for his ruse.

But where Benjamin had been calculated and methodical, West was patient. Content to let me come to him. I watched him from the corner of my eye as I went about my business. I tucked my knives away, washed my face, and got ready for bed. And West watched me.

Rain pattered against the windowpane, filling the room with its soft noise. After braiding my hair, I walked to my side of the bed and was about to climb in when West took my hand. His other hand pressed a button on the phone and the opening strains to a familiar song filtered through the space.

"Dance with me," he said with a soft smile.

"You can't be serious."

His only answer was an arched eyebrow and a gentle tug toward him. I huffed a small laugh and stepped toward him. He wrapped his arms around me as I rested my head against his chest. Our dancing wasn't elegant or practiced. It was just the two of us, swaying to the soft rhythm of Solomon Burke piping out of the phone.

I let myself get lost in his scent. The feel of him against me. I listened to the lyrics that filled the room in a passionate, pleading voice. West's arms held me close to him in an easy embrace as he stroked my waist with his thumb.

The music stopped. The room was once again quiet but for the sound of falling rain. But we stayed there. Swaying. Then he backed away a step, removing his arms to take my face in his hands.

I knew. Before he brushed his thumbs along my cheeks. Before he leaned in to kiss me. Before he backed me toward the bed to lay me gently on its soft linens. The look in his dusky green eyes let me know exactly what was coming. And that he wasn't going to hide it or run from it anymore. Just like he'd promised.

Coasting his hand along my jaw to thread his fingers into my hair, he pulled it to angle my mouth up as he kissed me. Not out of lust or claiming, but in question. A choice that had to be mine. Letting myself care for West terrified me. I couldn't bear losing him. That would shatter me.

I tugged the shirt over my head, our locked gaze only interrupted by the brief flash of cotton over my eyes. He stood and removed his own shirt, followed by everything else. Then leaned forward to hook his fingers around my panties, lowering them with heartbreaking gentleness and soft kisses to my raised knees, shins, and feet.

An ache started to build, not just between my thighs, but in my chest as I watched him climb over me. More soft kisses trailed up my stomach, worshiping the wolf tattoo and my breasts. I tangled my fingers in his hair to bring his mouth to mine.

"West," I whispered against his lips. The words were there. Stuck inside my mouth. I wondered if he could taste them as he kissed me. Every syllable on my tongue touched his. And I was a coward. Too afraid to gamble and lose everything. So I said, "I need you."

He said nothing. Instead, he shifted his weight onto an arm braced beside me to slide his other beneath my thigh. As he hooked my leg around his hip, he kissed me with gentle licks into my mouth. Another kiss accompanied the torturously slow press of his length inside me.

I wondered where the gasps dropping from my lips came from. Wondered where I got the air when every breath felt trapped inside me. He kept his hold of my leg, grasping my ass to angle my hips as they met his slow and steady assault. West was talking to me with his body, saying things that maybe neither of us was ready to admit. He grazed my neck with his nose, a soft touch that lit me from within. Another gasp was swallowed by the kiss that followed.

The hand that had been braced beside me drifted to my throat, but not in the dominating grasp Benjamin favored. Instead, his fingers found the inky black waves of hair at my nape. He touched me like I was a precious, breakable thing. Gentle, awed, worshiping. He threw his head back, his jaw tight with the groan he was biting back.

My first true friend. It was all so obvious to me now. Every day that felt a little bit dimmer without seeing him. Each small surge of joy I felt at his smile. The discomfort I felt at his disappointment. Every man I'd been with before had been prologue to this. To him.

An increasing tightness pulled on my lungs, stealing my breath. West leaned down toward me, near enough for our noses to brush against each other. I threaded my fingers into the soft locks of his beard as he searched my face for the truth I wasn't ready to say. One he seemed to already know.

I did want to say it. I wanted to lay it all at his feet. To give him everything. But the words felt to dangerous to say out loud. Maybe that didn't matter. He knew. He had to know it, didn't he? Knowing each other so well,

I had seen it in his eyes. Maybe it was in mine, too. If I could see it, then so could he. Still, fear kept the words from passing my lips.

The burning feeling in my chest coupled with his mouth pressing gentle kisses to my skin was all I needed to tip over the edge. As my climax peaked, a sob broke from my throat. I turned my face away, unable to contain my tears. Shaking in his arms, he kissed a tear away from my cheek and dropped his head to the crook of my neck as he came.

"Lili, I," he started.

"Not now," I whispered on an uneven breath. "Please."

West slowed his breathing with a measured exhale, collecting himself. That scarred eyebrow knit with the other, two small lines forming between them as he watched me cry beneath him. I squeezed my eyes shut, begging the tears to stop. His hair formed a curtain around us as he pressed his forehead to mine.

"You're safe, Lili," he panted.

The knowing beats of my heart. The ache in my chest filled me with fear, squeezing more tears from my eyes as it stole my breath. My words.

I was a fucking coward.

58

HYSSOPUS OFFICINALIS

My hand slid over the fine fabrics. Hugo Boss. Tom Ford. Handcrafted suits from some famous London tailor. I admired every stitch. Every carefully sartorial piece. Herringbone. Cashmere. Drago. All of it was carefully curated. Each item was selected to do the talking for a man who wanted to advertise how powerful he was without speaking. It's true what they say. Money talks. Wealth whispers. Benjamin Camden's closet whispered.

However, Benjamin Camden wouldn't be whispering anything to anyone anymore. No more filth. No seductive pleas and no soliloquies. Bare naked on the cold floor of his wood-paneled closet, strangled with an Hermès belt. His tongue sat on display with his rolled neckties, bleeding onto the soft velvet roll.

The emperor had no pulse.

SCALDING HOT WATER pounded down on my head as I tried to wash the remains of my dream from my mind. Even with West holding me, the nearness of Benjamin's demise had plagued my sleeping thoughts. I'd gone through the motions of washing. Scrubbing the blood from myself. The blood I had imagined. It had dried and even though it had been in my imagination, it left an unpleasant sensation on my seemingly clean skin.

A knock on the glass door jarred me from the fog. West held up his phone.

"Call for you. It's Juliet."

I held up my finger, asking for a minute while I turned off the shower and stepped out. West handed me a towel. His eyes lingered on the places where I had scrubbed, my skin still red and irritated. Tucking the tip of the towel into itself, I reached for the phone.

"Hello? Juliet?"

"They may have your sister in Joshua Tree."

I squinted, confused. Water soaked into the small rug beneath my feet. She wasn't in Joshua Tree. I was just there.

"No," I protested. "I was at the encampment. She wasn't there."

"What encampment? It's not an encampment. It's the house."

Oh, Jesus. I coughed and tried to reroute my thoughts. Explaining everything I knew to her was not the top priority. And who had the time? It was also guaranteed to melt her brain. While it would be a justified reaction, it was of very little use to me. I shook it off.

"What are you talking about?"

"There's a house they've been renting for some big investor. They reached out to me to send them some feminine products for a guest."

"What's strange about that? Do they not have women around?"

"They never have me get anything for anyone. Everything is supplied by the people on their end. They always bring everything with them."

So whoever she was, the female guest had been a surprise.

Then I remembered. Clayton said the guards from the encampment were moving to a second location in regular shifts. The men who were keeping us in trailers were also watching my sister who was only a few miles away. If she had been there...my sister would have been close. So fucking close.

"Can you give me the address?"

"Well, yes. But-"

"But what?"

"It's not the kind of house you can just drive up to."

"So what?"

"So there's no way inside without being invited in. That place is locked down and guarded like a prison."

I'd been distantly aware of hanging up. West pocketed his phone and leaned against the door frame, waiting for me to fill him in. Instead, I stood against the marble vanity and chewed the edges of my fingernails as my hair made little trails of water down my back.

When I was in my master's program, I had to do a survey course on differential equations. It was completely exhausting. One way or another, I would get stuck. Not able to see the answer in front of me. The professor guiding the course accused me of overthinking.

"You're getting ahead of yourself," she would say. "Get out of your head and work the problem."

I had all of the elements. All of the constants, variables, and operators. All I needed to do was work the problem.

Get out of my head and work the problem.

THE BLUE AND white paint sparkled in the fading sunlight. With West's work, my grandfather's Camero had started to purr. It growled and roared as it climbed up the winding road.

"This seems like more than a test drive," West observed.

I said nothing as our destination came into view.

"This is where you wanted to go?"

"Sometimes I come up here when I need to clear my head. It was one of the places my grandfather used to take me. In this car, actually."

The Griffith Observatory's domes were a stark black presence against the pink sky. The parking lot was half empty. Though the building was closed, it was a popular spot for watching the sunset. I shut off the engine and hopped out.

"What's on your mind?" West said as he rounded the car to walk beside me.

I looked around at the people within hearing distance and kept walking. Catching my cautious glance, West went quiet. Then a hand wrapped around mine, threading our fingers together.

The City of Los Angeles was cast in a tangerine glow by the setting sun as we strode past the building and over to the side. People had gathered here and there to watch. Take photos. Livestream it.

I just wanted to be here. To breathe it in. And get out of my head.

The terrace had only a few scattered people here and there. I leaned against the wall. West stood behind me, surrounding me with his warmth as he rested his arms on either side of mine. As he rested his chin on my shoulder, I looked out over the sprawl before me. My sister's kingdom that was handed down to her by our grandfather. The lights of the city sparked to life under the gradually darkening sky.

"You know, if you wanted a second date, you could have just asked," he hummed.

I gave an absent chuckle, leaning back to steal more of his body heat while the evening chill nipped at our cheeks.

As the sky turned from pink to periwinkle, I thought about all Juliet had said. All that I'd seen at the encampment. And everything Benjamin had said to me. The lies. And the truth buried within them. After trying all of the complicated solutions and failing miserably, the answer had to be simple.

I sighed and turned my head toward West's.

"I think I know where my sister is."

59

ROSA RUBIGINOSA

A bone-rattling growl cracked through the darkness. My feet were bare. The delicate pads felt every step through the cold dirt and dry leaves. Each movement brought me closer to the source. The snarling beast came closer. Teeth shining in the moonlight. Gold eyes glowing in the shadows. Ready to swallow me whole.

HOURS AFTER EVERYONE had gone to sleep, the house was still quiet as I snuck out in the middle of the night. A light poured out from under the guest room door, but Casey's heavy breaths let me know she'd been sound asleep. After what she'd been through, I wouldn't blame her for leaving the light on. I wondered if Clayton had gone to sleep in Daniel's bed or if he preferred the sofa as I took cautious, quiet steps down the stairs.

With no mercenary asleep in the living room, I was safe to leave without waking anyone. I wouldn't be going far. But I needed to get out.

It was all I thought about on the drive home. All I thought as I sat quietly through dinner. Through West and Clayton's conversation about surveilling the Joshua Tree compound for weaknesses after Casey excused herself halfway through the meal. As West slept beside me, I'd stared up at the ceiling imagining losing everyone I'd ever cared about. The thought drove me from our bed and out into the night.

The air on my skin felt like it pressed in on me. My fingers squeezed the puffy winter coat my sister never wore as I wrapped it around myself, hoping it was enough to block out the cold night air. The soles of my boots crunched on the gravel garden path as I walked toward the garage. Toward the only thing I could control. Toward my work.

"Lili."

I turned to find West standing on the terrace, sweatpants slung low on his hips like he'd hastily pulled them on. His hair was mussed with sleep, barely contained by the bun he'd tied it into. Tugging a shirt over his head, he approached me and whispered.

"What are you doing out here?"

"Just go inside. I'm fine."

"Tell me what's wrong. Did you have another nightmare?"

"No," I lied. "It's nothing. I can't sleep," I pulled the coat up as it slid down my shoulders, looking down at my feet. I needed to get some distance from my fears. From my thoughts. From him. "I just need some space."

"Space." The word was flat.

"I'm sorry." I walked with brisk steps toward the steps of the granny flat. The cloudless winter night turned my breath into hot puffs of steam before me. West hurried after me and grabbed my wrist, turning me to face him.

"Stop apologizing to me," he whispered.

"Look, you think you know me but you don't. I'm not some damsel in distress, waiting to be rescued," I said. West's laugh was cold and irritated.

"That's just fucking perfect. Just when I think we're getting past this bullshit, you go and do this."

"What am I supposed to say?" My throat closed around the words as tears stung my eyes. The stairs to the granny flat were only steps away. I hurried toward them to put distance between us. His hand circled my arm, turning me toward him again.

"You're supposed to tell me the truth. I've been there for you every fucking day. Damnit, I thought we were past this. I've bled for you and you can't just be honest with me?"

The rage in his eyes felt like a stone dropped into my center. I'd been waiting for this. For the moment when being with me would become too big of a burden to bear. Even for him. It was for his own good. He deserved better than that. Better than me.

"You want me to be honest with you? Fine. I'm terrified! Terrified, West. The things I love have a way of getting destroyed because of me. Every time," my voice broke as I whisper-shouted. Blinking through tears, I tried to steady myself. Still, I couldn't offer more than a whisper as I said, "I couldn't live with myself if you hated me."

"So you think we're fine just ignoring this? Lying to ourselves about what we're doing together? It's not going to go away and neither am I. I've been right here. Every day. Fighting it out with you."

Unable to think of anything to say, I shoved at his chest. Trying to get distance from him. From the rising tide that threatened to drown me. He shook his head, a look of disbelief washing over his features. West blew out a breath. For a moment, I thought that was it. He'd walk away and leave me in pieces.

But that's not what happened.

West stepped closer and I moved backward until my back hit the garage wall. I looked down at my shoes, too filled with fear and shame to look him in the eye. His voice was low and raw in a way that just made me feel worse as he spoke again.

"What's it going to take to convince you that I'm not going anywhere?"

I shrugged and shook my head. Everyone else had made it seem so easy to leave me. Made it seem like I was some disposable thing. But West wasn't everyone. He'd shown me exactly who he was, even when I was too stubborn to see it.

"Just admit it. Admit that you love me."

This was too much. I leaned back against the wall, letting it take my weight. I closed my eyes and let out a shaking breath. Tears left cool trails down my heated cheeks. Every inhale moved through my lungs in pressed agony. He wanted too much. West approached me, crowding me against the wall until I could feel his breath on my skin.

"Say it." A dare and a warning. Say it or break him. Break us. He stepped forward, bracing a forearm over my head as he bared his teeth. I was cornered. I'd never said it to any man. Not in the way he wanted. Maybe I had never felt it. This feeling was so alarming. But it was real. It was the feeling I'd been ignoring, too afraid to acknowledge. I looked up at him. His smoky green eyes burned into mine.

"I love you," I said, my throat tight enough to steal my voice. "Ride off into the sunset together love. *Let's fall in love,* love. I think I have for a long time." The words rushed out of me in a shaky whimper. I clapped my hands over my mouth, horrified at everything I'd just admitted.

For a long moment, neither of us spoke. West just stared at me. His jaw worked as his eyes bore down on me. The man was letting me stew in the words that were still hanging in the air. Then he grinned.

"I'm glad you finally said it. It took you long enough."

"Cocky bastard," I laughed as I wiped away my tears.

He circled his other arm around my waist and smiled down at me. I rested my hands on his chest and looked into his eyes, waiting to hear him return my words. Those three words. Eight damned letters that would change my life forever. And because he was West, he was going to make me wait for it.

"Well?" I said impatiently.

"What?"

"You're unbelievable," I groaned as I rolled my eyes and tried to pry myself out of his hold. He squeezed and pulled me close, bending down to whisper into my ear.

"I knew from the moment I met you. You had a black bruise right under one of the most beautiful eyes I've ever seen. I was a fucking goner. Right then and there."

I bit my lip, trying to ignore the rush of relief I felt. My wrists locked behind his neck as he moved to rest his forehead against mine.

"Lili, I love you. Every inch of you. Every goddamn bit. I'm fucking crazy about you."

"Crazy?" I asked with a watery laugh.

"Certifiable," he grinned.

60

SALVIA ROSMARINUS

Fine. The bastard made me fall in love with him. I'd been in love with him for longer than I'd even be able to say, but I could pinpoint the moment I knew it. The smirk I could taste on his lips told me West did, too. Down to the second.

Every hour I'd spent with West felt like a relief from the world. From the life I'd created with the decisions I'd made. Even when I was up all night. Even when I was exhausted by some daunting task set for me by my sister, seeing him was a priority. At the time, I told myself it was because I needed to train. To stay ready for any situation. That was true, to an extent.

But it was also the way he could make me laugh with just a look. Or how he helped me feel strong.

A small gasp left me as West's hands cupped my backside and hoisted me up. My legs wrapped around his waist as he carried me up the stairs and into the flat above the garage. Reaching backward, I fumbled for the doorknob as he pressed a needy kiss to my lips.

The scent of him. It overwhelmed the flowers hanging around us. The herbs drying in the window. All I could smell was cedar, salt, and something thoroughly West. I drank it in. Couldn't get enough of it. Realized now that I'd always needed it. Wanted it. Every inhale was like coming home.

Cool wood rose to meet the back of my thighs as West placed me on the worktable and backed away. Shifting my weight to one side and then the other, I shed the fluffy coat I'd wrapped myself in. Then the shirt I'd put on before bed. His shirt. I hadn't wanted to sleep in anything else.

West stepped out of his shoes and mine thudded to the floor as I toed them off. His eyes stayed locked on mine as my fingers curled around the waistband of my panties, tugging them off with a sense of anticipation I hadn't felt before. Like I was somehow more bare before him. Completely.

Our clothes were a pool of fabric on the floor as he approached again. The tips of his fingers shook as they traced my mouth with reverence, a touch gentle enough to bring more tears to my eyes. His mouth met mine again and everything we had been to each other unraveled completely. In his arms, I wasn't a Caccia. I wasn't a killer. I wasn't a dangerous, broken thing. I was just Lili. He was just West.

"Say it again," his voice was raw as he begged against my mouth, licking the curve of my lips with heated urgency. I let out a choked laugh and brushed the hair out of his eyes, feeling an ache in my chest at his unguarded gaze.

"West," I breathed, trying to calm the expanding strain I was feeling with every inhale. "I love you. I'm in love with you."

He didn't need to say anything. Not this time. He'd shown me every day. Every minute he was with me. Every single time he had shown up for me. When he made me breakfast or opened the door for me. I'd just been too blind to see it.

I was more than all of that, too. It was the way he pulled my hair to plant soft kisses on my shoulder. Like chili and chocolate, it burned and melted in my mouth. It was always going to be like this with him. Like a storm raging on the open sea. I stayed away because I was afraid I'd be dragged beneath the surface. His hand went to my throat, fingers stroking gently as he whispered sweetly in my ear.

"You're mine, Trouble."

It was everything, everything, everything. He pressed against me. Into me. Filling me until he was bottomed out and I couldn't help the whimper that left me. West seemed to be fighting himself for control, small breaths blowing hot against my shoulder. His groans were like wine. I wanted to swallow every drop.

My hands bracketed his jaw as it tightened, still fighting for control. His brows were knit together in concentration as his eyes peered into my own. West had nothing to fear from me. I would spare him hurt. Heartbreak. All of it, if I had any power to do so. I kissed him. Let him taste everything he'd begged to hear.

Listening to the way he was coming undone for me, mewling growls into my mouth as he took hold of my hip, and destroyed any defense I had left. Those little worries I'd had seemed stupid now. That he would get tired of me. Leave me for someone else. Someone easier. But it had never been easy. Not for him. He'd seen it all. Loved it all. Loved me.

My core tightened with every passing second, pressure building with a promise of release. With one hand gripping the worktable and the other still pinned to me, West spoke a stream of beautiful filthy words as he rolled his hips into my own.

"You feel like you were fucking made for me. Open those pretty lips and tell me," he panted. "Tell me you're mine."

I was. My body was his. My soul, if there was such a thing. And my heart.

"I'm yours."

AFTER QUITE LITERALLY leaving it all on the table. After a climax that had me glad we'd been in an entirely different building. After West tugged my ear with his teeth during his release. We snuck back into the house, careful not to wake the others.

His breaths were deep and even as I listened to them rush in and out beneath my head. Not sleeping. But chewing over what to say as I finished telling him about Ethan and the only time I'd thought I'd been in love with someone.

"That wasn't love."

"What do you mean? Of course it was. He broke my heart. You can't break someone's heart if they're not in love with you. He may not have been in love with me but I think I was in love with him."

"First of all, if you have to say 'I think,' then you know you didn't. Second, he didn't know you. He didn't know that you eat like a raccoon rooting through the garbage when you're exhausted, or that you clean when you've got a lot on your mind. You do this amazing little dance when you're about to eat, by the way."

I pushed myself up to look down at him. He gave me a lazy smile that said *I know you better than you think*. There wasn't a damned thing I could say to that. Brushing my lips over his was the only thing that even came close to a response. His hand threaded into the hair at my nape as he deepened the kiss, humming like every corner of my mouth was delicious.

Pulling away, I tried to remember that we needed to get some sleep, certain I wouldn't be able to control myself if I let the kiss go on any longer. He smirked, as though he knew exactly where my mind had gone.

"Do you know," I started. "For the first few weeks we trained together, I thought your eyes were brown. Like a light brown. Then we started training on the mat and I got closer to you. Literally. Now I know they're green. And it's my favorite color."

He smiled and I couldn't help myself. Kissing him was becoming addictive. Every part of it. The way he cupped my jaw every time. The soft hums that started in his chest. If he wasn't careful, I was going to drink him down until there was nothing left. As I sat back again, my eyes went to his tattoos and caught on the tentacled skull he'd gotten with his SEAL teammates.

"Also, there's a second part to this," I said as I traced the inked tentacles curling down his arm. "Memento mori. Remember that you must die. Memento vivere. Remember to live."

West let out a sigh and grabbed my hand, bringing my palm to his mouth for a soft kiss before he spoke.

"I think I'm starting to figure that second part out."

Settling down against him, I sucked in a deep breath and let it out as I closed my eyes. Maybe that darkness, the things he'd done, had threatened to crush him in its depths too. Just as that darkness had always threatened me. It was something he'd tried to hide from everyone, just as I had. But I'd felt drawn to his shadows. Like my own had recognized his. Our rough edges matched like puzzle pieces.

As I lay there letting sleep take me, my mind felt unlocked. Anxiety was replaced with certainty. About West, but also Benjamin and Kaia. For the first time in weeks, I knew exactly what I needed to do.

61

TURNERA DIFFUSA

The corridor was dark. Footsteps shuffled in the dirt path. His fine leather shoes weren't made for this sort of terrain.

"It's here," I said. "Follow me."

Only my candle provided light as we made our way through the catacombs. Surrounded by skulls who all looked on with eager anticipation. Uncertain steps became uneven as the breathing behind me turned feathery with fear.

There. The shadowed hollow.

"Here," I pointed. Curiosity and relief propelled him forward. Stepping beyond me and over the first few rows of brick. The ones I had already laid.

"Where?" His voice boomed in the cavernous emptiness.

I leaned forward.

"Here."

The needle punctured his neck with lethal efficiency. Thick panicked gasps sounded from within the space. My boot pressed between his shoulders, pushing him forward.

As he lay there in the darkness, in the dirt, I finished my work. Concealing him within the black grotto, brick by brick. His billions would scatter to the wind. His name would collapse. He would wither into ash.

And no one would remember the man named Benjamin Camden.

IT WAS DIFFICULT not to smile. Really. We had come downstairs for breakfast to find Casey and Clayton talking over coffee. Clayton had his laptop open on the counter. Casey seemed to be answering questions for him. Once he noticed the two of us entering the kitchen with stupid grins on our faces, Clayton turned to face us.

"You two finally done?"

I tried not to blush as I shared a look with West. He smirked. Maybe I hadn't been as quiet as I'd thought this morning. But I'd done my best to stifle the moans pouring out of my mouth with a pillow as West pounded into me.

"So what did you learn?" West asked, mercifully changing the direction of the conversation.

"A lot, actually. But you're not going to like it. Lilith, Juliet was right about the building. It's super heavily guarded. I've seen terrorist compounds less protected than this. You're sure this is where your sister is?"

"Juliet said that she had to send women's things to that house." I surveyed the house for what felt like the hundredth time, looking for something. A weakness. I'd crept into dozens of houses. Maybe a hundred. Never got caught. Always got my target.

"Women's things?"

"Tampons. Pads. Period shit," I said, still looking at the screen. "She had to have it delivered. Apparently, the bastards were too busy to do it themselves."

I stared at the screen, chewing on the edge of my thumb as I let the details sink in. Then turned to find West giving me a careful look.

"What."

"I've known you long enough to know that your mind is the sharpest weapon in your arsenal, Trouble. What are you thinking?"

The house was surrounded by guards. If they knew someone was coming, like an expected guest, they would back off. Possibly. But I also knew someone good with a sniper rifle.

"Juliet said there was no way in without an invitation. I need to go visit our little pet."

THE DOORMAN AT Benjamin's building remembered me. Probably because I wasn't Benjamin's usual type. Still, he let me in. Then I let myself into his penthouse. It had still been sparse. Barely lived in. All of the produce had gone bad. The putrid scent filled my nostrils as I made my way to his closet. Benjamin Camden was about to make his reappearance.

On the way over to Pals, I placed some calls. If I was in charge of the Caccia family for now, I was going to use it to my advantage and show up with a goddamned army. The heavy steel door swung open on squeaky hinges and the familiar stench of unwashed Benjamin made my eyes sting.

"You're going to make yourself useful, Benjamin. I'm going to give you a phone. You're going to set a meeting. Then I am going to accompany you to that meeting."

A garment bag and a pair of shoes landed at Benjamin's feet with an unceremonious thud.

"You think that's going to get your sister back, do you?"

"I have a hostage who's worth a bit of money. That may help matters."

"They'll never let you in the door if they know I'm your hostage."

He held up his bandaged finger to articulate his point. In that moment, I was grateful for Clayton's attention to those details because I found it difficult to give a flying fuck about this guy's wellbeing.

"Then I'll be your assistant. Shouldn't be hard. You've demonstrated that you're perfectly comfortable with pretending, haven't you?"

I walked back up the stairs to fetch the other things I'd brought. The bucket filled with cold water, a bar of soap, and a worn-out towel. After placing them within his reach, I took a step backward. Finally, I pulled Ozzie's gun from the waist of my jeans and cocked it. With my free hand, I tossed Benjamin the key to his bindings.

THE MESSAGE I'D sent on Benjamin's behalf was looked over and approved by him. Before leaving him in Carlo's care for the night, he gave me a crocodile grin. I saw a glimmer of the man I'd let myself get distracted by. My stomach roiled at the memory. It would never happen again.

My sister's kitchen island was covered in weapons. West and Clayton were taking an inventory of their artillery, checking them, cleaning them, and evaluating their ammunition supply. Sniper rifles. Pistols. Smoke bombs. I didn't know that the last one was actually real.

Compared to their war-worthy assembly, my collection of knives looked small. I sharpened, cleaned, and sheathed them for the brawl to come. My sister deserved every ounce of fight I had to give. Even if it was just a blade.

As I finished sharpening my last knife, the tacos we had picked up had started to sour in my stomach. I got up from the table swiftly and stepped outside. Winter's chill stung my cheeks as the moon covered the garden in its waning light. I heard the door close behind me.

"Are you alright?" West asked. He dropped a coat around my shoulders, rubbing them with his large hands.

I nodded.

His body was flush with mine as he wrapped his arms around me, resting his chin on the top of my head as he spoke again. I felt the rumble of his voice against my back.

"No matter what happens tomorrow, I need for you to know something."

I tried to turn but his hold kept my back to his chest.

"From the moment I thought I lost you, all I've wanted to do was protect you. And I know, I know. You can protect yourself, so don't start, but fuck. I can't help myself."

He paused, taking a shaky inhale.

"If it takes everything I have to give, you're going to make it out of there tomorrow."

My stomach plummeted at his words.

"If this is supposed to make me feel better," I started, my voice trembling. He kissed the top of my head and squeezed me.

"Listen to me. You're mine."

I nodded.

"And I'm yours."

West did everything he could to calm me down. We went inside and talked. Talked until I ran out of things to say. Until he did. Then we kissed. His kisses were languid and unhurried. West was taking his time. Tasting me. Memorizing me. He kissed me long and deep. The kind of kisses that said he didn't need me to tell him who I belong to anymore. He already knew.

We kissed until kissing turned into confessions of love whispered against bare skin. Long into the night, we talked and touched. Made love until I couldn't put a sentence together.

When we finally were ready for sleep, West pulled me into his arms. The security of his hold soothed me enough to fall into a state of threshold consciousness.

62

UNCARIA TOMENTOSA

Her voice was soft, just as I remembered it. My mother's black hair hung around her shoulders like spun silk. She was wearing her red dress. The one from her 30th birthday. It looked like she had stepped out of the photograph in my grandfather's office to speak to me. But only darkness surrounded us.

"Bambina."

Her hands gripped my shoulder as her deep brown eyes looked into mine. Dewy olive skin was marred by bruises and cuts. My father's work.

"Bambina, you cannot change what has happened."

Her gaze moved from my face to something behind me. Perhaps looking for something. Then I realized she was looking at someone. There was someone else in this dark between space. My head turned to follow her line of sight when she gripped my chin to recapture my attention.

"Listen to me."

Her eyes fixed on me again. They were softened with a sadness I had never seen. Her black brows with pulled together with worry.

"You cannot change what will happen."

Then I was sitting in the office. Kaia's office. Waiting. An important meeting was supposed to occur. How was I the first one here? Even my sister was late. Muse was completely quiet. No music pumped through the walls. No shouting or hooting rose to meet my ears. To occupy my time, I read the titles of the books lining the shelves behind her desk. The ones that framed the window. Still, no one came.

I stood and walked to the bar to pour myself a drink. The Japanese whiskey my sister often poured for me was empty. I picked up another bottle. Gin. Empty. Another. Vodka. Empty. Frustrated, I closed the cabinet and resumed my seat. Surely this wouldn't take all night, would it?

A knock sounded at the door. Carlo. Gino. Nico. They each filed in. Followed by everyone else. They all looked at me.

"Should we get started?"

"Aren't we waiting for my sister?"

"What do you mean, Boss?"

I looked down to find myself seated at the desk. But I wasn't wearing my usual jeans and boots. I was wearing a suit. The office was filled with every connected Caccia man in the family. Every eye was trained on me.

✦

THE SUN WAS making its way toward the horizon as we neared the house hidden in Joshua Tree. West sat beside Benjamin. I kept glancing at them in the rearview mirror from the passenger seat. West smirked at me every time our eyes met. As for Benjamin, well...

"I know where we're going. I still don't see why this hood is necessary."

"I wouldn't want you ratting out my friends, Benji."

Nico, Carlo, and Gino snickered. West huffed a laugh at Benjamin's side. On the way out to the house, the van had been silent except for the crunch of tires on the loose gravel road.

"Here," West said. The van rolled to a stop at his command. Tugging his pack onto his shoulder, he glanced at me. I gave him a small smile. The smile he returned as he pulled up the skull gaiter settled something in me. The door slid shut and the van soldiered on, leaving West to make his way up the trail ahead of him.

Benjamin stumbled out of the van. Carlo stayed close behind, pushing him to walk further from where I stood. With a swift tug, the hood came off. Carlo tucked it into his pocket as Benjamin looked around, confusion marring that perfect face. I loosed my hunting knife from my holster and gave it a casual flip.

"Hey, Benji. How fast can you run?"

"What?"

"I'm going to give you to the count of ten to get out of range."

"Out of range?" He glanced at my knife.

"One."

Benjamin's dress shoes slid on the dirt as he sprinted as quickly as he could on his impaled foot.

"Two," I said a bit louder.

Out into the open desert, far away from the eyes of the paparazzi, Benjamin Camden ran for his life.

"Three!"

I raised my blade high, letting it catch the sun. A soft crack sounded in the distance. Red mist floated on a gust of desert wind. West's shot from his perch atop the rocks had found its mark as Benjamin collapsed mid-stride.

Hope. I'd watched Benjamin's hurried strides, knowing he'd thought that the hours of torment had ended. That I had, out of the kindness of my heart, set him free. Giving him hope was the cruelest thing I could think of.

"Make sure his body is never found," I said to Carlo as I tucked away my knife. "Keep the watch if you want. Burn everything else if you have to."

Carlo nodded as he unrolled the large black bag. Benjamin Camden's last accessory.

THE HOUSE, IF you could call the structure a house, looked like a pill bug crawling over the rocks. Blades of roof overlapped one another, resulting in a bizarre shape that was like something from a sci-fi movie. Carlo looked up at the structure as our van pulled up to the entrance.

As Clayton had said, there was no way to drive up to the house. A walled-off walking path was the only way to get inside. The path was monitored by cameras. One back exit. One side exit. Each was heavily guarded. The best way in was through the front door. And I'd have to go in alone.

"This place looks weird as shit," Carlo muttered. I turned to him, Nico, and Gino.

"Remember, block the exits. Nico takes the back. Gino takes the east exit. West is covering from the peak. I'm not leaving this god-awful building without my sister. No one leaves. Carlo, keep the van running."

"You got it, Boss," Carlo replied.

I popped the door open and hopped out, wishing I hadn't left Clayton to keep watch over Casey. I could use all the help I could get.

"Make em' bleed," Nico said as he loaded his gun.

With a last look at all of them, I simply nodded and stepped toward the gate.

A beep came from the intercom.

"Name."

"Mr. Benjamin Camden. He has an appointment, but he's been detained. He sent me in his stead."

Static crackled from the speaker as I waited. Then the lock clicked.

Decomposed granite lined the path, crunching slightly under my careful footfalls. My fingertips loosed a dagger from my holster.

A dark man made his way toward me, pointing a pistol at me. Before he could take another step, he was downed with a bullet. I glanced up at the peak, thankful for my lethal guardian.

I entered a large courtyard circular. I could see the front door, though it was flanked by walls obscuring my view of the rest of the building ahead.

Four pairs of footsteps hustled toward me from behind the walls ahead. Four men surrounded me. I knew what needed to be done, confirmed by a small flutter in my gut.

"You're coming with us, Caccia."

"No."

They laughed with each other as the head idiot spoke again.

"No?"

"I'm not coming with you. Not when there are only four of you."

The head idiot turned to look at his second, whose neck was already a ragged mess of flesh and blood pierced by West's bullet. My blade plunged into the eye of his third as I tugged the head idiot toward me, shielding myself from the shots of his fourth. I'd been right to assume my human shield was wearing Kevlar.

It took another blade to quiet the fourth guard. One in his thigh. His femoral artery gushed as his moans of pain turned to whimpers. The man with my knife in his eye was still twitching as I retrieved the blade. A twinge of searing pain raged through my bicep as I tucked the knife away. A bullet had grazed me, leaving an angry gash in my skin.

"Fuck," I whined as I examined the wound. The bullet tore a hole in my jacket.

I kicked the twitching man. After wiping and re-sheathing my knife, I stood to retrieve the others. The fourth guard gaped with lifeless eyes at the cloudless sky above.

Two more men stepped into the path. With only one dagger, I wouldn't be able to take out both of them. I turned, grabbing the twitching man for a shield as I worked my way to the front door. Bullets chipped away at muscle and skin as I dragged his carcass across the ground, silently thanking West for all of the lunges and sled pushes he'd made me do. As though summoned by my thoughts, West's gun cracked through the air.

The first of the two men fell within reaching distance of me. I dragged the dead man as far as I could, but I needed to move faster. My steps went wider, harder. I was only a few feet from the front door. A second gunshot sounded. Only this time it struck me.

My thigh screamed as I shoved the dead man off of me. I reached for his gun, but a boot landed firmly on my wrist.

"He's been waiting for you."

63

ACHILLEA MILLEFOLIUM

Having a bullet wound dragged over a gravel path would not be on my list of pleasurable experiences. In fact, none of this was very pleasant at all. The gash in my shoulder didn't feel like it was bleeding much. My captor was pulling me by the opposite shoulder, which was a small mercy.

The inside of the house was just as strange as the outside. Big curved stone walls lead to large skylights. Rocks and concrete everywhere. Like some futuristic desert fortress. I was being brought into what looked like a dining room. A glass table with a strange base like a crawling centipede stretched through the room.

My blood made a long streak on the stone floor behind me. The hand that had been dragging me pushed me down.

"Wait here."

With the high concrete walls, I could hear his footsteps as they moved out of the room. My palms pressed into the ground. If I moved quickly, I could still find her. A boot pressed into my back.

"I don't think so, princess."

An electric hum came from a few steps away. The boot lifted from my back as a phone rang. He answered the phone.

"No. No. She's alone, sir."

Thank heaven for small mercies.

"Yes, sir." A rough hand grabbed me by the neck. "Alright, princess. Stand up. If you can."

His fingers threaded into my hair. A hard tug had me fighting to get to my feet. Through gritted teeth, I groaned. The bullet in my thigh protested as I fought to remain standing.

"Hello?"

At the head of the dining table, a large projector screen appeared. That must have been where the humming was coming from. A light flickered on, creating an image on the screen. A man.

"Ah, yes. Hello, there."

A refined accent. Possibly Scottish? Sandy red hair. Blue eyes. A beard. All perfectly groomed. Expensive-looking tortoiseshell glasses that whispered of his wealth.

"Who are you?" My voice was cracked and raw. Had I been screaming?

"I apologize, how rude of me. Well, officially my title is Duke Harrison Augustus-Stanley. The fifth. But you can call me Harry. All my friends call me Harry."

My teeth clenched as a fiery pain lanced through my leg.

"Aren't you going to introduce yourself?"

I sucked in a breath. Speaking was out of the question as another lash of pain whipped my thigh. I grunted.

"Oh, that looks painful." Soft tsks came from him. "Help the young lady into a chair, Mr. Jameson."

Definitely Scottish. The man behind me pulled out the chair next to me. Hands shoved me down to sit.

"That's much better, isn't it?" His smile was a dangerous thing. It lit up his face, but not his eyes.

I looked at him, then let my eyes drift around the room he was standing in. Actually, not a room. A terrace. Lush green hills. Thick, perfectly manicured hedges. A fountain? This guy was nowhere near here. In fact, I didn't think he was in the same country.

"You must be Lilith," he said, his voice metallic even through the sound system. But maybe that was just how he sounded. "Mr. Camden told me so much about you."

"Only good things, I'm sure," I managed to droll. The armed goon squeezed my shoulder, the gash in it screamed in agony. I didn't.

"He failed to mention how stunning you are. But I saw photos of you two together. You made a handsome couple."

The Duke took a seat on a plush cream sofa. The camera pivoted to capture his movements. In front of him was a full tea service. It was an effort not to roll my eyes. He fixed himself some tea in a blue toile China cup. The gold rim met his lips. He placed the cup back on the table and looked at the camera or what was likely a feed of the room I was sitting in.

"Where is Mr. Camden?"

"Dead."

"Pity. He was so useful."

I shrugged.

"Your kind is so uncivilized."

"Italians?"

"Oh, goodness no. No. I love Italians. I mean you mafioso types. Codes of honor. Cement shoes. Sleeping with the fishes. All that nonsense. You kill each other like dogs in the street and fail to see the bigger picture."

I rolled my lips together. Of course Benjamin had been reporting to someone else. Someone like this. A born aristocrat. This man was what Benjamin had likely always wanted to be. But this guy was likely selling women off like cattle and he had the nerve to criticize my behavior? I fantasized about drowning him in tea as he took another sip from his cup. Raising my eyebrows in agitation seemed enough to prompt him into continuing.

"I suppose I'll have to make some calls. Mr. Camden was a facilitator. A glorified operations manager, if you will. But he's replaceable. Easily replaceable. Do you know how many people in the world can do his job? And want to?"

"What job is that, exactly?" My question was shaky with barely contained rage. I knew.

This man was at the center of it all. I thought about what Clayton had said about Benjamin. Who he would answer to. Someone with political clout. Someone who could manipulate people at a higher level. He was at the center of what was an ever-expanding sex trafficking ring.

"There are those who have darker tastes. Those who control everything that matters. Money. War. Food. Energy. I give them what they want."

"Why?" I bit out. "Why do any of it?"

"Oh, if I don't someone else will. Why give up all of that power? With their secrets, I control them. I'll ask you this, Ms. Caccia. If I control the most powerful men in the world, who is truly the most powerful man?"

Did I somehow step into a Bond movie? Was I dead and this was hell? Another whip of pain lashed my leg. Nope, still very much alive. Trying to breathe through it, I focused on the screen instead of the pain. A drop of sweat rolled down my back, sending a shudder rolling through my muscles. Another lance of pain stabbed at me with the movement.

"Well," Augustus-Stanley shrugged casually. "You came all this way. Surely, you'd like to set eyes on your dear sister before you're both eliminated. I'm many things, but I'm not a monster. How about a little family reunion, hm?"

64

TAGETES

I'd been lost in my pain. I hadn't heard it, the sound of her footsteps. Normally clad in a pair of heels higher and sharper than her cheekbones, bare feet had silently padded in behind me. Into Augustus-Stanley's view but not my own. When I turned, my stomach dropped out completely. Kaia. Only a few steps away from me next to the table. I couldn't believe how she looked.

The usually clean, pin-straight strands of her hair were greasy and dirty. Her clothes were something they had shoved her into. Shabby sweatpants and a stained man's short-sleeved shirt. Not her at all. But the thing I couldn't tear my eyes away from, the thing that shredded me from the inside out, was the look on her face. Defeat. Fear. My sister, the imperious leader of the Caccia family, was terrified.

A tremor went through my hands. I fisted them at my sides.

"Now," Augustus-Stanley started. "The two remaining members of the infamous Caccia crime family of Los Angeles. Two beautiful women. I'm not as sexist as some of your fellow mafiosos. I know how powerful and dangerous a woman can be."

"Are you going to tell us how much you respect us before you have us killed?" My sister's voice was husky and dry. She glanced at the bleeding wound in my thigh.

My eyes darted around the room as the man on the screen roared with rich laughter. Nothing. I had nothing. With two guns on my sister and I, one of us would be down before I could disarm both men, even with West's training. Kaia and I locked eyes. We needed to buy time.

"So," I started. "Your center for a trafficking ring is in the middle of a desert? Seems inconvenient."

"You think this is the center? No, no, no. Silly girl. This is just one source of dozens. Like a franchise. Instead of burgers and fries, well... How would I keep all of the women in this house? Or the children?"

My gut churned. Why didn't I think it could be worse? It could always be worse.

"You have a child, don't you, Ms. Caccia? A boy."

My jaw clenched so hard I thought I might crack a molar. A glance at Kaia told me she'd reacted similarly.

"That old man won't be enough to keep him safe. Not with all of the dangers lurking in the world. He seems frail. Breakable. And that cancer he's got. He won't be around much longer, I think. You should have left him with someone more capable."

Kaia's knuckles went white, mirroring my own.

"Perhaps I'll send someone to fetch him for me. To make up for the inventory you'd cost me, Lilith. Children are much more valuable."

Acid filled my mouth. If this mother fucker laid a hand on my nephew, he'd never be able to comprehend the level of hell I was going to bring down on him. Kaia's eyes met mine. Slightly rounded corners were the only indication of any emotion. She was afraid. She was angry. And so was I.

"Mr. Jameson, please help her to her feet and take them to the courtyard. Then do something about her blood all over the floor. It's going to stain. Goodbye, Caccias."

The projector went dark. Humming began again as it rolled out of sight.

A rough hand found my collar and yanked me up. Pain coated my thigh in a web of lightning. Breath sawed through my teeth as I gritted them in agony. I couldn't fight my way out. Could barely walk.

I had nothing. Nothing. Nothing.

This was it. Time to say goodbye.

Guns popped nearby. Shouting started. Booted feet plodded through the stone halls. The man called Mr. Jameson lifted a radio to his lips to bark orders.

"What in the hell is going on out there?"

"We're taking fire. She didn't come alone. They're almost inside. They-"

A scream of pain from beyond the concrete walls followed more gunfire. Hope glimmered in me. Maybe we could fight our way out of this thing. Or at least I could get Kaia out. I had to get her out. A thread tugged in my chest as I tried to invent an escape, remembering the smoky green eyes I'd likely never see again.

Mr. Jameson had a gun and the first man who had brought me in still held my last blade, tucked into his belt. He had been the one to bring my sister into the room. And it was only a fingertip's distance from Kaia's grasp.

Kaia had always been faster than me. Faster to learn things from our grandfather. Faster to notice small details. It happened so quickly. Before I could blink. The knife was in her hand. In the chest of Mr. Jameson. Mr. Jameson had a pistol in his grip. He'd fired two shots. One hit the other man in the room, kneecapping him by accident. The other. That one had hit my sister. Right below her heart.

THE RIGHT AMOUNT of poison is the antidote. It's not exactly accurate, but it increases tolerance. After a lifetime of swallowing pain, I thought I was immune.

The kneecapped thug didn't take long to die. I took the knife from Jameson's chest and slit his throat. There was no time to make it hurt. To make them suffer for what they'd done to her. I had to get her out.

Threading my arms beneath hers, I hefted her up and moved toward the door. My thigh screamed in pain as I dragged her body out the way I'd come. Out the way I had been dragged in.

"Don't you fucking die on me, Kaia." I roared through clenched teeth. "*I'm* supposed to protect *you*!"

The door was still ajar. My feet barely moved as I collapsed on the stone just outside. The gunfire had stopped. My voice rasped and cracked as I screamed for help. For anyone.

Kaia's skin had gone pale. An ugly blue hue had started to permeate the rich olive complexion I'd always known. Blood spread through the dirty white cotton, even as I pressed my hands over the wound.

"Stop," I whispered toward my trembling hands, begging for the bleeding to slow. I racked my mind, looking for an excuse. Maybe it missed everything vital. Maybe it didn't puncture her lung. It could have missed.

"Lili," Kaia panted a rattling breath. Her hand cupped my cheek, her fingers weak and cold. The knot in my throat expanded as I watched her breathing slow. My eyes lined with tears as a frown dragged my lips down.

"No. Don't. Save your energy. Help is coming," I said, choking on the words. Her hand fell away from my face, like a limp bird crashing to the ground. Blood soaked the stone beneath us.

"You're supposed to protect the family, Lili," she said softly. The next words were firm.

"Protect him."

They were her last.

It's hard to tell a story without talking about breathing. It's the first notable thing we do. People who fill a hospital room eagerly await a first breath. Years later, someone will be there for the last. Kaia's last breaths were not in a hospital. They were not comfortable. They were against my arms. In spite of my pleading.

The sound that came out of me was filled with anger. A howl of rage and pain emanated from my very core. My mind and body felt like they were separating. I felt like I was somewhere else. This was happening to someone else. But the blood that bubbled from her lips. Her gaze locked on me before the light in it faded away. That was real. Kaia was dead. Nothing could change that now.

I clung to my sister, pulling her lifeless body against mine as though all of my energy and grief could bring her back to me. Tears soaked my sister's hair. Screaming sobs tore out of my mouth as I gasped, the air coming into my lungs like shards of glass. A shuffle in the dirt alerted me to an approaching presence and I released my knife from its holster, quick to protect the woman who was no longer there.

West held his hands up as he went to his knees beside me. I couldn't say anything. Couldn't find the tether to the human inside me. The one who could make sense of the world. There was only the girl who'd failed her sister.

I had failed.

65

EUCALYPTUS GLOBULUS

Death is a foreign thing to children. When you're little, the world stretches out before you. The ground rises to meet your feet and you can't imagine that one day you'll not take another step. Daniel was seated on Lupo's living room floor, looking at pictures of his father. I wondered what it must be like for him to get to know his father through second-hand accounts. He'd never know Dante like he knows his mother. Knew. Knew his mother.

The drive from the desert had been long. I could still feel the gravel embedded in my knees. West struggled to peel my grasp off Kaia's body as I fought to keep her with me. Our small band of Caccia men took her away. Every moment of increasing distance had coated my heart in the hoarfrost of grief.

"Zia!" His head snapped up, his pin-straight grin beaming at me.

"Hey, buddy," I sighed as I rustled the dark mop on his head. "You and I need to talk for a bit, alright?"

Lupo looked at me, his mouth tight with worry, and stood from his armchair. I sat down on the floor next to Daniel and picked up the photo he'd been looking at. In the photo, Dante is sitting next to Kaia on a bench outside my grandfather's house. He's looking at the camera and she's looking at him. They're both young. So young.

"I remember this," I said with a small smile. "This was Christmas at Nonno's house."

"Mama looks pretty."

"Yes, she does," I said, with another glance at the photo. My fingers traced the sharp edge of the print as I set it down on the floor again. "Daniel, I need to tell you something."

"Mama's not coming back, is she?"

My throat tightened as I tried to force down a breath. "Why do you think that?"

"Mama says goodnight to me every night. Even when she's at work, she calls to say goodnight. She never misses it. She promised," he said weakly. "Mama doesn't break promises."

"You're right about that," I nod. "She didn't want to leave you. Some bad men took her and she..." My voice trailed off. I wished I'd thought about this more. How could I explain what happened to her to someone whose world was so small?

I started again. "There are dangerous people in the world, and she was protecting us from them. She's not coming back because she died."

Daniel was silent for a long moment. I looked him over, not sure if he was even breathing. The color leached from his cheeks as he stared at the floor. I tried to think of something to say to him. Anything that would help. Then I remembered the night I lost my mother. I thought about Nonno sitting at the end of my bed, looking at me in the same way I was now looking at Daniel. No words would help. I put a hand on his shoulder and sat in silence with him.

"It's not fair," he said quietly.

"No," I agreed. "It's not fair."

* * *

WEST WAS SITTING at the table with Lupo when we finally went to the kitchen for some water. My legs were stiff from sitting on the floor, my thigh still aching with the freshly cleaned bullet wound. I gestured for Daniel to sit at the chair West pulled out for him. The room was silent except for the sound of water filling a small glass. I set the glass on the table in front of Daniel and leaned against the counter behind him.

Lupo let out a long sigh and gave a casual shrug that was completely manufactured for Daniel's comfort. He stood and headed for the refrigerator, opening the cabinet above it to reach for something I couldn't see. Patting my shoulder as he passed, Lupo returned to his seat.

A small white box with the label "Pal's" written on it in big blue letters was set in the center of the table. Lupo's large, weathered fingers gently lifted the lid to reveal frosting and rainbow sprinkles.

"It's alright to be angry," he said to the boy, whose grief made him look even smaller in the wooden kitchen chair. West nodded, looking into his glass as he turned it in his fingers. It had only been hours. Hours since my sister's light had flickered out and he'd not spoken much. Only let me stew in my pain. I was both grateful for his silence and tired of it.

"You can be sad, too. For as long as you need to be. I like to eat cookies when I'm sad," he said to Daniel. "These are your Zia's favorite."

⚔

"LILITH CACCIA," SAID the deep, rolling Irish voice. "I expect you're calling about my offer."

I stood on Lupo's porch, watching the stars flicker overhead. Inside I could hear Lupo talking to Daniel in the kitchen, West listening quietly to every word. My breath clouded before me as I spoke.

"You want my help to find the men who hurt your daughter and make them pay," I said in hushed words. "I have some conditions. One. One condition."

A glass being set on wood sounded in the background. Ronan Arawn sighed. "Let's hear it, then."

"We find them all. From the top man to the last miserable soldier. Tear them out, root and stem."

"You're a vicious little cunt, you know that?" He let out a rough laugh and took a drink of whatever it was, the sound clear through the receiver.

"Yes or no, Ronan."

The line went silent. Long enough that I thought the call had dropped. Then that voice became dark on the other end.

"Root and stem."

EPILOGUE

WEST

The house was quiet except for the occasional rustle of clothing falling to the floor and Lanna's feet padding out into the hallway from the closet. All of Kaia's clothes, except for a suit that Lili picked for the viewing, were being diligently packed away by my sister. A project my girl couldn't handle. Not now.

I didn't know what to do for her. Eyes that sparkled with mischief were now haunted with grief. The lush pink lips I used to lay awake thinking about were drained of color. Getting her to eat was an exercise in patience. All she did was sleep.

Her voice had pierced through everything. I'd heard her screaming for help. In the middle of the goddamned desert. Gino got into it with the guards on the side of the house. After doing what I could from the peak, I'd come down to help him. Then I heard it. Panicked, I ran to find her. Saw the gash on her arm. The wound in her thigh. And the look on her face. It shredded everything in me.

"Hey."

My sister's head poked over the banister, looking down at where I'd been sitting on the stairs. I'd planned on going outside after bringing food to Lili in the bedroom but found myself unable to get beyond the first few steps.

"Can you come help me with these boxes?"

I nodded and stood. The stairs creaked under the weight of my careful footfalls. Waking Lili didn't worry me, but the quiet felt insistent. Like a library. Or a mausoleum. Even Lanna was barely speaking above a whisper. The blackout shades had been closed for days. Joining her in bed at night felt like laying beside a fallen tree.

The bedroom was still shrouded in darkness. The only light was coming from the closet where my sister was keeping busy. Lili didn't seem to mind the light or Lanna's noise. A mass of black hair covered her face. Her arms were pulled up underneath to support her head. The points of her elbows nearly touched her knees. She was completely curled in on herself.

My throat tightened at the sight. It hadn't changed much. But it still hit me. A few steps had me in front of her. The plate of cheese and crackers I'd left for her was untouched, but the glass on the nightstand was empty. Gratitude filled me when I realized she'd at least been drinking the water I left for her. I picked up the glass and carried it to the carafe on the dresser. Lanna left it there next to a box of tissues. Completely untouched tissues.

"She hasn't cried," Lanna whispered, noticing me eyeing the unopened box.

"No."

She hadn't. Not since I found her kneeling in her sister's blood. She probably wouldn't. Tears would not be her way. Not for some time. Her sadness manifested in silence. It was a familiar song, the sound of it. The feel of grief's claws embedding in my gut was one I knew well.

I brought the water back to the nightstand and found a pair of gold eyes looking up at me.

"Hi," I said quietly.

She said nothing. I brushed the hair away from her face.

"Are you hungry?"

She said nothing. I knelt beside the bed and stroked her cheek as gently as I could manage. Barely a touch. But I couldn't not touch her. Not any-more.

"I'm right here, Trouble."

Kaia Caccia's funeral was in three days. In the days following her sister's death in Joshua Tree, Lili was a champion. She comforted Daniel. Con-tacted their lawyer and got Kaia's estate in order. Planned the funeral. Never let on that she was crumbling on the inside. But I knew. In the broken half-smiles she gave me. The untouched food. The tired kisses. I felt her falling apart.

She nestled into the pillow and shut her eyes again. Her skin was soft beneath my fingers. I wanted to feel her. Hold her. See her smile again. My heart cracked at the thought.

"West," my sister whispered from the doorway. She beckoned. With ev-ery step away, I felt pulled toward the woman I'd wanted from the moment I met her. Every bit of distance was agony. "She just needs time."

"I know," I said with a look back at her. My Trouble. Lanna put a hand on my shoulder.

"It's hard to watch the people we love suffer," she said quietly. With a glance at Lili, she looked at me with pitying eyes. "You do, don't you? Love her?"

I nodded, rubbing at the tugging ache in my chest. Lanna squeezed my shoulder and walked into the hallway, placing a jacket I hadn't seen her hold-ing into another box.

"Just keep doing what you're doing. It's enough."

It sure as hell didn't feel like it. Nothing I did felt like enough.

"Leave the shoes," I said. "They wear the same size shoe."

A pair of black high heels sat next to one of the boxes. I squatted to pick them up and carry them back into the closet. Soon Lili would be filling these shoes. Taking the role she told me she'd never wanted. Never dreamed of it for herself because it meant this painful reality. In this reality, I couldn't falter. Not now.

I looked back at her, sleeping in the shadows of her agony. My place would always be by her side. Lilith Rhamnusia Caccia. I thought about the name she'd told me in that bed as I watched her breaths become even with sleep. My beautiful dark angel. No matter how long it took, I would wait. Wait for her to come back to me.

And bring her bloody brand of justice with her.